THE CRITICS ARE PURRING
OVER THE CAT WHO . . . SERIES!

"Braun gives fans what they crave."

—*Publishers Weekly*

"Like dropping in on old and very dear friends."

—*The Tampa Tribune*

"Braun keeps both paws planted on the side of charming."

—*Los Angeles Times*

"Delightful . . . [The cats] steal the show." —*San Francisco Chronicle*

"Enjoyable."

—*People*

"Braun's fans devour these tales and keep coming back for more."

—*The Chattanooga Times*

"Thoroughly delightful . . . sheer reading enjoyment."

—*Detroit Free Press*

"The mix of crime and cats [is] catnip to readers who like both."

—*Chicago Sun-Times*

Titles by Lilian Jackson Braun

Two Cats, Three Tales

LILIAN JACKSON BRAUN

BERKLEY BOOKS, NEW YORK

THE BERKLEY PUBLISHING GROUP
Published by the Penguin Group
Penguin Group (USA) Inc.
375 Hudson Street, New York, New York 10014, USA
Penguin Group (Canada), 90 Eglinton Avenue East, Suite 700, Toronto, Ontario M4P 2Y3, Canada
(a division of Pearson Penguin Canada Inc.)
Penguin Books Ltd., 80 Strand, London WC2R 0RL, England
Penguin Group Ireland, 25 St. Stephen's Green, Dublin 2, Ireland (a division of Penguin Books Ltd.)
Penguin Group (Australia), 250 Camberwell Road, Camberwell, Victoria 3124, Australia
(a division of Pearson Australia Group Pty. Ltd.)
Penguin Books India Pvt. Ltd., 11 Community Centre, Panchsheel Park, New Delhi—110 017, India
Penguin Group (NZ), Cnr. Airborne and Rosedale Roads, Albany, Auckland 1310, New Zealand
(a division of Pearson New Zealand Ltd.)
Penguin Books (South Africa) (Pty.) Ltd., 24 Sturdee Avenue, Rosebank, Johannesburg 2196,
South Africa

Penguin Books Ltd., Registered Offices: 80 Strand, London WC2R 0RL, England

This is a work of fiction. Names, characters, places, and incidents are either the product of the author's imagination or are used fictitiously, and any resemblance to actual persons, living or dead, business establishments, events, or locales is entirely coincidental. The publisher does not have any control over and does not assume any responsibility for author or third-party websites or their content.

PRINTING HISTORY
Berkley trade paperback edition / April 2006

Berkley trade paperback ISBN: 0-425-20794-3

This book has been catalogued with the Library of Congress

PRINTED IN THE UNITED STATES OF AMERICA

10   9   8   7   6   5   4

CONTENTS

Two Cats, Three Tales

The Cat
Who Could
Read Backwards

CHAPTER 1

JIM QWILLERAN, whose name had confounded typesetters and proof-readers for two decades, arrived fifteen minutes early for his appointment with the managing editor of the *Daily Fluxion*.

In the reception room he picked up a copy of the early edition and studied the front page. He read the weather prediction (unseasonably warm) and the circulation figures (427,463) and the publisher's slogan snobbishly printed in Latin (*Fiat Flux*).

He read the lead story on a murder trial and the secondary lead on the gubernatorial race, in which he found two typographical errors. He noticed that the art museum had failed to get its million dollar grant, but he skipped the details. He bypassed another feature about a kitten trapped in a drainpipe, but he read everything else: *Cop Nabs Hood in Gun Tiff. Probe Stripper Feud in Loop. Stocks Soar as Tax Talk Irks Dems.*

Qwilleran could hear familiar noises beyond a glass-paneled door—typewriters clattering, teletypes jigging, telephones screaming. At the sound his ample pepper-and-salt moustache bristled, and he smoothed it with his knuckles. Aching for a sight of the bustle and clutter that consti-tuted the City Room before a deadline, he walked to the door for a squint through the glass.

The sounds were authentic, but the scene—he discovered—was all wrong. The Venetian blinds were straight. The desks were tidy and un-scarred. Crumpled copy paper and slashed newspapers that should have been on the floor were collected in wire wastebaskets. As he contemplated the scene with dismay, an alien sound reached his ears—one that did not harmonize with the background music of any city rooms he had known. Then he noticed a copyboy feeding yellow pencils into a small moaning contraption. Qwilleran stared at the thing. An electric pencil sharpener! He had never thought it would come to this. It reminded him how long he had been out of touch.

Another copyboy in tennis shoes bounced out of the City Room and said, "Mr. Qwilleran? You can come in now."

Qwilleran followed him to the cubicle where a young managing editor was waiting with a sincere handshake and a sincere smile. "So you're Jim Qwilleran! I've heard a lot about you."

Qwilleran wondered how much—and how bad. In the job résumé he had mailed to the *Daily Fluxion* his career traced a dubious curve: sports writer, police reporter, war correspondent, winner of the Publishers' Trophy, author of a book on urban crime. Then came a succession of short-term jobs on smaller and smaller newspapers, followed by a long period of unemployment—or no jobs worth listing.

The managing editor said, "I remember your coverage of the trial that won you the Publishers' Trophy. I was a cub reporter at the time and a great admirer of yours."

By the man's age and schooled manner, Qwilleran recognized him as the new breed of editor—one of the precision-honed generation who approached newspapering as a science rather than a holy cause. Qwilleran had always worked for the other kind—the old-fashioned nail-spitting crusaders.

The editor was saying, "With your background you may be disappointed in our offer. All we have for you is a desk in the Feature Department, but we'd like you to take it until something turns up cityside."

"And until I've proved I can stay on the job?" Qwilleran said, looking the man in the eye. He had been through a humbling experience; now the problem was to strike the right chord of humility and confidence.

"That goes without saying. How are you getting along?"

"So far, so good. The important thing is to get back on a newspaper. I wore out my welcome in several cities before I got smart. That's why I wanted to come here. Strange town—lively paper—new challenge. I think I can make it work."

"Sure you can!" said the editor, squaring his jaw. "And here's what we have in mind for you. We need an art writer."

"An art writer!" Qwilleran winced and mentally composed a headline: *Vet Newsman Put to Pasture.*

"Know anything about art?"

Qwilleran was honest. He said, "I don't know the Venus de Milo from the Statute of Liberty."

"You're exactly what we want! The less you know, the fresher your viewpoint. Art is booming in this town, and we need to give it more coverage. Our art critic writes a column twice a week, but we want an experienced newsman to scout stories about the artists themselves. There's plenty of material. These days, as you probably know, artists are more plentiful than cats and dogs."

Qwilleran combed his moustache with his knuckles.

The editor continued in a positive vein. "You'll report to the feature editor, but you can dig up your own assignments. We'll want you to get around on the beat, meet a lot of artists, shake a few hands, make friends for the paper."

Qwilleran silently composed another headline: *Journalist Sinks to Role of Glad-hander*. But he needed the job. Necessity battled with conscience. "Well," he said, "I don't know—"

"It will be a nice clean beat, and you'll meet some decent people for a change. You've probably had your fill of mobsters and con men."

Qwilleran's twitching moustache was trying to say who-the-hell-wants-a-nice-clean-beat, but its owner maintained a diplomatic silence.

The editor consulted his watch and stood up. "Why don't you go upstairs and talk it over with Arch Riker? He can—"

"Arch Riker! What's he doing here?"

"He's feature editor. Know him?"

"We worked together in Chicago—years ago."

"Good! He'll give you all the details. And I hope you decide to join the *Flux*." The editor extended his hand and smiled a measured smile.

Qwilleran wandered out through the City Room again—past the rows of white shirts with sleeves at three-quarter mast, past the heads bent obliviously over typewriters, past the inevitable girl reporter. She was the only one who gave him an inquisitive look, and he stretched to his full six-feet-two, reined in the superfluous ten pounds that pushed at his belt buckle, and passed a preening hand over his head. Like his upper lip, it still boasted three black hairs for every one that was gray.

Upstairs he found Arch Riker presiding over a roomful of desks, typewriters and telephones—all in a single shade of pea green.

"Pretty fancy, isn't it?" Arch said apologetically. "They call it Eye-Ease Olive. Everybody has to be pampered these days. Personally, I think it looks bilious."

The Feature Department was a small edition of the City Room—without the smolder of urgency. Serenity filled the room like a mist. Everyone seemed to be ten years older than the crew in the City Room, and Arch himself was plumper and balder than he used to be.

"Jim, it's great to see you again," he said. "Do you still spell your name with that ridiculous *W*?"

"It's a respectable Scottish spelling," Qwilleran protested.

"And I see you haven't got rid of that overgrown moustache."

"It's my only war souvenir." The knuckles smoothed it affectionately.

"How's your wife, Jim?"

"You mean my ex-wife?"

"Oh, I didn't know. Sorry."

"Let's skip that. . . . What's this job you've got for me?"

"It's a snap. You can do a Sunday piece for us if you want to start today."

"I haven't said I'll take the job yet."

"You'll take it," Arch said. "It's just right for you."

"Considering my recent reputation, you mean?"

"Are you going to be touchy? Forget it. Quit needling yourself."

Qwilleran parted his moustache thoughtfully. "I suppose I could give it a try. Want me to do a trial assignment?"

"Anything you say."

"Got any leads?"

"Yes." Arch Riker drew a pink sheet of paper from a tickler file. "How much did the boss tell you?"

"He didn't tell me anything," Qwilleran said, "except that he wants human-interest stuff on artists."

"Well, he sent up a pink memo suggesting a story on a guy called Cal Halapay."

"So?"

"Here at the *Flux* we have a color code. A blue memo means *For Your Information*. Yellow means *Casual Suggestion*. But pink means *Jump, Man, Jump*."

"What's so urgent about Cal Halapay?"

"Under the circumstances it might be better if you didn't know the background. Just go out there cold, meet this Halapay person, and write something readable. You know all the tricks."

"Where do I find him?"

"Call his office, I suppose. He's a commercial artist and head of a successful agency, but he does oil paintings in his spare time. He paints pictures of kids. They're very popular. Kids with curly hair and rosy cheeks. They look apoplectic, but people seem to buy them. . . . Say, do you want lunch? We could go to the Press Club."

Qwilleran's moustache sprang to attention. Once upon a time press clubs had been his life, his love, his hobby, his home, his inspiration.

This one was across the street from the new police headquarters, in a sooty limestone fortress with barred windows that had once been the county jail. The stone steps, bowl-shaped with age, held the evidence of an unseasonable February thaw. In the lobby the ancient woodwork gleamed red under countless coats of varnish.

"We can eat in the bar," Arch said, "or we can go upstairs to the dining room. They've got tablecloths up there."

"Let's eat down here," Qwilleran said.

It was dim and noisy in the bar. Conversation was high-key, with confidential undertones. Qwilleran knew it well. It meant that rumors were circulating, campaigns were being launched, and cases were getting solved unofficially over a beer and a hamburger.

They found two empty stools at the bar and were confronted by a bartender wearing a red vest and a conspiratorial smile that brimmed with inside information. Qwilleran recalled that some of his best story tips had come from Press Club bartenders.

"Scotch and water," Arch ordered.

Qwilleran said, "Double tomato juice on the rocks."

"Tom-tom on the rocks," said the bartender. "You want a squeeze of lime and a shot of Worcestershire?"

"No, thanks."

"That's the way I fix it for my friend the mayor when he comes in here." There was more of the authoritative smile.

"No, thanks."

"How about a drop of Tabasco to give it a bite?"

"No, just pour it straight."

The bartender's mouth turned down at the corners, and Arch said to him, "This is Jim Qwilleran, a new staffer. He doesn't realize you're an artist. . . . Jim, this is Bruno. He gives his drinks a lot of personal expression."

Behind Qwilleran an earsplitting voice said, "I'll take less expression and a bigger shot of liquor. Hey, Bruno, make me a martini, and leave out the garbage. No olive, lemon twist, anchovy or pickled unborn tomato."

Qwilleran turned and faced a cigar clamped between grinning teeth, its size vastly out of proportion to the slender young man who smoked it. The black cord hanging from his breast pocket was obviously attached to a light meter. He was noisy. He was cocky. He was enjoying himself. Qwilleran liked him.

"This clown," Arch said to Qwilleran, "is Odd Bunsen from the Photo Lab. . . . Odd, this is Jim Qwilleran, old friend of mine. We hope he's joining the *Flux* staff."

The photographer extended a quick hand. "Jim, glad to meet you. Care for a cigar?"

"I use a pipe. Thanks just the same."

Odd studied Qwilleran's luxuriant moustache with interest. "That shrubbery's getting out of hand. Aren't you afraid of brush fires?"

Arch said to Qwilleran, "That black string hanging out of Mr. Bunsen's pocket is what we use to tie his head on. But he's a useful man. He has more information than the reference library. Maybe he can fill you in on Cal Halapay."

"Sure," said the photographer. "What do you want to know? He's got a sharp-looking wife, 34-22-32."

"Who is this Halapay, anyway?" Qwilleran asked.

Odd Bunsen consulted his cigar smoke briefly. "Commercial artist. Runs a big ad agency. Personally worth a few million. Lives in Lost Lake Hills. Beautiful house, big studio where he paints, two swimming pools. Two, did you get that? With water being so scarce, he probably fills one with bourbon."

"Any family?"

"Two or three kids. Gorgeous wife. Halapay owns an island in the Caribbean and a ranch in Oregon and a couple of private planes. Everything money can buy. And he's not tight with his dough. He's a good joe."

"What about these pictures he paints?"

"Sharp! Real sharp," said Odd. "I've got one hanging in my living room. After I photographed Halapay's wife at a charity ball last fall, he gave me a painting. Couple of kids with curly hair. . . . Well, I've got to go and eat now. There's a one o'clock assignment on the board."

Arch drained his drink and said to Qwilleran, "Talk to Halapay and size up the photo possibilities, and then we'll try to assign Odd Bunsen. He's our best man. Maybe he could try some color shots. It wouldn't hurt to do this layout in color."

"That pink memo has you straining a bit, hasn't it?" Qwilleran said. "What's the connection between Halapay and the *Daily Fluxion*?"

"I'm having another drink," Arch said. "Want another tomato juice?"

Qwilleran let the question drop, but he said, "Just give me one straight answer, Arch. Why are they offering me this art beat? Me, of all people."

"Because that's the way newspapers do things. They assign baseball experts as drama critics and church news writers to the nightclub beat. You know that as well as I do."

Qwilleran nodded and stroked his moustache sadly. Then he said, "What about this art critic you have on the staff? If I take the job, do I work with him? Or her, as the case may be?"

"It's a guy," Arch told him. "He writes critical reviews, and you'll be doing straight reporting and personality stories. I don't think there'll be any conflict."

"Does he work in our department?"

"No, he never comes to the office. He does his column at home, puts it on tape and sends it down by messenger once or twice a week. We have to transcribe it. It's a fat nuisance."

"What keeps him away? Doesn't he like pea green?"

"Don't ask me. That's his arrangement with the front office. He has a neat contract with the *Flux*."

"What's the fellow like?"

"Aloof. Opinionated. Hard to get along with."

"That's nice. Is he young or old?"

"In between. He lives alone—with a cat, if you can picture that! A lot of people think the cat writes the column, and they may be right."

"Is his stuff any good?"

"*He* thinks so. And the brass evidently thinks so." Arch shifted around on the bar stool while he weighed his next remark. "There's a rumor that the *Flux* has the guy heavily insured."

"What's so valuable about an art critic?"

"This one's got that certain magic that newspapers love; he's controversial! His column pulls hundreds of letters a week. No, thousands!"

"What kind of letters?"

"Angry ones. Sugary ones. Hysterical ones. The arty readers hate his guts; the others think he's the greatest, and they get to brawling among themselves. He manages to keep the whole city stirred up. Do you know what our last survey showed? The art page has a bigger readership than the sports section! Now you know and I know that's an unnatural situation."

"You must have a lot of art buffs in this town," Qwilleran said.

"You don't have to like art to enjoy our art column; you just have to like blood."

"But what do they fight about?"

"You'll find out."

"I can understand controversy in sports and politics, but art is art, isn't it?"

"That's what I used to think," said Arch. "When I took over the feature desk, I had this simpleminded notion that art was something precious—for beautiful people who had beautiful thoughts. Man, did I lose that dream in a hurry! Art has gone democratic. In this town it's the greatest fad since canasta, and anybody can play. People buy paintings instead of swimming pools."

Qwilleran chewed the ice in his tomato juice and pondered the mysteries of this beat the *Daily Fluxion* was offering him. "By the way," he said, "what's the critic's name?"

"George Bonifield Mountclemens."

"Say that again, please?"

"George Bonifield Mountclemens—the Third!"

"That's a stickful! Does he use all three names like that?"

"All three names, all nine syllables, all twenty-eight letters plus the numerals! Twice a week we try to fit his by-line into a standard column width. It can't be done, except sideways. And he doesn't permit any abbreviations, hyphens, contractions or amputations!"

Qwilleran gave Arch a close look. "You don't like him much, do you?"

Arch shrugged. "I can take him or leave him. Actually I never see the guy. I just see the artists who come to the office wanting to punch him in the teeth."

"George Bonifield Mountclemens the Third!" Qwilleran shook his head in amazement.

"Even his name infuriates some of our readers," Arch said. "They want to know who does he think he is."

"Keep talking. I'm beginning to like this job. The boss said it was a nice wholesome beat, and I was afraid I'd be working with a bunch of saints."

"Don't let him kid you. All the artists in this town hate each other, and all the art-lovers take sides. Then everybody plays rough. It's like football only dirtier. Name-calling, back-biting, double-crossing—" Arch slid off his bar stool. "Come on, let's get a corned beef sandwich."

The blood of several old war-horses that flowed through Qwilleran's veins began to churn a little faster. His moustache almost smiled. "Okay, I'll take it," he said. "I'll take the job."

CHAPTER 2

IT WAS QWILLERAN'S first day on the job at the *Daily Fluxion*. He moved into one of the pea green desks in the Feature Department and got himself a supply of yellow pencils. He noticed that the pea green telephone was stenciled with an official reminder: *Be Nice to People*. He tried the pea green typewriter by poking out, "The time of many murders is after midnight." Then he telephoned the *Fluxion* garage to request a staff car for the trip to Lost Lake Hills.

To reach the fashionable exurb fifteen miles beyond the city limits, Qwilleran drove through complacent suburbs and past winter-brown farms patched with snow. He had plenty of time to think about this interview with Cal Halapay, and he wondered if the Qwilleran Method would still work. In the old days he had been famous for a brotherly approach that put interviewees at ease. It was composed of two parts sympathy, two parts professional curiosity, and one part low blood pressure, and it had won confidences from old ladies, juvenile delinquents, pretty girls, college presidents and crooks.

Nevertheless, he felt qualms about the Halapay assignment. It had been a long time since he had done an interview, and artists were not his specialty. He suspected they spoke a secret language. On the other hand, Halapay was an advertising executive, and he might hand over a mimeographed release prepared by his public-relations office. Qwilleran's moustache shuddered.

It had always been the newsman's habit to compose the opening paragraph of his story in advance. It never worked, but he did it as a limbering-up exercise. Now—on the road to Lost Lake Hills—he made a few starts at the Halapay story.

He thought he might say, "When Cal Halapay leaves his plush executive suite at the end of the day, he forgets the cutthroat competition of the advertising rat race and finds relaxation in—" No, that was trite.

He tried again. "A multimillionaire advertising man with a beautiful wife (34-22-32) and two swimming pools (one filled with champagne, according to legend) admits he lives a double life. In painting poignant portraits of children, he escapes—" No, that was sensationalism.

Qwilleran recalled his brief employment with a newsmagazine and made another attempt in the crunchy style favored by that publication. "With an ascot folded in the throatline of his custom-made Italian silk sports shirt, the handsome, graying, six-foot-two czar of an advertising empire spends his spare time—"

Qwilleran guessed that a man of Halapay's accomplishments must be that tall, that gray, and that impressive. He would probably have a winter tan as well.

"With a blue foulard ascot accentuating his Caribbean tan—"

Lost Lake Road ended abruptly at a massive iron gate set in a field-stone wall that looked impregnable and expensive. Qwilleran braked the car and glanced around for signs of a caretaker.

Almost immediately a recorded voice coming from the gatepost said pleasantly, "Please face the pylon at your left and announce your name clearly."

He rolled down the car window and said, "Qwilleran from the *Daily Fluxion*."

"Thank you," murmured the gatepost.

The gate swung open, and the newsman drove into the estate, following a road that meandered through a tall stand of pines. It ended in a severely landscaped winter garden—all pebbles, boulders and evergreens, with arched bridges crossing small frozen ponds. In this setting, bleak but picturesque, stood a rambling house. It was contemporary in style with gently curving rooflines and opaque glass walls that looked like rice paper. Qwilleran revised his opening line about the Italian sports shirt. Halapay probably knocked around his million-dollar pagoda in a silk kimono.

At the entrance door, which appeared to be carved out of ivory, Qwilleran found something that resembled a doorbell and reached toward it, but before his finger touched the button, the surrounding panel glowed with a blue-green light and chimes could be heard indoors. These were followed by the bark of a dog, or two or three. There was a sharp command, a moment of silent obedience, and a briskly opened door.

"Good morning. I'm Qwilleran from the *Daily Fluxion*," the newsman said to a curly-haired, pink-faced youth in sweat shirt and dungarees, and before he could add, "Is your father home?" the young man said amiably, "Come in, sir. Here's your passport." He handed over a fuzzy snapshot of a heavily moustached face peering anxiously from the window of a car.

"That's me!" said Qwilleran in astonishment.

"Taken at the gate before you drove in," the young man said with obvious delight. "It's spooky, isn't it? Here, let me take your topcoat. I hope you don't mind the dogs. They're sort of friendly. They love visitors. This one is the mother. She's four years old. The pups are from her last litter. Do you like blue terriers?"

Qwilleran said, "I—"

"Everyone wants Yorkshires these days, but I like the Kerry Blues. They've got beautiful coats, haven't they? Did you have any trouble finding the place? We have a cat, too, but she's pregnant, and she sleeps all the time. I think it's going to snow. I hope so. The skiing has been lousy this year—"

Qwilleran, who prided himself on conducting interviews without making notes, was taking mental inventory of the house: white marble foyer with fish pool and tropical tree probably fourteen feet high. Skylight two stories overhead. Sunken living room carpeted with something like white raccoon. Fireplace in a shiny black wall. Probably onyx. He noticed also that the boy had a hole in his sleeve and was padding around in sweat socks. The flow of chatter had not ceased.

"Would you like to sit in the living room, Mr. Qwilleran? Or do you want to go right to the studio? It's more comfortable in the studio, if you don't mind the smell. Some people are allergic to turpentine. Would you like a Coke or something? Allergies are funny things. I'm allergic to crustaceans. That burns me up, because I'm crazy about lobster—"

Qwilleran was waiting for a chance to say, "Is your father home?" when the young man said, "My secretary tells me you want to do a story on my paintings. Let's go into my studio. Do you want to ask questions, or shall I just talk?"

Qwilleran gulped and said, "Frankly, I was expecting you to be a much older—"

"I'm a boy wonder," said Halapay without smiling. "I made my first million before I was twenty-one. I'm twenty-nine now. I seem to have a genius for making money. Do you believe in genius? It's spooky, really. Here's a picture of me when I was married. My wife looks Oriental, doesn't she? She's out taking an art lesson this morning, but you'll meet her after lunch. We designed the house to go with her looks. Would you like some coffee? I'll stir up the housekeeper if you want coffee. Let's face it, I look boyish and I always will. There's a bar in the studio if you'd rather have a drink."

The studio had a painty aroma, a good deal of clutter, and one vast wall of glass overlooking a white frozen lake. Halapay flicked a switch, and a filmy shade unfolded from the ceiling to screen out the glare. He touched another control, and doors glided open to reveal a bigger liquor supply than the Press Club had on its backbar.

Qwilleran said he preferred coffee, so Halapay pressed a button and gave the order to a brass grille mounted on the wall. He also handed Qwilleran an odd-shaped bottle from the bar.

"This is a liqueur I brought back from South America," he said. "You can't buy it here. Take it home with you. How do you like the view from this window? Sensational, isn't it? That's a man-made lake. The landscaping alone cost me half a million. Do you want a doughnut with your coffee? These are my paintings on the wall. Do you like them?"

The studio walls were covered with framed canvases—portraits of small boys and girls with curly hair and cheeks like red apples. Everywhere Qwilleran looked there were red apples.

"Pick out a painting," said Halapay, "and take it home with you—compliments of the artist. The large ones sell for five hundred dollars. Take a big one. Do you have any kids? We have two girls. That's their picture on the stereo cabinet. Cindy is eight and Susan is six."

Qwilleran studied the photograph of Halapay's daughters. Like their mother they had almond eyes and classically straight hair, and he said, "How come you paint nothing but children with curly hair and rosy cheeks?"

"You should go to the Valentine Ball on Saturday night. We're having a great jazz combo. Do you know about the ball? It's the annual Valentine party at the art club. We're all going in costume representing famous lovers. Would you like to go? You don't have to dress up, if masquerading doesn't appeal to you. It's twenty dollars a couple. Here, let me give you a pair of tickets."

"Getting back to your paintings," said Qwilleran, "I'm curious to know why you specialize in kids. Why not landscapes?"

"I think you should write up the ball in your column," Halapay said. "It's the biggest event of the year at the club. I'm chairman, and my wife's very photogenic. Do you like art? Everyone in the art field will be there."

"Including George Bonifield Mountclemens the Third, I suppose," said Qwilleran, in a tone intended to be jocular.

Without any change in his expressionless delivery, Halapay said, "That fraud! If that fraud showed his face in the outer lobby of the club, they'd throw him out. I hope he isn't a close friend of yours. I have no use for that character. He doesn't know anything about art, but he poses as an authority, and your paper lets him crucify established artists. They're letting him corrupt the entire art atmosphere of the city. They should get smart and unload him."

"I'm new on this beat," said Qwilleran, as Halapay stopped for breath, "and I'm no expert—"

"Just to prove what a fraud your critic is—he builds up Zoe Lambreth as a great artist. Did you ever see her stuff? It's a hoax. You go and see her paintings at the Lambreth Gallery, and you'll see what I mean. No reputable gallery would accept her work, so she had to marry an art dealer. There are tricks in all trades. As for her husband, he's nothing but a bookkeeper who got into the art racket, and I do mean racket. Here comes Tom with the coffee."

A houseboy dressed in soiled chinos and a half-buttoned shirt appeared with a tray, which he banged down on a table with a lack of grace. He gave Qwilleran an unfriendly stare.

Halapay said, "I wonder if we ought to have a sandwich with this. It's almost lunchtime. What do you want to know about my work? Go ahead and ask some questions. Don't you want to make notes?"

"I'd like to know," said Qwilleran, "why you specialize in painting children."

The artist lapsed into a thoughtful silence, his first since Qwilleran's arrival. Then he said, "Zoe Lambreth seems to have this big connection with Mountclemens. It would be interesting to know how she manages it. I could make a few guesses—not for publication. Why don't you dig into the situation? You might come up with a juicy exposé and get Mountclemens fired. Then you could be art critic."

"I don't want—" Qwilleran began.

"If your paper doesn't clean up that mess—and clean it up soon— they're going to start feeling it where it hurts. I wouldn't mind a hot dog with this coffee. Do you want a hot dog?"

AT FIVE-THIRTY that afternoon Qwilleran fled to the warm, varnished sanctuary of the Press Club, where he had agreed to meet Arch Riker. Arch wanted a quick drink on the way home. Qwilleran wanted an explanation.

He told Bruno curtly, "Tomato juice on the rocks. No lime, no Worcestershire, no Tabasco." To Arch he said, "Thanks, pal. Thanks for the welcome celebration."

"What do you mean?"

"Was that an initiation gag?"

"I don't know what you're talking about."

"I'm talking about that assignment to interview Cal Halapay. Was that a practical joke? You couldn't have been serious. The guy's a nut."

Arch said, "Well, you know how artists are. Individualists. What happened?"

"Nothing happened. Nothing I could possibly use in a story—and it took six hours to find it out. Halapay lives in this rambling house about the size of a junior high school, only it's sort of Japanese. And it's wired to do all kinds of tricks. The inside is wild. There's one wall made of glass rods hanging like icicles. They move when you walk past and sound like a xylophone that needs tuning."

"Well, why not? He's got to spend his dough somehow."

"I know, but wait till I finish. There's all this expensive stage setting, and then out comes Cal Halapay padding around in stocking feet and wearing a sweat shirt with a big hole in the elbow. And he looks about fifteen years old."

"Yes, I've heard he's youthful-looking—for a millionaire," Arch said.

"That's another thing. He keeps boasting about his money and trying to force presents on you. I had to fight off cigars, liquor, a $500 painting, a frozen turkey from his ranch in Oregon, and a Kerry Blue puppy. After lunch his wife showed up, and I was afraid his generosity would exceed the bounds of propriety. Incidentally, Mrs. Halapay is quite a dish."

"You're making me envious. What did you have for lunch? Ostrich tongues?"

"Hot dogs. Served by a houseboy with the charm of a gorilla."

"You got a free lunch. What are you griping about?"

"Halapay. He won't answer questions."

"He refuses?" Arch asked in surprise.

"He ignores them. You can't pin him down. He wanders from progressive jazz to primitive masks he collected in Peru to pregnant cats. I had more luck communicating with the gatepost than with that boy wonder."

"Did you get anything at all?"

"I saw his paintings, of course, and I found out about a blast the art club is giving on Saturday night. I think I might go."

"What did you think of his paintings?"

"They're slightly monotonous. All those red-apple cheeks! But I made a discovery. In all those pictures of kids, Cal Halapay is painting himself. I think he's enchanted with his own looks. Curly hair. Pink complexion."

Arch said, "I agree this isn't going to make the kind of story the boss wants. It sounds like *The Arabian Nights.*"

"Do we have to run a story?"

"You saw the color of the memo. Pink!"

Qwilleran massaged his moustache. After a while he said, "The only time I got a direct answer to a question was when I mentioned George Bonifield Mountclemens."

Arch put down his drink. "What did Halapay say?"

"He exploded—in a controlled sort of way. Basically, he says Mountclemens isn't qualified to judge art."

"That figures. Halapay had a one-man show about a year ago, and our critic roasted him alive. The readers loved it. It cheered their black hearts to know that a successful money-man could be a failure at something. But it was a bitter blow to Halapay. He discovered his money could buy anything but a good art review."

"I weep for him. What about the other newspaper? Did they criticize his work, too?"

"They don't have a critic. Just a nice old lady reporter who covers the art openings and gushes about everything. They play it safe."

Qwilleran said, "So Halapay's a bad sport!"

"Yes, and you don't know how bad," said Arch, pulling his bar stool closer to Qwilleran's. "Ever since that episode, he's been trying to bankrupt the *Flux*. He's withdrawn a lot of advertising linage and switched it over to the other paper. That hurts! Especially since he controls most of the food and fashion advertising in town. He's even trying to turn other admen against the *Flux*. It's serious."

Qwilleran grimaced in disbelief. "And I'm supposed to write a story buttering up that skunk, so the advertising department can get the linage back again?"

"Frankly, it would help. It would take the heat off."

"I don't like it."

"Don't go fastidious on me," Arch pleaded. "Just write a folksy piece about an interesting guy who wears old clothes around the house, takes his shoes off, keeps cats and dogs, eats wieners for lunch. You know how to do it."

"I don't like it."

"I'm not asking you to lie. Just be selective, that's all. Skip the part about the glass icicles and the half-million-dollar lake and the visits in

South America, and bear down on the turkey farm and his lovely wife and the adorable kiddies."

Qwilleran brooded over it. "I suppose that's called practical newspapering."

"It helps pay the bills."

"I don't like it," said Qwilleran, "but if you're in that bad of a bind, I'll see what I can do." He raised his tomato juice glass. "Halapay or hell-to-pay!"

"Don't be cute. I've had a hard day."

"I'd like to read some of Mountclemens' reviews. Have you got them around?"

"On file in the library," Arch said.

"I want to see what he wrote about an artist named Zoe Lambreth. Halapay hinted at a shady connection between Mrs. Lambreth and Mountclemens. Know anything about that?"

"I just process his copy. I don't peek under his window shades," said Arch, and he gave Qwilleran a good-night slap on the back.

CHAPTER 3

QWILLERAN, wearing the newer and darker of his two suits, went alone to the Valentine Ball at the art club, which—he discovered—was called the Turp and Chisel. The club had originated forty years before in the back room of a blind pig. Now it occupied the top floor of the best hotel; its membership was large and fashionable; and the impecunious Bohemians who had founded the fraternity had become old, staid and full of dollars.

Upon his arrival at the ball, Qwilleran was able to wander unrecognized about the premises of the Turp and Chisel. He found a sumptuous lounge, a dining room, and a very busy bar. The games room, paneled with old barnwood, offered everything from darts to dominoes. In the ballroom, tables were draped with red and white cloths, and an orchestra played innocuous tunes.

He asked for the Halapay table and was greeted by Sandra Halapay wearing a white kimono of stiff embroidered silk. Exaggerated makeup made her almond eyes even more exotic.

"I was afraid you wouldn't come," she said, holding his hand long after the handshake had ended and delighting him with a rippling laugh.

"The invitation was irresistible, Mrs. Halapay," said Qwilleran. Then he surprised himself by bending over her hand and brushing it with his moustache.

"Please call me Sandy," she said. "Did you come alone? To a Lovers' Ball?"

"Yes. I represent Narcissus."

Sandy trilled with merriment. "You newspaper people are so clever!"

She was lyrically tall and lovely, Qwilleran decided, and tonight she was charmingly relaxed as wives often are when their husbands are absent.

"Cal is chairman of the ball," she said, "and he's flitting around, so you can be my date."

Her eyes were roguish as well as exotic.

Then Sandy, changing to a formal tone that rang hallow, introduced the others who were seated at the table. They were members of Cal's committee, she explained pointedly. A Mr. and Mrs. Riggs or Biggs were in French period costume. A short fleshy couple named Buchwalter, who seemed to be having a dull time, were garbed as peasants. There was also Mae Sisler, art reporter from the other newspaper.

Qwilleran gave her a fraternal bow, at the same time estimating that she was ten years past retirement age.

Mae Sisler gave him a bony hand and said in a thin voice, "Your Mr. Mountclemens is a very naughty boy, but you look like a nice young man."

"Thank you," said Qwilleran. "No one has called me a young man for twenty years."

"You'll like your new job," she predicted. "You'll meet lovely people."

Sandy leaned close to Qwilleran and said, "You look so romantic in that moustache. I wanted Cal to grow one so he would look halfway grown-up, but he resisted the suggestion. He looks like such an infant. Don't you think so?" she laughed musically.

Qwilleran said, "It's true he appears youthful."

"I think he's retarded somehow. In another few years people will think he's my son. Won't that be crushing?" Sandy gave Qwilleran an adoring look. "Are you going to ask me to dance? Cal is a terrible dancer. He thinks he's a killer, but he's really a clod on the dance floor."

"Can you dance in that costume?"

Sandy's stiff white kimono was bound about the middle with a wide black obi. More white silk was draped over her straight dark hair.

"Oh, sure." She squeezed Qwilleran's arm as they walked to the dance floor. "Do you know what my costume represents?"

Qwilleran said no.

"Cal's in a black kimono. We're the Young Lovers in a Snowy Landscape."

"Who are they?"

"Oh, *you* know. The famous print—by Harunobu."

"Sorry. I'm a dunce when it comes to art." Qwilleran felt he could be debonair about the admission because, at that moment, he was leading Sandy expertly through a fox-trot enhanced by a few Qwilleran flourishes.

"You're a fun dancer," she said. "It takes real coordination to fox-trot to a cha-cha. But we must do something about your art education. Would you like me to tutor you?"

"I don't know if I could afford you—on my salary," he said, and Sandy's laughter could be heard above the orchestra. "How about the little lady from the other newspaper? Is she an art expert?"

"Her husband was a camouflage artist in World War I," said Sandy. "I guess that makes her an expert."

"And who are the rest of the people at your table?"

"Riggs is a sculptor. He does stringy, emaciated things that are shown at the Lambreth Gallery. They look like grasshoppers. So does Riggs, when you come to think of it. The other couple, the Buchwalters, are supposed to be Picasso's famous pair of lovers. You can't tell they're in costume. They always dress like peasants." Sandy turned up her nicely tilted nose. "I can't stand *her*. She thinks she's such an egghead. Her husband teaches art at Penniman School, and he's having a one-man show at the Westside Gallery. He's a vegetable, but he does lovely watercolors." Then she frowned. "I hope newspapermen aren't eggheads. When Cal told me to— Oh, well, never mind. I talk too much. Let's just dance."

Qwilleran lost his partner shortly after, when a surly young man cut in. He was wearing a torn T-shirt and had the manners of a hoodlum. The face was familiar.

Later, back at the table, Sandy said, "That was Tom, our houseboy. He's supposed to be Stanley what's-his-name from that Tennessee Williams play, and his date is around here somewhere, dressed in a pink negligee. Tom is a boor, but Cal thinks he has talent, and so he's putting the kid through art school. Cal does a lot of wonderful things. You're going to write an article about him, aren't you?"

"If I can collect enough material," said Qwilleran. "He's difficult to interview. Perhaps you could help me."

"I'd love it. Did you know Cal is chairman of the State Council on Art? I think he wants to be the first professional artist to make the White House. He'll probably get there, too. He lets *nothing* stop him." She paused and became thoughtful. "You ought to write an article about the old man at the next table."

"Who's he?"

"They call him Uncle Waldo. He's a retired butcher who paints animals. He never held a paintbrush until he was sixty-nine."

"Where have I heard that before?" Qwilleran said.

"Oh, sure, every senior citizen wants to be a Grandma Moses, but Uncle Waldo is really talented—even if Georgie doesn't think so."

"Who's Georgie?"

"You know Georgie—your precious art critic."

"I haven't met the man yet. What's he like?"

"He's a real stinker, that's what he's like. When he reviewed Uncle Waldo's one-man show, he was absolutely cruel."

"What did he say?"

"He said Uncle Waldo should go back to operating a meat market and leave the cows and bunny rabbits to kids, who draw them with more imagination and honesty. He said Uncle Waldo butchered more livestock on canvas than he ever did in the meat business. Everyone was furious! Lots of people wrote letters to the editor, but the poor old man took it hard and stopped painting. It was a crime! He used to paint very charming primitives. I understand his grandson, who's a truck driver, went to the newspaper office and threatened to beat up George Bonifield Mountclemens, and I don't blame him. Your critic is completely irresponsible."

"Has he ever reviewed your husband's work?" Qwilleran asked with his best expression of innocence.

Sandy shuddered. "He's written some vicious things about Cal—just because Cal is a commercial artist and successful. Mountclemens classifies commercial artists with house painters and paperhangers. Actually Cal can draw better than any of those arty blotch-and-dribble kids who call themselves Abstract Expressionists. Not one of them could draw a glass of water!"

Sandy frowned and fell silent, and Qwilleran said, "You're prettier when you smile."

She obliged with a burst of laughter. "Look! Isn't that a panic? Cal is dancing with Mark Antony."

Qwilleran followed her pointing finger to the dance floor, where Cal Halapay in black Japanese kimono was guiding a husky Roman warrior through a slow fox-trot. The face under Antony's helmet was bold-featured but soft.

"That's Butchy Bolton," said Sandy. "She teaches sculpture at the art school—welded metal and all that sort of thing. She and her roommate came as Antony and Cleopatra. Isn't that a scream? Butchy welded her own armor. It looks like a couple of truck fenders."

Qwilleran said, "The paper should have sent a photographer. We should be getting pictures of all this."

Sandy did some acrobatics with her eyebrows and said, "Zoe Lambreth was supposed to handle publicity for the ball, but I guess she's only good at getting publicity for herself."

"I'm going to phone the picture desk," said Qwilleran, "and see if they'll send over a man."

Half an hour later, Odd Bunsen, who was working the one-to-eleven shift, arrived with a 35-mm reflex camera hanging around his neck and the usual cigar between his teeth.

Qwilleran met him in the foyer and said, "Be sure to get a good shot of Cal and Sandra Halapay."

Odd said, "You're telling me? They love to get their noodles in the paper."

"Try to get everybody in pairs. They're dressed up as famous lovers—Othello and Desdemona, Lolita and Humbert Humbert, Adam and Eve—"

"Cr-r-azy!" said Odd Bunsen as he readied his camera. "How long do you have to hang around here, Jim?"

"Just long enough to see who wins the costume prizes and phone something in to the desk."

"Why don't you meet me at the Press Club for a nightcap? I can quit after I print these."

Back at the Halapay table, Sandy introduced Qwilleran to an impressive woman in a beaded evening dress. "Mrs. Duxbury," Sandy explained, "is the most important collector in the city. You should write an article about her collection. It's eighteenth-century English—Gainsborough and Reynolds, you know."

Mrs. Duxbury said, "I'm not anxious to have my collection publicized, Mr. Qwilleran, unless it will help you personally in your new position. Frankly, I am overjoyed to welcome you among us."

Qwilleran bowed. "Thank you. It's a completely new field for me."

"I trust your presence here means that the *Daily Fluxion* has at last come to its senses and dropped Mountclemens."

"No," said Qwilleran, "we're simply expanding our coverage. Mountclemens will continue to write critical reviews."

"What a pity. We were all hoping the newspaper would dismiss that horrid man."

A fanfare of trumpets from the stage announced the presentation of costume prizes, and Sandy said to Qwilleran, "I've got to collect Cal for the judging and the grand march. Are you sure you won't stay longer?"

"Sorry, I have to file my copy, but don't forget you're going to help me write a profile on your husband."

"I'll phone you and invite myself to lunch," said Sandy, giving the newsman an affectionate hug. "It will be fun."

Qwilleran moved to the back of the room and jotted down names as the winners were announced, and he was looking for a telephone when a woman's voice—soft and low—said, "Aren't you the new man from the *Daily Fluxion*?"

His moustache tingled. Women's voices sometimes affected him that way, and this voice was like caressing fingers.

"I'm Zoe Lambreth," she said, "and I'm afraid I failed miserably in my assignment. I was supposed to notify the newspapers about this ball, and it slipped my mind completely. I'm getting ready for a one-man show and working awfully hard—if you'll accept a lame excuse. I hope you're not being neglected. Are you getting all the information you need?"

"I think so. Mrs. Halapay has been looking after me."

"Yes, I noticed," Zoe said with a slight tightening of well-shaped lips. "Mrs. Halapay was very helpful."

Zoe's eyebrows flickered. "I daresay."

"You're not in costume, Mrs. Lambreth."

"No. My husband didn't care to come tonight, and I just dropped in for a few minutes. I wish you would visit the Lambreth Gallery someday and meet my husband. Both of us would like to help you in any way we can."

"I'm going to need help. This is brand-new territory for me," Qwilleran said, and then slyly he added, "Mrs. Halapay has offered to supervise my art education."

"Oh, *dear*!" said Zoe with an intonation that suggested mild distress. "Don't you approve?"

"Well . . . Sandra is not the most *knowledgeable* of authorities. Forgive me. Sooner or later you'll find out that artists are notorious cats." Zoe's large brown eyes were being disarmingly frank, and Qwilleran drowned in them momentarily. "But I'm really sincere in my concern for you," she went on. "I wouldn't want to see you—misdirected. Much of the work being produced today in the name of art is spurious at its worst and shoddy at its best. You should insist on knowing the credentials of your advisers."

"What would you suggest?"

"Come and visit the Lambreth Gallery," she urged, and her eyes echoed the invitation.

Qwilleran pulled in his waistline and entertained the idea of losing a few pounds—beginning tomorrow. Then he made another attempt to find a telephone.

The grand march was over, and the guests were circulating. Word had spread about the club that the *Daily Fluxion*'s new reporter was attending the party and that he was easily recognized by his prominent moustache. Consequently, numerous strangers approached Qwilleran and introduced themselves. Each one wished him well and followed with something uncomplimentary about George Bonifield Mountclemens. Those who were art dealers added brief commercials for their galleries; artists mentioned their forthcoming exhibitions; the laymen invited Qwilleran to come and see their private collections—anytime—and to bring a photographer if he wished.

Among those who hailed the newsman was Cal Halapay. "Come out to the house for dinner some evening," he said. "Bring the whole family."

Now the drinking commenced in earnest, and the party grew boisterous. The greatest commotion could be heard in the games room, and Qwilleran followed the crowd in that direction. He found the room packed with laughing guests, standing rib to rib with barely enough room to raise a highball glass, and the center of attention was Mark Antony. She was standing on a chair. Without a helmet Mark Antony was more nearly a woman—pudgy-faced, with a short haircut set in tight waves.

"Step right up, folks," she was barking. "Try your skill!"

Qwilleran squeezed into the room. The crowd, he discovered, was focusing its attention on a game of darts. Players were trying their aim at a life-size sketch of a man, chalked on the barnwood wall with all features of the anatomy explicitly delineated.

"Step right up, folks," the woman warrior was chanting. "Doesn't cost a cent. One chance apiece. Who wants to play Kill the Critic?"

Qwilleran decided he had had enough. His moustache was feeling vaguely uncomfortable. He made a discreet exit, telephoned his story to the paper, and then joined Odd Bunsen at the Press Club.

"Mountclemens must be a pill," he said to the photographer. "Do you read his column?"

"Who reads?" said Odd. "I just look at the pictures and check my credit line."

"He seems to cause a lot of trouble. Do you know anything about the situation at the art museum?"

"I know they've got a cute chick in the checkroom," Odd said, "and some cr-r-razy nudes on the second floor."

"Interesting, but that's not what I mean. The museum just lost a million-dollar grant from some foundation, and the director was fired as a result. That's what I heard at the party tonight, and they say the whole ruckus was caused by the *Daily Fluxion*'s critic."

"I wouldn't doubt it. He's always raising hell in the Photo Lab. He phones in and tells us what he wants photographed for his column. Then we have to go to the galleries to make the pix. You should see the garbage he expects us to photograph! Last week I went back to the Lambreth Gallery twice, and I still couldn't get a shot worth printing."

"How come?"

"The painting was black and navy blue, for Pete's sake! My print looked like a coal bin on a dark night, and the boss thought it was my fault. Old Monty's always beefing about our photographs. If I ever get a chance, I'd like to bust a speed graphic over his skull."

CHAPTER 4

SUNDAY MORNING Qwilleran picked up a copy of the *Fluxion* at the hotel newsstand. He was living at an old, inexpensive hotel that had replaced its worn rugs and faded velvets with plastic floors and plastic-covered armchairs. In the coffee shop a countergirl in a plastic apron served his scrambled eggs on a cold plastic plate, and Qwilleran opened his newspaper to the art page.

George Bonifield Mountclemens III was reviewing the work of Franz Buchwalter. Qwilleran remembered the name. Buchwalter was the quiet man at the Halapay table—the husband of the social worker—the vegetable who painted lovely watercolors, in Sandy Halapay's estimation.

Two of the man's paintings had been photographed to illustrate the review, and Qwilleran thought they looked pretty good. They were sailboats. He had always liked sailboats. He began to read:

"Any gallery-goer who entertains an appreciation for fine craftsmanship must not miss Franz Buchwalter's one-man show at the Westside Gallery this month," wrote Mountclemens. "The artist, who is a watercolorist and instructor at Penniman School of Fine Art, has elected to exhibit an outstanding collection of picture frames.

"It is obvious even to the untrained eye that the artist has been working diligently at his framing in the last year. The moldings are well-joined and the corners meticulously mitered.

"The collection is also distinguished by its variety. There are wide moldings, narrow moldings, and medium-size moldings, finished in gold leaf, silver leaf, walnut, cherry and ebony, as well as a murky wash intended to be that fashionable counterfeit known as antique white.

"One of the best frames in the show is a wormy chestnut. It is difficult for an observer to determine—without actually inserting a darning needle in the holes—whether this was manufactured by worms in North Carolina or by electric drills in Kansas City. However, a picture-framer of Buchwalter's integrity would be unlikely to use inferior materials, and this critic rather feels that it is genuine wormy chestnut.

"The exhibition is well hung. And special praise must be given to the matting, the textures and tones of which are selected with taste and imagination. The artist has filled his remarkable picture frames with sailboats and other subjects that do not detract from the excellence of the moldings."

Qwilleran looked at the illustrations again, and his moustache made small mute protests. The sailboats were pleasant—very pleasant indeed.

He gathered up his newspaper and left. He was about to try something he had not done since the age of eleven, and at that time he had been under duress. In short, he spent the afternoon at the art museum.

The city's art collection was housed in a marble edifice copied from a

Greek temple, an Italian villa and a French chateau. In the Sunday sun it gleamed white and proud, sparkling with a fringe of dripping icicles.

He resisted an urge to go directly to the second floor for a look at the nudes recommended by Odd Bunsen, but he wandered into the checkroom for a glimpse of the cute chick. He found a long-haired, dreamy-faced girl wrestling with the coat hangers.

She said, glancing at his moustache, "Didn't I see you at the Turp and Chisel last night?"

"Didn't I see you in a pink negligee?"

"We won a prize—Tom LaBlanc and I."

"I know. It was a nice party."

"Real cool. I thought it would be a bomb."

In the lobby Qwilleran approached a uniformed attendant who wore the typical museum-guard expression of suspicion, disapproval and ferocity.

"Where can I find the museum director?" Qwilleran asked.

"He's not around on Sundays—as a rule—but I saw him walking through the lobby a minute ago. Probably came in to pack. He's leaving here, you know."

"Too bad. I hear he was a good man."

The guard wagged his head sympathetically. "Politics! And that muckraker down at the newspaper. That's what did it. I'm glad I'm civil service. . . . If you want to see Mr. Farhar, try his office—down this corridor and turn left."

The office wing of the museum was shrouded in its Sunday quiet. Noel Farhar, Director—according to the lettering on the door—was there alone.

Qwilleran walked through the unattended anteroom and into a paneled office adorned with art objects. "Excuse me," he said. "Mr. Farhar?"

The man rummaging in a desk drawer jumped back in a spasm of guilty acknowledgment. A more fragile young man Qwilleran had never seen. Although Noel Farhar seemed young for the job, his unhealthy thinness gave him a ghostly look of old age.

"Sorry to intrude. I'm Jim Qwilleran from the *Daily Fluxion*."

Noel Farhar's clenched jaw was all too obvious, and he was unable to control the tremor that afflicted one eyelid. "What do you want?" he demanded.

Amiably Qwilleran said, "Just wanted to introduce myself. I'm new on the art beat and trying to get acquainted." He extended a hand and received a reluctant, trembling hand from Farhar.

"If they added you to the staff to mend matters," the director said coldly, "it's too late. The damage is done."

"I'm afraid I don't understand. I've just arrived in this city."

"Sit down, Mr. Qwilleran." Farhar folded his arms and remained standing. "I presume you know the museum has just lost a million-dollar grant."

"I heard about it."

"That would have given us the incentive and the prestige to raise another five million from private donors and industry. It would have given us the country's outstanding pre-Hispanic Mexican collection and a new wing to house it, but *your newspaper* subverted the entire program. *Your critic*, by his continual harassment and ridicule, presented this museum in such an unfavorable light that the Foundation withdrew its consideration." Farhar spoke forcefully despite his visible trembling. "Needless to say, this failure—plus Mountclemens' personal attacks on my administration—has forced me to offer my resignation."

Qwilleran mumbled, "That's a serious charge."

"It is incredible that a single individual who knows nothing about art can pollute the city's art climate. But there's nothing you can do about it. I'm wasting my time talking to you. I have written to your publisher, demanding that this Mountclemens be stopped before he destroys our cultural heritage." Farhar turned back to the files. "Now I have some work to do—some papers to organize—"

"Sorry to interrupt," said Qwilleran. "Very sorry about this whole business. Not knowing the facts, I can't comment—"

"I've told you the facts." Farhar's tone put an end to the interview.

Qwilleran wandered about several floors of the museum, but his mind was not on the Renoirs and the Canalettos. The Toltec and Aztec cultures failed to capture his interest. Only the historic weapons stirred his enthusiasm—the left-handed daggers, German hunting knives, spiked maces, Spanish stylets and rapiers, Italian poniards. And repeatedly his thoughts went to the art critic that everyone hated.

Early the next morning Qwilleran was on the job at the *Fluxion*. In the reference library on the third floor he asked for the file of Mountclemens' reviews.

"Here it is," said the library clerk with a half-wink, "and when you finish with it, you'll find the first-aid room on the fifth floor—in case you need a bromo."

Qwilleran scanned twelve months of art reviews. He found the blistering appraisal of Cal Halapay's curly-haired kids ("drugstore art") and the cruel words about Uncle Waldo's primitives ("age is no substitute for talent"). There was a column, without mention of names, on private collectors who are less dedicated to art preservation than to tax avoidance.

Mountclemens had strong words to say about Butchy Bolton's life-size metal sculptures of the human figure, which reminded him of armor worn in a rural high-school performance of *Macbeth*. He deplored the mass production of third-rate artists at the Penniman School, whose assembly lines would do credit to a Detroit automobile factory.

He complimented the small suburban galleries for their role as afternoon social centers replacing the bridge club and the sewing circle, although he questioned their value as purveyors of art. And he inveighed against the museum: its policies, its permanent collection, its director, and the color of the uniforms worn by the guards.

Interspersed among the tirades, however, were the critic's enthusiastic endorsements of certain artists—especially Zoe Lambreth—but the jargon went over Qwilleran's head. "The complexity of eloquent dynamics in organic texture . . . internal subjective impulses expressed in compassionate linguistics."

There was also a column that had nothing to do with painting or sculpture but discussed cats (*Felis domestica*) as works of art.

Qwilleran returned the file to the library and looked up an address in the telephone book. He wanted to find out why Mountclemens thought Zoe Lambreth's work was so good—and why Cal Halapay thought it was so bad.

He found the Lambreth Gallery on the edge of the financial district, in an old loft building dwarfed by nearby office towers. It seemed to have class. The sign over the door was lettered in gold, and in the window there were only two paintings but thirty yards of gray velvet.

One of the canvases in the window was navy blue, sprinkled with black triangles. The other was a mysterious gravy of thick paint in tired browns and purples. Still, an image seemed to emerge from it, and Qwilleran felt a pair of eyes peering from its depths. As he stared, the expression in the eyes changed from innocence to awareness to savagery.

He opened the door and ventured inside. The gallery was long and narrow, furnished like a living room, rather richly, in uncompromising modern design. On an easel Qwilleran spotted another arrangement of triangles—gray scattered on white—which he preferred to the one in the window. The artist's signature was "Scrano." On a pedestal stood an elbow of drain tile spiked with bicycle spokes. It was titled "Thing #17."

A bell jangled somewhere when he entered the shop, and now

Qwilleran heard footsteps tapping on the treads of the spiral staircase at the rear of the gallery. The iron structure, painted white, resembled a huge sculpture. Qwilleran saw feet, then narrow-trousered legs, and then the crisp, formal, supercilious proprietor of the gallery. It was hard for him to imagine Earl Lambreth as the husband of the warm, womanly Zoe. The man appeared somewhat older than his wife, and he was painfully dapper.

Qwilleran said, "I'm the new art reporter from the *Daily Fluxion*. Mrs. Lambreth asked me to visit your gallery."

The man did something that started to be a smile but ended as an unpleasant mannerism: he raked his bottom lip with his teeth. "Mrs. Lambreth mentioned you," he said, "and I suppose Mountclemens has told you that this is the leading gallery in the city. In fact, it is the *only* gallery worthy of the name."

"I haven't met Mountclemens as yet, but I understand he speaks highly of your wife's work. I'd like to see some of it."

The dealer, standing stiffly with hands behind his back, nodded toward a brown rectangle on the wall. "That is one of Mrs. Lambreth's recent paintings. It has the rich painterly quality recognized as her signature."

Qwilleran studied the picture in cautious silence. Its surface had the texture of a heavily iced chocolate cake, and he unconsciously passed his tongue over his lips. Yet he was aware, once more, of a pair of eyes somewhere in the swirls of paint. Gradually there evolved the face of a woman.

"She uses a lot of paint," Qwilleran observed. "Must take a long time to dry."

The dealer cleaned his lower lip again and said, "Mrs. Lambreth employs pigment to capture the viewer and enmesh him sensually before making her statement. Her declamation is always elusive, nebulous— forcing her audience to participate vitally in the interpretation."

Qwilleran nodded vaguely.

"She is a great humanist," Lambreth continued. "Unfortunately we have very few of her canvases here at present. She is holding everything back for her one-man show in March. However, you saw one of her most lucid and disciplined works in the window."

Qwilleran remembered the paint-clouded eyes he had seen before entering the gallery—the eyes full of mystery and malice. He said, "Does she always paint women like that?"

Lambreth jerked one shoulder. "Mrs. Lambreth never paints to formula. She has great versatility and imagination. And the painting in the window is not intended to invoke human associations. It is a study of a cat."

"Oh," said Qwilleran.

"Are you interested in Scrano? He is one of the foremost contemporary artists. You saw one of his paintings in the window. Here is another on the easel."

Qwilleran squinted at the gray triangles on a white background. The painted surface was fine-grained and slick, with a gleam that was almost metallic; the triangles were crisp.

The newsman said, "He seems to be hooked on triangles. If you hung this one upside down, you'd have three sailboats in a fog."

Lambreth said, "The symbolism should be obvious. In his hard-edge paintings Scrano expresses succinctly the essential libidinous, polygamous nature of Man. The painting in the window is specifically incestuous."

"Well, I guess that clobbers my theory," Qwilleran said. "I was hoping I discovered some sailboats. What does Mountclemens say about Scarno?"

"S-c-r-a-n-o," Lambreth corrected him. "In Scrano's work Mountclemens finds an intellectual virility that transcends the lesser considerations of artistic expression and focuses on purity of concept and sublimation of medium."

"Pretty expensive, I suppose."

"A Scrano usually runs into five figures."

"Whoosh!" said Qwilleran. "How about some of these other artists?"

"They command considerably less."

"I don't see any price tags anywhere."

Lambreth straightened a picture or two. "A gallery of this caliber would hardly be expected to post prices like a supermarket. For our major exhibitions we print a catalog, but what you see today is merely an informal showing of our own group of artists."

"I was surprised to find you located in the financial district," Qwilleran said.

"Our most astute collectors are businessmen."

Qwilleran took a turn around the gallery and reserved comment. Many of the canvases presented drips and blobs of paint in screaming, explosive colors. Some were composed solely of wavy stripes. There was a six-by-eight-foot close-up of a gaping red maw, and Qwilleran recoiled instinctively. On a pedestal stood an egg-shaped ball of metal titled "Untitled." Some elongated shapes in reddish clay resembled grasshoppers, but certain bulges convinced Qwilleran that he was looking at underfed humans. Two pieces of scrap metal were labeled "Thing #14" and "Thing #20."

Qwilleran liked the furniture better: scooplike lounge chairs, sofas floated on delicate chromium steel bases, and low tables with white marble tops.

He said, "Do you have any paintings by Cal Halapay?"

Lambreth cringed. "You must be joking. We are not that kind of gallery."

"I thought Halapay's stuff was highly successful."

"It's easily sold to persons who have no taste," said the dealer, "but actually Halapay's stuff—as you aptly describe it—is nothing but commercial illustration rather presumptuously installed in a frame. It has no value as art. In fact, the man would be doing the public a favor if he would forget his pretensions and concentrate on the activity he does so well—making money. I have no quarrel with hobbyists who want to spend their Sunday afternoons pleasantly in front of an easel, but they should not pose as artists and degrade the public taste."

Qwilleran turned his attention to the spiral staircase. "Do you have another gallery upstairs?"

"Just my office and the framing shop. Would you like to see the framing shop? It might interest you more than the paintings and sculpture."

Lambreth led the way past a stock room, where paintings were stored in vertical slots, and up the stairs. In the framing shop there was a disarrayed workbench and a lingering aroma of glue or lacquer.

"Who makes your frames?" asked Qwilleran.

"A very talented craftsman. We offer the best workmanship and the largest selection of moldings in the city." Still standing stiffly with his hands clasped behind his back, Lambreth nodded at a molding on the workbench. "That one sells for $35 a linear foot."

Qwilleran's gaze wandered to a cluttered office adjoining the workroom. He stared at a painting of a dancer hung crookedly on the wall. A ballerina in a filmy blue garment was depicted in a moment of arrested motion—against a background of green foliage.

"Now there's something I can understand," he said. "I really go for that."

"And well you might! It's a Ghirotto, as you can see by the signature."

Qwilleran was impressed. "I saw a Ghirotto at the museum yesterday. This must be a valuable piece of art."

"It would be—if it were complete."

"You mean it isn't finished?"

Lambreth drew an impatient breath. "This is only half of the original canvas. The painting was damaged. I'm afraid I could not afford a Ghirotto in good condition."

Qwilleran then noticed a bulletin board well plastered with newspaper clippings. He said, "I see the *Daily Fluxion* gives you pretty good coverage."

"You have an excellent art column," said the dealer. "Mountclemens knows more about art than anyone else in the city—including the self-styled experts. And he has integrity—unimpeachable integrity."

"Hmm," said Qwilleran.

"You will no doubt hear Mountclemens denounced on all sides—because he is weeding out the quacks and elevating the standards of taste. Recently he did the city a great service by dislodging Farhar at the museum. A new regime will bring life back into that dying institution."

"But didn't they lose a juicy grant at the same time?"

Lambreth waved his hand. "Another year, another grant, and by that time the museum will merit it."

For the first time Qwilleran noticed the dealer's hands, their grimy nails out of keeping with his fastidious dress. The newsman said, "Mountclemens thinks well of Mrs. Lambreth's work, I've noticed."

"He has been very kind. Many people think he favors this gallery, but the truth is: we handle only the best artists."

"This guy who paints triangles—is he a local artist? I might like to get an interview."

Lambreth looked pained. "It is rather well-known that Scrano is a European. He has been a recluse—in Italy—for many years. For political reasons, I believe."

"How did you find out about him?"

"Mountclemens brought his work to our attention and put us in touch with the artist's American agent, for which we are grateful. We are Scrano's exclusive representative in the Midwest." He cleared his throat and said proudly, "Scrano's work has an intellectualized virility, a transcendent purity—"

"I won't take any more of your time," said Qwilleran. "It's almost noon, and I have a luncheon appointment."

Qwilleran left the Lambreth Gallery with several questions banging about in his head: How could you tell good art from bad art? Why did triangles get thumbs up while sailboats got thumbs down? If Mountclemens was as good as Lambreth said, and if the local art situation was so unhealthy, why did Mountclemens stay in this thankless environment? Was he really a missionary as Lambreth said? Or a monster, as everyone else implied?

Then one more question mark waved its curly tail. Was there really a man named George Bonifield Mountclemens?

At the Press Club, where he was meeting Arch Riker for lunch, Qwilleran said to the bartender, "Does the *Fluxion* art critic ever come in here?"

Bruno paused in wiping a glass. "I wish he did. I'd slip him a Mickey."

"Why? What's your complaint?"

"Only one thing," said Bruno. "He's against the whole human race." He leaned over the bar in a confidential manner. "I tell you he's out to ruin every artist in town. Look what he did to that poor old man, Uncle Waldo. And Franz Buchwalter in yesterday's paper! The only artists he likes are connected with the Lambreth Gallery. You'd think he owned it."

"Some people think he's a highly qualified authority."

"Some people think down is up." Then Bruno smiled wisely. "Just wait till he starts gunning for you, Mr. Qwilleran. As soon as Mountclemens finds out you're snooping around on his beat—" The bartender pulled an imaginary trigger.

"You seem to know a lot about the art situation here in town."

"Sure. I'm an artist myself. I do collage. I'd like you to look at it sometime and give me a critical opinion."

"I've just had this job two days," Qwilleran told him. "I don't even know what collage is."

Bruno gave him a patronizing smile. "It's a form of art. I soak labels off whiskey bottles, cut them in little pieces and paste them up to make presidential portraits. I'm working on Van Buren now. It would make a terrific one-man show." His expression changed to a chummy one. "Maybe you could help me line up a gallery. Do you think you could, like, pull a few strings?"

Qwilleran said, "I don't know if there's much acceptance for presidential portraits made out of whiskey labels, but I'll ask around. . . . Now how about the usual—on the rocks?"

"One of these days," said the bartender, "you'll get hives from all this tomato juice."

When Arch Riker arrived at the bar, he found the art writer chewing his moustache. Arch said, "How did everything go this morning?"

"Fine," said Qwilleran. "At first I was slightly confused about the difference between good art and bad art, but now I'm completely confused." He took a swallow of tomato juice. "However, I've reached a conclusion about George Bonifield Mountclemens III."

"Let's have it."

"He's a fake."

"What do you mean?"

"He doesn't exist. He's a legend, an invention, a concept, a corporation, a gleam in the publisher's eye."

Arch said, "Who do you think writes all that copy we print under his sesquipedalian by-line?"

"A committee of ghost-writers. A committee of three. Probably a Mr. George, a Mr. Bonifield, and a Mr. Mountclemens. No one man could cause so much trouble, or be so hated, or have such an ambiguous image."

"You just don't know about critics, that's all. You're used to cops and robbers."

"I have an alternate theory, if you don't buy my first one."

"What's that?"

"It's a phenomenon of the electronics age. The art column is turned out by a battery of computers in Rochester, N.Y."

"What did Bruno put in your tomato juice?" Arch said.

"Well, I'm telling you one thing: I won't believe George Bonifield Mountclemens until I see him."

"All right. How about tomorrow or Wednesday? He's been out of town, but he's back now. We'll line up an appointment for you."

"Let's make it for lunch—here. We can eat upstairs—off a tablecloth."

Arch shook his head. "He won't come to the Press Club. He never comes downtown. You'll probably have to go to his apartment."

"Okay, line it up," said Qwilleran, "and maybe I'll take Bruno's advice and rent a bulletproof vest."

CHAPTER 5

QWILLERAN SPENT TUESDAY morning at the Board of Education Building, viewing an exhibition of school children's art. He hoped to write something tenderly humorous about the crayoned sailboats floating in the sky, the purple houses with green chimneys, the blue horses that looked like sheep, and the cats—cats—cats.

After his venture into the uncomplicated world of juvenile art, Qwilleran returned to the office in a state of contented detachment. His arrival in the Feature Department caused an unnatural silence. Typewriters stopped chattering. Heads that had been bent over proofs were suddenly raised. Even the green telephones were respectfully quiet.

Arch said, "We've got news for you, Jim. We called Mountclemens to make an appointment for you, and he wants you to go tomorrow night. To *dinner*!"

"Huh?"

"Aren't you going to faint? The rest of the department did."

"I can see the headline now," said Qwilleran. "*Critic Poisons Reporter's Soup.*"

"He's supposed to be a great cook," Arch said. "A real gourmet. If you're lucky, he'll postpone the arsenic until dessert. Here's his address."

At six o'clock Wednesday night Qwilleran took a cab to 26 Blenheim Place. The address was in an old section of town, once a fashionable neighborhood of stately homes. Most of them had become cheap rooming houses or quarters for odd business enterprises. There was a mender of antique porcelain, for example; Qwilleran guessed he was a bookie. Next door was an old coin shop, probably a front for a dope ring. As for the manufacturer of burlesque costumes, there was no doubt in Qwilleran's mind as to the real nature of that establishment.

In the midst of it all, one proud and plucky town house was making a last stand. It had a respectable residential air. It was tall for its width and primly Victorian, even to the ornamental iron fence. This was No. 26.

Qwilleran dodged a pair of neighborhood drunks careening down the sidewalk and walked up the stone steps to the small portico, where three mailboxes indicated the building had been made into apartments.

He smoothed his moustache, which was lively with curiosity and anticipation, and rang the bell. A buzzer unlocked the front door, and he walked into a tile-floored vestibule. Before him was another door, also locked—until a buzzer of another tone released it.

Qwilleran stepped into a palatial but dimly lighted entrance hall that enveloped him with its furnishings. He was aware of large gilt picture frames, mirrors, statuary, a table supported by gold lions, a carved bench like a church pew. Red carpet covered the hall floor and the stairway, and from the top of the flight came a voice with a finely honed edge:

"Come right up, Mr. Qwilleran."

The man at the top of the stairs was excessively tall and elegantly slender. Mountclemens wore a dark red velvet jacket, and his face impressed the newsman as poetic; perhaps it was the way the thin hair was combed down on the high forehead. A fragrance of lime peel surrounded him.

"Apologies for the moat-and-drawbridge arrangement downstairs," said the critic. "In this neighborhood one takes no chances."

He gave Qwilleran a left-handed handshake and ushered him into a living room unlike anything the newsman had ever seen. It was crowded and shadowy. The only illumination came from a flagging blaze in the fireplace and from hidden spotlights beamed on works of art. Qwilleran's eye itemized marble busts, Chinese vases, many gilded picture frames, a bronze warrior and some crumbling wood carvings of angels. One wall of the high-ceilinged room was covered with a tapestry having life-size figures of medieval damsels. Over the fireplace was a painting that any moviegoer would recognize as a Van Gogh.

"You seem impressed by my little collection, Mr. Qwilleran," said the critic, "or appalled by my eclectic taste. . . . Here, let me take your coat."

"It's a pocket-size museum," said Qwilleran in awe.

"It is my life, Mr. Qwilleran. And I admit—quite without modesty— that it succeeds in having a certain *ambiance*."

Hardly an inch of dark red wall remained uncovered. The fireplace was flanked by well-stocked bookshelves. Other walls were stacked to the ceiling with paintings.

Even the red carpet, which had a luminosity of its own, was crowded— with oversize chairs, tables, pedestals, a desk, and a lighted cabinet filled with small carvings.

"Let me pour you an aperitif," said Mountclemens, "and then you can collapse into an easy chair and prop your feet up. I avoid serving anything stronger than sherry or Dubonnet before dinner, because I am rather proud of my culinary skill, and I prefer not to paralyze your taste buds."

"I can't have alcohol," said Qwilleran, "so my taste buds are always in first-class condition."

"Then how about a lemon and bitters?"

While Mountclemens was out of the room, Qwilleran became aware of other details: a dictating machine on the desk; music drifting from behind an Oriental screen; two deep-cushioned lounge chairs facing each other in front of the fire, sharing a plump ottoman between them. He tried one of the chairs and was swallowed up in the cushions. Resting his head back and putting his feet on the ottoman, he experienced an unholy kind of comfort. He almost hoped Mountclemens would never return with the lemon and bitters.

"Is the music satisfactory?" asked the critic, as he placed a tray at Qwilleran's elbow. "I find Debussy soothing at this time of day. Here is something salty to nibble with your drink. I see you have gravitated to the right chair."

"This chair is the next best thing to being unconscious," said Qwilleran. "What's it covered with? It reminds me of something they used to make boys' kneepants out of."

"Heather corduroy," said Mountclemens. "A miracle fabric not yet discovered by scientists. Their preoccupation with man-made materials amounts to blasphemy."

"I'm living in a hotel where everything is plastic. It makes an old flesh-and-blood character like me feel obsolete."

"As you can see, by looking around you, I ignore modern technology."

"I'm surprised," said Qwilleran. "In your reviews you favor modern art, and yet everything here is—" He couldn't think of a word that sounded complimentary.

"I beg to correct you," said Mountclemens. He gestured grandly toward a pair of louvered doors. "In that closet is a small fortune in twentieth-century art—under ideal conditions of temperature and humidity. Those are my investments, but these paintings you see on the walls are my friends. I believe in the art of today as an expression of its time, but I choose to live with the mellowness of the past. For the same reason I am attempting to preserve this fine old house."

Mountclemens—sitting there in his velvet jacket, with Italian pumps on his long narrow feet and a dark red aperitif in his long white fingers—looked smug, sure, safe and unreal. His nasal voice, the music, the comfortable chair, the warmth of the fire and the dimness of the room were making Qwilleran drowsy. He needed action.

"Mind if I smoke?" he said.

"Cigarettes in that cloisonné box at your elbow."

"I use a pipe." Qwilleran searched for his quarter-bend bulldog and his tobacco pouch and his matches and commenced the ritual of lighting up.

As the flame from his match flared in the darkened room, he jerked his head to the side. He stared at the bookshelves. He saw a red light. It was like a signal. No, it was two red lights. Blazing red—and alive!

Qwilleran gasped. The rush of breath extinguished the match, and the red signals disappeared.

"What was—*that*?" he said, when he stopped spluttering. "Something between the books. Something—"

"It was only the cat," said Mountclemens. "He likes to retire behind the books. The shelves are unusually deep because of my art books, and he can find a sanctum back there. Apparently he has had his afternoon nap behind the biographies. He seems to favor biographies."

"I never saw a cat with blazing red eyes," said Qwilleran.

"You will find that characteristic of Siamese cats. Shine a light in their eyes, and they turn ruby red. Ordinarily they are blue—like the blue in that Van Gogh. See for yourself when the cat decides to flatter us with his presence. For the moment he prefers seclusion. He is busy sensing you. Already he knows several things about you."

"What does he know?" Qwilleran squirmed in his chair.

"Having observed you, he knows you are unlikely to make any loud noises or sudden movements, and that is in your favor. So is your pipe. He likes pipes, and he knew that you smoked one, even before you extracted it from your pocket. He also realizes you are affiliated with a newspaper."

"How does he figure that?"

"Ink. He has quite a nose for printer's ink."

"Anything else?"

"At this moment he is flashing a message. He is telling me to serve the first course, or he will not get his own dinner until midnight."

Mountclemens left the room and returned with a tray of hot tarts.

"If you have no objection," he said, "we shall have the first course in the parlor. I have no servants, and you must forgive me if I employ a few informalities."

The crust was flaky; the filling was tender custard flecked with cheese and spinach. Qwilleran savored every mouthful.

"You may wonder," said the critic, "why I prefer to manage without servants. I have a morbid fear of robbery, and I want no strangers coming to the house and discovering the valuables I keep on the premises. Please be good enough not to mention my collection downtown."

"Certainly—if that's the way you feel."

"I know how you newspaper people function. You are purveyors of news by instinct and by habit."

"You mean we're a bunch of gossips," said Qwilleran amiably, enjoying the last forkful of cheese custard and wondering what would come next.

"Let us simply say that a great deal of information—correct and otherwise—is exchanged over the tables at the Press Club. Nevertheless, I feel I can trust you."

"Thank you."

"What a pity you don't drink wine. I had planned to celebrate this occasion by opening a bottle of Chateau Clos d'Estournel '45. It was a great vintage—very slow in maturing—even better than the '28's."

"Open it anyway," Qwilleran said. "I'll enjoy watching you enjoy it. Honestly!"

Mountclemens' eyes sparkled. "I need no further encouragement. And I shall pour you a glass of Catawba grape juice. I keep it in the house for—him."

"Who?"

"Kao K'o-Kung."

Qwilleran's face went momentarily blank.

"The cat," said Mountclemens. "Forgive me for forgetting you have not been formally introduced. He is very fond of grape juice, especially the white. And nothing but the best brand. He is a connoisseur."

"He sounds like quite a cat," Qwilleran said.

"A remarkable creature. He has cultivated an appreciation for certain periods of art, and although I disagree with his choice, I admire his independence. He also reads newspaper headlines, as you will see when the late edition is delivered. And now I believe we are ready for the soup." The critic drew aside some dark red velvet curtains.

An aroma of lobster greeted Qwilleran in the dining alcove. Plates of soup, thick and creamy, were placed on a bare table that looked hundreds of years old. Thick candles burned in iron holders.

As he seated himself in a lavishly carved, high-backed chair, he heard a thud in the living room. It was followed by throaty mutterings. A floorboard creaked, and a light-colored cat with a dark face and slanting eyes walked into the dining alcove.

"This is Kao K'o-Kung," said Mountclemens. "He was named after a thirteenth-century artist, and he himself has the dignity and grace of Chinese art."

Kao K'o-Kung stood motionless and looked at Qwilleran. Qwilleran looked at Kao K'o-Kung. He saw a long, lean, muscular cat with sleek fur and an unbearable amount of assurance and authority.

Qwilleran said, "If he's thinking what I think he's thinking, I'd better leave."

"He is only sensing you," said Mountclemens, "and he appears stern when he concentrates. He is sensing you with his eyes, ears, nose and whiskers. His findings from all four avenues of investigation will be relayed to a central point for evaluation and synthesis, and—depending upon the verdict—he may or may not accept you."

"Thanks," said Qwilleran.

"He is somewhat of a hermit and suspicious of outsiders."

The cat took his time and, when he had finished looking at the visitor, calmly and without visible effort rose in vertical flight to the top of a tall cabinet.

"Whoosh!" said Qwilleran. "Did you see that?"

On top of the cabinet Kao K'o-Kung arranged himself in an imperious posture and watched the scene below with intelligent interest.

"A seven-foot leap is not unusual for a Siamese," said Mountclemens. "Cats have many gifts that are denied humans, and yet we tend to rate them by human standards. To understand a cat, you must realize that he has his own gifts, his own viewpoint, even his own morality. A cat's lack of speech does not make him a lower animal. Cats have a contempt of speech. Why should they talk when they can communicate without words? They manage very well among themselves, and they patiently try to make their thoughts known to humans. But in order to read a cat, you must be relaxed and receptive."

The critic's manner was serious and scholarly.

"For the most part," he went on, "cats resort to pantomime when dealing with humans. Kao K'o-Kung uses a code which is not difficult to learn. He scratches objects to call attention. He sniffs to indicate suspicion. He rubs against ankles when he wants service, and he shows his teeth to express disapproval. He also has a catly way of thumbing his nose."

"That I've got to see."

"Very simple. When a cat, who is a picture of grace and beauty, suddenly rolls over in a hideous posture, contorts his face and scratches his ear, he is telling you, sir, to go to blazes!"

Mountclemens removed the soup plates and brought in a tureen of chicken in a dark and mysterious sauce. A piercing howl came from the top of the cabinet.

Qwilleran said, "You don't need an antenna to tune in that kind of message."

"The lack of an antenna in the human anatomy," said the critic, "impresses me as a vast oversight, a cosmic blunder. With some simple arrangement of feelers or whiskers, think what man might have achieved in communication and prognostication! What we call extrasensory perception is normal experience for a cat. He knows what you are thinking, what you are going to do, and where you have been. I would gladly trade one ear and one eye for a full set of cat's whiskers in good working condition."

Qwilleran put down his fork and wiped his moustache carefully with his napkin. "That's very interesting," he said. He coughed once or twice and then leaned toward his host. "Do you want to know something? I have a funny feeling about my moustache. I've never told this to anyone, but ever since I grew this set of lip whiskers I've had a weird idea that I'm more—more aware! Do you know what I mean?"

Mountclemens nodded encouragingly.

"It's something I wouldn't want to get around at the Press Club," Qwilleran said.

Mountclemens agreed.

"I seem to see things more clearly," said the newsman.

Mountclemens understood.

"Sometimes I seem to sense what's going to happen, and I turn up in the right place at the right time. It's uncanny."

"Kao K'o-Kung does the same thing."

A deep grumble came from the top of the cabinet, and the cat stood up, arched his back in a taut stretch, yawned widely, and jumped to the floor with a grunt and velvety thud.

"Watch this," said the critic. "In three or four minutes the doorbell will ring, and it will be the newspaper delivery. Right now the newsboy is riding his bicycle two blocks away, but Kao K'o-Kung knows he's on his way here."

The cat walked across the living room to the hall and waited at the top of the stairs. In a few minutes the doorbell rang.

Mountclemens said to Qwilleran, "Would you be good enough to pick up the newspaper downstairs? He likes to read it while the news is fresh. Meanwhile, I will toss the salad."

The cat waited on the top stair with a dignified display of interest while the newsman walked down to retrieve the paper that had been tossed on the front porch.

"Lay the paper on the floor," Mountclemens instructed him, "and Kao K'o-Kung will read the headlines."

The cat followed this procedure closely. His nose twitched with antic-ipation. His whiskers moved up and down twice. Then he lowered his head to the screamer head, which was printed in two-inch type, and touched each letter with his nose, tracing the words: DEBBAN RELLIK DAM.

Qwilleran said, "Does he always read backwards?"

"He reads from right to left," Mountclemens said. "By the way, I hope you like Caesar salad."

It was a man's salad, zesty and full of crunch. Then came a bittersweet chocolate dessert with a velvet texture, and Qwilleran felt miraculously in harmony with a world in which art critics could cook like French chefs and cats could read.

Later they had small cups of Turkish coffee in the living room, and Mountclemens said, "How are you enjoying your new milieu?"

"I'm meeting some interesting personalities."

"The artists in this city have more personality than talent, I regret to say."

"This Cal Halapay is a hard one to figure out."

"He is a charlatan," said Mountclemens. "His paintings belong in advertisements for shampoo. His wife is decorative, if she keeps her mouth shut, but unfortunately she finds this an impossible feat. He also has a houseboy or protégé—or whatever the charitable term may be—who has the insolence to want a retrospective exhibition of his life's work at the age of twenty-one. Have you met any other representatives of this city's remarkable art life?"

"Earl Lambreth. He seems to be—"

"There is a pathetic case. No talent whatever, but he hopes to reach the stars on his wife's apron strings. His one and only achievement has been to marry an artist. How he managed to win such an attractive woman is beyond my imagination."

"She's good-looking, all right," Qwilleran agreed.

"And an excellent artist, although she needs to clean up her palette. She has done some studies of Kao K'o-Kung, capturing all his mystery, magic, perversity, independence, playfulness, savagery and loyalty—in one pair of eyes."

"I met Mrs. Lambreth at the Turp and Chisel last weekend. There was a party—"

"Are those aging adolescents still dressing up in fancy costumes?"

"It was a Valentine party. They all represented great lovers. First prize went to a woman sculptor called Butchy Bolton. You know her?"

"Yes," said the critic, "and good taste prevents me from making any comment whatever. I suppose Madame Duxbury was also there, dripping with sables and Gainsboroughs."

Qwilleran got out his pipe and took a long time lighting it. Then Kao

K'o-Kung walked into the room from the direction of the kitchen and performed his after-dinner ritual for all to admire. In studious concentration he darted his long pink tongue over his face. Next he licked his right paw *well* and used it to wash his right ear. Then he changed paws and repeated the identical process on the left: one pass over the whiskers, one pass over the cheekbone, twice over the eye, once over the brow, once over the ear, once over the back of the head.

Mountclemens said to Qwilleran, "You may feel complimented. When a cat washes up in front of you, he is admitting you into his world. . . . Where are you planning to live?"

"I want to find a furnished apartment as soon as possible—anything to get sprung from that plastic-coated hotel."

"I have a vacancy downstairs," said Mountclemens. "Small but adequate—and furnished rather well. It has a gas fireplace and some of my second-best Impressionists. The rent would be insignificant. My chief interest is to have the place occupied."

"Sounds good," said Qwilleran from the depths of his lounge chair, with memories of Caesar salad and lobster bisque still soothing him.

"I travel a great deal, viewing exhibitions and serving on art juries, and in this dubious neighborhood it is a good idea to have signs of life in the front apartment downstairs."

"I'd like to have a look at it."

"Regardless of rumors that I am a monster," said Mountclemens in his most agreeable tone, "you will not find me a bad landlord. Everyone hates a critic, you know, and I imagine the gossips have described me as a sort of cultivated Beelzebub with artistic pretensions. I have few friends and, thankfully, no relatives, with the exception of a sister in Milwaukee who refuses to disown me. I am somewhat of a recluse."

Qwilleran made an understanding gesture with his pipe.

"A critic cannot afford to mix with artists," Mountclemens went on, "and when you hold yourself aloof, you invite jealousy and hatred. All my friends are here in this room, and I care for nothing else. My only ambition is to own works of art. I am never satisfied. Let me show you my latest acquisition. Did you know that Renoir painted window shades at one time in his career?" The critic leaned forward and lowered his voice, and a peculiar elation shone in his face. "I have two window shades painted by Renoir."

A shrill howl came from Kao K'o-Kung, who was sitting in a tall, compact posture, gazing into the fire. It was a Siamese comment that

Qwilleran could not translate. More than anything else it sounded like a portent.

CHAPTER 6

ON THURSDAY the *Daily Fluxion* published Qwilleran's first profile of an artist. His subject was Uncle Waldo, the elderly primitive and portrayer of livestock. Qwilleran had carefully avoided comment on the old man's artistic talent, building his story instead around the butcher's personal philosophy after a lifetime of selling chuck roasts to housewives in a lower-middle-class neighborhood.

The appearance of the story revived interest in Uncle Waldo's pictures, and on Friday the unimportant gallery that handled his work sold all their dusty canvases of beef cattle and woolly lambs and urged the old man to resume painting. Readers wrote to the editor commending Qwilleran's handling of the story. And Uncle Waldo's grandson, the truck driver, went to the offices of the *Daily Fluxion* with a gift for Qwilleran—ten pounds of homemade sausage that the retired butcher had made in his basement.

Friday evening Qwilleran himself was accorded some attention at the Press Club as he distributed links of knackwurst. He met Arch Riker and Odd Bunsen at the bar and ordered his usual tomato juice.

Arch said, "You must be quite a connoisseur of that stuff."

Qwilleran ran the glass under his nose and considered the bouquet thoughtfully. "An unpretentious vintage," he said. "Nothing memorable, but it has a naive charm. Unfortunately the bouquet is masked by the smoke from Mr. Bunsen's cigar. I would guess the tomatoes came from—" (he took a sip and rolled it on his tongue) "from Northern Illinois. Obviously a tomato patch near an irrigation ditch, getting the morning sun from the east and the afternoon sun from the west." He took another swallow. "My palate tells me the tomatoes were picked early in the day—on a Tuesday or Wednesday—by a farmhand wearing a Band-Aid. The Mercurochrome comes through in the aftertaste."

"You're in a good mood," said Arch.

"Yep," said Qwilleran. "I'm moving out of the plastic palace. I'm going to rent an apartment from Mountclemens."

Arch set his glass down with a thud of astonishment, and Odd Bunsen choked on cigar smoke.

"A furnished apartment on the first floor. Very comfortable. And the rent is only $50 a month."

"Fifty! What's the catch?" said Odd.

"No catch. He just doesn't want the house standing empty when he's out of town."

"There's gotta be a catch," Odd insisted. "Old Monty's too tightfisted to give anything away. Sure he doesn't expect you to be a cat-sitter when he's out of town?"

"Quit being a cynical press photographer," said Qwilleran. "Don't you know it's an outdated stereotype?"

Arch said, "Odd's right. When our messenger goes to pick up the tapes, Mountclemens sends him on all kinds of personal errands and never gives the kid a tip. Is it true he's got a houseful of valuable art?"

Qwilleran took a slow swallow of tomato juice. "He's got a lot of junk lying around, but who knows if it's worth anything?" He refrained from mentioning the Van Gogh. "The big attraction is the cat. He's got a Chinese name—something like Koko. Mountclemens says cats like to hear a repetition of syllables when they're being addressed, and their ears are particularly receptive to palatal and velaric sounds."

"Somebody's nuts," said Odd.

"This cat is a Siamese, and he's got a voice like an ambulance siren. Know anything about the Siamese? It's a breed of supercat—very intelligent. This one can read."

"*Read?*"

"He reads newspaper headlines, but they have to be fresh off the press."

"What does this supercat think of my photographs?" Odd said.

"It's questionable whether cats can recognize pictorial images, according to Mountclemens, but he thinks a cat can sense the *content* of a picture. Koko prefers modern art to old masters. My theory is that the fresher paint gets through to his sense of smell. Same way with fresh ink on a newspaper."

"What's the house like?" Arch asked.

"Old. Declining neighborhood. But Mountclemens cherishes his place like a holy relic. They're tearing down buildings all around him, but he says he won't give up his house. It's quite a place. Chandeliers, elaborate woodwork, high ceilings—all carved plaster."

"Dust-catchers," said Odd.

"Mountclemens lives upstairs, and the downstairs is made into two apartments. I'm taking the front one. The rear is vacant, too. It's a nice quiet place except when the cat lets out a shriek."

"How was the food Wednesday night?"

"When you taste Mountclemens' cooking, you forgive him for talking like a character in a Noel Coward play. I don't see how he turns out such dishes with his handicap."

"You mean his hand?"

"Yes. What's wrong with it?"

"That's an artificial hand he wears," said Arch.

"No kidding! It looks real, except for a little stiffness."

"That's why he tapes his column. He doesn't type."

Qwilleran thought about it for a few moments. Then he said, "I feel sorry for Mountclemens, in a way. He lives like a hermit. He thinks a critic shouldn't mix with artists, and yet art is his chief interest—that and the preservation of an old house."

"What did he say about the local art situation?" Arch asked.

"It's a funny thing. He didn't say much about art. We talked mostly about cats."

"See? What did I tell you?" said Odd. "Monty's lining you up for part-time cat-sitting. And don't expect a tip!"

THE UNSEASONABLE WEATHER, warm for February, ended that week. The temperature plunged, and Qwilleran bought a heavy pepper-and-salt tweed overcoat with his first full salary check.

For most of the weekend he stayed home, enjoying his new apartment. It had a living room with bed alcove, a kitchenette, and what Mountclemens would call *ambiance*. Qwilleran called it lots of junk. Still, he liked the effect. It was homey, and the chairs were comfortable, and there were gas logs in the fireplace. The picture over the mantel, according to the landlord, was one of Monet's less successful works.

Qwilleran's only complaint was the dim lighting. Light bulbs of low wattage seemed to be one of Mountclemens' economies. Qwilleran went shopping on Saturday morning and picked up some 75's and 100's.

He had a book from the library on how to understand modern art, and on Saturday afternoon he was coping with Dadaism in chapter nine, and chewing on a pipeful of unlighted tobacco, when an imperative wail sounded outside his door. Although it was clearly the voice of a Siamese cat, the cry was divided into syllables with well-placed emphasis, as if the command were "*Let* me *in!*"

Qwilleran found himself obeying the order punctually. He opened the door, and there stood Kao K'o-Kung.

For the first time Qwilleran saw the critic's cat in bright daylight, which streamed through the beveled glass windows of the hall. The light emphasized the luster of the pale fur, the richness of the dark brown face and ears, the uncanny blue of the eyes. Long brown legs, straight and slender, were deflected at the ends to make dainty feet, and the bold whiskers glinted with the prismatic colors of the rainbow. The angle of his ears, which he wore like a crown, accounted for his regal demeanor.

Kao K'o-Kung was no ordinary cat, and Qwilleran hardly knew how to address him. Sahib? Your Highness? On impulse he decided to treat the cat as an equal, so he merely said, "Won't you come in?" and stood aside, unaware that he was making a slight bow.

Kao K'o-Kung advanced to the threshold and surveyed the apartment carefully before accepting the invitation. This took some time. Then he stalked haughtily across the red carpet and made a routine inspection of the fireplace, the ashtray, the remains of some cheese and crackers on the table, Qwilleran's corduroy coat hanging on the back of a chair, the book on modern art, and an unidentified and almost invisible spot on the carpet. Finally satisfied with everything, he selected a place in the middle of the floor—at a carefully computed distance from the gas fire—and stretched out in a leonine pose.

"Can I get you something?" Qwilleran inquired.

The cat made no reply but looked at his host with a squeezing of the eyes that seemed to denote contentment.

"Koko, you're a very fine fellow," said Qwilleran. "Make yourself comfortable. Do you mind if I finish my reading?"

Kao K'o-Kung stayed half an hour, and Qwilleran relished the picture they made—a man, a pipe, a book, an expensive-looking cat—and he was disappointed when his guest arose, stretched, uttered a sharp adieu, and went upstairs to his own apartment.

Qwilleran spent the rest of the weekend anticipating his Monday lunch date with Sandra Halapay. He was circumventing the problem of interviewing her husband by writing a profile of Cal Halapay "through the eyes of his family and friends." Sandy was going to steer him to the right people, and she had promised to bring candid snapshots of her husband teaching the children to ski, feeding turkeys on the Oregon farm, and training a Kerry Blue to sit up.

All day Sunday Qwilleran felt that his moustache was transmitting messages to him—or perhaps it merely needed clipping. Just the same, its owner sensed that the coming week would be significant. Whether significantly good or significantly bad, the informed source did not reveal.

Monday morning arrived, and with it came an unexpected communication from upstairs.

Qwilleran was dressing and selecting a tie that Sandy might approve (a navy and green wool tartan, made in Scotland) when he first noticed the folded paper on the floor, half pushed under the door.

He picked it up. The handwriting was poor—like a child's scrawl—and the message was terse and abbreviated:

"Mr. Q—Pls del tapes to A.R. Save mess a trip—GBM."

Qwilleran had not seen his landlord since Friday evening. At that time he had moved his two suitcases from the hotel to the apartment and had paid a month's rent. A vague hope that Mountclemens would invite him to Sunday breakfast—perhaps eggs Benedict or a chicken liver omelet—had evaporated. It appeared that only the cat was going to be sociable.

After deciphering the note, Qwilleran opened the door and found the reels of tape waiting for him on the hall floor. He delivered them to Arch Riker, but he thought the request strange—and unnecessary. The Dispatch Room at the *Fluxion* had a benchful of messengers who sat around pitching pennies most of the time.

Arch said, "Making any headway with the Halapay profile?"

"I'm taking Mrs. Halapay to lunch today. Will the *Flux* be willing to pick up the check?"

"Sure, they'll go for a couple of bucks."

"Where's a good place to take her? Somewhere special."

"Why don't you ask the Hungry Photographers? They're always getting people to buy lunch on expense accounts."

In the Photo Lab Qwilleran found six pairs of feet propped on desks, tables, wastebaskets and filing cabinets—waiting for assignments, or waiting for prints to come off the dryer, or waiting for the dark room buzzer.

Qwilleran said, "Where's a good place to take someone to lunch for an interview?"

"Who's paying?"

"The *Flux*."

"Sitting Bull's Chop House," the photographers said in unison.

"The chopped sirloin weighs a pound," said one.

"The cheese cake's four inches thick."

"They have a double lamb chop as big as my shoe."

It sounded good to Qwilleran.

Sitting Bull's Chop House was located in the packinghouse district, and a characteristic odor seeped into the dining room to compete with the cigar smoke.

"Oh, what a fun place," Sandy Halapay squealed. "How clever of you to bring me here. So many *men*! I adore men."

The men adored Sandy, too. Her red hat topped with a proud black rooster tail was the center of attention. She ordered oysters, which the chop house could not supply, so she contented herself with champagne. But with each sip her laughter grew more shrill, rebounding from the antiseptic white tile walls of the restaurant, and the enthusiasm of her audience dwindled.

"Jim, dear, you must fly down to the Caribbean with me when Cal goes to Europe next week. I'll have the plane all to myself. Wouldn't it be *fun*?"

But she had forgotten to bring the information Qwilleran needed, and the snapshots of her husband were unusable. The lamb chop was indeed as big as a photographer's shoe and as flavorful. The waitresses, uniformed like registered nurses, were more efficient than cordial. The luncheon was not a success.

Back in the office that afternoon Qwilleran had to listen to telephone complaints about Mountclemens' review in Sunday's paper. The critic had called a watercolorist a frustrated interior decorator, and the watercolorist's friends and relatives were calling to castigate the *Daily Fluxion* and cancel their subscriptions.

Altogether Monday was not a halcyon day for Qwilleran. At the end of the tedious afternoon he fled to the Press Club for dinner, and Bruno, setting up a tomato juice, said, "I hear you've moved in with Mountclemens."

"I've rented one of his vacant apartments," Qwilleran snapped. "Anything wrong with that?"

"Not until he starts pushing you around, I guess."

Then Odd Bunsen stopped long enough to give the newsman an informed grin and say, "I hear old Monty's got you running errands for him already."

When Qwilleran returned home to 26 Blenheim Place, he was in no mood for what he found. There was another note under his door.

"Mr. Q," it read, "Apprec pick up plane ticket—reserv Wed 3 P.M. NY—chg my acct—GBM."

Qwilleran's moustache bristled. It was true that the airline office was across the street from the *Daily Fluxion* Building, and picking up a plane ticket was a small favor for his landlord to ask in return for a good dinner. What irked him was the abruptness of the request. Or was it an order? Did Mountclemens think he was Qwilleran's boss?

Tomorrow was Tuesday. The plane reservation was for Wednesday. There was no time to make an issue of it, so Qwilleran grumbled to himself and picked up the ticket the following morning on his way to work.

Later in the day Odd Bunsen met him on the elevator and said, "Going away somewhere?"

"No. Why?"

"Saw you going into the airline office. Thought you were skipping town." He added a taunting grin. "Don't tell me you're running errands for Monty again!"

Qwilleran groomed his moustache with his knuckles and tried to reflect calmly that curiosity and a keen sense of observation make a good news photographer.

When he arrived home that evening, the third note was waiting under his door. It was more to his liking:

"Mr. Q—Pls bkfst w me Wed 8:30—GBM."

Wednesday morning Qwilleran went upstairs with the plane ticket and knocked on Mountclemens' door.

"Good morning, Mr. Qwilleran," said the critic, extending a thin white hand, his left. "I hope you are not in a hurry. I have a ramekin of eggs with herbs and sour cream, ready to put in the oven, if you can wait. And some chicken livers and bacon en brochette."

"For that I can wait," said Qwilleran.

"The table is set in the kitchen, and we can have a compote of fresh pineapple while we keep an eye on the broiler. I was fortunate enough to find a female pineapple at the market."

The critic was wearing silk trousers and a short Oriental coat tied with a sash around his remarkably thin midriff. There was a scent of lime peel. His thong sandals slapped as he led the way down a long hall to the kitchen.

The walls of the corridor were completely covered with tapestries, scrolls and framed pictures. Qwilleran remarked about the quantity.

"Also quality," said Mountclemens, tapping a group of drawings as he walked past them. "Rembrandt . . . Holbein. Very fine . . . Millet."

The kitchen was large, with three tall narrow windows. Bamboo blinds kept the light subdued, but Qwilleran peered through them and saw an exterior stairway—evidently a fire escape—leading down to a brick-walled patio. In the alley beyond the high wall he could see the top of a station wagon.

"Is that your car?" he asked.

"That grotesquery," said Mountclemens with an implied shudder, "belongs to the junk dealer across the alley. If I kept a car, it would have some felicity of design—a Karmann Ghia, or a Citroën. As it is, I dissipate my fortune in taxicabs."

The kitchen had a mellow clutter of antiques, copper utensils and clumps of dried vegetation.

"I dry my own herbs," Mountclemens explained. "Do you appreciate a little mint marinated with the pineapple? I think it gives the fruit another dimension. Pineapple can be a little *too* direct. I grow the mint in a pot on the windowsill—chiefly for Kao K'o-Kung. His idea of a choice plaything is a bouquet of dried mint leaves tied in the toe of a sock. In a moment of rare wit we have named his toy Mintie Mouse. A rather free abstraction of a mouse, but that is the sort of thing that appeals to his artistic intellect."

Mountclemens was putting individual baking dishes into the oven one at a time, using his left hand.

"Where is Koko this morning?" Qwilleran asked.

"You should be able to feel his gaze. He is watching you from the top of the refrigerator—the only down-cushioned refrigerator west of the Hudson River. It is his bed. He refuses to sleep anywhere else."

The aroma of bacon, herbs and coffee was beginning to swirl about the kitchen, and Koko—on a blue cushion that matched his eyes—raised his nose to sniff. So did Qwilleran.

He said, "What do you do about the cat when you go to New York?"

"Ah, that is the problem," said the critic. "He requires a certain amount of attention. Would it be an imposition if I asked you to prepare his meals while I am away? I'll be gone less than a week. He takes only two meals a day, and his diet is simple. There is raw beef in the refrigerator. You merely carve it in small pieces the size of a lima bean, put it in a pan with a little broth, and warm it gently. A dash of salt and a sprinkling of sage or thyme will be appreciated."

"Well—" said Qwilleran, spooning up the last of the minted pineapple juice.

"To make it easier for you in the mornings, when you are headed for the office, he could have a slice of *pâté de la maison* for breakfast instead of beef. It makes a welcome change for him. Would you like your coffee now or later?"

"Later," said Qwilleran. "No—I'll take it now."

"And then there is the matter of his commode."

"What's that?"

"His commode. You'll find it in the bathroom. It needs very little attention. He is an immaculate cat. You will find the sand for the commode in the Chinese tea chest at the foot of the bathtub. Do you take sugar or cream?"

"Black."

"If the weather is not too inclement, he can take a little exercise in the patio, provided you accompany him. Normally he gets sufficient exercise by running up and down the front stairs. I leave my apartment door ajar for his comings and goings. To be on the safe side, I shall also give you a key. Is there anything I can do for you in New York?"

Qwilleran had just experienced the first forkful of chicken livers rolled in bacon and seasoned with a touch of basil, and he rolled his eyes gratefully heavenward. In doing so, he caught the gaze of Kao K'o-Kung, perched on the refrigerator. The cat slowly and deliberately closed one eye in an unmistakable wink.

CHAPTER 7

"I HAVE a complaint," Qwilleran told Arch at the Press Club on Wednesday night.

"I know what it is. Your name was spelled with a U yesterday, but we caught it in the second edition. You know what's going to happen, don't you? The next time the typographers' union meets with management, the spelling of your name is going to be one of their grievances."

"I have another beef, too. I wasn't hired to be an orderly for your art critic, but that's what he seems to think. Do you know he's leaving town tonight?"

"I guessed as much," said Arch. "That last batch of tapes included enough copy for three columns."

"First I delivered those tapes for him. And then I picked up his ticket for the three o'clock plane this afternoon. And now I'm expected to do latrine duty for his cat!"

"Wait till Odd Bunsen hears this!"

"Don't tell him! Nosy Bunsen will find out soon enough in his own devious way. I'm supposed to feed the cat twice a day, change his drinking water, and attend to his commode. Do you know what a commode is?"

"I can guess."

"It was new to me. I thought cats just ran out in the backyard."

"There's nothing in the Guild contract about reporters doing toidy service," Arch said. "Why didn't you decline?"

"Mountclemens didn't give me a chance. He's a sly operator! There I was, sitting in his kitchen, mesmerized by fresh pineapple, broiled chicken livers and eggs in sour cream. It was *female* pineapple, what's more. What could I do?"

"You'll have to choose between pride and gluttony, that's all. Don't you like cats?"

"Sure, I like animals, and this cat is more human than a few people I could name. But he gives me the uncomfortable feeling that he knows more than I do—and he's not telling what it is."

Arch said, "We have cats around the house all the time. The kids bring them home. But none of them ever gave me an inferiority complex."

"Your kids never brought home a Siamese."

"You can stand it for three or four days. If it gets too much for you, we'll send a copyboy with a master's degree. He should be able to cope with a Siamese."

"Knock it off. Here comes Odd Bunsen," said Qwilleran.

Even before the photographer appeared, the cigar could be detected and the voice could be heard, complaining about the frigid temperature outside.

Odd tapped Qwilleran on the shoulder. "Are those cat hairs on your lapel, or have you been dating a blonde with a crew cut?"

Qwilleran combed his moustache with a swizzle stick.

Odd said, "I'm still on nights. Any of you guys want to eat with me? I've got an hour for dinner, if nobody blows up City Hall."

"I'll eat with you," said Qwilleran.

They found a table and consulted the menu. Odd ordered Salisbury steak, complimented the waitress on the trimness of her waistline, and then said to Qwilleran, "Well, have you got old Monty figured out yet? If I went around insulting everybody the way he does, I'd get fired—or assigned to Society, what's worse. How does he get away with it?"

"Critic's license. Besides, newspapers like controversial writers."

"And where does he get all his money? I hear he lives pretty well. Travels a lot. Drives an expensive car. He doesn't do that on what the *Flux* pays him."

"Mountclemens doesn't drive," Qwilleran said.

"Sure, he does. I've seen him behind the wheel. I saw him this morning."

"He told me he didn't have a car. He rides taxis."

"Maybe he doesn't own one, but he drives one sometimes."

"How do you suppose he manages?"

"No sweat. Automatic transmission. Didn't you ever do any one-arm driving? You must be a lousy lover. I used to drive with one arm, shift gears and eat a hot dog all at the same time."

"I've got a few questions, too," Qwilleran said. "Are the local artists as bad as Mountclemens says? Or is he as phony as the artists think? Mountclemens says Halapay is a charlatan. Halapay says Zoe Lambreth's paintings are a hoax. Zoe says Sandy Halapay is uninformed. Sandy says Mountclemens is irresponsible. Mountclemens says Farhar is incompetent. Farhar says Mountclemens knows nothing about art. Mountclemens says Earl Lambreth is pathetic. Lambreth says Mountclemens is a monument of taste, truth and integrity. So . . . who's on first?"

"Listen!" said Odd. "I think they're paging me."

The voice mumbling over the public-address system could hardly be heard above the hubbub in the bar.

"Yep, that's for me," the photographer said. "Somebody must have blown up the City Hall."

He went to the telephone, and Qwilleran pondered the complexities of the art beat.

When Odd Bunsen returned from the telephone booth, he was taut with excitement.

Qwilleran thought, A press photographer for fifteen years, and he still lights up when there's a three-alarm fire.

"I've got news for you," said Odd, leaning over the table and keeping his voice down.

"What is it?"

"Trouble on your beat."

"What kind of trouble?"

"Homicide! I'm on my way to the Lambreth Gallery."

"The Lambreth!" Qwilleran stood up fast enough to knock over his chair. "Who is it? . . . Not Zoe!"

"No. Her husband."

"Know what happened?"

"They said he was stabbed. Want to come with me? I told the desk you were here, and they said it would be good if you could cover it. Kendall's out on a story, and both leg men are busy."

"Okay, I'll go."

"Better phone them back and say so. I've got my car outside."

When Qwilleran and Bunsen arrived in front of the Lambreth Gallery, there was an unwarranted calm in the street. The financial district was normally deserted after five-thirty, and even a murder had failed to draw much of a crowd. A sharp wind whipped down the canyon created by nearby office buildings, and only a few shivering stragglers stood about on the sidewalk, but they soon moved on. A loneliness filled the street. Isolated voices sounded unreasonably loud.

The newsmen identified themselves to the patrolman at the door. Inside, the expensive art and plush furnishings made an unlikely background for the assortment of uninvited guests. A police photographer was taking pictures of some paintings that had been viciously slashed. Bunsen pointed out the precinct inspector and Hames, a detective from the Homicide Bureau. Hames nodded at them and jerked a thumb upstairs.

The newsmen started up the spiral staircase at the rear and then backed away to let a fingerprint man come down. He was talking to himself. He was saying, "How can they get a stretcher down this thing? They'll have to take him out the window."

Upstairs a sharp voice was saying, "Come on, you fellows. You can take care of that downstairs. Let's thin out."

"That's Wojcik from Homicide," said Bunsen. "No fooling around with him."

The framing shop was approximately as Qwilleran remembered it—except for the men with badges, cameras and notebooks. A patrolman stood in the doorway to Lambreth's office, facing out. Over his shoulder

Qwilleran could see that the office had been fairly well wrecked. The body lay on the floor near the desk.

He got Wojcik's attention and flipped open a small notebook. "Murderer known?"

"No," said the detective.

"Victim: Earl Lambreth, director of the gallery?"

"Right."

"Method?"

"Stabbed with a tool from the workbench. A sharp chisel."

"Where?"

"Throat. A very wet job."

"Body discovered where?"

"In his office."

"By whom?"

"Victim's wife, Zoe."

Qwilleran took a second to gulp and grimace.

"That's spelled Z-o-e," said the detective.

"I know. Any sign of a struggle?"

"Office practically turned upside down."

"What about the vandalism in the gallery?"

"Several pictures damaged. A statue broken. You can see that downstairs."

"What time did it happen?"

"The electric clock—knocked off the desk—stopped at six-fifteen."

"The gallery was closed at that time."

"Right."

"Any evidence of forcible breaking and entering?"

"No."

"Then the murderer could have been someone who had legitimate access to the place."

"Could be. We found the front door locked. The alley door may or may not have been locked when Mrs. Lambreth arrived."

"Anything stolen?"

"Not immediately apparent." Wojcik started to move away. "That's all. You've got the story."

"One more question. Any suspects?"

"No."

Downstairs, while Bunsen scrambled around taking pictures, Qwilleran studied the nature of the vandalism. Two oil paintings had been ripped diagonally by a sharp instrument. A framed picture lay on the floor with its glass broken, as if a heel had been put through it. A reddish clay sculpture appeared to have been bounced off a marble-top table; there were scattered fragments.

Paintings by Zoe Lambreth and Scrano—the only two names that registered with Qwilleran—were unharmed.

He remembered the sculpture from his previous visit. The elongated shape with random swellings had apparently been a woman's figure. Its label, still affixed to the empty pedestal, said, "*Eve* by B. H. Riggs—terra cotta."

The watercolor on the floor was one Qwilleran had not noticed the week before. It resembled a jigsaw puzzle of many colors—just a pleasing pattern. It was titled "Interior," and the artist's name was Mary Ore. The label called it a gouache.

Then Qwilleran examined the two oils. Both were composed of wavy vertical stripes of color, applied on a white background with a wide brush. The colors were violent—red, purple, orange, pink—and the paintings seemed to vibrate like a plucked string. Qwilleran wondered who would buy these nerve-racking works of art. He preferred his second-rate Monet.

Stepping closer to check the labels, he noted that one was "Beach Scene #3 by Mary Ore—oil," while the other was "Beach Scene #2" by the same artist. In a way the titles were a help in appreciating the pictures. They began to remind Qwilleran of shimmering heat waves rising from hot sand.

He said to Bunsen, "Look at these two pictures. Would you say they were beach scenes?"

"I'd say the artist was drunk," said Odd.

Qwilleran moved back a few paces and squinted at the two oils. Suddenly he saw a crowd of standing figures. He had been looking at the red, orange and purple stripes, and he should have been seeing the white voids between them. The vertical stripes of white suggested the contours of female bodies—abstract but recognizable.

He thought, "Women's figures in those white stripes . . . a woman's torso in the broken clay. Let's have another look at the watercolor."

When he knew what he was searching for, it was not hard to find. In the jagged wedges of color that made up the pattern of Mary Ore's work, he could distinguish a window, a chair, a bed—on which reclined a human figure. Female.

He said to Odd Bunsen, "I'd like to go out to the Lambreth house and see if Zoe will talk to me. Also, she might have a photograph of the deceased. Shall we check with the desk?"

After phoning the details to a rewrite man and getting a go-ahead from the City Desk, Qwilleran folded himself into Odd Bunsen's cramped two-seater, and they drove to 3434 Sampler Street.

The Lambreth home was a contemporary town house in a new neighborhood—self-consciously well designed—that had replaced a former slum. The newsman rang the doorbell and waited. Draperies were drawn to cover the large windows, but it could be seen that lights were burning in every room, upstairs and downstairs. They rang the bell again.

When the door opened, the trousered woman who stood there—arms folded belligerently, feet planted solidly on the threshold—looked familiar to Qwilleran. She was tall and husky. Her soft face was set in a stern expression.

"Yes?" she said defiantly.

"I'm a friend of Mrs. Lambreth," said Qwilleran. "I wonder if I could see her and offer my assistance. Jim Qwilleran's the name. This is Mr. Bunsen."

"You're from the paper. She's not going to see any reporters tonight."

"This isn't an official visit. We were on our way home and thought there might be something we could do. Aren't you Miss Bolton?"

Inside the house a low, tired voice called, "Who is it, Butchy?"

"Qwilleran and another man from the *Fluxion*."

"It's all right. Ask them in."

The newsmen stepped into a room furnished in stark contemporary style. The furnishings were few, but fine, and there—leaning against a doorjamb—was Zoe Lambreth wearing purple silk trousers and a lavender blouse and looking gaunt and bewildered.

Butchy said, "She should be lying down and resting."

Zoe said, "I'm all right. I'm too keyed up to do any resting."

"She wouldn't take a sedative."

"Will you gentlemen sit down?" Zoe said.

Qwilleran's face reflected the sympathetic understanding for which he was famous. Even his moustache contributed to the expression of grave concern. He said, "I don't need to tell you my feelings. Even though our acquaintance was short, I feel a personal loss."

"It's terrible. Just terrible." Zoe sat on the extreme edge of the sofa, with her hands folded on her knees.

"I visited the gallery last week, as you suggested."

"I know. Earl told me."

"It's impossible to imagine what a shock this must have been."

Butchy interrupted. "I don't think she should be talking about it."

"Butchy, I've got to talk about it," said Zoe, "or I'll go crazy." She looked at Qwilleran with the full brown eyes that he remembered so well from their first meeting, and now they reminded him of the eyes in Zoe's own paintings at the gallery.

He said, "Was it your custom to go to the gallery after it was closed?"

"Quite the contrary. I seldom went there at any time. It looks unprofessional for an artist to hang around the gallery that handles her work. Especially in our case—husband and wife. It would look too folksy!"

"The gallery impressed me as very sophisticated," Qwilleran said. "Very suitable for the financial district."

Butchy said, with a frank show of pride, "That was Zoe's idea."

"Mrs. Lambreth, what caused you to go to the gallery tonight?"

"I was there twice. The first time was just before closing time. I had been shopping all afternoon and stopped in to see if Earl wanted to stay downtown for dinner. He said he couldn't leave until seven o'clock or later."

"What time was it when you were talking to him?"

"The front door was still open, so it must have been before five-thirty."

"Did he explain why he couldn't leave the gallery?"

"He had to work on the books—for a tax deadline or something—so I went home. But I was tired and didn't feel like cooking."

Butchy said, "She's been working night and day, getting ready for a one-man show."

"So I decided to have a bath and change clothes," Zoe went on, "and go back downtown at seven o'clock and drag Earl away from his books."

"Did you telephone him to say you were returning to the gallery?"

"I think so. Or maybe I didn't. I can't remember. I thought about phoning, but in the rush of getting dressed, I don't know whether I called or not. . . . You know how it is. You do things automatically—without thinking. Sometimes I can't remember whether I've brushed my teeth, and I have to look at the toothbrush to see if it's wet."

"When did you arrive at the gallery the second time?"

"Just about seven o'clock, I think. Earl had taken the car in for repairs, so I called a taxi and had the driver take me to the alley entrance of the gallery. I have a key for the back door—just in case of emergency."

"It was locked?"

"That's another thing I don't remember. It should have been locked. I put my key in the lock and turned the door handle without thinking much about it. The door opened, and I went in."

"Did you notice anything amiss on the ground floor?"

"No. The lights were out. I went right up the spiral staircase. As soon as I walked into the workroom, I sensed something wrong. It was deadly quiet. I was almost afraid to go into the office." She was remembering it painfully. "But I did. First I saw—papers and everything all over the floor. And then—" She put her face in her hands, and there was silence in the room.

After a while Qwilleran said gently, "Would you like me to notify Mountclemens in New York? I know he thought highly of you both."

"If you wish."

"Have the funeral plans been made?"

Butchy said, "There won't be a funeral. Zoe doesn't approve of funerals."

Qwilleran stood up. "We'll be going now, but please let me know—Mrs. Lambreth—if there's anything I can do. Sometimes it helps just to talk."

Butchy said, "I'm here. I'm looking after her."

Qwilleran thought the woman sounded possessive. He said, "Just one more thing, Mrs. Lambreth. Do you have a good photograph of your husband?"

"No. Just a portrait I painted last year. It's in my studio. Butchy will show you. I think I'll go upstairs."

She walked from the room without further ceremony, and Butchy led the newsmen to the studio at the rear of the house.

There on the wall was Earl Lambreth—cold, haughty, supercilious—painted without love.

"Perfect likeness," said Butchy with pride. "She really captured his personality."

Almost inaudible was the click of Odd Bunsen's camera.

CHAPTER 8

WHEN QWILLERAN and Odd Bunsen drove away from the Lambreth house, they shivered in silence until the heater in Odd's car gave out the first promising puff.

Then Odd said, "The Lambreths seem to be doing all right at that art racket. Wish I could live like that. I'll bet that sofa was worth a thousand bucks. Who was that big bruiser?"

"Butchy Bolton. Teaches sculpture at Penniman School of Fine Art."

"She really thought she was running the show. Enjoying it, too."

Qwilleran agreed. "Butchy didn't strike me as being exactly grief-stricken over the loss of Earl Lambreth. I wonder where she fits into the picture. Friend of the family, I suppose."

"If you ask me," said Odd, "I don't think that doll Zoe was taking it too hard, either."

"She's a calm, intelligent woman," Qwilleran said, "even if she is a doll. She's not the type to collapse."

"If my wife ever finds me lying in a pool of blood, I want her to collapse and collapse good! I don't want her running home and fixing her lipstick and putting on a sharp outfit to receive callers. Imagine a dame not remembering whether she telephoned her husband or not, and not remembering whether the gallery door was locked!"

"It was the shock. It leaves blanks in the memory. She'll remember tomorrow—or the next day. What did you think of the portrait she painted of her husband?"

"Perfect! He's a cold fish. I couldn't have taken a photograph that was any better."

Qwilleran said, "I used to think these modern artists painted drips and blots because they couldn't draw, but now I'm not so sure. Zoe is really talented."

"If she's so talented, why does she waste her time painting that modern garbage?"

"Probably because it sells. By the way, I'd like to meet our police reporter."

"Lodge Kendall? Haven't you met him yet? He's over at the Press Club just about every day for lunch."

"I'd like to have a talk with him."

"Want me to line it up for tomorrow?" Odd said.

"Okay. . . . Where are you headed now?"

"Back to the Lab."

"If it isn't out of your way, would you drop me at my apartment?"

"No sweat."

Qwilleran looked at his wristwatch in the glow from the instrument panel. "It's ten-thirty!" he said. "And I forgot to feed the cat."

"A-hah! A-hah!" said Odd. "I told you Monty wanted you for a cat-sitter." A few minutes later, when he turned the car into Blenheim Place, he said, "Doesn't this neighborhood scare the hell out of you? The characters you see on the streets!"

"They don't bother me," said Qwilleran.

"You wouldn't get *me* to live here! I'm a coward."

A folded newspaper lay on the porch of No. 26. Qwilleran picked it up, unlocked the front door and closed it quickly behind him, glad to get in out of the cold. He rattled the door handle to make sure it was locked again—as Mountclemens had warned him to do.

Using a second key, he unlocked the inner vestibule door. And that's when he recoiled in black fright!

Out of the dark came a wild scream. Qwilleran's mind went blank. The hairs of his moustache stood on end. His heart pounded. Instinctively he gripped the newspaper like a club.

Then he realized the source of the scream. Koko was waiting for him. Koko was scolding him. Koko was hungry. Koko was furious.

Qwilleran leaned against the doorjamb and gasped. He loosened his tie. "*Never* do that again!" he told the cat.

Koko was sitting on the table that was supported by golden lions, and he retorted with a torrent of abuse.

"All right! All right!" Qwilleran yelled at him. "I apologize. I forgot, that's all. Important business downtown."

Koko continued his tirade.

"Wait till I take my coat off, will you?"

Once Qwilleran started upstairs, the tumult ceased. The cat bounded ahead and led him into Mountclemens' apartment, which was in darkness. Qwilleran groped for a light switch. This delay irritated Koko, who commenced another vocal demonstration. Now the piercing cries had gravel-throated undertones signifying menace.

"I'm coming. I'm coming," said Qwilleran, following the cat down the long narrow hall to the kitchen. Koko led him directly to the refrigerator, where there was a chunk of beef waiting in a glass tray. It looked like a whole tenderloin.

Qwilleran put the meat on a built-in butcher's block and hunted for a sharp knife.

"Where does he keep his knives?" he said, pulling open one drawer after another.

Koko leaped lightly to the adjoining counter and nosed a knife rack, where five handsome blades hung point downward on a magnetized bar.

"Thanks," said Qwilleran. He started to carve the beef, marveling at the quality of the cutlery. Real chef's knives. They made meat-cutting a pleasure. How did Mountclemens say to cut the beef? The size of a kidney bean or the size of a navy bean? And how about the broth? He said to warm it in broth. Where was the broth?

The cat was sitting on the counter, supervising every move with what appeared to be an impatient scowl.

Qwilleran said, "How about eating it raw, old man? Since it's so late—"

Koko gargled a low note in his throat, which Qwilleran assumed was acquiescence. In a cupboard he found a plate—white porcelain with a wide gold band. He arranged the meat on it—attractively, he thought—and placed it on the floor alongside a ceramic water bowl decorated with the word "cat" in three languages.

Koko jumped to the floor with a grunt, walked to the plate and examined the beef. Then he looked up at Qwilleran with incredulity displayed in the tilt of his ears.

"Go ahead. Eat," said Qwilleran. "Enjoy it in good health."

Koko lowered his head once more. He sniffed. He touched the beef with his paw and gave a perceptible shudder. He shook his paw fastidiously and walked away, his tail pointed stiffly toward the North Star.

Later, after Qwilleran had found some thin gravy in the refrigerator and prepared the meal properly, Kao K'o-Kung consented to dine.

The newsman related the experience at the Press Club the following noon when he had lunch with Arch Riker and Lodge Kendall.

"But this morning I acquitted myself admirably," said Qwilleran. "Koko got me up at six-thirty by yelling outside my door, and I went up and prepared breakfast to his satisfaction. I think he's going to let me keep the job until Mountclemens comes home."

The police reporter was young, tense, earnest, literal and unsmiling. He said, "Do you mean to say you let a cat boss you around?"

"Actually, I feel sorry for him. Poor little rich cat! Nothing but tenderloin and *pâté de la maison*. I wish I could catch him a mouse."

Arch explained to Kendall, "You see, this is a Siamese, descended from an Egyptian god. It not only communicates and runs the show; it reads newspaper headlines. A cat that can read is obviously superior to a newspaperman who can't catch mice."

Qwilleran said, "He flies, too. When he wants to get to the top of an eight-foot bookcase, he just puts his ears back and zooms up like a jet. No wings. He's got some kind of aerodynamic principle that ordinary cats don't have."

Kendall regarded the two older men with wonder and suspicion.

"After Koko got me up at six-thirty," said Qwilleran, "I started thinking about the Lambreth murder. Any developments, Lodge?"

"Nothing released this morning."

"Have they reached any conclusions about the vandalism?"

"Not that I've heard."

"Well, I observed something last night that looks interesting. All four items that were damaged were portrayals of the female figure, more or less unclothed. Did the police notice that?"

"I don't know," said the police reporter. "I'll mention it at Headquarters."

"It isn't easy to spot. The stuff is pretty abstract, and a casual glance wouldn't tell anything."

"Then the vandal must have been someone who digs modern art," said Kendall. "Some kind of nut who hated his mother."

"That narrows it down," said Arch.

Qwilleran was in his element—on the fringe of the police beat where he had learned the newspaper craft. His face had a glow. Even his moustache looked happy.

Three corned beef sandwiches came to the table with a plastic squeeze bottle, and the newsmen concentrated on applying mustard, each in his fashion: Arch squirting it on the rye bread in concentric circles, Kendall limning a precise zigzag, and Qwilleran squeezing out a reckless abstraction.

After a while Kendall said to him, "Know much about Lambreth?"

"I just met him once. He was sort of a stuffed shirt."

"Was the gallery successful?"

"Hard to say. It was sumptuously furnished, but that doesn't prove anything. Some of the paintings were priced in five figures, although I wouldn't give you five cents for them. I imagine investors were buying this kind of art; that's why Lambreth set up shop in the financial district."

"Maybe some sucker thought he'd been taken and got into a fatal argument with the dealer."

"That doesn't fit in with the nature of the vandalism."

Arch said, "Do you think the choices of weapon indicates anything?"

"It was a chisel from the workbench," said Kendall.

"Either the killer seized on that in a moment of passion, or he knew in advance it would be there for the purpose."

"Who was employed in the workroom?"

"I don't think anyone was employed," said Qwilleran. "I suspect Lambreth made the frames himself—in spite of the fancy front he put on for customers. When I was there, I noticed definite evidence of work in progress—but no workman. And when I asked who made the frames, he gave me an evasive answer. Then I noticed that his hands were grimy— you know, stained and battered as if he did manual labor."

"Then maybe the gallery wasn't too successful, and he was cutting corners."

"On the other hand, he was living in a good neighborhood, and his house appeared to be furnished expensively."

Kendall said, "I wonder if Lambreth admitted the killer to the premises after hours. Or did the killer let himself in the back way—with a key?"

"I'm sure it was someone Lambreth knew," Qwilleran said, "and I think the evidence of a struggle was rigged after the murder."

"How do you figure that?"

"From the position of the body. Lambreth seemed to have gone down between his swivel chair and his desk, as if he had been sitting there when the murderer took him by surprise. He wouldn't engage in a brawl and then go and sit at his desk, waiting to be polished off."

"Well, let the police solve it," said Arch. "We've got work to do."

As the men left the lunch table, the bartender beckoned to Qwilleran. "I read about the Lambreth murder," he said and paused significantly before adding, "I know that gallery."

"You do? What do you know about it?"

"Lambreth was a crook."

"What makes you think so?"

Bruno gave a hasty glance up and down the bar. "I know a lot of painters and sculptors, and any one of them can tell you how Lambreth operated. He'd sell something for $800 and give the artist a measly $150."

"You think one of your pals wiped him out?"

Bruno was suitably indignant. "I wasn't saying anything like that. I just thought you'd like to know what kind of a guy he was."

"Well, thanks."

"And his wife isn't much better."

"What do you mean by that?"

The bartender picked up a towel and wiped the bar where it didn't need wiping. "Everybody knows she's been playing around. You've got to hand it to her, though. She tiddley-winks where it'll do the most good."

"Like where?"

"Like upstairs over where you live. I understand it's quite a cozy apartment up there." Bruno stopped wiping the bar and gave Qwilleran a significant look. "She goes up there to paint the cat!"

Qwilleran shrugged a no comment and started to leave.

Bruno called him back. "Something else, too, Mr. Qwilleran," he said. "I heard about some funny business at the museum. There's a valuable art object missing, and they're hushing it up."

"Why would they hush it up?"

"Who knows? A lot of funny things go on at that place."

"What's missing?"

"A dagger—from the Florentine Room! This friend of mine—he's a guard at the museum—he discovered the dagger was missing and reported it, but nobody wants to do anything about it. I thought it might be a scoop for you."

"Thanks. I'll look into it," said Qwilleran. Some of his best tips had come from Press Club bartenders. Also some of the worst.

On the way out of the building he stopped in the lobby where the ladies of the press were running a benefit sale of secondhand books. For a half-dollar he picked up a copy of *Keeping Your Pet Happy*. He also bought *A Study of Crests and Troughs in American Business from 1800 to 1850* for a dime.

Back at the office he telephoned the Lambreth home. Butchy answered and said no, Zoe couldn't come to the phone . . . yes, she had managed to get some sleep . . . no, there was nothing Qwilleran could do.

He finished his afternoon's work and went home with his coat collar turned up against the snow that had started to fall. He thought he would feed the cat, go out and grab a hamburger somewhere, and then wander over to the art museum to look at the Florentine Room. It was Thursday, and the museum was open late.

When he arrived at No. 26, shaking the snow from his shoulders and stamping his feet, he found Koko waiting for him. The cat greeted him in the front hall—not with a noisy bill of complaints this time but an appreciative squeak. The way his whiskers tilted upward gave him a pleasant look of expectancy. The newsman felt flattered.

"Hello, old fellow," he said. "Did you have an eventful day?"

From Koko's noncommittal murmur, Qwilleran decided the cat's day had been somewhat less interesting than his own. He started upstairs to carve the tenderloin—or whatever one called the cut of beef that Mountclemens supplied for catfood—and noted that Koko did not bound ahead of him. Instead the cat was dogging his heels and getting between his ankles as he climbed the stairs.

"What are you trying to do? Trip me?" Qwilleran said.

He prepared the beef according to official instructions, placed the dish on the floor, and sat down to watch Koko eat. He was beginning to appreciate the fine points of Siamese design—the elegant proportions of the body, the undulating muscles beneath the fine coat, and the exquisite shading of the fur from off-white to pale fawn to the darkest of velvety browns. Qwilleran decided it was the finest shade of brown he had ever seen.

To his surprise, the cat showed no interest in food. He wanted to rub ankles and utter plaintive high-pitched mews.

"What's the matter with you?" said Qwilleran. "You're a hard one to figure out."

The cat looked up with a beseeching expression in his blue eyes, purred loudly and raised one paw to Qwilleran's knee.

"Koko, I'll bet you're lonesome. You're used to having someone around all day. Are you feeling neglected?"

He lifted the willing bundle of warm fur to his shoulder, and Koko purred in his ear with a rasping undertone that denoted extreme satisfaction.

"I think I'll stay home tonight," Qwilleran told the cat. "Weather's bad. Snow's getting deep. Left my rubbers at the office."

Scrounging for something to eat, he helped himself to a slice of Koko's *pâté de la maison*. It was the best meat loaf he had ever tasted. Koko sensed that this was a party and began to race from one end of the apartment to the other. He seemed to be flying low over the carpet, his feet moving but never touching the floor—up over the desk in a single leap, then from chair to bookshelf to table to another chair to cabinet top—all with bewildering speed. Qwilleran began to realize why there were no table lamps in the apartment.

He too wandered around—at a more leisurely rate. He opened a door in the long narrow hall and found a bedroom with a four-poster bed that had red velvet side curtains and a canopy. In the bathroom he found a green flask labeled *Essence of Lime*; he took a sniff and recognized the scent. In the living room he strolled with his hands in his pants pockets, enjoying a close inspection of Mountclemens' treasures; engraved brass labels on the picture frames said *Hals, Gauguin, Eakins*.

So this was a love nest, according to Bruno. Qwilleran had to agree it was well equipped for the purpose: dim lights, soft music, candles, wine, big loungy chairs—everything to induce a mellow mood.

And now Earl Lambreth was dead! Qwilleran blew through his moustache as he considered the possibilities. It was not difficult to visualize Mountclemens as a wife-stealer. The critic had a suave charm that would appeal to any woman he chose to impress—and an authority that would never take no for an answer. Wife-stealer, yes. Murderer, no. Mountclemens was too elegant, too fastidious for that.

Eventually Qwilleran returned to his own apartment, followed by a genial Koko. For the cat's amusement, Qwilleran tied a wad of folded paper to a length of string and dangled it. At nine o'clock the final edition of the *Daily Fluxion* was delivered, and Koko perused the headlines. When the newsman finally settled down in an easy chair with a book, the cat took possession of his lap, the silky fur testifying to a state of contentment. It was with apparent reluctance that Koko took leave at midnight and went upstairs to his cushion on top of the refrigerator.

Qwilleran described his evening of cat-sitting the next day when he stopped at Arch Riker's desk to pick up his paycheck.

Arch said, "How are you hitting it off with the critic's cat?"

"Koko was lonesome last night, so I stayed home and entertained him. We played Sparrow."

"Is this some parlor game I'm not familiar with?"

"It's something we invented—like tennis, with one player and no net," said Qwilleran. "I make a sparrow out of paper and tie it to a piece of string. Then I swing it back and forth while Koko bats it with his paw. He's got a substantial backhand, I want you to know. Every time he connects, he gets one point. If he strikes and misses, that's a point for me. Twenty-one points is game. I'm keeping a running score. After five games last night it was Koko 108 and Qwilleran 92."

"I'm betting on the cat all the way," said Arch. He reached for a sheet of pink paper. "I know that cat consumes a lot of your time, attention and physical strength, but I wish you'd give me some action on that Halapay profile. Another pink memo came up this morning."

"I'll be all set as soon as I have one more meeting with Mrs. Halapay," said Qwilleran.

Returning to his desk, he called Sandy and suggested lunch the following Wednesday.

"Let's make it for dinner," she suggested. "Cal is in Denmark, and I'm all alone. I'd love to go to dinner where there's a dance band. You're such a wonderful dancer." Her laughter left the sincerity of her compliment in doubt.

Be Nice to People, said the slogan on his telephone, and he replied, "Sandy, I'd enjoy that very much—but not next week. I'll be working nights." The telephone said nothing about lying to people. "Let's just have lunch on Wednesday and discuss your husband's charities and civic activities. They've given me a firm deadline on this profile."

"All right," she said. "I'll pick you up, and we'll drive out somewhere. We'll have scads to talk about. I want to hear all about the Lambreth murder."

"I'm afraid I don't know much about it."

"Why, I think it's all perfectly obvious."

"What's obvious?"

"That it's a family affair." Weighted pause. "You know what was going on, don't you?"

"No, I don't."

"Well, I wouldn't want to discuss it on the phone," she said. "See you Wednesday at noon."

Qwilleran spent the morning finishing up odds and ends. He wrote a short humorous piece about a local graphics artist who had switched to watercolors after dropping a hundred-pound lithograph stone on his foot. Then he did an inspirational story about a prizewinning textile weaver who was also a high-school math teacher, author of two published novels, licensed pilot, cellist, and mother of ten. Next he considered the talented poodle who paw-painted pictures. The poodle was having a show at the humane society shelter.

Just as Qwilleran was visualizing the headline (*One-Dog Exhibition of Poodle Doodles*), the telephone on his desk rang. He answered, and a low, breathy voice gave him a ripple of pleasure.

"This is Zoe Lambreth, Mr. Qwilleran. I must speak softly. Can you hear me?"

"Yes. Is anything wrong?"

"I need to talk with you—in person—if you can spare the time. Not here. Downtown."

"Would the Press Club be all right?"

"Is there some place more private? I'd like to talk confidentially."

"Would you mind coming to my apartment?"

"That would be better. You live in Mountclemens' building, don't you?"

"No. 26 Blenheim Place."

"I know where it is."

"How about tomorrow afternoon? Take a taxi. It isn't a nice neighborhood."

"Tomorrow. Thank you so much. I need your advice. I must hang up now."

There was an abrupt click, and the voice was gone. Qwilleran's moustache virtually danced. *Widow of Slain Art Dealer Reveals Story to* Flux *Reporter*.

CHAPTER 9

IT HAD BEEN a long time since Qwilleran had entertained a woman in his apartment, and he waked Saturday morning with a mild case of stage fright. He swallowed a cup of instant coffee, gnawed on a stale doughnut, and wondered if he should serve Zoe something to eat or drink. Coffee seemed suitable under the circumstances. Coffee and what? Doughnuts would look frivolous; why, he couldn't explain. Cake? Too pretentious. Cookies?

There was a grocery in the neighborhood that specialized in beer, cheap wine and gummy white bread. Dubiously Qwilleran inspected their packaged cookies, but the ingredients listed in small type (artificial flavoring, emulsifier, glycerine, lecithin and invert syrup) dampened his interest.

He inquired for a bakery and walked six blocks through February slush to a shop where the merchandise appeared edible. Vetoing *petit fours* (too fancy) and oatmeal cookies (too hearty), he settled on chocolate chip cookies and bought two pounds.

There was an old-fashioned percolator in his kitchenette, but how it operated was a mystery to him. Zoe would have to accept instant coffee. He wondered if she used sugar and cream. Back he went to the grocery store for a pound of sugar, a half-pint of coffee cream and some paper napkins.

By that time it was noon, and a reluctant February sun began slanting into the apartment, exposing dust on the tables, lint on the rug, and cat hair on the sofa. Qwilleran dusted with paper napkins, then hurried upstairs to Mountclemens' apartment to hunt for a vacuum cleaner. He found one in a broom closet in the kitchen.

One o'clock came, and he was ready—except for cigarettes. He had forgotten cigarettes. He rushed out to the drugstore and bought something long, mild and unfiltered. After debating about the filter, he decided Zoe was not one to compromise.

At one-thirty he lighted the gas logs in the fireplace and sat down to wait.

Zoe arrived promptly at four. Qwilleran saw a lovely woman in a soft brown fur coat step from a taxi, look up and down the street, and hurry up to the portico. He was there to meet her.

"Thank you so much for letting me come," she said in a low-pitched, breathless voice. "Butchy has been watching me like a hawk, and I had to sneak out of the house. . . . I shouldn't complain. At a time like this you need a friend like Butchy." She dropped her brown alligator handbag. "I'm sorry. I'm very much upset."

"Just take it easy," said Qwilleran, "and gather yourself together. Would a cup of coffee feel good?"

"I'd better not have coffee," she said. "It makes me nervous, and I'm jumpy enough as it is." She gave Qwilleran her coat and took a seat in a straight-backed pull-up chair, crossing her knees attractively. "Do you mind if we close the door?"

"Not at all, although there's no one else in the house."

"I had an uneasy feeling I was being followed. I took a cab to the Arcade Building, then walked through and picked up another one at the other entrance. Do you think they might have someone following me? The police, I mean."

"I don't see why they should. What gave you that idea?"

"They came to the house yesterday. Two of them. Two detectives. They were perfect gentlemen, but some of their questions were upsetting, as if they were trying to trap me. Do you suppose they suspect *me*?"

"Not really, but they have to cover every possibility."

"Butchy was there, of course, and she was quite antagonistic toward the detectives. It didn't look good at all. She's so protective, you know. Altogether it was a terrible experience."

"What did they say when they left?"

"They thanked me for my cooperation and said they might want to talk to me again. After that I telephoned you—while Butchy was down in the basement. I didn't want her to know."

"Why not?"

"Well . . . because she's so sure she can handle everything herself in this—this crisis. And also because of what I'm going to tell you. . . . You don't suppose the police would be watching my movements, do you? Maybe I shouldn't have come here."

"Why shouldn't you come here, Mrs. Lambreth? I'm a friend of the family. I'm professionally connected with the art field. And I'm going to help you with details concerning the gallery. How does that sound?"

She smiled bleakly. "I'm beginning to feel like a criminal. One has to be careful in talking to the police. If you use the wrong word or put the wrong inflection in your voice, they pounce on it."

"Well, now," said Qwilleran in his most soothing way, "put that episode out of your mind and relax. Wouldn't you like a more comfortable chair?"

"This is fine. I have a better command of myself when I sit up straight."

She was wearing a pale blue dress of fuzzy wool that made her look soft and fragile. Qwilleran tried not to stare at the provocative indention just below her kneecap.

He said, "I find this a very comfortable apartment. My landlord has a knack for furnishing a place. How did you know I was staying here?"

"Oh . . . things get around in art circles."

"Apparently you've been to this house before."

"Mountclemens had us to dinner once or twice."

"You must know him better than most artists do."

"We've been fairly friendly. I did several studies of his cat. Did you notify him—about the—?"

"I haven't been able to find out where he stays in New York. Do you know his hotel?"

"It's near the Museum of Modern Art, but I can't remember the name." She was twisting the handle of her handbag that lay on her lap.

Qwilleran brought a plate from the kitchenette. "Would you care for some cookies?"

"No, thanks. I have to—count—calories—" Her voice trailed away.

He sensed her preoccupation and said, "Now what is it that you want to tell me?" With the other half of his mind he was taking Zoe's measurements and wondering why she worried about calories.

"I don't know how to begin."

"How about a cigarette? I'm forgetting my manners."

"I gave them up a few months ago."

"Mind if I light my pipe?"

Abruptly Zoe said, "I didn't tell the police everything."

"No?"

"It may have been wrong, but I couldn't bring myself to answer some of their questions."

"What kind of questions?"

"They asked if Earl had any enemies. How could I point a finger at someone and say he was an enemy? What would happen if I started naming people all over the city? Acquaintances . . . fellow club members . . . important people. I think that was a terrible thing to ask, don't you?"

"It was a necessary question. In fact," said Qwilleran, in a kind but firm way, "I'm going to ask you the same question. Did he have many enemies?"

"I'm afraid so. A lot of people disliked him. . . . Mr. Qwilleran, it's all right to talk confidentially to you, isn't it? I must confide in someone. I'm sure you're not one of those sneaky reporters who would—"

"Those characters are only in the movies," he assured her. His attitude was all sympathy and interest.

Zoe sighed heavily and began. "There's a lot of competition and jealousy in the art field. I don't know why it should be."

"That's true in all fields."

"It's worse among artists. Believe me!"

"Could you be more specific?"

"Well . . . the gallery directors, for example. The other galleries in town felt that Earl was luring their best artists away from them."

"Was he?"

Zoe bristled slightly. "Naturally, the artists wanted to be represented by the foremost gallery. As a result, Earl showed better work, and the Lambreth exhibitions got better reviews."

"And the jealousy increased."

Zoe nodded. "Besides, Earl often had to reject the work of second-rate artists, and that didn't win him any friends! It made him a villain. An artist's ego is a precious thing. People like Cal Halapay and Franz Buchwalter—or Mrs. Buchwalter, to be exact—did a lot of talking about my husband at the club, and it wasn't nice. That's why Earl would never go to the Turp and Chisel."

"So far," said Qwilleran, "you've mentioned only outsiders who were unfriendly. Was there anyone within the organization who didn't get along with your husband?"

Zoe hesitated. She looked apologetic. "Nobody really warmed up to him. He had an aloof manner. It was only a facade, but few people understood that."

"There's the possibility that the crime was committed by someone who had a key to the gallery or was willingly admitted to the premises."

"That's what Butchy said."

"Did anyone but you have a key?"

"N-no," said Zoe, groping in the depths of her handbag.

Qwilleran said, "Can I get you something?"

"Maybe I'll have a glass of water—with some ice. It's rather warm—"

He turned down the flame in the fireplace and brought Zoe a drink of ice water. "Tell me about your friend Butchy. I understand she's a sculptor."

"Yes. Welded metal," Zoe said in a bleak voice.

"You mean she uses a torch and all that? It might make a story. Lady welders are always good for some space—with a photograph of sparks flying."

Zoe nodded slowly as she considered the idea. "Yes, I wish you would write something about Butchy. It would do her a lot of good—psychologically. Not long ago she lost a $50,000 commission, and it was a damaging setback. You see, she teaches at Penniman School, and the commission would have enhanced her prestige."

"How did she lose out?"

"Butchy was being considered to do the outdoor sculpture for a new shopping center. Then suddenly the commission was awarded to Ben Riggs, who shows at the Lambreth Gallery."

"Was the switch justified?"

"Oh, yes. Riggs is a much better artist. He works in clay and casts in bronze. But it was a blow to Butchy. I'd like to do something to help her. Would you write her up for the paper?"

"She's a good friend of yours?" Qwilleran was comparing the soft, attractive Zoe with the mannish character who had been guarding her on the night of the murder.

"Yes and no. We grew up together and went to art school at the same time, and Butchy was my best friend when we were both at the tomboy age. But Butchy never outgrew that stage. She was always big and husky for a girl, and she bluffed it off by acting boyish. I feel sorry for Butchy. We don't have much in common anymore—except old times."

"How did she happen to be at your house Wednesday night?"

"She was the only one I could think of to call. After finding Earl and notifying the police, I was in a daze. I didn't know what to do. I needed someone, and so I called Butchy. She came right away and drove me home and said she'd stay with me for a few days. Now I can't get rid of her."

"How come?"

"She enjoys being my protector. She needs to feel needed. Butchy doesn't have many friends, and she has an annoying way of clutching at the few she has."

"What did your husband think of her?"

"He didn't like her at all. Earl wanted me to drop Butchy, but it's hard to break off with someone you've known all your life—especially when your paths are crossing all the time. . . . I don't know why I'm telling you these personal details. I must be boring you."

"Not at all. You're—"

"I needed to talk to someone who's disinterested and sympathetic. You're very easy to talk to. Is that typical of newspapermen?"

"We're good listeners."

"I feel much better now, thanks to you." Zoe leaned back in her chair and was silent, and a tenderness crept into her face.

Qwilleran smoothed his moustache with the stem of his pipe and beamed inwardly. He said, "I'm glad I could—"

"Are you looking for material for your column?" Zoe interrupted, the radiance of her expression seeming inappropriate for the question.

"Of course, I'm always—"

"I'd like to tell you about Nino." She pronounced the name "Nine-oh."

"Who's Nino?" said Qwilleran, camouflaging a mild disappointment with a brisk tone.

"He's a Thingist. Some people call him a junk sculptor. He makes meaningful constructions out of junk and calls them Things."

"I saw them at the gallery. One was a piece of sewer pipe stuck with bi-cycle spokes."

Zoe gave him a luminous smile. "That's 'Thing #17.' Isn't it eloquent? It affirms life while repudiating the pseudoworld around us. Weren't you gripped by its rebellious tensions?"

"To tell you the truth . . . no," said Qwilleran, a trifle peevishly. "It looked like a piece of sewer pipe and some bicycle spokes."

Zoe gave him a sweet look in which reproach mingled with pity. "Your eye isn't tuned to contemporary expression as yet, but you'll develop ap-preciation in time."

Qwilleran squirmed and scowled down at his moustache.

Enthusiastically Zoe went on. "Nino is my protégé, more or less. I dis-covered him. This city has some talented artists, but I can honestly say that Nino has more than talent. He has genius. You should visit his stu-dio." She leaned forward eagerly. "Would you like to meet Nino? I'm sure he'd make good material for a story."

"What's his full name?"

"Nine Oh Two Four Six Eight Three," she said. "Or maybe it's Five. I can never remember the last digit. We call him Nino for short."

"You mean he has a number instead of a name?"

"Nino is a disaffiliate," she explained. "He doesn't subscribe to the conventions of ordinary society."

"He wears a beard, of course."

"Yes, he does. How did you know? He even speaks a language of his own, but we don't expect conformity of a genius, do we? Using a number instead of a name is part of his Protest. I think only his mother and the So-cial Security people know his real name."

Qwilleran stared at her. "Where does this character hang out?"

"He lives and works in an alley garage at Twelfth and Somers, behind an iron foundry. His studio may shock you."

"I don't think I shock easily."

"I mean you may be disturbed by his collection of Found Objects."

"Junk?"

"It isn't all junk. He has a few very fine things. Heaven knows where he gets them. But mostly it's junk—beautiful junk. Nino's talent for alley-picking amounts to a divine gift. If you go to see him, try to understand the nature of his artistic vision. He sees beauty where others see only trash and filth."

Qwilleran studied Zoe with fascination—her quiet animation, her obvious conviction. He didn't understand what she was talking about, but he enjoyed being under her spell.

"I think you'll like Nino," she went on. "He is elemental and real—and sad, in a way. Or perhaps you and I are the sad ones, conducting ourselves according to a prescribed pattern. It's like following the steps of a dance composed by a dictatorial dancing master. The dance of life should be created from moment to moment with individuality and spontaneity."

Qwilleran roused himself from a rapt stare and said, "May I ask you a personal question? Why do you paint such incomprehensible things when you have the ability to make real pictures of real things?"

Zoe gazed at him sweetly again. "You are so naïve, Mr. Qwilleran, but you are honest, and that is refreshing. Real pictures of real things can be done by a camera. I paint in the exploratory spirit of today. We don't have all the answers, and we know it. Sometimes I'm bewildered by my own creations, but they are my artistic response to life as I see it today. True art is always an expression of its time."

"I see." He wanted to be convinced, but he wasn't sure that Zoe had succeeded.

"Someday we must discuss this subject at great length." There was an unaccountable yearning in her expression.

"I'd enjoy that," he said softly.

A self-conscious silence loomed between them. Qwilleran breached it by offering her a cigarette.

"I've given them up," she reminded him.

"Cookie? They're chocolate chip."

"No, thanks." She sighed.

He pointed to the Monet over the fireplace. "What do you think of that? It came with the apartment."

"If it were a good one, Mountclemens wouldn't squander it on a tenant," she said with an abrupt edge to her voice, and her quick change of mood astonished Qwilleran.

"But it has a nice frame," he said. "Who makes the frames at the Lambreth Gallery?"

"Why do you ask?"

"Just curious. People have remarked about their fine workmanship." It was a lie but the kind of lie that always elicited confidences.

"Oh . . . Well, I might as well tell you. It was Earl. He made all the frames himself, although he never wanted it known. It would have destroyed the prestige image of the gallery."

"He was a hard worker—making frames, keeping the books, tending shop."

"Yes. The last time I saw him alive he was complaining about the work-load."

"Why didn't he hire help?"

Zoe shrugged and shook her head.

It was an unsatisfactory answer, but Qwilleran let it pass. He said, "Have you remembered anything that might help the investigation? Anything your husband said when you were there at five-thirty?"

"Nothing of any importance. Earl showed me some graphics that had just come in, and I told him—" She stopped abruptly. "Yes, there was a phone call—"

"Anything unusual about that?"

"I wasn't listening particularly, but there was something Earl said—now that I remember it—that doesn't make sense. It was about the station wagon."

"Did your husband have a wagon?"

"Every dealer has to have one. I hate them."

"What did he say about the wagon?"

"I wasn't paying too much attention, but I heard something about putting paintings in the station wagon for delivery. Earl said the wagon was in the alley; in fact, he repeated it rather emphatically. That's why it comes to mind. . . . I didn't think of it at the time, but now it seems strange."

"Why does it strike you as strange?"

"Our car was at the repair shop, having a tune-up. It's still there. I never picked it up. Earl had dropped it off at the garage that morning. And yet he was insisting—on the telephone—that it was in the alley, as if the other party was giving him an argument."

"Do you know who was on the line?" Qwilleran asked.

"No. It sounded like long distance. You know how people shout when it's long distance. Even when it's a perfectly good connection they think they have to pitch their voices higher."

"Maybe your husband was telling a little white lie—for business reasons."

"I don't know."

"Or maybe he was referring to some other dealer's station wagon."

"I really don't know."

"You didn't see anything parked in the alley?"

"No. I went in the front door and left the same way. And when I went back at seven o'clock, there was no car of any kind in the alley. Do you think the phone call has any bearing on what happened?"

"It wouldn't hurt to tell the police about it. Try to remember as much as you can."

Zoe lapsed into a reverie.

"By the way," Qwilleran said, "does Mountclemens have a car?"

"No," she murmured.

Qwilleran took a long time to refill his pipe, tapping it noisily on the ashtray. As if in answer to his signal, there was a prolonged, desolate wail outside the apartment door.

"That's Koko," said Qwilleran. "He objects to being excluded. Mind if he comes in?"

"Oh, I adore Kao K'o-Kung!"

Qwilleran opened the door, and the cat—after his usual reconnaissance—walked in, his tail moving from side to side in graceful arabesques. He had been sleeping and had not yet limbered his muscles. Now he arched his back in a taut curve, after which he extended two forward legs in a luxurious stretch. He concluded by making a long leg to the rear.

Zoe said, "He limbers up like a dancer."

"You want to see him dance?" said Qwilleran. He folded a piece of paper and tied it to a string. In anticipation Koko took a few small steps to the left and a few to the right, then rose on his hind feet as the bauble started to swing. He was all grace and rhythm, dancing on his *pointes*, leaping, executing incredible acrobatic feats in midair, landing lightly, and leaping again, higher than before.

Zoe said, "I've never seen him perform like that. Such elevation! He's a real Nijinsky."

"Mountclemens stresses intellectual pursuits," Qwilleran said, "and this cat has spent too much time on the bookshelves. I hope to broaden his range of interests. He needs more athletics."

"I'd like to make some sketches." She dived into her handbag. "He does a *grand battement* just like a ballet dancer."

A ballet dancer. *A ballet dancer.* The words brought a picture to Qwilleran's mind: a cluttered office, a painting hung crookedly on the wall. The second time he had seen that office, over a patrolman's shoulder, there was a body on the floor. And where was the painting? Qwilleran could not remember seeing the ballet dancer.

He said to Zoe, "There was a painting of a ballet dancer at the Lambreth Gallery—"

"Earl's famous Ghirotto," she said, as she sketched rapidly on a pad. "It was only half of the original canvas, you know. It was his one great ambition to find the other half. It would have made him rich, he thought."

Qwilleran was alerted. "How rich?"

"If the two halves were joined and properly restored, the painting would probably be worth $150,000."

The newsman blew astonishment through his moustache.

"There's a monkey on the other half," she said. "Ghirotto painted ballerinas or monkeys during his celebrated Vibrato Period, but only once did he paint both dancer and monkey in the same composition. It was a unique piece—a collector's dream. After the war it was shipped to a New York dealer and damaged in transit—ripped down the middle. Because of the way the picture was composed, the importer was able to frame the two halves and sell them separately. Earl bought the half with the dancer and hoped to trace the half with the monkey."

Qwilleran said, "Do you suppose the owner of the monkey has been trying to trace the ballet dancer?"

"Could be. Earl's half is the valuable one; it has the artist's signature." As she talked, her pencil skimmed over the paper, and her glance darted between sketch pad and performing cat.

"Did many people know about the Ghirotto?"

"Oh, it was quite a conversation piece. Several people wanted to buy the ballerina—just on speculation. Earl could have sold it and made a nice little profit, but he was holding out for his dream of $150,000. He never gave up hope of finding the monkey."

Qwilleran proceeded circumspectly. "Did you see the ballerina on the night of the crime?"

Zoe laid down her pencil and pad. "I'm afraid I didn't see much of anything—that night."

"I was there, snooping around," Qwilleran said, "and I'm pretty sure the painting was gone."

"Gone!"

"It had been hanging over the desk on my previous visit, and now I remember—the night the police were there—that wall was vacant."

"What should I do?"

"Better tell the police. It looks as if the painting's been stolen. Tell them about the phone call, too. When you get home, call the Homicide Bureau. Do you remember the detectives' names? Hames and Wojcik."

Zoe clapped both hands to her face in dismay. "Honestly, I had forgotten all about that Ghirotto!"

CHAPTER 10

WHEN ZOE had gone from Qwilleran's apartment—leaving him with a can of coffee, a pound of sugar, a half-pint of cream, a pack of cigarettes, and two pounds of chocolate chip cookies—he wondered how much information she had withheld. Her nervousness suggested she was sifting the facts. She had stammered when asked if anyone else had a key to the Lambreth Gallery. Admittedly she had avoided telling the police everything that occurred to her. And she claimed to have forgotten the existence of a painting valuable enough—possibly—to make murder worthwhile.

Qwilleran went upstairs to prepare Koko's dinner. Slowly and absently he diced meat while pondering other complications in the Lambreth case. How valid was Sandy's hint that this was "a family affair"? And how would that connect with the disappearance of the Ghirotto? There was also the vandalism to take into account, and Qwilleran reflected that the missing painting fell in the same category as the damaged subjects; it depicted the female figure in skimpy attire.

He opened the kitchen door and looked out. The night was crisp, and the neighborhood smells were made more pungent by the cold. Carbon monoxide hung in the air, and oily rags had been burned at the corner garage. Down below him was the patio, a dark hole, its high brick walls cutting off any light from distant streetlamps.

Qwilleran turned on the exterior light, which cast a weak yellow glow on the fire escape, and thought, What does that guy have against using a little extra electricity? He remembered seeing a flashlight in the broom closet, and he went to get it—an efficient, long-handled, well-balanced, powerful, chrome-plated beauty. Everything Mountclemens owned was well-designed: knives, pots and pans, even the flashlight. It threw a strong beam on the walls and floor of the empty patio, on the ponderous wooden gate, on the wooden fire escape. Patches of frozen slush clung to the steps, and Qwilleran decided to postpone further investigation until daylight. Tomorrow he might even take Koko down there for a romp.

That evening he went to dinner at a nearby Italian restaurant, and the brown-eyed waitress reminded him of Zoe. He went home and played Sparrow with Koko, and the cat's movements reminded him of the missing ballet dancer. He lighted the gas logs in the fireplace and scanned the second-hand book on economics that he had bought at the Press Club; the statistics reminded him of Nine Oh Two Four Six Eight Three—or was it Five?

ON SUNDAY he went to visit Nino.

The artist's studio-home in an alley garage was as dismal as it sounded. A former occupant had left the building coated with grease, to which was added the blight of Nino's collection of junk.

Having knocked and received no answer, Qwilleran walked into the agglomeration of joyless castoffs. There were old tires, bushels of broken glass, chunks of uprooted concrete sidewalk, tin cans of every size, and dispossessed doors and windows. He made note of a baby carriage without wheels, a store window mannequin with arms and head missing, a kitchen sink painted bright orange inside and out, an iron gate covered with rust, and a wooden bedstead in the depressing modernistic design of the 1930s.

A heater suspended from the ceiling belched warm fumes in Qwilleran's face, while the cold drafts at ankle level were paralyzing. Also suspended from the ceiling by a rope was a crystal chandelier of incredible beauty.

Then Qwilleran saw the artist at work. On a platform at the rear stood a monstrous Thing made of wooden oddments, ostrich plumes and bits of shiny tin. Nino was affixing two baby carriage wheels to the monster's head.

He gave the wheels a twirl and stood back, and the spinning spokes, glinting under a spotlight, became malevolent eyes.

"Good afternoon," said Qwilleran. "I'm a friend of Zoe Lambreth. You must be Nino."

The sculptor appeared to be in a trance, his face illumined with the thrill of creation. His shirt and trousers were stiff with paint and grease, his beard needed trimming, and his hair had not recently known a comb. In spite of it all, he was a good-looking brute—with classic features and an enviable physique. He looked at Qwilleran without seeing him, then admiringly he turned back to the Thing with spinning eyes.

"Have you given it a title?" asked the newsman.

"'Thirty-six,'" said Nino, and he put his face in his hands and cried. Qwilleran waited sympathetically until the artist had recovered and then said, "How do you create these works of art? What is your procedure?"

"I live them," said Nino. "Thirty-six is what I am, I was and I will be. Yesterday is gone, and who cares? If I set fire to this studio, I live—in every leaping flame, flash, flare, floriferous flourish."

"Do you have your materials insured?"

"If I do, I do. If I don't, I don't. It's all relative. Man loves, hates, cries, plays, but what can an artist do? BOOM! That's the way it goes. A world beyond a world beyond a world beyond a world."

"A cosmic concept," Qwilleran agreed, "but do people really understand your ideas?"

"They wear out their brains trying, but I know, and you know, and we all know—what do we know? Nothing!"

Nino was edging closer to the newsman in his enthusiasm for this conversation, and Qwilleran backed away discreetly. He said, "Nino, you appear to be a pessimist, but doesn't your success at the Lambreth Gallery help to give you an affirmative attitude toward life?"

"Warm, wanton, wary, weak woman! I talk to her. She talks to me. We communicate."

"Did you know her husband is dead? Murdered."

"We are all dead," said Nino. "Dead as doorknobs . . . *Doorknobs*!" he shouted and plunged into a mountain of junk in desperate search.

"Thank you for letting me see your studio," said Qwilleran, and he started toward the door. As he passed a littered shelf, a gleam of gold signaled to him, and he called back over his shoulder, "Here's a doorknob, if that's what you're hunting for."

There were two doorknobs on the shelf, and they looked like pure gold. With them were other pieces of bright metal, as well as some startling pieces of carved ivory and jade, but Qwilleran did not stop to examine them. The fumes from the heater had made his head throb, and he was making a dash for the fresh air. He wanted to go home and spend a sane, sensible, sanitary Sunday with Koko. He was becoming attached to that cat, he told himself, and he would be sorry when Mountclemens returned. He wondered if Koko really liked the cultural climate upstairs. Were the pleasures of reading headlines and sniffing old masters preferable to an exhilarating game of Sparrow? After four days of play, the score was 471 for the cat, 409 for the man.

When Qwilleran arrived home, anticipating a friendly, furry, frolicsome fuss at the door, he was disappointed. Koko was not waiting for him. He went upstairs to Mountclemens' apartment and found the door closed. He heard music within. He knocked.

There was a delay before Mountclemens, wearing a dressing gown, answered the knock.

"I see you're home," said Qwilleran. "Just wanted to be sure the cat was getting his supper."

"He has finished the entrée," said Mountclemens, "and is now relishing a poached egg yolk as a savory. Thank you for taking care of him. He looks well and happy."

"We had some good times together," said Qwilleran. "We played games."

"Indeed! I have often wished he would learn mah-jongg."

"Did you hear the bad news about the Lambreth Gallery?"

"If they had a fire, they deserve it," said the critic. "That loft building is a tinderbox."

"Not a fire. A murder."

"Indeed!"

"Earl Lambreth," said Qwilleran. "His wife found him dead in his office last Wednesday night. He had been stabbed."

"How untidy!" Mountclemens' voice sounded bored—or tired—and he stepped back as if preparing to close the door.

"The police have no suspects," Qwilleran went on. "Do you have any theories?"

Curtly Mountclemens said, "I am in the process of unpacking. And I am about to bathe. There is nothing further from my mind than the identity of Earl Lambreth's murderer." His tone terminated the conversation.

Qwilleran accepted the dismissal and went downstairs, pulling at his moustache and reflecting that Mountclemens had a talent for being obnoxious when it suited his whim.

Down the street at a third-rate restaurant he later scowled at a plate of meatballs, picked at a limp salad, and contemplated a cup of hot water in which floated a tea bag. Added to his irritation with his landlord was a nagging disappointment; Koko had not come to the door to greet him. He returned home unsatisfied and disgruntled.

Qwilleran was about to unlock the vestibule door when a scent of lime peel came through the keyhole, and he was not surprised to find Mountclemens in the entrance hall.

"Oh, there you are!" said the critic amiably. "I had just come downstairs to invite you for a cup of Lapsang Souchong and some dessert. Rather laboriously I transported home a Dobos torte from a very fine Viennese bakery in New York."

The sun broke through Qwilleran's clouds, and he followed the velvet jacket and Italian pumps upstairs.

Mountclemens poured tea and described current exhibitions in New York, while Qwilleran let rich buttery chocolate melt slowly on his tongue.

"And now let us hear the gruesome details," said the critic. "I assume they are gruesome. I heard nothing about the murder in New York, where art dealers are more or less expendable. . . . Forgive me if I sit at my desk and open mail while you talk."

Mountclemens faced a stack of large and small envelopes and wrappered publications. Placing each envelope face down on the desk, he rested his right hand on it, while his left hand wielded the paper knife and extracted the contents, most of which he dropped contemptuously in the wastebasket.

Qwilleran recounted the details of Lambreth's murder briefly, as it had appeared in the newspaper. "That's the story," he said. "Any guesses as to motive?"

"Personally," said Mountclemens, "I have never been able to appreciate murder for revenge. I find murder for personal gain infinitely more appealing. But what anyone could possibly gain by dispatching Earl Lambreth to the hereafter is beyond my comprehension."

"He had quite a few enemies, I understand."

"All art dealers and all art critics have enemies!" Mountclemens gave an envelope a particularly vicious rip. "The first one who comes to mind, in this case, is that indescribable Bolton woman."

"What did the lady welder have against Lambreth?"

"He robbed her of a $50,000 commission—or so she says."

"The outdoor sculpture for the shopping center?"

"Actually Lambreth did the innocent public a favor by convincing the architects to commission another sculptor. Welded metal is a fad. If we are fortunate, it will soon die—put to death by practitioners like the Bolton creature."

Qwilleran said, "Someone suggested I write a human-interest story about her."

"By all means, interview the woman," said Mountclemens, "if only for your own education. Wear tennis shoes. If she stages one of her insane tantrums, you may have to sprint for your life or dodge metal ingots."

"She sounds like a good murder suspect."

"She has the motive and the temperament. But she did not commit the crime, I can assure you. She would be incapable of doing anything successfully—especially murder, which requires a certain amount of finesse."

Qwilleran lingered over the last few bittersweet crumbs of torte, and then he said, "I've also been wondering about the junk sculptor they call Nino. Know anything about him?"

"Brilliant, odoriferous and harmless," said Mountclemens. "Next suspect?"

"Someone has suggested it was a family affair."

"Mrs. Lambreth has too much taste to indulge in anything as vulgar as a stabbing. A shooting, perhaps, but not a stabbing. A shooting with a dainty little cloisonné pistol—or whatever women carry in those cavernous handbags. I have always had the impression those handbags were stuffed with wet diapers. But surely there would be room to accommodate a dainty little pistol in cloisonné or tortoise shell inlaid with German silver—."

Qwilleran said, "Have you ever seen the portrait she painted of her husband? It's as lifelike as a photograph and not very complimentary."

"I thank the fates I have been spared that experience.... No, Mr. Qwilleran, I am afraid your murderer was no artist. The textural experience of plunging a cutting tool into flesh would be extremely repugnant to a painter. A sculptor would have a greater feeling for anatomy, but he would vent his hostilities in a manner more acceptable to society—by mauling clay, chiseling stone, or torturing metal. So you might better search for an irate customer, a desperate competitor, a psychotic art-lover, or a rejected mistress."

"All of the vandalized art depicted the female figure," said Qwilleran.

R-r-rip went the letter knife. "A nice sense of discipline," said the critic. "I begin to suspect a jealous mistress."

"Did you ever have reason to suspect Earl Lambreth of unethical business dealings?"

"My dear man," said Mountclemens, "any good art dealer has the qualifications to make an outstanding jewel thief. Earl Lambreth chose to divert his talents into more orthodox channels, but beyond that I am not in a position to say. You newspapermen are all alike. Once you get your teeth into a piece of news, you must worry it to death.... Another cup of tea?"

The critic poured from the silver teapot and then returned to the attack on his mail. "Here is an invitation that might interest you," he said.

"Have you ever been unfortunate enough to attend a Happening?" He tossed a magenta-colored announcement card to Qwilleran.

"No. What's a Happening?"

"An evening of utter boredom, perpetrated by artists and inflicted on a public that is gullible enough to pay admission. However, the invitation will admit you without charge, and you might find it a subject for a column. You might even be mildly amused. I advise you to wear old clothes."

The Happening had a name. It was called *Heavy Heavy Hangs Over Your Head*, and it was scheduled for the following evening at the Penniman School of Fine Art. Qwilleran said he would attend.

Before the newsman left Mountclemens' apartment, Koko graced the occasion with a moment of his time. The cat appeared from behind the Oriental screen, looked at Qwilleran with a casual glance, yawned widely and left the room.

CHAPTER 11

MONDAY MORNING Qwilleran telephoned the director of the Penniman School and asked permission to interview a member of the faculty. The director was pleased. In the man's manner Qwilleran recognized the ringing bells and flashing lights that always accompanied the anticipation of free publicity.

At one o'clock the newsman appeared at the school and was directed to the welding studio—a separate building at the rear, the ivy-covered carriage house of the former Penniman estate. Inside, the studio had a mean look. It bristled with the sharp edges and thorny points of welded metal sculpture; whether the pieces were finished or unfinished, Qwilleran could not tell. Everything seemed designed to puncture flesh and tear clothing. Around the walls were gas cylinders, lengths of rubber hose, and fire extinguishers.

Butchy Bolton, formidable in coveralls and ludicrous in her tightly waved hair, was sitting alone, eating lunch from a paper sack.

"Have a sandwich," she said with a gruffness that failed to conceal her pleasure at being interviewed for the paper. "Ham on rye." She cleared a space on an asbestos-topped workbench, pushing aside wrenches, clamps, pliers and broken bricks, and she poured Qwilleran a cup of coffee strong as tar.

He ate and drank, although he had lunched well a half hour before. He knew the advantages of chewing during an interview; casual conversation replaced formal questions and answers.

They talked about their favorite restaurants and the best way to bake a ham. From there they went to diets and exercise. That led to oxyacetylene welding. While Qwilleran ate a large red apple, Butchy put on skullcap, goggles and leather gloves and showed how to puddle a metal bar and lay an even bead.

"The first semester we're lucky if we can teach the kids not to set themselves on fire," she said.

Qwilleran said, "Why do you weld metal instead of carving wood or modeling clay?"

Butchy looked at him fiercely, and it was not clear to Qwilleran whether she was going to hit him with a welding rod or whether she was thinking of a trenchant reply. "You must have been talking to that fellow Mountclemens," she said.

"No. I'm just curious. For my own education I want to know."

Butchy kicked a workbench with one of her high-laced boots. "Off the record, it's faster and cheaper," she said. "But for the paper you can say that it's something that belongs to the twentieth century. We've discovered a new sculptor's tool. Fire!"

"I suppose it appeals mostly to men."

"Nope. Some little bitty girls take the course."

"Was Nino, the junk sculptor, one of your students?"

Butchy looked back over her shoulder as if searching for a place to spit. "He was in my class, but I couldn't teach him anything."

"I understand he's considered somewhat of a genius."

"Some people think he's a genius. I think he's a phony. How he ever got accepted by Lambreth Gallery is hard to figure."

"Mrs. Lambreth thinks highly of his work."

Butchy exhaled loudly through her nose and said nothing.

"Did Earl Lambreth share her enthusiasm?"

"Maybe so. I don't know. Earl Lambreth was no expert. He just conned a lot of people into thinking he was an expert—if you'll pardon me for slandering the dead."

"From what I hear," said Qwilleran, "quite a few people agree with you."

"Of course they agree with me. I'm right! Earl Lambreth was a phony, like Nino. They made a great pair, trying to out-phony each other." She grinned wickedly. "Of course, everybody knows how Lambreth operated."

"How do you mean?"

"No price labels. No catalog—except on big one-man shows. It was part of the so-called prestige image. If a customer liked a piece of art, Lambreth could quote any figure the traffic would bear. And when the artist got his percentage, he had no proof of the actual selling price."

"You think there was some juggling going on?"

"Of course there was. And Lambreth got away with it because most artists are fools. Nino was the only one who accused Lambreth of rooking him. It takes a phony to know a phony."

Smugly, Butchy patted the tight waves on her head.

Qwilleran went back to the office and wrote a requisition to the Photo Department for a close-up of a lady welder at work. He also typed a rough draft of the interview—minus references to Lambreth and Nino—and put it aside to ripen. He felt pleased with himself. He felt he was on the trail of something. Next he would visit the art museum to check out the missing Florentine dagger, and after dinner he would attend the Happening. For a Monday, this was turning out to be an interesting day.

The art museum assaulted Qwilleran with its Monday afternoon quiet. In the lobby he picked up a catalog of the Florentine Collection and learned that most of it had been the generous gift of the Duxbury family. Percy Duxbury was museum commissioner. His wife was president of the fundraising group.

At the checkroom, where Qwilleran left his hat and coat, he asked Tom LaBlanc's girl where to find the Florentine Collection.

She pointed dreamily to the far end of the corridor. "But why do you want to waste your time *there*?"

"I've never seen it, that's why. Is that a good reason?" He used an amiable, bantering tone.

She looked at him through a few strands of long hair that had fallen over one eye. "There's a loan exhibit of Swedish contemporary silver that's much more stimulating."

"Okay. I'll see both."

"You won't have time. The museum closes in an hour," she said. "The Swedish stuff is real cool, and this is the last week it will be here."

For a checkroom attendant she was taking more than routine interest in directing him, Qwilleran thought, and his professional suspicion started wigwagging to him. He went to the Florentine Room.

The Duxbury gift was a hodgepodge of paintings, tapestries, bronze reliefs, marble statues, manuscripts and small silver and gold objects in glass cases. Some were displayed behind sliding glass doors fitted with tiny, almost invisible locks; others stood on pedestals under glass domes that seemed permanently affixed.

Qwilleran ran his finger down the catalog page and found the item that interested him: a gold dagger, eight inches long, elaborately chased, sixteenth century, attributed to Benvenuto Cellini. In the glass cases—among the salt cellars and chalices and religious statues—it was not to be seen.

Qwilleran went to the director's office and asked for Mr. Farhar. A middle-aged secretary with a timid manner told him that Mr. Farhar was out. Could Mr. Smith be of assistance? Mr. Smith was chief curator.

Smith was sitting at a table covered with small jade objects, one of which he was putting under a magnifying glass. He was a handsome dark-haired man with sallow skin and eyes that were green like the jade. Qwilleran remembered him as Humbert Humbert, Lolita's escort at the Valentine Ball. The man had a slyness in his eyes, and it was easy to suspect that he might be misbehaving in some unspeakable way. Furthermore, his first name was John; anyone called John Smith would arouse doubts in the most trusting nature.

Qwilleran said to him, "I understand there is a valuable item missing from the Florentine Room."

"Where did you hear that?"

"It was a tip that came to the paper. I don't know its source."

"The rumor is unfounded. I'm sorry you've wasted a trip. If you're looking for story material, however, you could write about this private collection of jade that has just been given to the museum by one of our commissioners."

"Thank you. I'll be glad to do that," said Qwilleran, "but at some future date. Today I'm interested in Florentine art. I'm looking particularly for a chased gold dagger attributed to Cellini, and I can't seem to find it."

Smith made a deprecating gesture. "The catalog is overly optimistic. Very little of Cellini's work has come down to us, but the Duxburys like to think they bought a Cellini, and so we humor them."

"It's the dagger itself I want to see, regardless of who made it," said Qwilleran. "Would you be good enough to come with me and point it out?"

The curator leaned back in his chair and threw his arms up. "All right.

Have it your way. The dagger is temporarily misplaced, but we don't want any publicity on it. It might touch off a wave of thefts. Such things happen, you know." He had not offered the newsman a chair.

"How much is it worth?"

"We prefer not to state."

"This is a city museum," said Qwilleran, "and the public has a right to be told about this. It might lead to its recovery. Have you notified the police?"

"If we notified the police and called the newspapers every time some small object happened to be misplaced, we would be a major nuisance."

"When did you first notice it was missing?"

Smith hesitated. "It was reported by one of the guards a week ago."

"And you've done nothing about it?"

"A routine report was placed on Mr. Farhar's desk, but—as you know—he is leaving us and has many other things on his mind."

"What time of day did the guard notice its absence?"

"In the morning when he made his first inventory check."

"How often does he check?"

"Several times a day."

"And was the dagger in the case when he made the previous check?"

"Yes."

"When was that?"

"The evening before, at closing time."

"So it disappeared during the night."

"It would seem so." John Smith was being tight-lipped and reluctant.

"Was there any evidence that someone had broken into the museum or had been locked up in the place all night?"

"None."

Qwilleran was warming up. "In other words, it could have been an inside job. How was it removed from the case? Was the case broken?"

"No. The vitrine had been properly removed and replaced."

"What's a vitrine?"

"The glass dome that protects the objects on a pedestal."

"There were other objects under the same dome, were there?"

"Yes."

"But they were not touched."

"That's right."

"How do you remove one of those domes? I looked at them, and I couldn't figure it out."

"It fits down over the pedestal, secured by a molding attached with concealed screws."

"In other words," said Qwilleran, "you'd have to know the trick in order to get the thing apart. The dagger must have been taken by somebody in the know—after hours, when the museum was closed. Wouldn't you say it looks like an inside job?"

"I dislike your reference to an *inside job*, Mr. Qwilleran," said the curator. "You newspapermen can be extremely obnoxious, as this museum has discovered—to its sorrow. I forbid you to print anything about this incident without permission from Mr. Farhar."

"You don't tell a newspaper what to print and what not to print," said Qwilleran, keeping his temper in check.

"If this item appears," Smith said, "we will have to conclude that the *Daily Fluxion* is an irresponsible, sensational press. First, you may be spreading a false alarm. Second, you may encourage an epidemic of thefts. Third, you may impede the recovery of the dagger if it has actually been stolen."

"I'll leave that up to my editor," said Qwilleran. "By the way, do you move up the ladder when Farhar leaves?"

"His successor has not yet been announced," Smith said, and his sallow skin turned the color of parchment.

Qwilleran went to dinner at the Artist and Model, a snug cellar hideaway favored by the culture crowd. The background music was classical, the menu was French, and the walls were hung with works of art. They were totally unviewable in the cultivated gloom of the basement, and even the food—small portions served on brown earthenware—was difficult for the fork to find.

It was an atmosphere for conversation and handholding, rather than eating, and Qwilleran allowed himself a moment of self-pity when he realized he was the only one dining alone. He thought, Better to be at home sharing a slice of meat loaf with Koko and having a fast game of Sparrow. Then he remembered dolefully that Koko had deserted him.

He ordered *ragôut de boeuf Bordelaise* and entertained himself by brooding over the golden dagger. The Smith person had been furtive. He had admittedly lied at the beginning of the interview. Even the girl in the checkroom had tried to deter Qwilleran from visiting the Florentine Room. Who was covering up for whom?

If the dagger had been stolen, why had the thief selected this particular memento of Renaissance Italy? Why steal a weapon? Why not a goblet or bowl? It was hardly the kind of trinket that a petty thief could peddle for a meal ticket, and professional jewel thieves—big operators—would have made a bigger haul. Someone had coveted the dagger, Qwilleran told himself, because it was gold, or because it was beautiful.

It was a poetic thought, and Qwilleran blamed it on the romantic mood of the restaurant. Then he let his thoughts drift pleasantly to Zoe. He wondered how long it would be before he could conventionally invite her out to dinner. A widow who didn't believe in funerals and who wore purple silk trousers as mourning attire apparently did not cling to convention.

All around him couples were chattering and laughing. Repeatedly one female voice rose in a trill of laughter. There was no doubt about that voice. It belonged to Sandy Halapay. She had evidently found a dinner date to amuse her while her husband was in Denmark.

When Qwilleran left the restaurant, he stole a glance at Sandy's table and at the dark head bending toward her. It was John Smith.

Qwilleran plunged his hands in his overcoat pockets and walked the few blocks to Penniman School, his mind flitting from the Cellini dagger to the sly-eyed John Smith—to the conniving Sandy—to Cal Halapay in Denmark—to Tom, the Halapay's surly houseboy—to Tom's girl in the museum checkroom—and back to the dagger.

This mental merry-go-round gave Qwilleran a mild vertigo, and he tried to shake the subject out of his mind. After all, it was none of his business. Neither was the murder of Earl Lambreth. Let the police solve it.

AT PENNIMAN SCHOOL, Qwilleran found other mysteries to confound him. The Happening was a roomful of people, things, sounds and smells that seemed to have no purpose, no plan and no point.

The school was lavishly endowed (Mrs. Duxbury had been a Penniman before her marriage), and among its facilities was an impressive sculpture studio. It had been described in one of Mountclemens' columns as "big as a barn and artistically productive as a haystack." This sculpture studio was the scene of the Happening, to attend which students paid a dollar and the general public paid three. Proceeds were earmarked for the scholarship fund.

When Qwilleran arrived, the vast room was dark except for a number of spotlights that played on the walls. These shafts and puddles of light revealed a north wall of opaque glass and a lofty ceiling spanned by exposed girders. There was also a network of temporary scaffolding overhead.

Below, on the concrete floor, persons of all ages stood in clusters or promenaded among the stacks of huge empty cartons that transformed the room into a maze. These cardboard towers, painted in gaudy colors and piled precariously high, threatened to topple at the slightest instigation.

Other threats dangled from the scaffolding. A sword hung from an invisible thread. There were bunches of green balloons, red apples tied by the stems, and yellow plastic pails filled with nobody-knew-what. A garden hose dribbled in desultory fashion. Suspended in a rope sling was a nude woman with long green hair who sprayed cheap perfume from an insecticide gun. And in the center of the scaffold, presiding over the Happening like an evil god, was "Thing #36" with its spinning eyes. Something had been added, Qwilleran noted; the Thing now wore a crown of doorknobs, Nino's symbol of death.

Soon the whines and bleeps of electronic music filled the room, and the spotlights began to move in coordination with the sound, racing dizzily across the ceiling or lingering on upturned faces.

In one passage of light Qwilleran recognized Mr. and Mrs. Franz Buchwalter, whose normal dress was not unlike the peasant costumes they had worn to the Valentine Ball. The Buchwalters immediately recognized his moustache.

"When does the Happening start?" he asked them.

"It has started," said Mrs. Buchwalter.

"You mean this is it? This is all there is?"

"Other things will Happen as the evening progresses," she said.

"What are you supposed to do?"

"You can stand around and let them Happen," she said, "or you can cause things to Happen, depending on your philosophy of life. I shall probably shove some of those cartons around; Franz will just wait until they fall on him."

"I'll just wait until they fall on me," said Franz.

As more people arrived, the crowd was being forced to circulate. Some were passionately serious; some were amused; others were masking discomfiture with bravado.

"What is your opinion of all this?" Qwilleran asked the Buchwalters, as the three of them rambled through the maze.

"We find it an interesting demonstration of creativity and development of a theme," said Mrs. Buchwalter. "The event must have form, movement, a dominant point of interest, variety, unity—all the elements of good design. If you look for these qualities, it adds to the enjoyment."

Franz nodded in agreement, "Adds to the enjoyment."

"The crew is mounting the scaffold," said his wife, "so the Happenings will accelerate now."

In the flashes of half-light provided by the moving spotlights, Qwilleran saw three figures climbing the ladder. There was the big figure of Butchy Bolton in coveralls, followed by Tom LaBlanc, and then Nino, no less unkempt than before.

"The young man with a beard," said Mrs. Buchwalter, "is a rather successful alumnus of the school, and the other is a student. Miss Bolton you probably know. She teaches here. It was her idea to have that goggle-eyed Thing reigning over the Happening. Frankly, we were surprised, knowing how she feels about junk sculpture. Perhaps she was making a point. People worship junk today."

Qwilleran turned to Franz. "You teach here at Penniman, don't you?"

"Yes, he does," said Mrs. Buchwalter. "He teaches watercolor."

Qwilleran said, "I see you're having a show at the Westside Gallery, Mr. Buchwalter. Is it a success?"

"He's sold almost everything," said the artist's wife, "in spite of that remarkable review by George Bonifield Mountclemens. Your critic was unable to interpret the symbolism of Franz's work. When my husband paints sailboats, he is actually portraying the yearning of the soul to escape, white-winged, into a tomorrow of purest blue. Mountclemens used a clever device to conceal his lack of comprehension. We found it most amusing."

"Most amusing," said the artist.

"Then you're not offended by that kind of review?"

"No. The man has his limitations, as we all do. And we understand his problem. We are most sympathetic," said Mrs. Buchwalter.

"What problem do you mean?"

"Mountclemens is a frustrated artist. Of course, you know he wears a prosthetic hand—remarkably realistic—actually made by a sculptor in Michigan. It satisfies his vanity, but he is no longer able to paint."

"I didn't know he had been an artist," Qwilleran said. "How did he lose his hand?"

"No one seems to know. It happened before he came here. Obviously the loss has warped his personality. But we must learn to live with his eccentricities. He is here to stay. Nothing, we understand, could uproot him from that Victorian house of his—"

A series of squeals interrupted Mrs. Buchwalter. The garden hose suspended overhead had suddenly doused a number of spectators.

Qwilleran said, "The Lambreth murder was shocking news. Do you have any theories?"

"We don't allow our minds to dwell on that sort of thing," said Mrs. Buchwalter.

"We don't dwell on it," said her husband.

Now laughter filled the studio as the crew released a bale of chicken feathers and an electric fan sent them swirling like snow.

"It seems like good clean fun," Qwilleran commented.

He changed his mind a moment later when a noxious wave of hydrogen sulfide was released by the crew.

"It's all symbolic," said Mrs. Buchwalter. "You don't have to agree with the fatalistic premise, but you must admit they are thinking and expressing themselves."

Shots rang out. There were shouts, followed by a small riot among the spectators. The crew on the scaffold had punctured the green balloons, showering favors on the crowd below.

Qwilleran said, "I hope they're not planning to drop that sword of Damocles."

"Nothing really dangerous ever happens at a Happening," said Mrs. Buchwalter.

"No, nothing dangerous," said Mr. Buchwalter.

The crowd was milling about the floor, and the towers of cartons were beginning to topple. A shower of confetti descended from above. Then a volley of rubber balls, dumped from one of the yellow plastic buckets. Then—

"*Blood!*" shrieked a woman's voice. Qwilleran knew that scream, and he rammed his way through the crowd to reach her side.

Sandy Halapay's face dripped red. Her hands were red. She stood there helplessly while John Smith tenderly dabbed at it with his handkerchief. She was laughing. It was ketchup.

Qwilleran went back to the Buchwalters. "It's getting kind of wild," he said. The crowd had started throwing the rubber balls at the crewmen on the scaffold.

The rubber balls flew through the air, hit the scaffolding, bounced back, ricocheted off innocent skulls, and were thrown again by jeering spectators. The music screeched and blatted. Spotlights swooped in giddy arcs.

"Get the monster!" someone yelled, and a hail of balls pelted the Thing with spinning eyes.

"No!" shouted Nino. "Stop!"

Seen in flashes of light, the Thing rocked on its perch.

"Stop!"

Crew members rushed to save it. The planks of the scaffold rattled.

"Look out!"

There was a scream from the girl in the rope sling.

The crowd scattered. The Thing fell with a crash. And with it a body plunged to the concrete floor.

CHAPTER 12

TWO NEWS ITEMS rated headlines in the Tuesday morning edition of the *Daily Fluxion*.

A valuable gold dagger, attributed to Cellini, had disappeared from the art museum. Although its absence had been noted by a guard more than a week ago, the matter was not reported to the police until a *Flexion* reporter discovered that the rare treasure was missing from the Florentine Room. Museum officials gave no satisfactory explanation for the delay.

The other item reported a fatal accident.

"An artist plunged to death Monday night at the Penniman School of Fine Art during an audience-participation program called a Happening. He was a sculptor known professionally as Nine Oh Two Four Six Eight Five, whose real name was Joseph Hibber.

"Hibber was perched on a high scaffold in the darkened room when unruly activity on the floor below caused a near-accident to one of the mammoth props in the show.

"Eyewitnesses reported that Hibber attempted to save the object from falling on the spectators. In the effort he apparently lost his footing, falling 26 feet to a concrete floor.

"Mrs. Sadie Buchwalter, wife of Franz Buchwalter, a faculty member, was injured by a flying doorknob when the object crashed. Her condition was described as satisfactory.

"Some 300 students, faculty members and art patrons attending the benefit event witnessed the accident."

Qwilleran threw the newspaper on the bar at the Press Club that afternoon, when Arch Riker met him for a five-thirty pick-me-up.

"Plunged to his death," said Qwilleran, "or was pushed."

"You've got a criminous mind," said Arch. "Isn't one murder on your beat enough to keep you happy?"

"You don't know what I know."

"Let's have it. Who was this character?"

"A beatnik who happened to like Zoe Lambreth. And she was pretty fond of him, although you'd find this hard to believe if you could see the guy—a nature boy straight from the city dump."

"You never know about women," said Arch.

"And yet I've got to admit the boy had possibilities."

"So who pushed him?"

"Well, there's this woman sculptor, Butchy Bolton, who seemed to resent him. I think Butchy was jealous of this beatnik's friendship with Zoe and jealous of him professionally. He enjoyed more critical success than she did. Butchy also has a crush on Zoe."

"Oh, one of those!"

"Zoe was trying to brush her off—subtly—but Butchy is as subtle as a bulldog. And here's an interesting point: both Butchy and Nino, the deceased, had serious grudges against Zoe's husband. Suppose one of them killed Earl Lambreth; did Butchy consider Nino a competitor for Zoe's attention and push him off the scaffold last night? The whole crew rushed out on those flimsy boards to stop the Thing from crashing. Butchy would have had a beautiful opportunity."

"You seem to know more than the police."

"I don't have any answers. Just questions. And here's another one: Who stole the painting of a ballet dancer from Earl Lambreth's office? Last weekend I suddenly remembered it was missing on the night of the murder. I told Zoe, and she reported it to the police."

"You've been a busy boy. No wonder you haven't finished that profile on Halapay."

"And one more question: Who stole the dagger at the museum? And why are they being so cagey about it?"

"Do you have any more yarns?" asked Arch. "Or can I go home to my wife and kiddies?"

"Go home. You're a lousy audience. Here comes a couple of guys who'll be interested."

Odd Bunsen and Lodge Kendall were walking through the bar single file.

"Hey, Jim," said Odd, "did you write that piece about the missing dagger at the museum?"

"Yeah."

"They've found it. I went up and got some shots of it. The Picture Desk thought people would like to see what the thing looked like—after all the hullabaloo you stirred up."

"Where'd they find it?"

"In the safe in the Education Department. One of the instructors was writing a piece on Florentine art for some magazine, and he took the dagger out of the case to examine. Then he went off to a convention somewhere and parked it in the safe."

"Oh," said Qwilleran. His moustache drooped.

"Well, that solves one of your problems," Arch told him. He turned to the police reporter. "Anything new in the Lambreth case?"

"A major clue just fizzled out," said Kendall. "The police found a valuable painting that Lambreth's wife said was missing."

"Where'd they find it?" Qwilleran demanded.

"In the stock room of the gallery, filed under G."

"Oh," said Qwilleran.

Arch slapped him on the back. "As a detective, Jim, you're a great art writer. Why don't you bear down on that Halapay profile and leave crime to the police? I'm going home."

Arch left the Press Club, and Odd Bunsen and Lodge Kendall drifted away, and Qwilleran sat alone, peering unhappily into his tomato juice.

Bruno, wiping the bar, said with his wise smile, "You want another Bloody Mary without vodka, lime, Worcestershire or Tabasco?"

"No," snapped Qwilleran.

The bartender lingered. He tidied up the bar. He gave Qwilleran another paper napkin. Finally he said, "Would you like to see a couple of my presidential portraits?"

Qwilleran glowered at him.

"I've finished Van Buren," said Bruno, "and I've got him and John Quincy Adams here under the bar."

"Not tonight. I'm not in the mood."

"I don't know anybody else who makes collage portraits out of whiskey labels," Bruno persisted.

"Look, I don't care if you make mosaic portraits out of used olive pits! I don't want to look at them tonight!"

"You're beginning to sound like Mountclemens," said Bruno.

"I've changed my mind about that drink," said Qwilleran. "I'll take one. Make it a Scotch—straight."

Bruno shrugged and began filling the order in slow motion.

"And snap it up," said Qwilleran.

Over the loudspeaker came a muffled voice that he did not hear.

"Mr. Qwilleran," said Bruno. "I think they're paging you."

Qwilleran listened, wiped his moustache, and in bad humor went to the telephone.

A soft voice said, "Mr. Qwilleran, I hope I'm not intruding, but I wonder if you have any plans for dinner tonight?"

"No, I haven't," he said, shifting gears.

"Would you come out and have dinner with me at the house? I'm feeling blue, and it would help if I could talk with someone who is understanding. I promise not to dwell on my troubles. We'll talk about pleasant things."

"I'll grab a cab and be right there."

On the way out of the Press Club, Qwilleran threw Bruno a dollar. "Drink the Scotch yourself," he said.

WHEN QWILLERAN returned home from Zoe's house sometime after midnight, he was in a congenial mood. The night was bitter cold, and yet he felt warm. He gave a quarter to a frozen-looking panhandler shuffling down Blenheim Place, and he whistled a tune as he unlocked the outer door of No. 26.

Even before he inserted the second key in the inner door, he could hear a wail from Koko in the hall.

"Ha! fair-weather friend," he said to the cat. "You snubbed me yesterday. Don't expect a game of Sparrow tonight, old fellow."

Koko was sitting on the bottom step in a tall posture. No prancing. No ankle-rubbing. He was strictly business. He spoke again urgently.

Qwilleran looked at his watch. The cat should have been asleep at this hour, curled on the refrigerator cushion in Mountclemens' apartment. But there he was, wide awake and speaking in long, loud terms. It was not the

complaining whine he used when dinner was slightly delayed, nor the
scolding tone he assumed when dinner was unforgivably late. It was a cry
of desperation.

"Quiet, Koko! You'll wake up the house," Qwilleran said in a hushed
voice.

Koko lowered his volume but persisted in the urgency of his message.
He stalked back and forth on taut legs, rubbing against the newel-post.

"What's the matter, Koko? What are you trying to say?"

The cat's sleek side ground against the newel-post as if to gouge out
chunks of fur. Qwilleran reached down and stroked the arched back; the
silky fur had become strangely coarse and bristling. At the touch of the
hand, Koko bounded up five or six stairs, then lowered his head and
twisted his neck until he could rub the back of his ears against the front
edge of a tread.

"Are you locked out, Koko? Let's go up and see."

Immediately the cat scampered to the top of the flight, with the man
following.

"The door's open, Koko," Qwilleran whispered. "Go in. Go to sleep."

The cat squeezed through the narrow opening, and Qwilleran was
halfway downstairs again when the wailing resumed. Koko had come out
and was rubbing his head violently against the doorjamb.

"You can't keep that up all night! Come on home with me. I'll find you
a snack." Qwilleran grabbed the cat under the middle and carried him to
his own apartment, where he tossed him lightly on the sofa, but Koko was
gone again in a white blur of speed, flying up the stairs and wailing desperately from the top.

At that point Qwilleran's moustache quivered without explanation.
What was this all about? Without another word, he followed the cat upstairs. First he knocked on the open door. When there was no answer, he
went in. The living room was dark.

As he pressed the switch, all the hidden spotlights flicked their tiny
beams on paintings and objects of art. Koko was quiet now, watching
Qwilleran's feet as they walked through the living room, into the dining
alcove, then out again. The heavily draped and carpeted rooms had a stifling hush. When the feet stopped moving, Koko rushed off down the
long hall to the dark kitchen. The feet followed. Bedroom and bathroom
doors stood open. Qwilleran turned on the kitchen light.

"What is it, you devil?"

The cat was rubbing against the back door that led to the fire escape.

"If you just want to go for a walk, I'll wring your neck. Is that what you want?"

Koko rose on his hind feet and pawed at the doorknob.

"Well, I'm not taking you out. Where's your roommate? Let *him* take you out. . . . Besides, it's too cold for cats out there."

Qwilleran switched off the kitchen light and started back down the long hallway, only to have Koko come racing after him with a chesty growl. The cat threw himself at the man's legs.

Qwilleran's moustache sent him another message. He returned to the kitchen, turned on the light and took the flashlight from the broom closet. He reached for the night latch on the back door and found it unlocked. Strange, he thought.

Opening the door, he met a blast of wintry air, crackling cold. There was a wall switch just inside the door, and he flicked it with a finger, but the exterior light made only a sick puddle of yellow on the upper landing. Qwilleran thumbed the flashlight, and its powerful beam leaped about the scene below. It explored the three brick walls. It studied the closed gate. It crept over the brick paving until it pounced on the sprawled body—the long, dark, spidery body of George Bonifield Mountclemens.

Qwilleran made his way cautiously down the icy treads of the wooden staircase. He flashed the center beam of the flashlight on the side of the face. Mountclemens was lying cheek to the pavement, his body hunched. No doubt about it; he was dead.

The alley was deserted. The night was quiet. There was a fragrance of lime peel. And within the patio the only movement was a pale shadow just beyond the flashlight's range. It moved in circles. It was the cat, behaving oddly, performing some private ritual. With back arched and tail stiff and ears laid back, Kao K'o-Kung walked around and around and around.

Qwilleran grabbed the cat in one arm and got up the wooden staircase as fast as the icy treads would permit. At the telephone his finger hesitated over the dial, but he called the police first and after that the night city editor of the *Daily Fluxion*. Then he sat down to wait, composing his own wry versions of appropriate headlines for tomorrow's paper.

First to arrive at Blenheim Place were two officers in a patrol car.

Qwilleran told them, "You can't reach the patio from the front of the house. You have to go upstairs through his apartment and down the fire escape, or else go around the block and come in the alley gate. It may be locked."

"Who lives in the downstairs rear?" they asked.

"No one. It's used for storage."

The officers tried the door of the rear apartment and found it locked. They went upstairs and down the fire escape.

Qwilleran told them, "At first I thought he'd fallen down the steps. They're treacherous. But he's lying too far from the bottom."

"Looks like a body wound," they said. "Looks like it might have been a knife."

Upstairs the cat arched his back and made long legs and stepped lightly in a pattern of ever-narrowing circles.

CHAPTER 13

THE DAY AFTER the murder of Mountclemens, there was only one topic of conversation at the *Daily Fluxion*. One by one they stopped at Qwilleran's desk: the members of the City Room, the Women's Department, Editorial, the Photo Lab, and the Sports Department. The head librarian, the foreman of the Composing Room, and the elevator starter paid unexpected visits.

Qwilleran's telephone rang incessantly. Women readers cried in his ear. Several anonymous callers said they were glad; Mountclemens had it coming to him. Some urged the newspaper to offer a reward for the killer. Six galleries telephoned to inquire who would review their March exhibitions, now that the critic was out of the picture. A crank called with a phony-sounding tip on the murder and was referred to the Homicide Bureau. A twelve-year-old girl applied for the job of art critic.

One call was from Sandy Halapay's maid, canceling the lunch date scheduled with Qwilleran; there was no explanation. So at noon he went to the Press Club with Arch Riker, Odd Bunsen and Lodge Kendall.

They took a table for four, and Qwilleran went over the incident in detail, starting with Koko's unusual behavior. Mountclemens had been knifed in the stomach. The weapon had not been found. There was no sign of a tussle. The gate to the alley was locked.

"The body's being sent to Milwaukee," Qwilleran told his audience.

"Mountclemens mentioned that he had a sister there, and the police found her address. They also impounded the tape reels he had been working on."

Arch said, "They've been looking at back files of his reviews, but I don't know what they hope to find. Just because he insulted half the artists in town, that doesn't make them all suspects, does it? Or maybe it does!"

"Every scrap of information helps," said Lodge.

"A lot of people hated Mountclemens. Not only artists but dealers, museum people, teachers, collectors—and at least one bartender that I know," said Qwilleran. "Even Odd wanted to bust a camera over his head."

Arch said, "The switchboard has been jumping. Everybody wants to know who did it. Sometimes I think our readers are all morons."

"Mountclemens wasn't wearing his artificial hand when he was killed," said Odd. "I wonder why."

"That reminds me," said Qwilleran. "I got quite a jolt this morning. Went upstairs to Mountclemens' apartment to get the cat's meat, and there on the top shelf of the refrigerator was that plastic hand! I jumped a foot!"

"What does the cat think about all the uproar?"

"He's edgy. I'm keeping him in my apartment, and he jumps at the slightest sound. After the police had gone last night and everything quieted down, I put a blanket on the sofa and tried to make him bed down, but he just walked the floor. I think he prowled all night."

"I'd like to know what that cat knows."

Qwilleran said, "I'd like to know what Mountclemens was doing in the patio on a cold winter night—in his velvet house jacket. That's what he was wearing—and a glove on his good hand. Yet he had taken his topcoat with him. There was a British tweed lying on the bricks in a corner of the patio. They assume it was his—right size, New York label, and a shoulder cape! Who else would wear a cape?"

"Exactly where did you find the body?"

"In a corner of the yard, close to the gate that leads into the alley. It looked as if he'd had his back to the brick wall—the side wall, that is—when someone plunged the knife into his gut."

"It went into the abdominal aorta," said Lodge. "He didn't have a chance."

"Now we've got to find a new art critic," said Arch. "Do you want the job, Jim?"

"Who? Me? Are you crazy?"

"That gives me an idea," Lodge said. "Was there anyone in town who wanted to get Mountclemens' job for himself?"

"It doesn't pay enough to be worth the risk of a murder rap."

"But it has prestige," said Qwilleran, "and some art expert might see it as a chance to play God. A critic can make or break an artist."

"Who would be qualified for such a job?"

"A teacher. A curator. Someone who contributes to art journals."

Arch said, "He'd have to know how to write. Most artists can't write. They think they can, but they can't."

"It'll be interesting to see who applies for the job."

Someone said, "Any more dope on the Lambreth case?"

"Nothing that they've seen fit to reveal," said Lodge.

"Know who'd make a good critic?" Qwilleran said. "He's currently unemployed, too."

"Who?"

"Noel Farhar from the museum."

"Think he'd be interested?" Arch said. "Maybe I should give him a buzz."

After lunch Qwilleran spent most of the afternoon taking telephone calls, and at the end of the day his urge to go back to the Press Club for dinner was less powerful than his urge to go home and see Koko. The cat, he told himself, was now an orphan. Siamese were particularly needful of companionship. The bereaved animal had been locked up alone in Qwilleran's apartment all day. There was no telling what kind of breakdown he might have suffered.

When Qwilleran unlocked the door of his apartment, there was no sign of Koko on the sofa or the big chair, no leonine pose on the red carpet, no pale bundle of fur on the bed in the alcove.

Qwilleran called the cat's name. He got down on hands and knees and looked under things. He searched behind draperies and behind the shower curtain in the bathtub. He peered up the chimney.

He thought, I've accidentally shut him up in a cabinet or closet. But a frantic banging of doors and drawers produced no cat. He couldn't have escaped. The apartment door had been locked. There were no open windows. He's got to be in this apartment, Qwilleran thought. If I start fixing his dinner, he may come crawling out of the woodwork.

Qwilleran went to the kitchenette, approached the refrigerator, and found himself face to face with a calm, cool-eyed Koko.

Qwilleran gasped, "You devil! Were you sitting there all the time?"

Koko, huddled in an awkward pose on the refrigerator top, answered with a curt syllable.

"What's the matter, old fellow? Are you unhappy?"

The cat shifted position irritably. Now he crouched with his body hovering above the hard porcelain surface. His haunches angled up like fins, and the fur over his shoulder blades spread open like a huge dandelion gone to seed.

"You're uncomfortable! That's what's wrong. After dinner we'll go upstairs and get your cushion. Is that okay?"

Koko squeezed both eyes.

Qwilleran started to mince the beef. "When this hunk of meat is gone, you'll have to start eating something I can afford—or else move to Milwaukee. You live better than I do."

After Koko had chewed his beef and Qwilleran had downed a salami sandwich, they went upstairs to get the blue cushion from the top of Mountclemens' refrigerator. The place was locked now, but Qwilleran still had the key the critic had given him a week ago.

Koko entered the apartment with a wondering hesitation. He wandered aimlessly, smelled the carpet here and there, and moved gradually toward one corner of the living room. The louvered doors seemed to attract him. He sniffed their edges, the hinges, the louvers—in rapt concentration.

"What are you looking for, Koko?"

The cat stretched tall on his hind legs and scratched the door. Then he pawed the red carpet.

"Do you want to get into that closet? What for?"

Koko dug vigorously at the rug, and Qwilleran took the suggestion. He opened the double doors.

In the early life of the house, this closet might have been a small sewing room or study. Now the windows were shuttered, and the space was filled with racks holding paintings in vertical slots. Some were framed; some were merely stretched canvases. Here and there Qwilleran caught glimpses of wild, meaningless splotches of color.

Once inside the closet, Koko sniffed avidly, his nose taking him to one rack after another. One particular slot interested him keenly; he tried to insert his paw.

"I'd like to know what this demonstration is all about," Qwilleran said.

Koko yowled in excitement. He tried first one paw and then the other. He took time out to brush against Qwilleran's pant leg, after which he resumed the quest.

"You want some help, I suppose. What's in that rack?" Qwilleran withdrew the framed painting that filled the narrow slot, and Koko reached in to snag a small dark object with his claws.

Qwilleran took the thing away from the cat to examine it. What could it be? Soft . . . fuzzy . . . lightweight. Koko howled in indignation.

"Sorry," said Qwilleran. "Just curious. So this is Mintie Mouse!" He tossed the mint-perfumed toy back to the cat, who clutched it with both paws, rolling on his side and pummeling it with his hind feet.

"Come on, let's get out of here." Qwilleran returned the painting to its slot but not without giving it a quick perusal. It was a dreamlike landscape filled with headless bodies and disembodied heads. He grimaced and put it away. So these were Mountclemens' blue-chip stocks!

He looked at a few more. One was a series of black lines ruled across a white background—some parallel, some intersecting. He raised his eyebrows. Another canvas was covered with gray paint—just gray paint and a signature in the lower corner. Then there was a vivid purple sphere on a red field that gave Qwilleran the beginning of a headache.

The next painting caused a peculiar sensation in the roots of his moustache. Impulsively, he swooped down on Koko, gathered him up and ran downstairs.

He went to the telephone and dialed a number that he had come to know by heart. "Zoe? This is Jim. I've found something here at the house that I want you to see. . . . A painting—one that will interest you. Koko and I went up to Mountclemens' apartment to get something, and the cat led me to this closet. He was very insistent. You'll never believe what we found. . . . A monkey. A painting of a monkey! . . . Can you come over?"

Minutes later, Zoe arrived by taxi, wearing her fur coat over slacks and a sweater. Qwilleran was watching for her. He had brought the monkey painting down to his own apartment, where it was propped on the mantel over the Monet.

"That's it!" cried Zoe. "That's the other half of Earl's Ghirotto!"

"You're sure?"

"It's obviously a Ghirotto. The brushwork is unmistakable and the background is the same yellow-green. Notice how the design is poorly balanced; the monkey is too far to the right, and he's reaching out of the picture. Also—can't you see a scrap of the dancer's tutu showing at the right-hand edge?"

They both stared at the canvas, their thoughts taking shape.

"If this is the missing half—"

"What does it mean?"

Zoe suddenly looked hollow-cheeked. She sat down and bit her lower lip. It was the mannerism that Qwilleran had found so unpleasant in Earl Lambreth. In Zoe it was appealing.

She said, slowly, "Mountclemens knew Earl was hunting for the monkey. He was one of those who offered to buy the ballerina. And no wonder! He had found the monkey!"

Qwilleran was making short stabs at his moustache with a thumbnail. He was asking himself, Would Mountclemens kill to get the ballerina? And if that were the case, why leave the painting on the premises? Because it had been removed to the stock room and he couldn't find it? Or because—?

With a crawling sensation in his moustache, Qwilleran remembered the gossip he had heard about Zoe and Mountclemens.

Zoe was gazing down at her hands clasped tightly in her lap. As if she felt Qwilleran's questioning stare, she suddenly raised her eyes and said, "I despised him! I *despised* him!"

Qwilleran waited patiently and sympathetically for anything she wanted to say.

"He was an arrogant, avaricious, overbearing man," said Zoe. "I loathed Mountclemens, and yet I had to play along—for obvious reasons."

"Obvious reasons?"

"Can't you see? My paintings were enjoying his critical favor. If I had made him angry, he could have ruined my career. He would have ruined Earl, too. What could I do? I flirted—discreetly, I thought—because that was the way Mountclemens wanted to play." Zoe fussed with her handbag—clasping, unclasping, clasping. "And then he got the idea that I should leave Earl and go with him."

"How did you handle that proposition?"

"It was a delicate maneuver, believe me! I said—or I implied—that I would like to accept his proposal, but an old-fashioned sense of loyalty bound me to my husband. What an act! I felt like the heroine in one of those old silent movies."

"Did that settle the matter?"

"Unfortunately, no. He continued his campaign, and I got in deeper and deeper. It was a nightmare! There was the constant strain of acting out a lie."

"Didn't your husband know what was going on?"

Zoe sighed. "For a long time he didn't suspect. Earl was always so preoccupied with his own problems that he was blind and deaf to everyone else. But eventually he heard the gossip. And then we had a horrible scene. I convinced him—finally—that I was trapped in a nasty situation." There was prolonged business with the handbag clasp. Falteringly she said, "You know—Earl seemed to cling to me. Even though we were no longer— close—if you know what I mean. I found it *safer* to be married, and Earl clung to me because I was a success. He was born to be a failure. His only achievement was a happy accident—finding half a Ghirotto—and it was his life's ambition to find the other half and be rich!"

Qwilleran said, "You don't think Mountclemens killed your husband, do you?"

Zoe looked at him helplessly. "I don't know. I just don't know. He wouldn't have done anything so drastic merely to get me. I'm positive of that! He wasn't capable of loving that passionately. But he might have done it to get me *and* the other half of the Ghirotto."

That would be quite a package, Qwilleran reflected. He said, "Mount-clemens had a passion for art."

"Only as a form of wealth, to be accumulated and hoarded. He didn't share his possessions. He didn't even want people to know he owned fabulous treasures."

"Where did he get the dough to buy them? Certainly not from writing art columns for the *Daily Fluxion*."

Zoe left his question dangling. She seemed to shrink into her chair. "I'm tired," she said. "I'd like to go home. I didn't mean to talk like this."

"I know. It's all right," Qwilleran said. "I'll call you a cab."

"Thank you for being so understanding."

"I'm complimented to have you confide in me."

Zoe bit her lip. "I feel I can say this to you: When Earl was killed, my reaction was more fear than grief—fear of Mountclemens and what would happen next. Now that fear has been removed, and I can't be anything but glad."

Qwilleran watched Zoe's taxi disappear into the darkness. He wondered if she had suspected Mountclemens from the start. Was the critic one of Earl's enemies—one of the "important people" she had been afraid to name to the police? On the other hand, would a man like Mountclemens—enjoying a good life and with so much to lose—take the risk of committing murder to gain a woman and a valuable painting? Qwilleran doubted it.

Then his thoughts went back to the monkey propped on the mantel in his apartment. What would happen to it now? Along with the Rembrandt drawings and the Van Gogh, the Ghirotto monkey would go to that woman from Milwaukee. She would be unlikely to know its significance. In all probability she would loathe the ugly thing. How easy it would be—

An idea began to take shape in his mind. "Keep it . . . Say nothing . . . Give it to Zoe."

He returned to the apartment to look at the monkey. On the mantel in front of the canvas sat Kao K'o-Kung, straight as a sentinel, giving Qwilleran a reproachful stare.

"Okay. You win," said the newsman. "I'll report it to the police."

CHAPTER 14

THURSDAY MORNING Qwilleran telephoned Lodge Kendall at the pressroom in police headquarters.

He said, "I've picked up some information on Lambreth and Mountclemens. Why don't you bring the Homicide guys to lunch at the club?"

"Make it dinner. Hames and Wojcik are working nights."

"Do you think they're willing to discuss the case?"

"Oh, sure. Especially Hames. He's a relaxed type. Never underestimate him, though. He's got a mind like a computer."

Qwilleran said, "I'll get to the club early and snag a quiet table upstairs. Is six o'clock okay?"

"Make it six-fifteen. I won't promise, but I'll try to have them there."

Qwilleran wrote six-fifteen on his desk calendar and reluctantly considered the possibility of starting his day's work. He sharpened a handful of pencils, cleaned out his paper clip tray, filled his glue pot, straightened his stack of copy paper. Then he pulled out his draft of the Butchy Bolton interview and put it away again. No hurry; the Photo Department had not yet produced any pictures to accompany the story. Without much effort he found similar excuses to postpone most of the other chores in his "next" file.

He was in no mood to work. He was too busy wondering how the *Daily Fluxion* would react to the idea of a murderer on the staff—on the culture beat, no less! He could visualize the editorial embarrassment if the police pinned Lambreth's murder on Mountclemens, and he could picture the other newspaper gleefully capitalizing on the scandalous news. . . . No, it was unthinkable. Newspaper writers reported on homicide; they never indulged in it.

Qwilleran had liked Mountclemens. The man was a delightful host, clever writer, unashamed egotist, cat-worshipper, fearless critic, miser with electric light bulbs, sentimentalist about old houses, and an unpredictable human being. He could be curt one minute, genial the next—as he was on the night he heard the news of Lambreth's murder.

The newsman looked at his calendar. There was nothing on his schedule until six-fifteen. Six-fifteen—the hour the clock stopped for Earl Lambreth. Six-fifteen? Qwilleran felt a prickling sensation in his moustache. *Six-fifteen!* Then Mountclemens had an alibi!

It was six-twenty that evening when the police reporter turned up with the two men from the Homicide Bureau: Hames, blandly amiable, and Wojcik, all business.

Hames said, "Aren't you the fellow with the cat that can read?"

"He can not only read," said Qwilleran, "he can read backwards, and don't laugh. I'm sending him to the FBI Academy when he grows up, and he may get your job."

"He'll do all right, too. Cats are born snoopers. Our kids have a cat that gets into everything. He'd make a good cop—or a good newspaperman." Hames scanned the menu. "Before I order, who's paying for this meal? The *Daily Fluxion* or us underpaid guardians of the public welfare?"

Wojcik said to Qwilleran, "Kendall tells us you want to talk about the art murders."

"I've picked up a few facts. Do you want to hear them now, or do you want to order first?"

"Let's hear."

"Well, it's like this: Lambreth's widow seems to have made me her confidant, and she told me a few things last night after I discovered something unusual in Mountclemens' apartment."

"What were you doing up there?"

"Looking for the cat's toy mouse. It's an old sock filled with dried mint. He was going crazy because he couldn't find it."

Hames said, "Our cat's wild for catnip, too."

"This isn't catnip. It's fresh mint that Mountclemens grew in a pot on the windowsill."

"Same thing," said Hames. "Catnip's a member of the mint family."

"So what did you find that was unusual?" said Wojcik.

"A painting of a monkey that seemed to ring a bell. I called Mrs. Lambreth, and she came over and identified it."

"What's with this monkey?"

"It has to do with that painting of a ballet dancer by Ghirotto at the Lambreth Gallery."

Hames said, "We have one of those Ghirotto dancers at home. My wife bought it for $14.95 at Sears."

"Ghirotto painted a lot of dancers," said Qwilleran, "and the reproductions are quite popular. But this one is unique. It's only half a painting. The canvas was ripped and the two halves sold separately. Lambreth owned the half with Ghirotto's signature and was hunting for the other half, which had a monkey on it. Combined and restored, they'd be worth $150,000."

Hames said, "They get ridiculous prices for art these days. . . . Does anybody want one of these poppy-seed rolls?"

Wojcik said, "And you found the missing half—"

"In a closet in Mountclemens' apartment," said Qwilleran.

"In a closet? You were really snooping, weren't you?"

Qwilleran's moustache rebelled and he smoothed it. "I was looking for the cat's—"

"Okay, okay. So it looks like Mountclemens killed a man to get a picture of a dame in a short skirt. What else do you know?"

Qwilleran, irritated by Wojcik's brusqueness, found his spirit of cooperation flagging. He said to himself, Let him dig up his own lousy clues. With a degree of reluctance he told the detective, "Mountclemens had apparently been making eyes at Mrs. Lambreth."

"Did she tell you that?"

Qwilleran nodded.

"Women always say that. Was she interested in Mountclemens?"

Qwilleran shook his head.

"Foiled!" said the jovial Hames. "So the villain went home and committed hara-kiri in his backyard, after which he swallowed the knife to conceal the evidence of suicide and throw suspicion on the poor widow. Will someone please pass the butter?"

Wojcik threw his partner an impatient scowl.

"However," said Qwilleran coolly, "I have an alibi for Mountclemens." He paused and waited for the reaction.

Kendall was all eyes and ears; Wojcik was twiddling a spoon; Hames was buttering another roll.

Qwilleran proceeded. "Lambreth was murdered at six-fifteen, according to the electric desk clock that stopped at that hour, but Mountclemens was on the three o'clock plane to New York. I bought his ticket for him."

"You bought his ticket," said Hames, "but do you know whether he used it? Perhaps he changed his reservation and went on the seven o'clock plane after killing Lambreth at six-fifteen. . . . Funny thing about that clock stopping at six-fifteen. It wasn't damaged. It was merely unplugged from the wall socket. It appears that the murderer went to some pains to stage signs of a violent shindy, place the clock on the floor and disconnect the juice, thus pinpointing the hour of the crime. Had the struggle been genuine and had the clock been knocked to the floor accidentally in the heat of battle, it would probably have been damaged, and if it had *not* been damaged, it would have continued to run, *unless* its fall had yanked the plug from the wall socket. However, considering the position of the desk and the location of the wall socket and the spot where the clock was found, it is doubtful whether such a fall could have disconnected the plug *accidentally*. So it appears that the murderer made a special effort to register the hour of the murder by means of the clock—for the purpose of establishing an alibi—after which he took a later flight . . . all of this assuming that your art critic with a three o'clock plane ticket was actually the killer."

Wojcik said, "We'll check the airline."

After the detectives had left, Qwilleran had another cup of coffee with Lodge Kendall and said, "Did you say Hames had a mind like a computer? It's more like a cement mixer."

Kendall said, "I think he's right. I'll bet Mountclemens had you pick up his plane ticket for the express purpose of emphasizing that three o'clock departure. Then he took a later flight. Lambreth would have no qualms about letting him in the gallery after hours, and Mountclemens probably took the man completely by surprise."

"With only one hand?"

"He was tall. He came up behind Lambreth, got a stranglehold with his right arm, and plunged the chisel in Lambreth's exposed throat with his good left hand. Then he roughed up the office, disconnected the clock, damaged some art to leave a false clue, and took a later plane."

Qwilleran shook his head. "I can't picture Mountclemens on the other end of that chisel."

"Got a better theory?"

"I'm playing with one. It hasn't jelled yet. But it might explain all three deaths. . . . What's in that package?"

"The tapes the police impounded. There's nothing on them—just an art review. Are they any good to you?"

"I'll give them to Arch," Qwilleran said. "And maybe I'll write some kind of memorial piece to go with Mountclemens' last column."

"Careful how you phrase it. You might be writing a memorial to a murderer," Kendall said.

Qwilleran's moustache made a stubborn stand. He said, "I have a hunch you'll find Mountclemens was on that three o'clock plane."

When Qwilleran arrived home with the tape reels under his arm, it was nearing eight o'clock, and Koko met him at the door with an impatient clamor. Koko was not in favor of Qwilleran's casual meal schedule.

"If you'd learn to talk, I wouldn't have to hang around the Press Club so much," the newsman explained, "and you'd get your dinner on time."

Koko passed one paw over his right ear and gave his left shoulder blade two short licks with his tongue.

Qwilleran studied the signals thoughtfully. "I guess you can talk, all right. I'm just not bright enough to read you."

After dinner, cat and man went upstairs to the dictating machine on the critic's desk, and Qwilleran slipped a reel on the spindle. The sharp voice of the late George Bonifield Mountclemens—made more nasal by the quality of the equipment—filled the room:

"For publication Sunday, March 8—Serious collectors of contemporary art are secretly acquiring all available works by the celebrated Italian painter Scrano, it was learned this week. For reasons of ill health, the artist—for twenty years a recluse in the Umbrian Hills—is no longer able to produce the paintings that have earned him the accolade of modern master.

"Scrano's final works are now en route to the United States, according to his New York agent, and prices may be expected to soar. In my own modest collection I have a small Scrano painted in 1958, and I have been offered twenty times its original cost. Needless to say, I would not part with it."

There was a pause in the dictation, while a few inches of tape unwound thoughtfully. Then the ringing voice dropped to a more casual tone.

"Correction! Editor, delete the last two sentences."

There was another pause. Then:

"Scrano's work is handled locally by the Lambreth Gallery, which will reopen soon, it has been announced. The gallery closed following the tragedy of February 25, and the art world mourns . . . correction, the *local* art world mourns . . . the passing of a respected and influential figure.

"The quality of Scrano's work has not wavered, despite age and illness. He combines the technique of an old master, the hubris of youth, the insight of a sage, the expressiveness . . ."

Koko sat on the desk, regarding the spinning tape with fascination and purring a rich throaty accompaniment.

"Recognize your old roommate?" asked Qwilleran with a note of sadness. He himself was affected by the sound of Mountclemens' last words, and he smoothed his moustache pensively.

As the tape reel rewound at high speed, Koko lowered his head and fervently rubbed his jaw against the edge of the machine.

Qwilleran said, "Who killed him, Koko? You're supposed to be able to sense things."

The cat sat tall on the desk, with forelegs close to his body, and stared at Qwilleran with wide eyes. The blue disappeared, and they were large black voids. He swayed slightly.

"Go ahead. Talk! You must know who killed him."

Koko closed his eyes and uttered a tentative squeak.

"You must have seen it happen! Tuesday night. Out the back widow. Cats can see in the dark, can't they?"

The cat's ears waggled, one forward and one back, and he jumped to the floor. Qwilleran watched while he prowled about the room—aimlessly at first—looking under a chair here and a cabinet there, peering into the cold black fireplace, touching an electric cord with a wary paw. Then he thrust his head forward and down. He began to zigzag down the long hall to the kitchen, and Qwilleran followed.

At the bedroom door Koko gave a perfunctory sniff. At the threshold of the kitchen, he stopped and murmured something in his throat. Then he backtracked down the long hall to the tapestry that covered much of the wall space opposite the bedroom door. Woven into the tapestry was the scene of a royal hunting party, with horses, falcons, dogs and small game. Dim light and the fading of age made the figures almost indistinguishable, but Koko showed pronounced interest in the rabbits and wildfowl that filled one corner of the design. Was it true, Qwilleran wondered, that cats could sense the content of a picture?

Koko touched it experimentally with his paw. He reared on his hind legs and waved his head from side to side like a cobra. Then dropping to all fours, he sniffed the lower edge of the tapestry where it grazed the floor.

Qwilleran said, "Is there something behind that thing?" He lifted one corner of the heavy hanging and saw nothing but plain wall. Yet Koko gave a joyous cry. Qwilleran raised the corner higher, and the cat pushed his way behind the tapestry, proclaiming his delight in positive tones.

"Wait a minute." Qwilleran went for the flashlight and shone a wedge of light between the tapestry and wall. It revealed the edge of a doorframe, and that was where Koko was rubbing and sniffing and voicing his excitement.

Qwilleran followed, burrowing with some difficulty between the heavy textile and the wall, until he came to the bolted door. The catch slid open easily, and the door swung out over a narrow stairway. It made a sharp turn and descended to the floor below, where it was closed off by a second door. At one time this would have been the servants' stairs.

There was a light switch, but no light bulb responded. Qwilleran was not surprised. He descended with the aid of the flashlight—thoughtfully. If this led to the rear apartment—which the critic had claimed to use for storage—there was no telling what treasures might be found.

Koko had already scampered to the bottom and was waiting impatiently. Qwilleran picked him up and opened the door.

He found himself in a large old-fashioned kitchen with drawn window shades and the aroma of disuse. Yet the room was comfortably warm. It was more studio than kitchen. There was an easel, a table, a chair and—against one wall—a cot. Many unframed canvases stood on the floor, face to the wall.

One door led to the patio. Another, toward the front of the house, opened into a dining room. Qwilleran ran the flashlight over a marble fireplace and an ornate built-in sideboard. Otherwise the room was bare.

Koko wriggled to get free, but there was dust everywhere, and Qwilleran kept a tight hold on the cat while he turned his attention back to the kitchen.

One painting stood on the sink counter, propped against the cupboards above. It was a portrait of a steely-blue robot against a rusty-red background, disturbingly real and signed by the artist, O. Narx. There was a three-dimensional quality about the work, and the robot itself had the glint and texture of actual metal. It was covered with dust. Qwilleran had heard it said that old houses manufacture their own dust.

Alongside the back door a kitchen table, well-crusted with dried paint of many colors, held a jar of brushes, a palette knife and some twisted tubes. The easel stood near the window, and on it was another square-headed mechanical man in a menacing pose. The painting was unfinished, and a brushful of white paint splashed across the canvas had disfigured it.

Koko squirmed and squealed and made himself a troublesome armful, and Qwilleran said, "Let's get upstairs. There's nothing down here but dirt."

At the top, after bolting the door and groping his way out from under the tapestry, Qwilleran said, "False alarm, Koko. You're losing your knack. There were no clues down there."

Kao K'o-Kung gave him a withering look, then turned his back and licked himself extensively.

CHAPTER 15

FRIDAY MORNING Qwilleran sat at his typewriter and stared at the row of keys that spelled q-w-e-r-t-y-u-i-o-p. He hated that word *qwertyuiop*; it meant that he was stymied, that he should be writing brilliant copy, and that he hadn't an idea in his head.

It was three days since he had found the body of Mountclemens sprawled in the patio. It was four days since Nino had fallen to his death. It was nine days since the murder of Earl Lambreth.

Qwilleran's moustache was twitching and sending him signals. It kept suggesting that the three deaths were connected. One person had killed the art dealer, pushed Nino off the scaffolding, and knifed Mountclemens. And yet—to spoil his argument—there was the possibility that Mountclemens had committed the first murder.

The telephone on his desk rang three times before it won his attention.

Lodge Kendall was on the line, saying, "Thought you'd like to know what Homicide found out at the airline."

"Huh? Oh, yes. What did they find out?"

"The alibi holds. The passenger list indicates Mountclemens was on that afternoon flight."

"Did it depart on time?"

"Right on schedule. Did you know the airline puts passenger lists on microfilm and keeps them for three years?"

"No. I mean—yes. That is—thanks for filling me in."

So Mountclemens had an alibi, and Qwilleran had some support for his new theory. Only one person, he told himself, had a motive in all three crimes and the strength to plunge a blade into a man and the opportunity to push Nino to his death. Only Butchy Bolton. And yet it was all too neat, too pat. Qwilleran was reluctant to trust his suspicions.

He went back to his typewriter. He looked at the blank sheet of paper waiting expectantly. He looked at the ten green typewriter keys: qwertyuiop.

Butchy, he was aware, had a serious grudge against Earl Lambreth. She thought he had cheated her out of a lucrative commission and considerable prestige. Furthermore, Lambreth was encouraging his wife to drop Butchy. Grievances like these could build up in the imagination of a woman who had a personality problem and was given to violent fits of temper. With Lambreth out of the way, she might reason, Zoe would again be her "best friend" as in the old days. But there was another obstacle in Butchy's way: Zoe was showing inordinate interest in Nino. If Nino were to meet with a fatal accident, Zoe might have more time and enthusiasm for her girlhood friend.

Qwilleran whistled through his moustache as he remembered another fact: It had been Butchy's idea, according to Mrs. Buchwalter, to put that piece of junk sculpture on the scaffolding.

After Nino's death Butchy faced other complications. Mountclemens was posing a threat to Zoe's happiness and her career, and Butchy—fiercely protective—might see a chance to eliminate this distressing dilemma . . . qwertyuiop.

"Do you always look so puzzled when you write?" asked a soft voice.

Startled, Qwilleran could only sputter. He jumped to his feet.

Zoe said, "I'm sorry. I shouldn't have come to your office without telephoning first, but I was downtown having my hair done, and I took a chance on finding you here. The girl at the desk said I could walk right in. Am I interrupting something important?"

"Not at all," Qwilleran said. "Glad you dropped in. Let's go to lunch."

Zoe was looking strikingly handsome. He pictured himself ushering her into the Press Club, basking in curious stares, answering questions later.

But Zoe said, "Not today, thanks. I have another appointment. I'd just like to talk to you for a few minutes."

Qwilleran found a chair for her, and she pulled it close to his.

In a low voice she said, "There's something I should tell you—something that's been on my conscience—but it isn't easy to discuss."

"Will it help the investigation?"

"I don't know, really." She glanced around the room. "Is it all right to talk here?"

"Perfectly safe," Qwilleran said. "The music critic has his hearing aid turned off, and the man at the next desk has been in a fog for two weeks. He's writing a series on income tax."

Zoe smiled meagerly and said, "You asked me how Mountclemens could afford to buy his art treasures, and I evaded the question. But I've decided that you should be told, because indirectly it reflects on this newspaper."

"In what way?"

"Mountclemens was taking the profits from the Lambreth Gallery."

"You mean your husband paid him off?"

"No. Mountclemens owned the Lambreth Gallery."

"He *owned* it?"

Zoe nodded. "Earl was only an employee."

Qwilleran puffed through his moustache. "What a setup! Mountclemens could write free plugs for his own merchandise and blast competition—and the *Flux* paid him to do it! Why didn't you tell me this before?"

Zoe's hands fluttered. "I was ashamed of Earl's connection in the deal. I guess I hoped the secret would die with him."

"Did your husband discuss gallery business at home?"

"Not until recently. I had no idea of Mountclemens' connection with the gallery until a few weeks ago. When Earl and I had the showdown over Mountclemens. It was then he told me what kind of operator Mountclemens really was. It came as a complete shock."

"That I can believe."

"I was even more appalled at Earl's involvement. After that he began to tell me more about the gallery operation. He had been under a terrible strain, and he was overworked. Well paid, but overworked. Mountclemens wouldn't hire any help—or didn't dare. Earl did everything. Besides meeting the public and coping with artists, he made the picture frames and kept the books. My husband used to work for an accounting firm."

"Yes, I'd heard that," said Qwilleran.

"Earl had to take care of all the government red tape and juggle the figures on the tax returns."

"Juggle them, did you say?"

Zoe smiled bitterly. "You don't suppose a man like Mountclemens reported all his income, do you?"

"What did your husband think about that bit of snookery?"

"He said it was Mountclemens' funeral—not his. Earl merely did what he was told, and he wasn't liable." Zoe bit her lip. "But my husband kept a complete record of actual sales."

"You mean he kept two sets of books?"

"Yes. For his own information."

Qwilleran said, "Was he intending to use that information—?"

"Earl was getting to the end of his rope. Something had to be done—some change in the arrangement. And then there was this—this unpleasantness about me. That's when Earl confronted Mountclemens with some demands."

"Did you hear their discussion?"

"No, but Earl told me about it. He threatened Mountclemens—if he didn't leave me alone."

Qwilleran said, "I don't imagine our late art critic would scare very easily."

"Oh, yes, he was scared," said Zoe. "He knew my husband wasn't joking. Earl threatened to tip off the Internal Revenue people. He had the records that would prove fraud. He would even get a commission from the government for informing."

Qwilleran leaned back in his chair. "Wow!" he said softly. "That would have blown the whole mess wide open."

"The ownership of the gallery would have been exposed, and I'm afraid the *Daily Fluxion* would have looked rather bad."

"That's putting it mildly! The other newspaper would really make hay out of a thing like that. And Mountclemens—"

"Mountclemens would have to stand trial, Earl said. It would mean a jail term for fraud."

"It would have been the end of Mountclemens—here or anywhere else."

They stared at each other in silence, and then Qwilleran said, "He was a complex character."

"Yes," Zoe murmured.

"Did he really know art?"

"He had a brilliant knowledge. And in spite of his crooked streak, there was no misrepresentation in his column. Whatever he praised at the Lambreth Gallery was praiseworthy—the stripe paintings, the graphics, Nino's junk sculpture—"

"What about Scrano?"

"His concept is obscene, but the technique is flawless. His work has a classic beauty."

"All I see is a flock of triangles."

"Ah, but the proportions—the design—the depth and mystery in a flat composition of geometrics! Superb! Almost too good to be true."

Qwilleran challenged her boldly. "What about your own painting? Is it as good as Mountclemens said?"

"No. But it will be. The dirty colors I used expressed my inner turmoil, and that's all over now." Zoe showed Qwilleran a cold-blooded little smile. "I don't know who killed Mountclemens, but it's the best thing that could have happened." Venom darted from her eyes. "I don't think there's any doubt that he killed my husband. That night when Earl had to stay in his office to work on the books . . . I think he was expecting Mountclemens."

"But the police say Mountclemens left for New York at three o'clock that afternoon—by plane."

"I don't think so. I think he drove to New York—in that station wagon that was parked in the alley." Zoe stood up to leave. "But they'll never prove anything now that he's gone."

As Qwilleran rose, she extended a hand in a soft leather glove. She did it almost with gaiety. "I must hurry. I have an appointment at Penniman School. They're taking me on the faculty." Zoe smiled radiantly and walked from the office with a light step.

Qwilleran watched her go and said to himself, She's free now, and she's happy. . . . Who freed her? Then he hated himself for his next thought. And if it was Butchy, I wonder if the plot was entirely Butchy's idea.

For a while Professional Suspicion argued with Personal Inclination.

The latter said, *"Zoe is a lovely woman, incapable of such a heinous plot. And she sure knows how to wear clothes!"*

To which Professional Suspicion replied, "She's pretty eager to have her husband's murder blamed on the critic, now that he's gone and can't defend himself. She keeps coming up with scraps of information—strictly afterthoughts—that make Mountclemens look like a heel."

"But she's so gentle and appealing and talented and intelligent! and that voice! Like velvet."

"She's a smart dame, all right. Two people stabbed . . . and she gets the jackpot. It would be interesting to know how those maneuvers were engineered. Butchy may have done the dirty work, but she isn't bright enough to hatch the plot. Who gave her the key to the back door of the gallery? And who told Butchy to vandalize the female figure—in order to throw suspicion on a cockeyed male? Zoe wasn't even interested in Butchy; she was just using her."

"Yes, but Zoe's eyes! So deep and honest."

"You can't trust a woman with eyes like that. Just stop and think what probably happened on the night of Mountclemens' murder. Zoe phoned him to arrange a rendezvous, saying she'd drive into the deserted alley and sneak in the back way. That's probably the way she always did it. She'd blow the horn, and Mountclemens would go out and unlock the patio gate. But the last time it happened, it wasn't Zoe standing there in the dark; it was Butchy—with a short, wide, sharp, pointed blade."

"But Zoe is such a lovely woman. And that gentle voice! And those knees!"

"Qwilleran, you're a dope. Don't you remember how she got you out of the way on the night of Mountclemens' murder by inviting you to dinner?"

That evening Qwilleran went home and sat down and said to Qwilleran, "You fell for that helpless-female act and let her make you a stooge. . . . Remember how she sighed and bit her lip and stammered and called you so *understanding*? All the time she was building up her case with hints, alibis, painful revelations. . . . And did you notice that nasty gleam in her eye today? It was the same savage look she put in that cat picture at the Lambreth Gallery. Artists always paint themselves. You've found that out."

Qwilleran was plunged in the depths of his big armchair, pulling on a pipe that had burned out some minutes before. His silence weighted the atmosphere, and a shrill protest eventually came from Koko.

"Sorry, old fellow," said Qwilleran. "I'm not very sociable tonight."

Then he sat up straight and asked himself, What about that station wagon? Did Mountclemens drive it to New York? And whose was it?

Koko spoke again, this time from the hallway. His conversation was a melodic succession of cat sounds that had a certain allure. Qwilleran walked out to the hall and found Koko frolicking on the staircase. The cat's slender legs and tiny feet, looking like long-stemmed musical notes, were playing tunes up and down the red-carpeted stairs. When he saw Qwilleran, he raced to the top of the flight and looked down with an engaging follow-me invitation in his stance and the tilt of his ears.

Qwilleran suddenly felt indulgent toward this friendly little creature who knew when companionship was needed. Koko could be more entertaining than a floor show and, at times, better than a tranquilizer. He gave much and demanded little.

Qwilleran said, "Want to visit your old stamping ground?" He followed Koko and unlocked the critic's door with the key he carried.

Trilling with delight, the cat walked in and explored the apartment, savoring every corner.

"Have a good smell, Koko. That woman from Milwaukee will be coming soon, and she'll sell the place and take you home with her, and then you'll have to live on beer and pretzels."

Koko—as if he understood and wished to comment—paused in his tour and sat down on his spine for a brief but significant washup of his nether parts.

"I gather you'd rather live with me."

The cat ambled toward the kitchen, sprang to his old post on the refrigerator, found it cushionless, complained and jumped down again. Hopefully he reconnoitered the corner where his dinner plate and water bowl used to be. Nothing there. He hopped lightly to the stove, where the burners tantalized him with whiffs of last week's boiled-over broth. From there he stepped daintily to the butcher's block, redolent with memories of roasts and cutlets and poultry. Then he nuzzled the knife rack and dislodged one blade from the magnetic bar.

"Careful!" said Qwilleran. "You could cut off a toe." He put the knife back on the magnet.

As he lined it up with the other three blades, his moustache flagged him, and Qwilleran had a sudden urge to go down to the patio.

He went to the broom closet for the flashlight and wondered why Mountclemens had gone down the fire escape without it. The steps were dangerous, with narrow treads partly iced.

Had the critic thought he was going down to meet Zoe? Had he thrown his tweed coat over his shoulders and gone down *without* a flashlight? Had he taken a knife instead? The fifth knife that belonged on the magnetic rack?

Mountclemens had left his prosthetic hand upstairs. A man so vain would have worn it to meet his paramour, but he wouldn't need it to kill her.

Qwilleran turned up the collar of his corduroy jacket and stepped carefully down the fire escape, accompanied by a curious but unenthusiastic cat. The night was cold. The alley kept its after-hours silence.

The newsman wanted to see how the patio gate opened, in what direction the shadows fell, how visible an arriving visitor would be in the darkness. He examined the solid plank gate with its heavy Spanish lock and strap hinges. Mountclemens would have remained partly hidden behind the gate as he opened it. One swift movement by the visitor would have pinned him to the wall. Somehow Mountclemens had failed to take his intended victim by surprise. Somehow the murderer had managed to get the jump on him.

While Qwilleran mused and ran the flashlight over the weathered bricks of the patio, Koko discovered a dark stain on the brick floor and sniffed it intently.

Qwilleran grabbed him roughly about the middle. "Koko! Don't be disgusting!"

He went back up the fire escape, carrying the cat, who writhed and squalled as if he were being tortured.

In Mountclemens' kitchen Koko sat down in the middle of the floor and had a pedicure. His brief walk in the unclean outdoors had soiled his toes, his claws, the pads of his dainty feet. Spreading the brown toes like petals of a flower, he darted his pink tongue in and out—washing, brushing, combing and deodorizing with one efficient implement.

Suddenly the cat paused in the middle of a lick, his tongue extended and his toes spread in midair. A faint rumble came from his throat, and he unfolded to standing position—tense with subdued excitement. Then deliberately he walked to the tapestry in the long hall and pawed the corner.

"There's nothing down in that old kitchen except dust," said Qwilleran, and then his moustache tingled, and he had a singular feeling that the cat knew more than he himself did.

He picked up the flashlight, rolled up the corner of the tapestry, unbolted the door and went down the narrow service stairs. Koko was waiting at the bottom, making no sound, but when Qwilleran picked him up, he felt the cat's body vibrating, and he felt tension in every muscle.

Qwilleran opened the door and let it swing into the old kitchen, quickly flashing his light around the entire room. There was nothing there to warrant Koko's restlessness. Qwilleran trained the flashlight on the easel, the littered table, the canvases stacked against the walls.

And then with a disturbing sensation on his upper lip he realized there were fewer canvases than he had seen the night before. The easel was empty. And the robot propped on the sink was gone.

Momentarily off his guard, he lost his hold on Koko, and the cat jumped to the floor. Qwilleran swung around and flashed the light into the dining room. It was empty, as before.

In the kitchen Koko was stalking something—with stealth in every line of his body. He jumped first to the sink, teetered on the edge while he scanned the area, then noiselessly down to a chair, then up to the table. As he ran his nose over the clutter on the tabletop, his mouth opened, his whiskers flared, and he showed his teeth, while with one paw he scraped the table around the palette knife.

Qwilleran stood in the middle of the room and tried to assemble his thoughts. Something was happening here that made no sense. Who had been in this kitchen? Who had removed the paintings—and why? The two pictures of robots had disappeared. What else had been taken?

Qwilleran placed the flashlight on a tiled counter, so that the light fell on the few remaining canvases in the room, and he turned one around.

It was a Scrano! A blaze of orange and yellow triangles, the canvas was painted in the Italian artist's smooth, slick style, and yet it had a feeling of depth that made Qwilleran reach out to touch the surface. Down in the corner was the famous signature, daubed in block letters.

Qwilleran set it aside and turned another painting around to face the room. Again, triangles! These were green on blue. Behind this canvas there were more—gray on brown, brown on black, white on cream. Proportions and arrangements varied, but the triangles were all pure Scrano.

A throaty murmur from Koko attracted Qwilleran's attention. The cat was sniffing the orange triangles on the yellow background. Qwilleran wondered what it was worth. Ten thousand? Twenty thousand? Perhaps even more, now that Scrano would paint no more.

Had Mountclemens been cornering the market? Or were these forgeries? And in either case . . . who was stealing them?

Koko's nose covered the surface of the painting in great detail, as if he were experiencing the texture of the canvas, visible under the pigment. When he came to the signature, his neck was stretched, and he tilted his head first to one side and then to the other, as he strained to get close to the letters.

His nose moved from right to left, first tracing the *O*, then studying the *N*, moving on to the *A*, sniffing the *R* with gusto as if it were something special, then on to the *C*, and finally lingering over the *S*.

"Remarkable!" said Qwilleran. "Remarkable!"

He hardly heard the turning of a key in the back door, but Koko heard it. The cat vanished. Qwilleran froze, as the door slowly opened.

The figure that stood in the doorway made no move. In the half light Qwilleran saw square shoulders, heavy sweater, square jaw, high square brow.

"Narx!" said Qwilleran.

The man came to life. He sidled into the room, reaching for the table. His eyes were on Qwilleran. With a lunge he seized the palette knife and rushed forward.

Suddenly . . . shrieks . . . snarls! The room was full of flying things—swooping down, across, back, up, over!

The man ducked. The hurtling bodies were quicker than the eye. They screamed like harpies. They flew down, under, up, across. Something hit him in the arm. He faltered.

In that half moment Qwilleran pounced on the flashlight and swung it with all his force.

Narx staggered back, went down. There was a sharp, rending *crack* as his head struck the tiled counter. He slumped slowly to the floor.

CHAPTER 16

IT WAS FIVE-THIRTY at the Press Club, and Qwilleran was relating the story for the hundredth time. All day Monday the personnel of the *Daily Fluxion* had been filing past his desk to hear the details firsthand.

At the Press Club bar Odd Bunsen said, "I wish I'd been there with my camera. I can picture our hero phoning the police with one hand and holding up his pants with the other."

"Well, I had to tie Narx with my belt," Qwilleran explained. "When his head hit the tile counter, he was out cold, but I was afraid he'd come around while I was phoning the police. I'd already tied his wrists with my necktie—my good Scotch tie—and the only thing I had for his ankles was my belt."

"How did you know it was Narx?"

"When I saw that square face and those square shoulders, I thought of those pictures of robots, and I knew this man must be the artist. Painters, I've been told, always put some quality of themselves on canvas—whether they paint kids or cats or sailboats. But Koko was the one who made it all clear when he read Scrano's signature backwards."

Arch said, "How does it feel to be playing Dr. Watson to a cat?"

Odd said, "What about the signature? That's something I missed?"

"Koko read the signature on this painting," Qwilleran explained, "and he spelled it out backwards. He always reads backwards."

"Oh, naturally. It's an old Siamese custom."

"That's when I realized that Scrano, the painter of the triangles, was also O. Narx, the painter of the robots. Their painted surfaces had the same slick metallic effect. A few minutes later the robot himself walked into the house and came at me with a palette knife. He would have got me, too, if Koko hadn't come to the rescue."

"Sounds as if that cat's in line for a Civilian Citation. What did he do?"

"He went berserk! And one Siamese flying around in a panic looks and sounds like a pack of wildcats. Zoom—screech—wham! I thought there were six animals in that room, and that fellow Narx was one bewildered guy."

"So Scrano is a fake," said Arch.

"Yep. There's no Italian recluse hiding out in the Umbrian Hills," said Qwilleran. "There's only Oscar Narx manufacturing triangle pictures for Mountclemens to plug in his column and sell in his art gallery."

"Funny why he wouldn't use his own name," said Odd.

Then Arch said, "But Mountclemens' last column said there wouldn't be any more stuff from Scrano."

"I think Mountclemens was planning to eliminate Oscar Narx," said Qwilleran. "Maybe Narx knew too much. I suspect our critic was not on that three o'clock plane the day of Lambreth's murder. I suspect he had an accomplice who used the plane ticket and entered Mountclemens' name on the passenger list. And I'll bet that accomplice was Narx."

"And then Mountclemens took a later flight," said Arch.

"Or drove to New York," said Qwilleran, "in the mysterious station wagon that was parked behind the gallery in the late afternoon. Zoe Lambreth heard her husband talking about it on the phone."

Odd Bunsen said, "Mountclemens was crazy to let another guy in on the plot. If you're going to commit murder, go it alone, I always say."

"Mountclemens wasn't stupid," said Qwilleran. "He probably had a clever alibi figured out, but something went wrong."

Arch, who had been hearing fragments of Qwilleran's story all day, said, "What makes you so sure Mountclemens was going to kill somebody when he went down to his backyard?"

"Three reasons." Qwilleran was enjoying himself. He was speaking with authority and making large gestures. "First, Mountclemens went down to the patio to meet someone, and yet this vain man left his prosthetic hand upstairs. He wasn't going to greet a guest, so he didn't need it. Second, he did not take the flashlight, although the steps were icy and treacherous. Third, I suspect he took a kitchen knife instead; there's one missing."

Qwilleran's audience was hanging on every word.

"Apparently," he went on, "Mountclemens failed to take Narx by surprise. Unless he could surprise him and sink the knife in his back as Narx came through the gate, there was a good chance that the younger man would overpower the critic. Narx is a powerful-looking adversary, and it was one hand against two."

"How do you know Mountclemens went downstairs to meet someone?"

"He had on his lounging coat. He probably had his topcoat over his shoulders while waiting for Narx, then threw it off to get ready for action. Narx would unlock the gate, which swings into the patio, and Mountclemens would be waiting behind it, ready to knife him in the back. He probably planned to deposit the body in the alley, where the murder would be blamed on a tramp. It's that kind of neighborhood."

"If Narx is as formidable as you say," said Arch, "how did that fool think he could pull off the job with one hand?"

"Vanity. Everything Mountclemens did, he did superbly. It gave him an impossible conceit. . . . And I think I know why he failed this time. It's only a guess, but here's how I figure it: When Narx was unlocking that patio gate, he was alerted to Mountclemens' presence."

"How?"

"He smelled that lime-peel scent that Mountclemens always wore."

"Cr-r-razy!" said Odd Bunsen.

Arch said, "Narx might have gotten away with murder if he hadn't come back for those paintings."

"Two murders," said Qwilleran, "if it hadn't been for Koko."

"Anybody want another drink?" Arch said. "Bruno, let's have two more martinis and a tomato juice. . . . Make it three martinis. Here comes Lodge Kendall."

"Skip the tomato juice," said Qwilleran. "I've got to leave in a couple of minutes."

Kendall was hurrying with news. "Just came from Headquarters," he said. "Narx is finally able to make a statement, and the police have his story. It's just the way Qwill said. Narx painted the Scrano pictures. Every time he came to town, he camped out in Mountclemens' vacant apartment, but mostly he worked in New York. He brought the stuff here by station wagon, posing as Scrano's New York agent."

"Did he mention the three o'clock plane flight?"

"Yes. He was the one who used Mountclemens' ticket."

Odd said, "Then Mountclemens—that hammerhead—let him in on the plot."

"No. Narx was innocent at that stage of the game. You see, he had just come to town with the wagon, and Mountclemens told him to fly right back to New York to meet a big buyer who was due in unexpectedly from Montreal. Mountclemens said he had just arranged this deal by phone—in Narx's name, the way he conducted all Scrano business. Narx understood he was to hustle back and meet the Canadian in New York at five o'clock and sell him a flock of Scrano paintings. It sounded logical enough to Narx. After all, he was front man for the operation. So Mountclemens turned his own ticket over to Narx, drove with him to the airport, and saw him off on the three o'clock plane."

"How come Mountclemens' name was on the passenger list?"

"According to Narx, they barely made it to the airport by flight time, and Mountclemens said, 'Don't bother to change the name on the ticket. Just go directly to the gate and check in.' He said he had decided to drive. He claimed he would start out immediately in Narx's station wagon, stop in Pittsburgh overnight, and arrive in New York Thursday morning."

Qwilleran said, "I can guess what went wrong."

"Well," said Kendall, "the sucker from Montreal was nuts about those triangles. He wanted all he could get. So Narx phoned Earl Lambreth and asked him to airfreight some of the older stock that hadn't sold."

"That's the phone call Zoe overheard."

"Lambreth said he'd send them by wagon, but Narx told him that Mountclemens and the station wagon were already halfway to Pittsburgh. Lambreth said no, the car was still there, parked in the alley behind the gallery."

"So Narx smelled a rat."

"Not until he heard the news of Lambreth's murder and realized Mountclemens had lied. Then he decided to capitalize on it. He hated Mountclemens anyway; he felt like a flunkey—a robot—always carrying out the great man's orders. So he decided to hit him for a bigger cut of the dough that Mountclemens was raking in from Scrano sales."

Odd said, "Narx was dumb to think he could blackmail a sharp operator like Monty."

"So Mountclemens laid for him in the patio," said Kendall, "but Narx got the jump and grabbed the knife."

"Did he say why he returned to the scene?"

"Mostly to collect some paintings that had his own signature on them. He was afraid the police might start checking. But he also took some Scrano pictures and was going back for more when he ran into Qwill—and that cat!"

Arch said, "What will happen to the value of Scrano pictures when this story breaks? A lot of investors are going to be jumping out of high windows."

"Well, I'll tell you something," said Qwilleran. "I've looked at a lot of art in the last few weeks, and if I had some dough to squander, I think I'd buy some nice gray and white triangles by Scrano."

"Man, you're lost!" said Odd.

"I forgot to tell you," said Kendall. "Those triangle pictures were a collaboration. Narx says he painted them, but Mountclemens designed them."

"Very clever," said Qwilleran. "Mountclemens had lost a hand and couldn't paint; Narx had a great technique but no creative imagination. Pretty slick."

"I'll bet a lot of artists have ghost-painters," said Odd.

"Come on, have another tomato juice," Arch invited. "Live it up."

"No thanks," said Qwilleran. "I'm having dinner with Zoe Lambreth, and I've got to go home and change my shirt."

"Before you go," said Odd, "maybe I should explain about that lady welder and why I didn't get any pix last week."

"No rush," said Qwilleran.

"I went to the school, but she wasn't there. She was home with a couple of sore flippers."

"What happened?"

"Remember that guy that fell and killed himself? The Bolton dame tried to save him. He fell against her hands and sprained her wrists. But she'll be back this week, and I'll get your shots."

"Make them good," Qwilleran said. "Flatter the gal, if you can."

When Qwilleran arrived home to feed the cat, he found Koko sprawled on the living room carpet taking a bath.

"Dressing for dinner?" said Qwilleran.

The pink tongue darted over white breast, brown paws, and fawn flanks. Moistened pads were wiped over velvety brown ears. The lustrous brown tail was clutched between forepaws and groomed with painstaking care. Koko looked surprisingly like a cat and not the supernal creature who read minds, knew what was going to happen, smelled what he couldn't see, and sensed what he couldn't smell.

Qwilleran said, "They should have given you a headline, Koko. *Cat Sleuth Sniffs Out Double Murder Clue*. You were right every time, and I was wrong every time. Nobody stole the gold dagger. Mountclemens didn't take the three o'clock plane. Butchy didn't commit any crimes. Nino wasn't murdered. And Zoe didn't lie to me."

Koko went on licking his tail.

"But I still don't have all the answers. Why did you lead me to that closet upstairs? To get Mintie Mouse or to help me find the Ghirotto monkey?

"Why did you call attention to the knife rack Friday night? Did you want me to know one was missing? Or were you just suggesting some chopped tenderloin?

"And why did you insist on going downstairs to that kitchen? Did you know Narx was coming?

"And how about the palette knife? Why were you trying to cover it up? Did you know what was going to happen?"

Koko went on licking his tail.

"And another thing: When Oscar Narx came at me with that blade, did you really panic? Were you just a scared cat, or were you trying to save my life?"

Koko finished his tail and gazed at Qwilleran with a faraway look, as if some divine answer was forming in his glossy brown head. Then he twisted his lithe body into a tortured shape, turned up his nose, crossed his eyes, and scratched his ear with one hind leg and an expression of catly rapture.

The Cat
Who Ate
Danish Modern

CHAPTER 1

JIM QWILLERAN prepared his bachelor breakfast with a look of boredom and distaste, accentuated by the down-curve of his bushy moustache. Using hot water from the tap, he made a cup of instant coffee with brown lumps floating on the surface. He dredged a doughnut from a crumb-filled canister that was beginning to smell musty. Then he spread a paper napkin on a table in a side window where the urban sun, filtered through smog, emphasized the bleakness of the furnished apartment.

Here Qwilleran ate his breakfast without tasting it, and considered his four problems:

At the moment he was womanless. He had received an eviction notice, and in three weeks he would be homeless. At the rate the moths were feeding on his neckwear, he would soon be tieless. And if he said the wrong thing to the managing editor today, he might very well be jobless. Over forty-five and jobless. It was not a cheerful prospect.

Fortunately, he was not friendless. On his breakfast table—along with a large unabridged dictionary, a stack of paperback books, a pipe rack with a single pipe, and a can of tobacco—there was a Siamese cat.

Qwilleran scratched his friend behind the ears, and said, "I'll bet you weren't allowed to sit on the breakfast table when you lived upstairs."

The cat, whose name was Koko, gave a satisfied wiggle, tilted his whiskers upward, and said, "YOW!"

He had lived with the newsman for six months, following the unfortunate demise of the man on the second floor. Qwilleran fed him well, conversed sensibly, and invented games to play—unusual pastimes that appealed to the cat's extraordinary intelligence.

Every morning Koko occupied one small corner of the breakfast table, arranging himself in a compact bundle, brown feet and tail tucked fastidiously under his white-breasted fawn body. In the mild sunshine Koko's slanted eyes were a brilliant blue, and his silky fur, like the newly spun spider web that spanned the window, glistened with a rainbow of iridescence.

"You make this apartment look like a dump," Qwilleran told him.

Koko squeezed his eyes and breathed faster. With each breath his nose changed from black velvet to black satin, then back to velvet.

Qwilleran lapsed again into deep thought, absently running a spoon handle through his moustache. This was the day he had promised himself to confront the managing editor and request a change of assignment. It was a risky move. The *Daily Fluxion* was known as a tight ship. Percy preached teamwork, team spirit, team discipline. Shoulder to shoulder, play the game, one for all. Ours not to question why. A long pull, a strong pull, a pull all together. We happy few!

"It's like this," Qwilleran told the cat. "If I walk into Percy's office and flatly request a change of assignment, I'm apt to land out in the street. That's the way he operates. And I can't afford to be unemployed—not right now—not till I build up a cash reserve."

Koko was listening to every word.

"If the worst came to the worst, I suppose I could get a job at the *Morning Rampage*, but I'd hate to work for that stuffy sheet."

Koko's eyes were large and full of understanding. "Yow," he said softly.

"I wish I could have a heart-to-heart talk with Percy, but it's impossible to get through to him. He's programmed, like a computer. His smile—very sincere. His handshake—very strong. His compliments—very gratifying. Then the next time you meet him on the elevator, he doesn't know you. You're not on his schedule for the day."

Koko shifted his position uneasily.

"He doesn't even look like a managing editor. He dresses like an advertising man. Makes me feel like a slob." Qwilleran passed a hand over the back of his neck. "Guess I should get a haircut."

Koko gurgled something in his throat, and Qwilleran recognized the cue. "Okay, we'll play the game. But only for a few innings this morning. I've got to go to work."

He opened the big dictionary, which was remarkable for its tattered condition, and he and Koko played their word game. The way it worked, the cat dug his claws into the pages, and Qwilleran opened the books where he indicated, reading aloud the catchwords—the two boldface entries at the top of the columns. He read the right-hand page if Koko used his right paw, but usually it was the left-hand page. Koko was inclined to be a southpaw.

"*Design* and *desk*," Qwilleran read. "Those are easy. Score two points for me. . . . Go ahead, try again."

Koko cocked his brown ears forward and dug in with his claws.

"*Dictyogenous* and *Dieguéños*. You sneaky rascal! You've stumped me!" Qwilleran had to look up both definitions, and that counted two points for the cat.

The final score was 7 to 5 in Qwilleran's favor. Then he proceeded to shower and dress, after preparing Koko's breakfast—fresh beef, diced and heated with a little canned mushroom gravy. The cat showed no interest in food, however. He followed the man around, yowling for attention in his clarion Siamese voice, tugging at the bath towel, leaping into dresser drawers as they were opened.

"What tie shall I wear?" Qwilleran asked him. There were only a few neckties in his collection—for the most part Scotch plaids with a predominance of red. They hung about the apartment on door handles and chairbacks. "Maybe I should wear something funereal to impress Percy favorably. These days we all conform. You cats are the only real independents left."

Koko blinked his acknowledgment.

Qwilleran reached for a narrow strip of navy-blue wool draped over the swing-arm of a floor lamp. "Damn those moths!" he said. "Another tie ruined!"

Koko uttered a small squeak that sounded like sympathy, and Qwilleran, examining the nibbled edge of the necktie, decided to wear it anyway.

"If you want to make yourself useful," he told the cat, "why don't you go to work on the moths and quit wasting your time on spider webs?"

Koko had developed a curious aberration since coming to live with Qwilleran. In this dank old building spiders were plentiful, and as fast as they spun their webs, Koko devoured the glistening strands.

Qwilleran tucked the ragged end of the navy-blue tie into his shirt and pocketed his pipe, a quarter-bend bulldog. The he tousled Koko's head in a rough farewell and left the apartment on Blenheim Place.

When he eventually arrived in the lobby of the *Daily Fluxion*, his hair was cut, his moustache was lightly trimmed, and his shoes rivaled the polish on the black marble walls. He caught a reflection of his profile in the marble and pulled in his waistline; it was beginning to show a slight convexity.

More than a few eyes turned his way. Since his arrival at the *Fluxion* seven months before—with his ample moustache, picturesque pipe, and unexplained past—Qwilleran had been a subject for conjecture. Everyone knew he had had a notable career as a crime reporter in New York and Chicago. After that, he had disappeared for a few years, and now he was holding down a quiet desk on a Midwestern newspaper, and writing, of all things, features on art!

The elevator door opened, and Qwilleran stepped aside while several members of the Women's Department filed out on their way to morning assignments or coffee breaks. As they passed, he checked them off with a calculating eye. One was too old. One was too homely. The fashion writer was too formidable. The society writer was married.

The married one looked at him with mock reproach. "You lucky dog!" she said. "Some people get all the breaks. I hate you!"

Qwilleran watched her sail across the lobby, and then he jumped on the elevator just before the automatic doors closed.

"I wonder what *that* was all about," he mumbled.

There was one other passenger on the car—a blonde clerk from the Advertising Department. "I just heard the news," she said. "Congratulations!" and she stepped off the elevator at the next floor.

A great hope was rising under Qwilleran's frayed tie as he walked into the Feature Department with its rows of green metal desks, green typewriters, and green telephones.

Arch Riker beckoned to him. "Stick around," the feature editor said. "Percy's calling a meeting at ten thirty. Probably wants to discuss that ridiculous *w* in your name. Have you seen the first edition?" He pushed a newspaper across the desk and pointed to a major headline: *Judge Qwits Bench After Graft Qwiz.*

Riker said: "No one caught the error until the papers were on the street. You've got the whole staff confused."

"It's a good Scottish name," Qwilleran said in defense. Then he leaned over Riker's desk, and said: "I've been getting some interesting vibrations this morning. I think Percy's giving me a new assignment."

"If he is, it's news to me."

"For six months I've been journalism's most ludicrous figure—a crime writer assigned to the art beat."

"You didn't have to take the job if it didn't appeal to you."

"I needed the money. *You* know that. And I was promised a desk in the City Room as soon as there was an opening."

"Lots of luck," Riker said in a minor key.

"I think something's about to break. And whatever it is, everyone knows it but you and me."

The feature editor leaned back in his chair and folded his arms. "It's axiomatic in the communications industry," he said, "that the persons most directly concerned are the last ones to know."

When the signal came from the City Room, Riker and Qwilleran filed into the managing editor's office, saying, "Morning, Harold." The boss was called Percy only behind his back.

The advertising director was there, shooting his cuffs. The photo chief was there, looking bored. The women's editor was there, wearing a brave hat of zebra fur and giving Qwilleran a prolonged friendly stare that embarrassed him. Fran Unger had a syrupy charm that he distrusted. He was wary of women executives. He had been married to one once.

Someone closed the door, and the managing editor swiveled his chair to face Qwilleran.

"Qwill, I owe you an apology," he said. "I should have discussed this with you ten days ago. You've probably been hearing rumors, and it was unfair of me to leave you in the dark. I'm sorry. I've been involved with the mayor's Civilian Committee on Crime, but that is no excuse per se."

He's really not a bad guy, Qwilleran thought, as he wriggled anxiously in his chair.

"We promised you another assignment when the right opportunity presented itself," the editor went on, "and now we have a real challenge for you! We are about to launch a project of significance to the entire newspaper industry and, I might add, a bonanza for the *Daily Fluxion* per se."

Qwilleran began to realize why everyone called the boss Percy.

The editor continued: "This city has been selected for an experiment to determine if national advertising ordinarily carried in magazines can be diverted to daily papers in major cities."

The advertising director said, "If it works, our linage will double. The revenue for the experimental year alone will be upward of a million dollars."

"The *Morning Rampage* also will be making a bid for this plum," said the editor, "but with our new presses and our color reproduction process, we can produce a superior product."

Qwilleran stroked his moustache nervously.

"It will be your job, Qwill, to produce a special Sunday supplement for fifty-two weeks—in magazine format, with plenty of color!"

Qwilleran's mind raced ahead to the possibilities. He pictured great court trails, election campaigns, political exposés, sports spectaculars, perhaps overseas coverage. He cleared his throat, and said, "This new magazine—I suppose it will be general interest?"

"General interest in its approach," said Percy, "but specific in content. We want you to publish a weekly magazine on interior design."

"On *what*?" Qwilleran said in an unintended falsetto.

"On interior decorating. The experiment is being conducted by the home-furnishings industry."

"Interior decorating!" Qwilleran felt a chill in the roots of his moustache. "I should think you'd want a woman to handle it."

Fran Unger spoke up sweetly. "The Women's Department wanted the assignment very badly, Qwill, but Harold feels a great many *men* are interested in the home today. He wants to avoid the women's slant and attract general readership to the *Gracious Abodes* magazine."

Qwilleran's throat felt as if it had swallowed his moustache. "*Gracious Abodes*? Is that the name of the thing?"

Percy nodded. "I think it conveys the right message: charm, livability, taste! You can do stories on luxury homes, high-rent apartments, residential status symbols, and the Upper Ten Percent and how they live."

Qwilleran fingered his frayed tie.

"You'll love this assignment, Qwill," the women's editor assured him. "You'll be working with decorators, and they're delightful people."

Qwilleran leaned toward the managing editor earnestly. "Harold, are you sure you want me for this beat? You know my background! I don't know the first thing about decorating."

"You did such an outstanding job on the art beat without knowing the first thing about art," said Percy. "In our business, expertise can be a drawback. What this new job needs is nothing more nor less than a seasoned newsman, creative and resourceful. If you have any trouble at the start, Fran will be glad to lend a hand, I'm sure."

Qwilleran squirmed in his chair.

"Yes, of course," said the women's editor. "We can work together, Qwill, and I can steer you in the right direction." Ignoring Qwilleran's bleak reaction, she went on. "For example, you could start with the Sorbonne Studio; they do society work. Then Lyke and Starkweather; they're the largest decorating firm in town." She made a swooning gesture. "David Lyke is absolutely adorable!"

"I'll bet he is," said Qwilleran in a sullen growl. He had his private opinion of decorators, both male and female.

"There's also Mrs. Middy, who does cozy Early American interiors. And there's a new studio called PLUG. It specializes in Planned Ugliness."

Then Percy made a remark that cast a new light on the proposal. "This assignment will carry more responsibility," he said to Qwilleran, "and naturally your classification will be adjusted. You will be advanced from senior writer to junior editor."

Qwilleran made a quick computation and came up with a figure that would finance a decent place to live and pay off some old debts. He tugged at his moustache. "I suppose I could give it a try," he said. "How soon would you want me to start?"

"Yesterday! We happen to know that the *Morning Rampage* is breaking with their supplement on October first. We'd like to beat them to the wire."

That turned the trick. The prospect of scoring a beat on the competition stirred the ink in Qwilleran's veins. His first horrified reaction to *Gracious Abodes* dissolved into a sudden sense of proprietorship. And when Fran Unger gave him a chummy smile and said, "We'll have fun with this assignment, Qwill," he felt like saying, Sister, just keep your hands off *my magazine*.

That day, during the lunch hour, Qwilleran went out and celebrated the raise in salary. He bought a can of crabmeat for Koko and a new tie for himself. Another red wool plaid.

CHAPTER 2

WEARING HIS new tie and the better of his two suits, Qwilleran set forth with some apprehension for his first visit to a decorating studio, bracing himself for an overdose of the precious and the esoteric.

He found the firm of Lyke and Starkweather in an exclusive shopping area, surrounded by specialty shops, art galleries, and tearooms. The entrance was impressive. Huge double doors of exotically grained wood had silver door handles as big as baseball bats.

The interior displayed furniture in room settings, and Qwilleran was pleased to find one room wallpapered in a red plaid that matched his tie. Moose antlers were mounted above a fireplace made of wormeaten driftwood, and there was a sofa covered in distressed pigskin, like the hides of retired footballs.

A slender young man approached him, and the newsman asked to see Mr. Lyke or Mr. Starkweather. After a delay that seemed inauspicious, a gray-haired man appeared from behind an Oriental screen at the rear of the shop. He had a blank appearance and a bland manner.

"Mr. Lyke is the one you should talk to, if it's about publicity," he told Qwilleran, "but he's busy with a client. Why don't you just look around while you're waiting?"

"Are you Mr. Starkweather?" Qwilleran asked.

"Yes, but I think you should talk to Mr. Lyke. He's the one. . . ."

"I'd appreciate it if you'd tell me about these displays while I'm waiting." Qwilleran motioned toward the moose antlers.

"There isn't much to tell," said Starkweather with a helpless gesture.

"What's selling these days?"

"Just about everything."

"Is there any particular color that's popular?"

"No. They're all good."

"I see you have some modern stuff over there."

"We have a little of everything."

Qwilleran's interviewing technique was not working. "What do you call that thing?" he asked, pointing to a tall secretary-desk with a bulbous base and an inlaid design of exotic birds and flowers.

"It's a desk," said Starkweather. Then his expressionless face brightened a fraction of a degree. "Here comes Mr. Lyke."

From behind the Oriental screen came a good-looking man in his early thirties. He had his arm around an elaborately hatted middle-aged woman who was smiling and blushing with pleasure.

Lyke was saying in a deep, chesty voice: "You go home, my dear, and tell the Old Man you've got to have that twelve-foot sofa. It won't cost him a cent more than the last car he bought. And remember, dear, I want you to invite me to dinner the next time you're having that *superb* chocolate cake. Don't let your cook bake it. I want you to bake it yourself—for David."

While he talked, David Lyke was walking the woman rapidly toward the front door, where he stopped and kissed her temple. Then he said a beautifully timed goodbye, meaningful but not lingering.

When he turned toward Qwilleran, he recomposed his face abruptly from an expression of rapture to one of businesslike aplomb, but he could not change his eyes. He had brooding eyes with heavy lids and long lashes. Even more striking was his hair—snow white and somewhat sensational with his young suntanned face.

"I'm David Lyke," he growled pleasantly, extending a cordial hand. His eyes flickered downward for a second, but Qwilleran felt they had appraised his plaid tie and the width of his lapel. "Come into my office, and we'll talk."

The newsman followed him into a room that had deep-gray walls. A leopard rug sprawled on the polished ebony floor. Lounge chairs, square and bulky and masculine, were covered in fabric with the texture of popcorn. On the back wall was a painting of a nude figure, her skin tones a luminous blue-gray, like steel.

Qwilleran found himself nodding in approval. "Nice office."

"Glad you like it," the decorator said. "Don't you think gray is terribly civilized? I call this shade Poppy Seed. The chairs are sort of Dried Fig. I'm sick to death of Pablum Beige and Mother's Milk White." He reached for a decanter. "How about a splash of cognac?"

Qwilleran declined. He said he would rather smoke his pipe. Then he stated his mission, and Lyke said in his rumbling voice: "I wish you hadn't called your magazine *Gracious Abodes*. It gives me visions of lavender gloves and *pêche Melba*."

"What kind of decorating do you do?" the newsman asked.

"All kinds. If people want to live like conquistadors or English barons or little French kings, we don't fight it."

"If you can find an important house for us to photograph, we'll put it on the cover of our first issue."

"We'd like the publicity," said the decorator, "but I don't know how our clients will react. You know how it is; whenever the boys in Washington find out a taxpayer has wall-to-wall carpet in his bathroom, they audit his tax returns for the last three years." He was flipping through a card index. "I have a magnificent Georgian Colonial job, done in Champagne and Cranberry, but the lamps haven't arrived. . . . And here's an Edwardian town house in Benedictine and Plum, but there's been a delay on the draperies; the fabric manufacturer discontinued the pattern."

"Could the photographer shoot from an angle that would avoid the missing drapes?"

Lyke looked startled, but he recovered quickly and shook his head.

"No, you'd have to include the windows." He browsed through the file and suddenly seized an index card. "Here's a house I'd like to see you publish! Do you know G. Verning Tait? I did his house in French Empire with built-in vitrines for his jade collection."

"Who is this Tait?" Qwilleran asked. "I'm new in this city."

"You don't know the Taits? They're one of the old families living in pseudocastles down in Muggy Swamp. You know Muggy Swamp, of course—very exclusive." The decorator made a rueful face. "Unfortunately, the clients with the longest pedigrees are the slowest to pay their bills."

"Are the Taits very social?"

"They used to be, but they live quietly now. Mrs. Tait is unwell, as they say in Muggy Swamp."

"Do you think they'd let us photograph?"

"People with Old Money always avoid publicity on their real estate," Lyke said, "but in this case I might be able to use a little persuasion."

Other possibilities were discussed, but both the decorator and newsman agreed the Tait house would be perfect: important name, spectacular décor, brilliant color, and a jade collection to add interest.

"Besides that," said Lyke with a smug smile, "it's the only job I've succeeded in getting away from the Sorbonne Studio. It would give me a lot of satisfaction to see the Tait house on the cover of *Gracious Abodes*."

"If you succeed in lining it up, call me immediately," Qwilleran said. "We're working against time on the first issue. I'll give you my home phone."

He wrote his number on a *Daily Fluxion* card and stood up to leave.

David Lyke gave him a parting handshake that was hearty and sincere. "Good luck with your magazine. And may I give you some fatherly advice?"

Qwilleran eyed the younger man anxiously.

"Never," said Lyke with an engaging smile, "*never* call draperies *drapes*."

Qwilleran returned to his office, pondering the complexities of his new beat and thinking fondly of lunch in the familiar drabness of the Press Club, where the wall color was Sirloin, Medium Rare.

On his desk there was a message to call Fran Unger. He dialed her number reluctantly.

"I've been working on our project," said the women's editor, "and I have some leads for you. Have you got a pencil ready? . . . First, there's a Greek Revival farmhouse converted into a Japanese teahouse. And then there's a penthouse apartment with carpet on the walls and ceiling, and an aquarium under the glass floor. And I know where there's an exciting master bedroom done entirely in three shades of black, except for the bed, which is brass. . . . That should be enough to fill the first issue!"

Qwilleran felt his moustache bristling. "Well, thanks, but I've got all the material I need for the first book," he said, aware that it was a rash lie.

"Really? For a beginner you're a fast worker. What have you lined up?"

"It's a long, involved story," Qwilleran said vaguely.

"I'd love to hear it. Are you going to the Press Club for lunch?"

"No," he said with hesitation. "As a matter of fact, I'm having lunch . . . with a decorator . . . at a private club."

Fran Unger was a good newspaperwoman, and not easy to put down. "In that case, why don't we meet for drinks at the Press Club at five thirty?"

"I'm sorry," Qwilleran said in his politest voice, "but I've got an early dinner date uptown."

At five thirty he fled to the sanctuary of his apartment, carrying a chunk of liver sausage and two onion rolls for his dinner. He would have preferred the Press Club. He liked the dingy atmosphere of the club, and the size of the steaks, and the company of fellow newsmen, but for the last two weeks he had been driven to avoiding his favorite haunt. The trouble had started when he danced with Fran Unger at the Photographers' Ball. Apparently there was some magic in Qwilleran's vintage fox trot that gave her aspirations. She had been pursuing him ever since.

"I can't get rid of that woman!" he told Koko, as he sliced the liver sausage. "She's not bad-looking, but she isn't my type. I've had all the bossy females I want! Besides, I like zebra fur on zebras."

He cut some morsels of the sausage as an appetizer for Koko, but the cat was busy snapping his jaws at a thin skein of spider web that stretched between two chair legs.

Only when the telephone rang, a moment later, did Koko pay attention. Lately he had shown signs of jealousy toward the phone. Whenever Qwilleran talked into the instrument, Koko untied his shoelaces or bit the telephone cord. Sometimes he jumped on the desk and tried to nudge the receiver away from Qwilleran's ear.

The telephone rang, and the newsman said to the mouthpiece, "Hello? . . . Yes! What's the good news?"

Immediately Koko jumped to the desk top and started making himself a pest. Qwilleran pushed him away.

"Great! How soon can we take pictures?"

Koko was pacing back and forth on the desk, looking for further mischief. Somehow he got his leg tangled in the cord, and howled in indignation.

"Sorry, I can't hear you," said Qwilleran. "The cat's raising the roof. . . . No, I'm not beating him. Hold the line."

He extricated Koko and chased him away, then wrote down the address that David Lyke gave him. "See you Monday morning in Muggy Swamp," Qwilleran said. "And thanks. This is a big help."

The telephone rang once more that evening, and the friendly voice of Fran Unger came on the wire. "Well, hello! You're home!"

"Yes," said Qwilleran. "I'm home." He was keeping an eye on Koko, who had leaped up on the desk.

"I thought you had a big date tonight."

"Got home earlier than I expected."

"I'm at the Press Club," said the sugary voice. "Why don't you come over? We're all here, drinking up a storm."

"Scram!" said Qwilleran to Koko, who was trying to dial the phone with his nose.

"What did you say?"

"I was talking to the cat." Qwilleran gave Koko a push, but the cat slanted his eyes and stood his ground, looking determined as he devised his next move.

"By the way," the wheedling voice was saying, "when are you going to invite me up to meet Koko?"

"YOW!" said Koko, aiming his deafening howl directly into Qwilleran's right ear.

"Shut up!" said Qwilleran.

"What?"

"Oh, hell!" he said, as Koko pushed an ashtray full of pipe ashes to the floor.

"Well!" Fran Unger's voice became suddenly tart. "Your hospitality overwhelms me!"

"Listen, Fran," said Qwilleran. "I've got a mess on my hands right now." He was going to explain, but there was a click in his ear. "Hello?" he said.

A dead silence was his answer, and then a dial tone. The connection had been cut. Koko was standing with one foot planted firmly on the plunger button.

CHAPTER 3

WHEN QWILLERAN reported to the Photo Lab on Monday morning to pick up a man for the Muggy Swamp assignment, he found Odd Bunsen slamming gear into a camera case and voicing noisy objections. Bunsen was the *Daily Fluxion*'s specialist in train wrecks and five-alarm fires, and he had just been assigned on a permanent basis to *Gracious Abodes*.

"It's an old man's job," he complained to Qwilleran. "I'm not ready to come down off the flagpoles yet."

Bunsen, who had recently climbed a skyscraper's flagpole to get a close-up of the Fourth of July fireworks, had an exuberance of qualities and defects that amused Qwilleran. He was the most daring of the photographers, had the loudest voice, and smoked the longest and most objectionable cigars. At the Press Club he was the hungriest and the thirstiest. He was raising the largest family, and his wallet was always the flattest.

"If I wasn't broke, I'd quit," he told Qwilleran as they walked to the parking lot. "For your private information, I hope this stupid magazine is a fat flop." With difficulty and mild curses he packed the camera case, tripod, lights and light stands in his small foreign two-seater.

Qwilleran, jackknifing himself into the cramped space that remained, tried to cheer up the photographer. He said, "When are you going to trade in this sardine can on a real car?"

"This is the only kind that runs on lighter fluid," said Bunsen. "I get ten miles to the squirt."

"You photographers are too cheap to buy gas."

"When you've got six kids and mortgage payments and orthodontist bills . . ."

"Why don't you cut out those expensive cigars?" Qwilleran suggested. "They must cost you at least three cents apiece."

They turned into Downriver Road, and the photographer said, "Who lined up this Muggy Swamp assignment for you? Fran Unger?"

Qwilleran's moustache bristled. "I line up my own assignments."

"The way Fran's been talking at the Press Club, I thought she was calling the plays."

Qwilleran grunted.

"She does a lot of talking after a couple of martinis," said Bunsen. "Saturday night she was hinting that you don't like girls. You must have done something that really burned her up."

"It was my cat! Fran called me at home, and Koko disconnected the phone."

"That cat's going to get you into trouble," the photographer predicted.

They merged into the expressway traffic and drove in speed and silence until they reached the Muggy Swamp exit.

Bunsen said, "Funny they never gave the place a decent name."

"You don't understand upper-class psychology," said Qwilleran. "You probably live in one of those cute subdivisions."

"I live in Happy View Woods. Four bedrooms and a big mortgage."

"That's what I mean. The G. Verning Taits wouldn't be caught dead in a place called Happy View."

The winding roads of Muggy Swamp offered glimpses of French châteaux and English manor houses, each secluded in its grove of ancient trees. The Tait house was an ornate Spanish stucco with an iron gate opening into a courtyard and a massive nail-studded door flanked by iron lanterns.

David Lyke greeted the newsmen at the door, ushering them into a foyer paved with black and white marble squares and sparkling with crystal. A bronze sphinx balanced a white marble slab on which stood a seventeen-branch candelabrum.

"Crazy!" said Bunsen.

"I suppose you want some help with your equipment," Lyke said. He signaled to a houseboy, who gave the young white-haired decorator a worshipful look with soft black eyes. "Paolo, pitch in and help these splendid people from the newspaper, and maybe they'll take your picture to send home to Mexico."

Eagerly the houseboy helped Bunsen carry in the heavy camera case and the collection of lights and tripods.

"Are we going to meet the Taits?" Qwilleran asked.

The decorator lowered his voice. "The old boy's holed up somewhere, clipping coupons and nursing his bad back. He won't come out till we yell *Jade!* He's an odd duck."

"How about his wife?"

"She seldom makes an appearance, for which we can all be thankful."

"Did you have much trouble getting their permission?"

"No, he was surprisingly agreeable," said Lyke. "Are you ready for the tour?"

He threw open double doors and led the newsmen into a living room done in brilliant green with white silk sofas and chairs. A writing desk was in ebony ornamented with gilt, and there was a French telephone on a gilded pedestal. Against the far wall stood a large wardrobe in beautifully grained wood.

"The Biedermeier wardrobe," said Lyke, raising an eyebrow, "was in the family, and we were forced to use it. The walls and carpet are Parsley Green. You can call the chairs Mushroom. The house itself is Spanish, circa 1925, and we had to square off the arches, rip up tile floors, and re-plaster extensively."

As the decorator moved about the room, straightening lampshades and smoothing the folds of the elaborately swagged draperies, Qwilleran stared at the splendor around him and saw dollar signs.

"If the Taits live quietly," he whispered, "why all this?"

Lyke winked. "I'm a good salesman. What he wanted was a setting that would live up to his fabulous collection of jade. It's worth three quarters of a million. That's not for publication, of course."

The most unusual feature in the living room was a series of niches in the walls, fronted with plate glass and framed with classic moldings. On their glass shelves were arranged scores of delicately carved objects in black and translucent white, artfully lighted to create an aura of mystery.

Odd Bunsen whispered, "Is that the jade? Looks like soap, if you ask me."

Qwilleran said, "I expected it to be green."

"The green jade is in the dining room," said Lyke.

The photographer started to set up his tripod and lights, and the decorator gave Qwilleran notes on the interior design.

"When you write up this place," he said, "call the Biedermeier ward-robe an *armoire*, and call the open-arm chairs *fauteuils*."

"Wait till the guys at the *Fluxion* read this," said Qwilleran. "I'll never hear the end of it."

Meanwhile, Bunsen was working with unusual concentration, taking both color and black-and-white shots. He shifted lights and camera angles, moved furniture an inch one way or another, and spent long periods under the focusing cloth. The houseboy was a willing assistant. Paolo was almost too eager. He got in the way.

Finally Bunsen sank into a white silk chair. "I've got to park for a minute and have a smoke." He drew a long cigar from his breast pocket.

David Lyke grimaced and glanced over his shoulder. "Do you want us all to get shot? Mrs. Tait hates tobacco smoke, and she can smell it a mile away."

"Well, that squelches *that* little idea!" Bunsen said irritably, and he went back to work.

Qwilleran said to him, "We need some closeups of the jades."

"I can't shoot through the glass."

"The glass can be removed," said Lyke. "Paolo, will you tell Mr. Tait we need the key to the cases?"

The jade collector, a man of about fifty, came at once, and his face was radiant. "Do you want to see my jades?" he said. "Which cases do you want me to open? These pictures will be in color, won't they?" His face had a scrubbed pink gleam, and he kept crimping the corners of his mouth in an abortive smile. He looked, Qwilleran thought, like a powerful man who had gone soft. His silk sports shirt exposed a heavy growth of hair on his arms, and yet there was a complete absence of hair on his head.

The plate-glass panels in the vitrines were ingeniously installed without visible hardware. Tait himself opened them, wearing gloves to prevent smudging.

Meanwhile Lyke recited a speech with affected formality: "Mr. Tait has generously agreed to share his collection with your readers, gentlemen. Mr. Tait feels that the private collector—in accumulating works of art that would otherwise appear in museums—has an obligation to the public. He is permitting these pieces to be photographed for the education and esthetic enjoyment of the community."

Qwilleran said, "May I quote you to that effect, Mr. Tait?"

The collector did not answer. He was too absorbed in his collection. Reverently he lifted a jade teapot from its place on a glass shelf. The teapot was pure white and paper-thin.

"This is my finest piece," he said, and his voice almost trembled. "The pure white is the rarest. I shouldn't show it first, should I? I should hold it back for a grand finale, but I get so excited about this teapot! It's the purest white I've ever seen, and as thin as a rose petal. You can say that in the article: thin as a rose petal."

He replaced the teapot and began to lift other items from the shelves. "Here's a Chinese bell, almost three thousand years old. . . . And here's a Mexican idol that's supposed to cure certain ailments. Not backache, unfortunately." He crimped the corners of his mouth as if enjoying a private joke that was not very funny.

"There's a lot of detail on those things," Qwilleran observed.

"Artists used to spend a whole lifetime carving a single object," Tait said. "But not all my jades are works of art." He went to the writing table and opened a drawer. "These are primitive tools made of jade. Axheads, chisels, harpoons." He laid them out on the desk top one by one.

"You don't need to take everything out," said Qwilleran. "We'll just photograph the carved pieces," but the collector continued to empty the drawer, handling each item with awe.

"Did you ever see jade in the rough?" he said. "This is a piece of nephrite."

"Well, let's get to work," said Bunsen. "Let's start shooting this crazy loot."

Tait handed a carved medallion to Qwilleran. "Feel it."

"It's cold," said the newsman.

"It's sensuous—like flesh. When I handle jade, I feel a prickle in my blood. Do you feel a prickle?"

"Are there many books on jade?" Qwilleran asked. "I'd like to read up on it."

"Come into my library," said the collector. "I have everything that has ever been written on the subject."

He pulled volume after volume from the shelves: technical books, memoirs, adventure, fiction—all centered upon the cool, sensuous stone.

"Would you care to borrow a few of these?" he said. "You can return them at your leisure." Then he reached into a desk drawer and slipped a button-shaped object into Qwilleran's hand. "Here! Take this with you for luck."

"Oh, no! I couldn't accept anything so valuable." Qwilleran fingered the smooth rounded surface of the stone. It was green, the way he thought jade should be.

Tait insisted. "Yes, I want you to have it. Its intrinsic value is not great. Probably just a counter used in some Japanese game. Keep it as a pocket piece. It will help you write a good article about my collection." He puckered the corners of his mouth again. "And who knows? It may give you ideas. You may become a collector of jade . . . and that is the best thing that could happen to a man!"

Tait spoke the words with religious fervor, and Qwilleran, rubbing the cool green button, felt a prickle in his blood.

Bunsen photographed several groups of jade, while the collector hovered over him with nervous excitement. Then the photographer started to fold up his equipment.

"Wait!" said Lyke. "There's one more room you should see—if it's permissible. Mrs. Tait's boudoir is magnificent." He turned to his client. "What do you think?"

Qwilleran caught a significant exchange of glances between the two men.

"Mrs. Tait is unwell," the husband explained to the newsmen. "However, let me see . . ."

He left the room and was gone several minutes. When he returned, his bald head as well as his face was unduly flushed. "Mrs. Tait is agreeable," he said, "but please take the picture as quickly as possible."

With the photographer carrying his camera on a tripod and Paolo carrying the lights, the party followed Tait down a carpeted corridor to a secluded wing of the house.

The boudoir was a combined sitting room and bedroom, lavishly decorated. Everything looked soft and downy. The bed stood under a tentlike canopy of blue silk. The chaise longue, heaped with pillows, was blue velvet. There was only one jarring note, and that was the wheelchair standing in the bay window.

Its occupant was a thin, sharp-featured woman. Her face was pinched with either pain or petulance, and her coloring was an unhealthy blond. She acknowledged the introductions curtly, all the while trying to calm a dainty Siamese cat that sat on a cushion on her lap. The cat had large lavender-blue eyes, slightly crossed.

Bunsen, with an attempt at heartiness, said, "Well, look what we've got here! A pussycat. A cross-eyed pussycat. Woof, woof!"

"Stop that!" Mrs. Tait said sharply. "You're frightening her."

In a hushed sickroom voice her husband said: "The cat's name is Yu. That's the ancient Chinese word for jade."

"Her name is not Yu," said the invalid, giving her husband a venomous look. "Her name is Freya." She stroked the animal, and the small furry body shrank into the cushion.

Bunsen turned his back to the wheelchair and started to whistle softly while adjusting the lens of his camera.

"It's taken you a long time to snap a few pictures," the woman observed. She spoke in a peculiarly throaty voice.

In defense Bunsen said, "A national magazine would take two days to photograph what I've done in one morning."

"If you're going to photograph my room," she said, "I want my cat in the picture."

A prolonged silence hung quivering in the air as everyone turned to look at the photographer.

"Sorry," he said. "Your cat wouldn't hold still long enough for a time exposure."

Cooly the woman said, "Other photographers seem to have no difficulty taking pictures of animals."

Bunsen's eyes snapped. He spoke with strained patience. "This is a long time exposure, Mrs. Tait. I've got to stop the lens down as far as possible to get the whole room in focus."

"I'm not interested in your technical problems. I want Freya in the picture!"

The photographer drew a deep breath. "I'm using a wide angle lens. The cat will be nothing but a tiny dot unless you put it right in front of the camera. And then it'll move and ruin the time exposure."

The invalid's voice became shrill. "If you can't take the picture the way I want it, don't take it at all."

Her husband went to her side. "Signe, calm yourself," he said, and with one hand waved the others out of the room.

As the newsmen drove away from Muggy Swamp, Bunsen said: "Don't forget to give me a credit line on those pictures. This job was a blinger! Do you realize I worked for three hours without a smoke? And that biddy in the wheelchair was the last straw! Besides, I don't like to photograph cats."

"That animal was unusually nervous," Qwilleran said.

"Paolo was a big help. I slipped him a couple of bucks."

"He seemed to be a nice kid."

"He's homesick. He's saving up to go back to Mexico. I'll bet Tait pays him in peanuts."

"Lyke told me the jades are worth $750,000."

"That burns me," said Bunsen. "A man like Tait can squander millions on teapots, and I have trouble paying my milk bill."

"You married guys think you've got all the problems," Qwilleran told him. "At least you've got a home! Look at me—I live in a furnished apartment, eat in restaurants, and haven't had a decent date for a month."

"There's always Fran Unger."

"Are you kidding?"

"A man your age can't be too fussy."

"Huh!" Qwilleran contracted his waistline an inch and preened his moustache. "I still consider myself a desirable prospect, but there seems to be a growing shortage of women."

"Have you found a new place to live yet?"

"I haven't had time to look."

"Why don't you put that smart cat of yours to work on it?" Bunsen suggested. "Give him the classified ads and let him make a few phone calls."

Qwilleran kept his mouth shut.

CHAPTER 4

THE FIRST ISSUE of *Gracious Abodes* went to press too smoothly. Arch Riker said it was a bad omen. There were no ad cancellations, the copy dummied in perfectly, cutlines spaced out evenly, and the proofs were so clean it was eerie.

The magazine reached the public Saturday night, sandwiched between several pounds of Sunday paper. On the cover was an exclusive Muggy Swamp residence in bright Parsley Green and Mushroom White. The editorial pages were liberally layered with advertisements for mattresses and automatic washers. And on page two was a picture of the *Gracious Abodes* editor with drooping moustache and expressionless eyes—the mug shot from his police press card.

On Sunday morning David Lyke telephoned Qwilleran at his apartment. "You did a beautiful job of writing," said the decorator in his chesty voice, "and thanks for the overstuffed credit line. But where did they get that picture of you? It makes you look like a basset hound."

For the newsman it was gratifying day, with friends calling constantly to offer congratulations. Later it rained, but he went out and bought himself a good dinner at a seafood restaurant, and in the evening he beat the cat at the word game, 20 to 4. Koko clawed up easy catchwords like *block* and *blood*, *police* and *politely*.

It was almost as if the cat had a premonition; by Monday morning *Gracious Abodes* was involved with the law.

The telephone jolted Qwilleran awake at an early hour. He groped for his wristwatch on the bedside table. The hands, after he had blinked enough to see them, said six thirty. With sleep in his bones he shuffled stiffly to the desk.

"Hello?" he said dryly.

"Qwill! This is Harold!"

There was a chilling urgency in the managing editor's voice that paralyzed Qwilleran's vocal cords for a moment.

"Is this Qwilleran?" shouted the editor.

The newsman made a squeaking reply. "Speaking."

"Have you heard the news? Did they call you?" The editor's words had the sound of calamity.

"No! What's wrong?" Qwilleran was awake now.

"The police just phoned me here at home. Our cover story—the Tait house—it's been burglarized!"

"*What!* . . . What did they get?"

"Jade! A half million dollars' worth, at a rough guess. And that's not the worst. Mrs. Tait is dead. . . . Qwill! Are you there? Did you hear me?"

"I heard you," Qwilleran said in a hollow voice, as he lowered himself slowly into a chair. "I can't believe it."

"It's a tragedy per se, and our involvement makes it even worse."

"Murder?"

"No, thank God! It wasn't quite as bad as *that*. Apparently she had a heart attack."

"She was a sick woman. I suppose she heard the intruders, and—"

"The police want to talk to you and Odd Bunsen as soon as possible," said the editor. "They want to get your fingerprints."

"They want *our* fingerprints? They want to question *us*?"

"Just routine. They said it will help them sort out the prints they find in the house. When were you there to take pictures?"

"Monday. Just a week ago." Then Qwilleran said what they were both thinking. "The publicity isn't going to do the magazine any good."

"It could ruin it! What have you got lined up for next Sunday?"

"An old stable converted into a home. It belongs to a used-car dealer who likes to see his name in the paper. I've found a lot of good houses, but the owners don't want us to use their names and addresses—for one reason or another."

"And now they've got another reason," said the editor. "And a damn good one!"

Qwilleran slowly hung up and gazed into space, weighing the bad news. There had been no interference from Koko during this particular telephone conversation. The cat was huddled under the dresser, watching the newsman intently, as if he sensed the gravity of the situation.

Qwilleran alerted Bunsen at his home in Happy View Woods, and within two hours the two newsmen were at Police Headquarters, telling their stories.

One of the detectives said, "What's your newspaper trying to do? Publish blueprints for burglary?"

The newsmen told how they had gone about the photographing the interior of the house in Muggy Swamp and how Tait had produced a key and supervised the opening of the jade cases. They told how he had wanted the rarest items to be photographed.

"Who else was there when you were taking pictures?"

"Tait's decorator, David Lyke . . . and the houseboy, Paolo . . . and I caught a glimpse of a servant in the kitchen," said Qwilleran.

"Did you have any contact with the houseboy?"

"Oh, sure," said Bunsen. "He worked with me for three hours, helping with the lights and moving furniture. A good kid! I slipped him a couple of bucks."

After the brief interrogation Qwilleran asked the detectives some prying questions, which they ignored. It was not his beat, and they knew it.

On the way out of Headquarters, Bunsen said: "Glad that's over! For a while I was afraid they suspected us."

"Our profession is above suspicion," said Qwilleran. "You never hear of a newsman turning to crime. Doctors bludgeon their wives, lawyers shoot their partners, and bankers abscond with the assets. But journalists just go to the Press Club and drown their criminal inclinations."

When Qwilleran reached his office, his first move was to telephone the studio of Lyke and Starkweather. The rumbling voice of David Lyke came quickly on the line.

"Heard the news?" Qwilleran asked in tones of gloom.

"Got it on my car radio, on the way downtown," said Lyke. "It's a rough deal for you people."

"But what about Tait? He must be going out of his mind! You know how he feels about those jades!"

"You can bet they're heavily insured, and now he can have the fun of collecting all over again." The decorator's lack of sympathy surprised Qwilleran.

"Yes, but losing his wife!"

"That was inevitable. Anything could have caused her death at any moment—bad news on the stock market, a gunfight on television! And she was a miserable woman," said Lyke. "She'd been in that wheelchair for years, and all that time she made her husband and everyone else walk a tightrope. . . . No, don't waste any tears over Mrs. Tait's demise. You've got enough to worry about. How do you think it will affect *Gracious Abodes*?"

"I'm afraid people will be scared to have their homes published."

"Don't worry. I'll see that you get material," Lyke said. "The profession needs a magazine like yours. Why don't you come to my apartment for cocktails this evening? I'll have a few decorators on tap."

"Good idea! Where do you live?"

"At the Villa Verandah. That's the new apartment house that looks like a bent waffle."

Just as Qwilleran hung up, a copyboy threw a newspaper on his desk. It was the Metro edition of the *Morning Rampage*. The *Fluxion*'s competitor had played up the Tait incident on the front page, and there were pointed references to "a detailed description of the jade collection, which appeared in another newspaper on the eve of the burglary." Qwilleran smoothed his moustache vigorously with his knuckles and went to the City Room to see the managing editor, but Percy was in conference with the publisher and the business manager.

Moodily, Qwilleran sat at his desk and stared at his typewriter. He should have been working. He should have been shooting for the next deadline, but something was bothering him. It was the *timing* of the burglary.

The magazine had been distributed Saturday evening. It was some time during the following night—late Sunday or early Monday—that the burglary occurred. Within a matter of twenty-four short hours, Qwilleran figured, someone had to (*a*) read the description of the jades and (*b*) dream up the idea of stealing them and (*c*) make elaborate preparations for a rather complex maneuver. They had to devise a plan of entering the house without disturbing the family or servants, work out a method of silent access to the ingeniously designed glass-covered niches, arrange for fairly careful packing of the loot, provide a means of transporting it from the house, and schedule all this so as to elude the private police. Undoubtedly Muggy Swamp had private police patrolling the community.

There had been very little time for research, Qwilleran reflected. It would require a remarkably efficient organization to carry out the operation successfully . . . unless the thieves were acquainted with the Tait house or had advance knowledge of the jade story. And if that was the case, had they deliberately timed the burglary to make *Gracious Abodes* look bad?

As Qwilleran pondered the possibilities, the first edition of the Monday *Fluxion* came off the presses, and the copyboy whizzed through the Feature Department, tossing a paper on each desk.

The Tait incident was discreetly buried on page four, and it bore an astounding headline. Qwilleran read the six short paragraphs in six gulps. The by-line was Lodge Kendall's; he was the *Fluxion*'s regular man at Police Headquarters. There was no reference to the *Gracious Abodes* story. The estimated value of the stolen jades was omitted. And there was an incredible statement from the Police Department. Qwilleran read it with a frown, then grabbed his coat and headed for the Press Club.

The Press Club occupied a soot-covered limestone fortress that had once been the county jail. The windows were narrow and barred, and mangy pigeons roosted among the blackened turrets. Inside, the old wood-paneled walls had the lingering aroma of a nineteenth-century penal institution, but the worst feature was the noise. Voices swooped across the domed ceiling, collided with other voices, and bounced back, multiplying into a deafening roar. To the newsmen this was heaven.

Today the cocktail bar on the main floor resounded with discussion and speculation on the happening in Muggy Swamp. Jewel thefts were crimes that civilized newsmen could enjoy with relish and good conscience. They appealed to the intellect, and as a rule nobody got hurt.

Qwilleran found Odd Bunsen at that end of the bar traditionally reserved for *Fluxion* staffers. He joined him and ordered a double shot of tomato juice on the rocks.

"Did you read it?" he asked the photographer.

"I read it," said Bunsen. "They're nuts."

They talked in subdued tones. At the opposite end of the mahogany bar the voices of *Morning Rampage* staffers suggested undisguised jubilation. Qwilleran glanced with annoyance at the rival crew.

"Who's that guy down there in the light suit—the one with the loud laugh?" he demanded.

"He works in their Circulation Department," Bunsen said. "He played softball against us this summer, and take my word for it—he's a creep."

"He irritates me. A woman is dead, and he's crowing about it."

"Here comes Kendall," said the photographer. "Let's see what he thinks about the police theory."

The police reporter—young, earnest, and happy in his work—was careful to exhibit a professional air of boredom.

Qwilleran beckoned him to the bar, and said, "Do you believe that stuff you wrote this morning?"

"As far as the police are concerned," said Kendall, "it's an open-and-shut case. It had nothing to do with your publication of the Tait house. It had to be an inside job. Somebody had to know his way around."

"I know," said Qwilleran. "That's what I figured. But I don't like their choice of suspect. I don't believe the houseboy did it."

"Then how do you explain his disappearance? If Paolo didn't swing with the jades and take off for Mexico, where is he?"

Bunsen said: "Paolo doesn't fit the picture. He was a nice kid—quiet and shy—very anxious to help. He's not the type."

"You photographers think you're great judges of character," Kendall said. "Well, you're wrong! According to Tait, the boy was lazy, sly, and deceitful. On several occasions Tait threatened to fire him, but Mrs. Tait always came to Paolo's defense. And because of her physical condition, her husband was afraid to cross her."

Bunsen and Qwilleran exchanged incredulous glances, and Kendall wandered away to speak to a group of TV men.

For a while Qwilleran toyed with the jade button that Tait had given him. He kept it in his pocket with his loose change. Finally he said to Bunsen, "I called David Lyke this morning."

"How's he taking it?"

"He didn't seem vitally upset. He said the jades were insured and Mrs. Tait was a miserable creature who made her husband's life one long hell."

"I'll buy that. She was a witch-and-a-half. What did he think about Paolo being mixed up in it?"

"At the time I talked to Lyke, that hadn't been announced."

Bruno, the Press Club bartender, was hovering in the vicinity, waiting for the signal.

"No more," Qwilleran told him. "I've got to eat and get back to work."

"I saw your magazine yesterday," the bartender said. "It gave me and my wife a lot of decorating ideas. We're looking forward to the next issue."

"After what happened in Muggy Swamp, you may never see a next issue," Qwilleran said. "Nobody will want to have his house published."

Bruno gave the newsman a patronizing smile. "Maybe I can help you. If you're hard up for material, you can photograph my house. We did it ourselves."

"What kind of place have you got?" Qwilleran waited warily for the answer. Bruno was known as the poor man's Leonardo da Vinci. His talents were many, but slender.

"I have what they call a monochromatic color scheme," said the bartender. "I've got Chartreuse carpet, Chartreuse walls, Chartreuse drapes, and a Chartreuse sofa."

"Very suitable for a member of your profession," said Qwilleran, "but allow me to correct you on one small detail. We *never* call draperies *drapes*."

CHAPTER 5

BEFORE GOING to the cocktail party at David Lyke's apartment, Qwilleran went home to change clothes and give the cat a slice of corned beef he had bought at the delicatessen.

Koko greeted him by flying around the room in a catly expression of joy—over chairs, under tables, around lamps, up to the top of the bookshelves, down to the floor with a thud and a grunt—making sharp turns in midair at sixty miles an hour. Lamps teetered. Ashtrays spun around. The limp curtains rippled in the breeze. Then Koko leaped on the dictionary and scratched for all he was worth—with his rear end up, his front end down, his tail pointed skyward, like a toboggan slide with a flag on top. He scratched industriously, stopped to look at Qwilleran, and scratched again.

"No time for games," Qwilleran said. "I'm going out. Cocktail party. Maybe I'll bring you home an olive."

He put on a pair of pants that had just come from the cleaner, unpinned a newly purchased shirt, and looked for his new tie. He found it draped over the arm of the sofa. There was a hole in it, center front, and

Qwilleran groaned. That left only one plaid tie in good condition. He whipped it off the doorknob where it hung and tied it around his neck, grumbling to himself. Meanwhile, Koko sat on the dictionary, hopefully preparing for a game.

"No game tonight," Qwilleran told him again. "You eat your corned beef and then have a nice long nap."

The newsman set out for the party with three-fold anticipation. He hoped to make some useful contacts; he was curious about the fashionable and expensive Villa Verandah; and he was looking forward to seeing David Lyke again. He liked the man's irreverent attitude. Lyke was not what Qwilleran had expected a decorator to be. Lyke was neither precious nor a snob, and he wore his spectacular good looks with a casual grace.

The Villa Verandah, a recent addition to the cityscape, was an eighteen-story building curved around a landscaped park, each apartment with a balcony. Qwilleran found his host's apartment alive with the sound of bright chatter, clinking glasses, and music from hidden loudspeakers.

In a pleasant rumbling voice Lyke said: "Is this your first visit to the Villa Verandah? We call this building the Architects' Revenge. The balconies are designed to be too sunny, too windy, and too dirty. The cinders that hurtle through my living room are capable of putting out an eyeball. But it's a good address. Some of the best people live in this building, several of them blind in one eye."

He opened a sliding glass door in the glass wall and showed Qwilleran the balcony, where metal furniture stood ankle-deep in water and the wind made ripples on the surface.

"The balconies become wading pools for three days after every rain," he said. "When there's a high wind, the railings vibrate and play 'Ave Maria' by the hour. And notice our unique view—a panorama of ninety-two other balconies."

The apartment itself had a warmly livable atmosphere. Everywhere there were lighted candles, books in good leather bindings, plants of the exotic type, paintings in important frames, and heaps of pillows. A small fountain in one corner was busy splashing. And the wallpaper was the most sumptuous Qwilleran had ever seen—like silver straw with a tracery of peacocks.

The predominant note was Oriental. He noticed an Oriental screen, some bowlegged black tables, and a Chinese rug in the dining room. Some large pieces of Far Eastern sculpture stood in a bed of pebbles, lighted by concealed spotlights.

Qwilleran said to Lyke, "We should photograph this."

"I was going to suggest something else in this building," said the decorator. "I did Harry Noyton's apartment—just a *pied-à-terre* that he uses for business entertaining, but it's tastefully done in wall-to-wall money. And the colors are smart—in a ghastly way. I've used Eggplant, Spinach, and Overripe Melon."

"Who is Harry Noyton?" Qwilleran asked. "The name sounds familiar."

"You must have heard of him. He's the most vocal 'silent partner' in town. Harry owns the ballpark, a couple of hotels, and *probably* the City Hall."

"I'd like to meet him."

"You will. He's dropping in tonight. I'd really like to see you publish Harry's country house in Lost Lake Hills—all artsy-craftsy contemporary—but there's an awkward situation in the family at the moment, and it might not be advisable. . . . Now, come and meet some of the guests. Starkweather is here—with his lovely wife, who is getting to be a middle-aged sot, but I can't say that I blame her."

Lyke's partner was sitting quietly at one end of the sofa, but Mrs. Starkweather was circulating diligently. There was a frantic gaiety in her aging face, and her costume was a desperate shade of pink. She clung to Lyke in an amorous way when he introduced Qwilleran.

"I'm in love with David," she told the newsman, waving a cocktail glass in a wide arc. "Isn't he just too overwhelming? Those eyes! And that sexy voice!"

"Easy, sweetheart," said Lyke. "Do you want your husband to shoot me?" He turned to Qwilleran. "This is one of the hazards of the profession. We're so lovable."

After Lyke disengaged himself from Mrs. Starkweather's grip, she clung to Qwilleran's arm and went on prattling. "Decorators give marvelous parties! There are always lots of *men*! And the food is always so good. David has a marvelous caterer. But the drinks are too potent." She giggled. "Do you know many decorators? They're lots of fun. They dress so well and they dance so well. My husband isn't really a decorator. He used to be in the wholesale carpet business. He handles the money at L&S. David is the one with talent. I adore David!"

Most of the guests were decorators, Qwilleran discovered. All the men were handsome, the majority of them young. The women were less so, but what they lacked in beauty and youth they made up in vivacity and impressive clothes. Everyone had an easy charm. They complimented Qwilleran on his new magazine, the luxuriance of his moustache, and the fragrance of his pipe tobacco.

Conversation flitted from one subject to another: travel, fashion, rare wine, ballet, and the dubious abilities of other decorators. Repeatedly, the name of Jacques Boulanger came up and was dismissed with disapproval.

No one, Qwilleran noticed, was disposed to discuss the November election or the major-league pennant race or the situation in Asia. And none of the guests seemed disturbed by the news of the Tait theft. They were merely amused that it should have happened to a client of David's.

One young man of fastidious appearance approached Qwilleran and introduced himself as Bob Orax. He had an oval aristocratic face with elevated eyebrows.

"Ordinarily," he told the newsman, "I don't follow crime news, but my family knew the Taits, and I was fascinated by the item in today's paper. I had no idea Georgie had amassed so much jade. He and Siggy haven't entertained for years! Mother went to school with Siggy in Switzerland, you know."

"No, I didn't know."

"Siggy's family had more brains than influence, Mother says. They were all scientists and architects. And it was rather a coup when Siggy married a rich American. Georgie had *hair* in those days, according to Mother."

"How did the Taits make their money?" Qwilleran asked.

"In a rather quaint and charming way. Georgie's grandfather made a mint—an absolute *mint*—manufacturing buggy whips. But Mother says Georgie himself has never had a taste for business. Monkey business, perhaps, but nothing that you can put in the bank."

"Tait was devoted to his jade collection," said Qwilleran. "I felt very bad about the theft."

"That," said Orax loftily, "is what happens when you hire cheap help. When Father was alive, he always insisted on English butlers and Irish maids. My family had money at one time. Now we get by on our connections. And I have a little shop on River Street that helps to keep the wolf from the door."

"I'd like to call on you some day," said Qwilleran. "I'm in the market for story material."

"Frankly, I doubt whether your readers are quite ready for me," said the decorator. "I specialize in Planned Ugliness, and the idea is rather advanced for the average taste. But do come! You might find it entertaining."

"By the way, who is this Jacques Boulanger I keep hearing about?"

"Boulanger?" The Orax eyebrows elevated a trifle higher. "He does work for the Duxburies, the Pennimans, and all the other old families in Muggy Swamp."

"He must be good."

"In our business," said the decorator, "success is not always an indication of excellence. . . . Bless you! You have no drink! May I get you something from the bar?"

It was not the bar that interested Qwilleran. It was the buffet. It was laden with caviar, shrimp, a rarebit in a chafing dish, marinated mushrooms, stuffed artichoke hearts, and savory meatballs in a dill sauce. As he loaded his plate for the third time, he glanced into the kitchen and saw the large stainless-steel warming oven of a professional caterer. A smiling Oriental caught his eye and nodded encouragement, and Qwilleran signaled a compliment in the man's direction.

Meanwhile a guest with a big, ungainly figure and a craggy face sauntered over to the buffet and started popping tidbits into his mouth, washing them down with gulps from a highball glass.

"I like these kids—these decorators," he said to the newsman. "They invite me to a lot of their parties. But how they ever make a living is beyond me! They live in a dream world. I'm a businessman myself—in and out of a dozen enterprises a year—and I make every investment pay off. I'm not in the racket for kicks—like these kids. *You* understand. You're a newspaperman, aren't you?"

"Jim Qwilleran from the *Daily Fluxion*."

"You newspaper guys are a good breed. You've got your feet on the ground. I know a lot of journalists. I know the managing editors of both papers, and the *Fluxion* sports editor, and your financial writer. They've all been up to my hunting lodge. Do you like hunting and fishing?"

"I haven't done much of it," Qwilleran admitted.

"To tell the truth, all we do is sit around with a bottle and shoot the breeze. You ought to come up and join us some time. . . . By the way, I'm Harry Noyton."

They shook hands, and Qwilleran said, "David tells me you have a house that might make good story material for the *Fluxion*'s new decorating magazine."

Noyton stared at his shoes for a long minute before answering. "Come in the other room where it's quiet," he said.

They went into the breakfast room and sat at a marble-topped table—the promoter with his highball glass and Qwilleran with a plate of shrimp and mushrooms.

Noyton said: "Whatever you've heard about my house in the Hills is no lie. It's terrific! And I give David all the credit—that is, Dave and my wife. She's got talent. I don't have any talent myself. All I did was go to engine college for a couple of years." He paused and gazed out of the window. "But Natalie is artistic. I'm proud of her."

"I'd like to see this house."

"Well . . . here's the problem," said Noyton, taking a long drink from his glass. "The house is going to be sold. You see, Natalie and I are getting a divorce."

"Sorry to hear it," said Qwilleran. "I've been over that course myself."

"There's no trouble between us, you understand. She just wants out! She's got this crazy idea that she wants an artistic career. Can you imagine that? She's got everything in the world, but she wants to be creative, wants to starve in an attic studio, wants to make something of her life. That's what she says. And she wants it bad! Bad enough to give up the boys. I don't understand this art bug that gets into women these days."

"You have children?"

"Two sons. Two fine boys. I don't know how she can have the heart to get up and walk away from them. But those are my terms: I get complete custody of the boys, and the divorce is forever. No willy-wagging. She can't change her mind and decide to come back after a couple of months. I won't play the fool for anyone! Especially not a woman. . . . Tell me, am I right?"

Qwilleran stared at the man—aggressive, rich, lonely.

Noyton drained his drink, and said, "I'll send the boys to military school, of course."

"Is Mrs. Noyton a painter?" Qwilleran asked.

"No, nothing like that. She's got these big looms, and she wants to weave rugs and things for decorators to sell. I don't know how she's going to make a living. She won't take any money from me, and she doesn't want the house. Know anybody wants a quarter-million dollars' worth of real estate?"

"It must be quite a place."

"Say, if you want to write it up for the paper, it might help me to unload the joint. I'm leveling with you, understand."

"Is anyone living there now?"

"Caretaker, that's all. Natalie's in Reno. I'm living here at the Villa Verandah . . . Wait'll I flavor these ice cubes."

Noyton dashed to the bar, and while he was gone the Japanese caterer quietly removed Qwilleran's plate and replaced it with another, piled high.

"Like I was saying," Noyton went on, "I have this apartment that Dave decorated. That boy's got taste! Wish I had that boy's taste. I've got a wood floor imported from Denmark, a built-in bar, a fur rug—the works!"

"I wouldn't mind seeing it."

"Come on and have a look. It's right here on this floor, in the north wing."

They left the party, Noyton carrying his highball glass. "I should warn you," he said as they walked around the curving corridor, "the colors are kind of wild."

He unlocked the door to 15-F and touched a wall switch. Qwilleran gasped.

Pleasant music burst forth. Rich color glowed in pools of light. Everything looked soft, comfortable, but rugged.

"Do you go for this modern stuff?" Noyton asked. "Expensive as hell when it's done right."

With awe in his voice Qwilleran said: "This is great! This really gets to me."

The floor consisted of tiny squares of dark wood with a velvety oiled finish. There was a rug as shaggy as unmown grass and half as big as a squash court.

"Like the rug?" Noyton asked. "Genuine goat hair from Greece."

It was surrounded on three sides by a trio of sofas covered in natural tan suede. A chair with inviting body curves was upholstered in something incredibly soft.

"Vicuña," said Noyton. "But try that green chair. That's my favorite."

When Qwilleran relaxed in the green chair and propped his feet on the matching ottoman, an expression of beatitude spread over his face. He stroked the sculptured woolly arms. "I'd sure like to have an apartment like this," he murmured.

"And this is the bar," said Noyton with unconcealed pride as he splashed some liquor in his glass. "And the stereo is in that old Spanish chest—the only antique in the place. Cost me a fortune." He sank into the vicuña chair. "The rent for this apartment is nothing to sneeze at, either, but some good people live in this building—good people to know." He named two judges, a banker, the retired president of the university, a prominent scientist. "I know them all. I know a lot of people in this town. Your managing editor is a good friend of mine."

Qwilleran's eyes were roving over the wall of cantilevered bookshelves, the large desk topped with rust-colored leather, the sensuous rug, and the three—not one, but three—deep-cushioned sofas.

"Yes, Lyke did a great job on the decorating," he said.

"Say, you look like a regular guy," Noyton remarked with a crafty look. "How are you getting along with these decorators?"

"They seem to be a congenial bunch," said Qwilleran, ignoring the innuendo.

"That's not what I mean. Have you met Bob Orax? He's got a real problem."

"I'm used to meeting all kinds," Qwilleran said, more curtly than he had intended. He had a newsman's capacity for identifying with his beat and defending its personnel, and he resented Noyton's aspersions.

Noyton said, "That's what I admire about you news guys. Nobody throws you. You take everything in your stride."

Qwilleran swung his feet off the ottoman and hoisted himself out of the green chair. "Well, what do you say? Shall we go back where the action is?"

They returned to the party, Noyton carrying two bottles of bourbon from his own stock, which he added to Lyke's supply.

Qwilleran complimented the decorator on the Noyton job. "Wish I could afford an apartment like his. What does a layout like that cost, anyway?"

"Too much," said the decorator. "By the way, if you ever need anything, I'll get it for you at cost, plus freight."

"What I need," said Qwilleran, "is a furnished apartment. The place where I live is being torn down to make a parking lot, and I've got to be out in ten days."

"Why don't you use Harry's apartment for a few weeks—if you like it so much?" Lyke suggested. "He's leaving for Europe, and he'll be gone a month or more."

Qwilleran blinked. "Do you think he'd be willing to sublet—at a price I could afford?"

"Let's ask him."

Noyton said, "Hell, no, I won't sublet, but if you want to use the joint while I'm gone, just move in."

"No, I'd insist on paying rent," Qwilleran said.

"Don't give me that integrity jive! I've had a lot of good treatment from the papers, and this'll give me a chance to say thanks. Besides, it's no skin off my back. Why should I take your money?"

Lyke said to Qwilleran, "There's a catch, of course. He'll expect you to forward his mail and take telephone messages."

Qwilleran said, "There's another catch, too. I've got a cat."

"Bring him along!" said Noyton. "He can have his own room and bath. First class."

"I could guarantee that he wouldn't scratch the furniture."

"It's a deal. I'm leaving Wednesday. The keys will be at the manager's desk, including the one for the bar. Help yourself to anything. And don't be surprised if I call you twice a day from Europe. I'm a telephone bug."

Later, Lyke said to the newsman: "Thanks for getting me off the hook. Harry was expecting *me* to do his secretary service. I don't know why, but clients think they've hired a wet nurse for life when they call in a decorator."

It had happened so fast that Qwilleran could hardly believe his good fortune. Rejoicing inwardly, he made two more trips to the buffet before saying good night to his host.

As he left the apartment, he felt a tug at his sleeve. The caterer was standing at his elbow, smiling.

"You got a doggie at home?" he asked the newsman.

"No," said Qwilleran, "but—"

"Doggie hungry. You take doggie bag," said the caterer, and he pushed a foil-wrapped package into Qwilleran's hand.

CHAPTER 6

"KOKO, OLD FELLOW, we're moving!" Qwilleran announced happily on Tuesday morning, as he took the doggie bag from the refrigerator and prepared a breakfast for the cat and himself. Reviewing the events of the previous evening, he had to admit that the decorating beat had its advantages. Never had he received so many compliments or tasted such good food, and the offer of an apartment was a windfall.

Koko was huddling on a cushion on top of the refrigerator—the blue cushion that was his bed, his throne, his Olympus. His haunches were sticking up like fins. He looked uncomfortable, apprehensive.

"You'll like it at the Villa Verandah," Qwilleran assured him. "There are soft rugs and high bookshelves, and you can sit in the sun on the balcony. But you'll have to be on your best behavior. No flying around and busting lamps!"

Koko shifted weight. His eyes were large troubled circles of blue.

"We'll take your cushion and put it on the new refrigerator, and you'll feel right at home."

At the *Daily Fluxion* an hour later, Qwilleran reported the good news to Odd Bunsen. They met in the employees' lunchroom for their morning cup of coffee, sitting at the counter with pressmen in square paper hats, typesetters in canvas aprons, rewrite men in white shirts with the cuffs turned up, editors with their cuffs buttoned, and advertising men wearing cufflinks.

Qwilleran told the photographer, "You should see the bathrooms at the Villa Verandah! Gold faucets!"

"How do you walk into these lucky breaks?" Bunsen wanted to know.

"It was Lyke's idea, and Noyton likes to make generous gestures. He likes to be liked, and he's fascinated by newspaper people. You know the type."

"Some newspapers wouldn't let you accept a plum like that, but on a *Fluxion* salary you have to take all you can get," the photographer said. "Was there any conversation about the robbery?"

"Not much. But I picked up a little background on the Taits. Did it strike you that Mrs. Tait had a slight foreign accent?"

"She sounded as if she'd swallowed her tongue."

"I think she was Swiss. She apparently married Tait for his money, although I imagine he was a good-looking brute before he went bald."

"Did you notice his arms?" the photographer said. "Hairiest ape I ever saw! Some women go for that."

There was a tap on Bunsen's shoulder, and Lodge Kendall sat down on the next stool. "I knew I'd find you here, goldbricking as usual," he said to the photographer. "The detectives on the Tait case would like a set of the photos you took. Enlargements, preferably. Especially any shots that show the jades."

"How soon do they want them? I've got a lot of printing to do for Sunday."

"Soon as you can."

Qwilleran said, "Any progress on the case?"

"Tait has reported two pieces of luggage missing," said Kendall. "He's going away for a rest after the funeral. He's pretty shook up. And last night he went to the storeroom to get some luggage, and his two large over-seas bags were gone. Paolo would need something like that to transport the jade."

"I wonder how he'd get a couple of large pieces of luggage to the airport."

"He must have had an accomplice with a car. By the time Tait found the stuff missing, Paolo had time to fly to Mexico and disappear forever in the mountains. I doubt whether they'll ever be able to trace the jades down there. Eventually they may turn up on the market, a piece at a time, but nobody will know anything about anything. You know how it is down there."

"I suppose the police have checked the airlines?"

"The passenger lists for the Sunday-night flights showed several Mexican or Spanish names. Of course, Paolo would use an alias."

Bunsen said: "Too bad I didn't take his picture. Lyke suggested it, but I never gave it another thought."

"You photographers are so stingy with your film," Kendall said, "anyone would think you had to buy it yourself."

"By the way," said Qwilleran, "exactly when did Tait discover the jades were missing?"

"About six o'clock in the morning. He's one of those early risers. He likes to go down into his workshop before breakfast and polish stones, or whatever it is he does. He went into his wife's room to see if she needed anything, found her dead, and called the doctor from the bedside phone. Then he rang for Paolo and got no response. Paolo was not in his room, and there were signs of hurried departure. Tait made a quick check of all the rooms, and that's when he discovered the display cases had been rifled."

"After which," said Qwilleran, "he called the police, and the police called Percy, and Percy called me, and it was still only six thirty. It all happened pretty fast. When Tait called the police, did he tell them about the story in *Gracious Abodes*?"

"He didn't have to. The Department had already spotted your story and questioned the advisability of describing valuable objects so explicitly."

Qwilleran snorted his disdain. "And where was the cook when all this was happening?"

"The housekeeper gets Sundays off, doesn't come back until eight o'clock Monday morning."

"And how do they account for Mrs. Tait's heart attack?"

"They assume she waked in the night, heard some kind of activity in the living room, and suspected prowlers. Evidently the fright was enough to stop her ticker, which was in bad shape, I understand."

Qwilleran objected. "That's a rambling house. The bedroom wing is half a mile from the living room. How come Mrs. Tait heard Paolo getting into the display cases—and her husband didn't?"

Kendall shrugged. "Some people are light sleepers. Chronic invalids always have insomnia."

"Didn't she try to rouse her husband? There must be some kind of buzzer system or intercom between the two rooms."

"Look, I wasn't there!" said the police reporter. "All I know is what I hear at Headquarters." He tapped his wristwatch. "I'm due there in five minutes. See you later. . . . Bunsen, don't forget those enlargements."

When he had gone, Qwilleran said to the photographer, "I wonder where Tait's going for a rest. Mexico, by any chance?"

"You do more wondering than any three guys I know," said Bunsen, rising from the lunch counter. "I've got to do some printing. See you upstairs."

Qwilleran could not say when his suspicions first began to take a definite direction. He finished his coffee and wiped his moustache roughly with a paper napkin. Perhaps that was the moment that the gears meshed and the wheels started to turn and the newsman's deliberation began to focus on G. Verning Tait.

He went upstairs to the Feature Department and found the telephone on his desk ringing urgently. It was a green telephone, matching all the desks and typewriters in the room. Suddenly Qwilleran saw the color scheme of the office with new eyes. It was Pea Soup Green, and the walls were painted Roquefort, and the brown vinyl floor was Pumpernickel.

"Qwilleran speaking," he said into the green mouthpiece.

"Oh, Mr. Qwilleran! Is this Mr. Qwilleran himself?" It was a woman's voice, high-pitched and excited. "I didn't think they'd let me talk to you personally."

"What can I do for you?"

"You don't know me, Mr. Qwilleran, but I read every word you write, and I think your new decorating magazine is simply elegant."

"Thanks."

"Now, here's my problem. I have Avocado carpet in my dining room and Caramel *toiles de Jouy* on the walls. Should I paint the dado Caramel Custard or Avocado? And what about the lambrequins?"

When he finally got rid of his caller, Arch Riker signaled to him. "The boss is looking for you. It's urgent."

"He probably wants to know what color to paint his dado," said Qwilleran.

He found the managing editor looking thin-lipped. "Trouble!" said Percy. "That used-car dealer just phoned. You have his horsebarn scheduled for next Sunday. Right?"

"It's a remodeled stable," Qwilleran said. "Very impressive. It makes a good story. The pages are made up, and the pictures have gone to the engraver."

"He wants the story killed. I tried to persuade him to let it run, but he insists on withdrawing it."

"He was hot for it last week."

"Personally he doesn't object. He doesn't blame us for the mishap in Muggy Swamp, but his wife is worried sick. She's having hysterics. The man threatens to sue if we publish his house."

"I don't know what I can substitute in a hurry," said Qwilleran. "The only spectacular thing I have on hand is a silo painted like a barber pole and converted into a vacation home."

"Not exactly the image we want to project for *Gracious Abodes*," said the editor. "Why don't you ask Fran Unger if she has any ideas?"

"Look, Harold!" said Qwilleran with sudden resolve. "I think we should take the offensive!"

"What do you mean?"

"I mean—conduct our own investigation! I don't buy the police theory. Pinning the crime on the houseboy is too easy. Paolo may have been an innocent dupe. For all anybody knows, he could be at the bottom of the river!"

He stopped to get the editor's reaction. Percy only stared at him.

"That was no petty theft," said Qwilleran, raising his voice, "and it was not pulled off by an unsophisticated, homesick mountain boy from an underdeveloped foreign country! Something more is involved here. I don't know who or what or why, but I've got a hunch—" He pounded his moustache with his knuckles. "Harold, why don't you assign me to cover this case? I'm sure I could dig up something of importance."

Percy waved the suggestion away impatiently. "I'm not opposed to investigate journalism per se, but we need you on the magazine. We don't have the personnel to waste on amateur sleuthing."

"I can handle both. Just give me the credentials to talk to the police—to ask a few questions here and there."

"No, you've got enough on your hands, Qwill. Let the police handle crime. We've got to concentrate on putting out a newspaper."

Qwilleran went on as if he had not heard. He talked fast. "There's something suspicious about the timing of that incident! Someone wanted to link us with it. And that's not the only strange circumstance! Too much happened too fast yesterday morning. You called me at six thirty. What time did the police call you? And what time did they get the call from Tait? . . . And if Mrs. Tait heard sounds of prowlers, why didn't she signal her husband? Can you believe there was no intercom in that house? All that plush decorating, and not even a simple buzzer system between the invalid's bed and the sleeping quarters of her devoted husband?"

Percy looked at Qwilleran coldly. "If there's evidence of conspiracy, the police will uncover it. They know what they're doing. You keep out of it. We've got troubles enough."

Qwilleran calmed his moustache. There was no use arguing with a computer. "Do you think I should make an appearance at the funeral tomorrow?" he asked.

"It won't be necessary. We'll be adequately represented."

Qwilleran went back to his office muttering into his moustache: "Play it safe! Don't offend! Support the Advertising Department! Make money!"

"Why not?" said Arch Riker. "Did you think we were in business to disseminate news?"

At his desk Qwilleran picked up the inoffensive green telephone that was stenciled with the reminder Be Nice to People. He called the Photo Lab.

"When you make those enlargements of the jades," he said to Bunsen, "make a set of prints for me, will you? I've got an idea."

CHAPTER 7

QWILLERAN KILLED the cover story about the car dealer's remodeled stable and started to worry about finding a substitution. He had an appointment that morning with another decorator, but he doubted that she would be able to produce a cover story on short notice. He had talked with her on the telephone, and she seemed flustered.

"Oh, dear!" Mrs. Middy had said. "Oh, dear! Oh, dear!"

Qwilleran went to her studio without any buoyant hope.

The sign over the door, lettered in Specerian script, said *Interiors by Middy*. The shop was located near Happy View Woods, and it had all the ingredients of charm: window boxes filled with yellow mums, bay windows with diamond-shaped panes, a Dutch door flanked by picturesque carriage lanterns, a gleaming brass door knocker. Inside, the cozy charm was suffocating but undeniable.

As Qwilleran entered, he heard Westminster chimes, and then he saw a tall young woman emerge from behind a louvered folding screen at the back of the shop. Her straight brown hair fell like a blanket to her shoulders, hiding her forehead, eyebrows, temples and cheeks. All that was visible was a pair of roguish green eyes, an appealing little nose, an intelligent mouth, a dainty chin.

Qwilleran brightened. He said, "I have an eleven o'clock appointment with Mrs. Middy, and I don't think you're Mrs. Middy."

"I'm her assistant," said the young woman. "Mrs. Middy is a little late this morning, but then Mrs. Middy is always a little late. Would you care to sit it out?" She waved a hand dramatically around the studio. "I can offer you a Chippendale corner chair, a combback Windsor, or a mammy settle. They're all uncomfortable, but I'll talk to you and take your mind off your anguish."

"Talk to me, by all means," said Qwilleran, sitting on the mammy settle and finding that it rocked. The girl sat in the combback Windsor with her skirt well above her knees, and Qwilleran was pleased to see that they were leanly upholstered. "What's your name?" he asked, as he filled his pipe and lighted it.

"Alacoque Wright, and you must be the editor of the new Sunday supplement. I forget what you call it."

"*Gracious Abodes*," said Qwilleran.

"Why do newspapers insist on sounding like warmed-over Horace Greeley?" Her greens eyes were kidding him, and Qwilleran liked it.

"There's an element of tradition in newspapering." He glanced around the studio. "Same as in your business."

"Decorating is not really my business," said the girl crisply. "Architecture is my field, but girl architects are not largely in demand. I took this job with Mrs. Middy in desperation, and I'm afraid these imitation worm-eaten hutches and folksy-hoaxy mammy settles are warping my personality. I prefer design that reflects the spirit of our times. Down with French Empire, Portuguese Colonial and Swahili Baroque!"

"You mean you like modern design?"

"I don't like to use the word," said Miss Wright. "It's so ambiguous. There's Motel Modern, Miami Beach Modern, Borax Danish, and a lot of horrid mutations. I prefer the twentieth-century classics—the work of Saarinen, Mies van der Rohe, Breuer, and all that crowd. Mrs. Middy doesn't let me meet clients; she's afraid I'll sabotage her work. . . . And I believe I would," she added with a feline smile. "I have a sneaky nature."

"If you don't meet clients, what do you do?"

"Renderings, floor plans, color schemes. I answer the telephone and sort of sweep up. . . . But tell me about you. Do you like contemporary design?"

"I like anything," said Qwilleran, "as long as it's comfortable, and I can put my feet on it."

The girl appraised him frankly. "You're better looking than your picture in the magazine. You look serious and responsible, but also interesting. Are you married?"

"Not at the moment."

"You must feel crushed about what happened this weekend."

"You mean the theft in Muggy Swamp?"

"Do you suppose Mr. Tait will sue the *Daily Fluxion*?"

Qwilleran shook his head. "He wouldn't get to first base. We printed nothing that was untrue or libelous. And, of course, we had his permission to publish his house in the first place."

"But the robbery will damage your magazine's image, you must admit," said Miss Wright.

Just then the Dutch door opened, and a voice said, "Oh, dear! Oh, dear! Am I late?"

"Here comes Mother Middy," said the girl with the taunting eyes.

The dumpling of a woman who bustled into the studio was breathless and apologetic. She had been hurrying, and wisps of gray hair were escaping in all directions from the confinement of her shapeless mouse-gray hat.

"Get us some coffee, dear," she said to her assistant. "I'm all upset. I just got a ticket for speeding. But the officer was so kind! They have such nice policemen on the force."

The decorator sat down heavily in a black and gold rocking chair. "Why don't you write a nice article about our policemen, Mr.—Mr.—"

"Qwilleran. Jim Qwilleran," he said. "I'm afraid that's not my department, but I'd like to write a nice article about you."

"Oh, dear! Oh, dear!" said Mrs. Middy, as she removed her hat and patted her hair.

The coffee came in rosebud-covered cups, and Miss Wright served it with her eyebrows arched in disapproval of the design. Then the decorator and the newsman discussed possibilities for *Gracious Abodes*.

"I've done some lovely interiors lately," said Mrs. Middy. "Dr. Mason's house is charming, but it isn't quite finished. We're waiting for lamps. Professor Dewitt's house is lovely, too, but the draperies aren't hung."

"The manufacturers discontinued the pattern," said Qwilleran.

"Yes! How did you know?" She rocked her chair violently. "Oh, dear! Oh, dear! What to do?"

"The housing?" her assistant whispered.

"Oh, yes, we've just finished some dormitories for the university," Mrs. Middy said, "and a sorority house for Delta Thelta, or whatever it's called. But those are out of town."

"Don't forget Mrs. Allison's," said Miss Wright.

"Oh, yes, Mrs. Allison's is really lovely. Would you be interested in a residence for career girls, Mr. Qwillum? It shows what can be done with a boardinghouse. It's one of those turn-of-the-century mansions on Merchant Street—all very gloomy and grotesque before Mrs. Allison called me in."

"It looked like a Victorian bordello," said Miss Wright.

"I used crewelwork in the living room and canopied beds in the girls' rooms. And the dining room turned out very well. Instead of one long table, which looks so institutional, I used lots of little skirted tables, like a café."

Qwilleran had been considering only private residences, but he was willing to publish anything that could be photographed in a hurry.

"What is the color scheme?" he asked.

"The theme is Cherry Red," said Mrs. Middy, "with variations. Upstairs it's all Cherry Pink. Oh, you'll love it! You'll just love it."

"Any chance of photographing this afternoon?"

"Oh, dear! That's too soon. People like to tidy up before the photographer comes."

"Tomorrow morning, then?"

"I'll call Mrs. Allison right away."

The decorator bustled to the telephone, and Alacoque Wright said to Qwilleran: "Mother Middy has done wonders with the Allison house. It doesn't look like a Victorian bordello anymore. It looks like an Early American bordello."

While the arrangements were being made, Qwilleran made an arrangement of his own with Miss Wright for Wednesday evening, at six o'clock, under the City Hall clock, and he left the Middy studio with a lilting sensation in his moustache. On the way back to the office he stopped at a gourmet shop and bought a can of smoked oysters for Koko.

That evening Qwilleran packed his books in three corrugated cartons from the grocery store and dusted his two pieces of luggage. Koko watched the process with concern. He had not touched the smoked oysters.

Qwilleran said, "What's the matter? Dieting?"

Koko began to prowl the apartment from one end to the other, occasionally stopping to sniff the cartons and utter a long, mournful howl.

"You're worried!" Qwilleran said. "You don't want to move." He picked up the cat and stroked his head reassuringly, then placed him on the open pages of the dictionary. "Come on, let's have a good rousing game to chase away the blues."

Koko dug his claws into the pages halfheartedly.

"*Balance* and *bald*," Qwilleran read. "Elementary! Two points for me. You'll have to try harder."

Koko grabbed again.

"*Kohistani* and *koolokamba*." Qwilleran knew the definition of the first, but he had to look up *koolokamba*. "A West African anthropoid ape with the head nearly bald and the face and hands black," he read. "That's great! That'll be a handy addition to my everyday vocabulary. Thanks a lot!"

At the end of nine innings Qwilleran had won, 14 to 4. For the most part Koko had turned up easy catchwords like *rook* and *root*, *frame* and *frank*.

"You're losing your knack," Qwilleran told him, and Koko responded with a long, indignant howl.

CHAPTER 8

ON WEDNESDAY MORNING Qwilleran and Bunsen drove to the Allison house on Merchant Street. Qwilleran said he hoped some of the girls would be there. Bunsen said he'd like to photograph one of the canopied beds with a girl in it.

The house was a Victorian monster—the love-song of a nineteenth-century carpenter enamored of his jigsaw—but it was freshly painted, and the windows exhibited perky curtains. Mrs. Middy met them at the door, wearing her shapeless hat and a frilly lace collar.

"Where's the girls?" Bunsen shouted. "Bring on the girls!"

"Oh, they're not here in the daytime," said Mrs. Middy. "They're working girls. Now, what would you like to see? Where would you like to start?"

"What I want to see," said the photographer, "is those bedrooms with canopied beds."

The decorator bustled around, plumping cushions and moving ashtrays. Then a haggard woman came from the rear of the house. Her face was colorless, and her hair was done up in rollers, covered by a net cap. She wore a housecoat of a depressing floral pattern, but her manner was hearty.

"Hello, boys," she said. "Make yourselves at home. I've unlocked the sideboard, if you want to pour a drink."

"It's too early for hooch," said Bunsen, "even for me."

"You want some coffee?" Mrs. Allison turned her face toward the rear of the house, and shouted. "*Elsie, bring some coffee!*" To her guests she said, "Do you boys like sticky buns? . . . *Elsie, bring some sticky buns!*"

There was a piping, unintelligible reply from the kitchen.

"*Then find something else!*" yelled Mrs. Allison.

"It's a nice place you've got here," Qwilleran said.

"It pays to run a decent establishment," said the house mother, "and Mrs. Middy knows how to make a place comfortable. She doesn't come cheap, but she's worth every penny."

"Why did you choose Early American for your house?"

For an answer Mrs. Allison turned to the decorator. "Why did I choose Early American?"

"Because it's homey and inviting," said Mrs. Middy. "And because it is part of our national heritage."

"You can quote me," Mrs. Allison said to Qwilleran with a generous gesture. She went to the sideboard. "Sure you don't want a drink? I'm going to have one myself."

She poured a straight rye, and as the decorator showed the newsmen about the house, Mrs. Allison trailed after them, carrying her glass in one hand and the bottle in the other. Qwilleran made notes on crewelwork, dry sinks, and Queen Anne candlesticks. The photographer formed an attachment for a ship's figurehead over the living-room mantel—an old wood carving of a full-busted mermaid with chipped nose and peeling paint.

He said, "Reminds me of a girl I used to date."

"That's one I caught and had stuffed," said Mrs. Allison. "You should've seen the one that got away."

Mrs. Middy said: "Look at the skirts on these little café tables, Mr. Qwillum. Aren't they sweet? They're slightly Victorian, but Mrs. Allison didn't want the interior to be too *pure*."

"It's all pretty elegant," Qwilleran said to the house mother. "I suppose you're fussy about the kind of girls you get in here."

"You better believe it. They gotta have references and at least two years of college." She poured another ounce in her glass.

The bedrooms were vividly pink. They had pink walls, pink carpet, and even pinker side curtains on the four-poster beds.

"Love this shade of green!" said Bunsen.

"How do the girls react to all this pink?" Qwilleran asked.

Mrs. Allison turned to the decorator. "How do the girls react to all this pink?"

"They find it warm and stimulating," said the decorator. "Notice the hand-painted mirror frames, Mr. Qwillum."

Bunsen photographed one bedroom, the living room, a corner of the dining room, and a close-up of the ship's figurehead. He was finished before noon.

"Come around and meet the girls some evening," Mrs. Allison said, as the newsmen made their goodbyes.

"Got any blondes?" asked the photographer.

"You name it. We got it."

"Okay, some night when I can get out of washing the dishes and helping the kids with their homework, I'll be around to collect that drink."

"Don't wait too long. You're not getting any younger," Mrs. Allison said cheerily.

As the newsmen carried the photographic equipment to the car, Mrs. Middy came hurrying after them. "Oh, dear! Oh, dear!" she said. "I forgot to tell you: Mrs. Allison doesn't want you to use her name or address."

"We always use names," Qwilleran said.

"Oh, dear! I was afraid so. But she thinks the girls will get crank phone calls if you print the name and address. And she wants to avoid that."

"It's a newspaper policy to tell who and where," Qwilleran explained. "A story is incomplete without it."

"Oh, dear! Then we'll have to cancel the story. What a pity!"

"Cancel it! We can't cancel it! We're right on deadline!"

"Oh, dear! Then you'll have to write it up without the name and address," said Mrs. Middy.

She no longer looked like a dumpling to Qwilleran. She looked like a granite boulder in a fussy lace collar.

Bunsen said to his partner in a low voice: "You're trapped. Do what the old gal wants."

"You think I should?"

"We don't have time to pick up another cover story."

Mrs. Middy said: "Just say that it's a residence for professional girls. That sounds nicer than career girls, don't you think? And don't forget to mention the name of the decorator!" She shook a playful finger at the newsmen.

As they drove away from the house on Merchant Street, Bunsen said, "You can't win 'em all."

Qwilleran was not cheered by this philosophy, and they drove in silence until Bunsen said, "They buried the Tait woman this morning."

"I know."

"The chief assigned two photographers. That's pretty good coverage for a funeral. He only sent *one* to the international boat races last week."

Bunsen lit a cigar, and Qwilleran opened his window wide.

The photographer said, "Have you moved into the Villa Verandah with the bigwigs yet?"

"I'm moving in this afternoon. And then I've got a dinner date with Mrs. Middy's assistant."

"I hope she's got references and two years of college."

"She's quite a dish. Clever, too!"

"Look out for the clever ones," the photographer warned him. "The dumb ones are safer."

Late that afternoon Qwilleran went home, packed his two suitcases, and called a taxi. Then he proceeded to stuff the cat into a canned tuna fish carton with airholes punched in the sides. Suddenly Koko had seventeen legs, all grabbing and struggling at once, and his verbal protests added to the confusion.

"I know! I know!" shouted Qwilleran above the din. "But it's the best I can do."

When the seventeen paws, nine ears, and three tails were tucked in, and the cover clapped shut and roped, Koko found himself in a snug, dark, sheltered place, and he settled down. The only sign of life was a glistening eye, seen through one of the airholes.

Once, during the brief ride to the Villa Verandah, the taxi swerved to avoid hitting a bus, and from the back seat came an outraged scream.

"My God!" yelled the driver, slamming on the brakes. "What'd I do?"

"It's only my cat," said Qwilleran. "I've got a cat in one of these boxes."

"I thought I hit a pedestrian. What is it? A bobcat?"

"He's a Siamese. They're inclined to be outspoken."

"Oh, yeah. I've seen 'em on television. Ugly buggers."

Qwilleran's moustache curled. He was never overly generous with gratuities, but he remembered to give the driver a tip lighter than usual.

At the Villa Verandah, Koko produced earsplitting howls in the elevator, but as soon as he was released from his box in the Noyton apartment, he was speechless. For a moment he stood poised with one forepaw lifted, and the place was filled with breathless, listening cat-silence. Then his head swung from side to side as he observed the general features of the room. He walked cautiously across the sleek wood floor. He sniffed the edge of the thick-piled rug and extended one paw experimentally, but withdrew it at once. He nosed the corner of one sofa, examined the hem of the draperies, looked in the wastebasket near the desk.

Qwilleran showed Koko the new location of his sandbox and gave him his old toy mouse. "Your cushion's on the refrigerator," he told the cat. "Make yourself at home."

An unfamiliar bell rang, and Koko jumped in alarm.

"It's only the phone," Qwilleran said, picking up the receiver and seating himself importantly behind the fine leather-topped desk.

From the instrument came a voice speaking in careful English. "I have a transatlantic call for Mr. James Qwilleran."

"Speaking."

"Copenhagen calling."

Then came the excited voice of Harry Noyton. "Would you believe it? I'm in Copenhagen already! How's everything? Did you move in? Did you get settled?"

"Just got here. How was the flight?"

"Some turbulence east of Gander, but it was a good trip on the whole. Don't forward any mail till I give the signal. I'll keep in touch. And one of these days I'll have a scoop for the *Daily Fluxion*."

"A news story?"

"Something fantastic! Can't talk about it yet . . . But here's why I called: Do you like baseball? There's a pair of tickets for the charity game, stuck in my desk calendar. It's a shame to let them go to waste—especially at thirty bucks a throw."

"I'll probably have to work Saturday."

"Then give them to your pals at the paper."

"How do you like Copenhagen?"

"It looks very clean, very tidy. Lots of bicycles."

"How soon will your news break?"

"Hopefully, within a week," said Noyton. "And when it does, the *Fluxion* gets the first crack at it!"

After hanging up, Qwilleran looked for Noyton's calendar. He found it in the desk drawer—a large leather-bound book with a diary on one side and an index for telephone numbers on the other. The baseball tickets

were clipped to September 26—box seats behind the dugout—and
Qwilleran wondered whether he should use them or give them away. He
could invite Alacoque Wright, break away from the office at noon on Saturday . . .

"Koko!" he snapped. "Get away from that book!"

The cat had risen noiselessly to the top of the desk and was sinking his
claws in the edge of the telephone index. He was trying to play the game.
Qwilleran's moustache twitched. He could not resist opening the book to
the page Koko had selected.

On it he found the telephone numbers of a Dr. Thomas and the well-
known law firm of Teahandle, Burris, Hansblow, Maus, and Castle.

"Congratulations!" Qwilleran said to the cat. "You've cornered a
Maus."

There was also Tappington, the stockbroker, and the phone number
of Toledo, the most expensive restaurant in town. And at the bottom of
the list there was the name Tait. Not George Tait or Verning Tait, but
Signe Tait.

Qwilleran stared at the hastily scrawled name as if it were the ghost of
the dead woman. Why had Noyton listed Signe and not her husband?
What business did a big-time promoter have with the invalid wife of a
rich, idle collector of jades?

Qwilleran recalled his conversation with Noyton at David's party. The
jade theft had been discussed, but the promoter had not mentioned his acquaintance with the late Mrs. Tait. And yet he was an unabashed name-
dropper, and the Tait name would have been an impressive one to drop.

Qwilleran closed the book slowly and opened it again quickly. He
went through the diary, checking Noyton's appointments day by day. He
started with September 20 and worked backward to January 1. There was
no entry concerning Signe Tait or Muggy Swamp. But the color of ink
changed around the first of September. For most of the year it had been
blue. Then Noyton switched to black. Signe Tait's phone number was
written in black; it had been added within the last three weeks.

CHAPTER 9

BEFORE LEAVING the apartment for his date with Alacoque Wright, Qwilleran telephoned David Lyke to inquire about Mrs. Tait's funeral.

"You should have been there," said the decorator. "There was enough blue blood to float a ship. All the Old Guard who knew Tait's pappy and grandpappy. You never saw so many pince-nez and Queen Mary hats."

"How was Tait taking it?"

"I wish I could say he looked pale and haggard, but with that healthy flush of his he always looks as if he'd just won at tennis. Why weren't you there?"

"I was working on a cover story. And this afternoon I moved into Harry Noyton's apartment."

"Good! We're neighbors," David said. "Why don't you come over Saturday night and meet Natalie Noyton? She just got back from Reno, and I'm having a few people in for drinks."

Qwilleran recalled the excellence of the buffet at the decorator's last party and accepted the invitation with alacrity. After that, he prepared a hasty dinner for Koko—half a can of red salmon garnished with a raw egg yolk—and said: "Be a good cat. I'll be home late and fix you a snack."

At six o'clock sharp he met Alacoque Wright under the City Hall clock; her punctuality had an architectural precision. She was wearing a curious medley of a green skirt, turquoise top, and blue cape in a weave that reminded Qwilleran of dining-room chair seats somewhere in his forgotten past.

"I made it myself—out of upholstery samples," she said, peering at him from under a quantity of glossy brown hair that enveloped her head, shoulders, and much of her face.

He took her to the Press Club for dinner, aware that he was being observed by all the regulars at the bar and would have to account, the next day, for his taste in women. Nevertheless, it had to be the Press Club. He had a charge account there, and payday was not until Friday. He ushered his date—she asked Qwilleran to call her Cokey—upstairs to the main dining room, where the atmosphere was quieter and the rolls were sprinkled with poppy seeds.

"Have a cocktail?" Qwilleran invited. "I'm on the wagon myself, but I'll have a lemon and seltzer to keep you company."

Cokey looked keenly interested. "Why aren't you drinking?"

"It's a long story, and the less said about it, the better." He put a matchbook under one table leg; all the Press Club tables had a built-in wobble.

"I'm on a yoga kick myself," she said. "No liquor. No meat. But I'll make us one of nature's own cocktails if you'll order the ingredients and two champagne glasses."

When the tray arrived, she poured a little cream into each glass, filled it with ginger ale, and then produced a small wooden device from her handbag.

"I carry my own nutmeg and grate it fresh," she said, dusting the surface of the drinks with brown spice. "Nutmeg is a stimulant. The Germans put it in everything."

Qwilleran took a cautious sip. The drink had a bite. It was like Cokey—cool and smooth, with an unexpected pepperiness. "How did you decide to become an architect?" he asked.

"Maybe you haven't noticed," said Cokey, "but there are more architects named Wright than there are judges named Murphy. We seem to gravitate to the drafting board. However, the name is getting me nowhere." She stroked her long hair lovingly. "I may have to give up the struggle and find a husband."

"Shouldn't be difficult."

"I'm glad you're so confident." She set her jaw and ground some more nutmeg on her cocktail. "Tell me what you think of the decorating profession after two weeks in the velvet jungle?"

"They seem to be likable people."

"They're children! They live in a world of play." A shadow passed over Cokey's face—the sliver of face that was visible. "And, just like children, they can be cruel." She studied the grains of nutmeg clinging to the inside of her empty glass and, catlike, darted out a pink tongue to lick it clean.

A man walked past the table and said, "Hi, there, Cokey."

She looked up abruptly. "Well, hello!" she said with meaning in the inflection.

"You know him?" Qwilleran asked in surprise.

"We've met," said Cokey. "I'm getting hungry. May we order?"

She looked at the menu and asked for brook trout with a large garnish of parsley, and a small salad. Qwilleran compared her taut figure with his own well-padded beltline and felt guilty as he ordered bean soup, hefty steak and a baked potato with sour cream.

"Are you divorced?" Cokey asked suddenly.

Qwilleran nodded.

"That's cool. Where do you live?"

"I moved into the Villa Verandah today." He waited for her eyes to open wide, and then added in a burst of honesty, "The apartment belongs to a friend who's gone abroad."

"Do you like living alone?"

"I don't live alone," said Qwilleran. "I have a cat. A Siamese."

"I adore cats," Cokey squealed. "What's your cat's name?"

Qwilleran beamed at her. People who really appreciated animals always asked their names. "His real name is Kao K'o-Kung, but he's called Koko for everyday purposes. I considered myself a dog man until I met Koko. He's a remarkable animal. Perhaps you remember the murder on Blenheim Place last spring. Koko is the cat who was involved, and if I told you some of his intellectual feats you wouldn't believe me."

"Oh, I'd believe anything about cats. They're uncanny."

"Sometimes I'm convinced Koko senses what's going to happen."

"It's true! Cats tune in with their whiskers."

"That's what I've been told," said Qwilleran, preening his moustache absently. "Koko always gives the impression that he knows more than I do, and he has clever ways of communicating. Not that he does anything uncatlike, you understand. Yet, somehow he gets his ideas across. . . . I'm not explaining this very well."

"I know exactly what you mean."

Qwilleran looked at Cokey with appreciation. These were matters he could not discuss with his friends at the *Fluxion*. With their beagles and boxers as a frame of reference, how could they understand about cats? In this one area of his life he experienced a kind of loneliness. But Cokey understood. Her mischievous green eyes had mellowed into an expression of rapport.

He reached over and took her hand—the slender, tapering hand that was playing tiddledywinks with stray poppyseeds on the tablecloth. He said, "Have you ever heard of a cat eating spider webs—or glue? Koko has started licking gummed envelopes. One day he chewed up a dollar's worth of postage stamps."

"I used to have a cat who drank soapsuds," Cokey said. "They're individualists. Does Koko scratch furniture? It was noble of your friend to let you move into his apartment with a cat."

"Koko does all his scratching on an old unabridged dictionary," Qwilleran said with a note of pride.

"How literary of him!"

"It's not really an *old* dictionary," he explained. "It's the new edition. The man Koko used to live with bought it for himself and then decided he preferred the old edition, so he gave the new one to the cat for a scratching pad."

"I admire men who admire cats."

Qwilleran lowered his voice and spoke confidentially. "We have a game we play with this dictionary. Koko exercises his claws, and I add a few words to my vocabulary . . . This is something I wouldn't want to get around the Press Club, you understand."

Cokey looked at him mistily. "I think you're wonderful," she said. "I'd love to play the game sometime."

When Qwilleran arrived home that evening, it was late, and he was exhausted. Girls like Cokey made him realize he was not so young as he used to be.

He unlocked the door of his apartment and was groping for the light switch when he saw two red sparks in the darkened living room. They glowed with supernatural light. He had seen them before, and he knew what they were, but they always gave him a scare.

"Koko!" he said. "Is that you?"

He flipped the lights on, and the mysterious red lights in Koko's eyes were extinguished.

The cat approached with arched back, question-mark tail, and the backswept whiskers of disapproval. He made vehement one-note complaints.

"I'm sorry," said Qwilleran. "Did you think you were abandoned? You'll never believe this, but we went for a walk—a long walk. That's what lady architects like to do on a date—take you for a walk, looking at buildings. I'm bushed!" He sank into a chair and kicked off his shoes without untying the laces. "For three hours we've been looking at architecture: insensitive massing, inefficient site-planning, trite fenestration . . ."

Koko was howling impatiently at his knee, and Qwilleran picked up the cat, laid him across his shoulder, and patted the sleek fur. He could feel the muscles struggling beneath the pelt, and Koko wriggled away and jumped down.

"Is something wrong?" Qwilleran asked.

"YOW-OW!" said Koko.

He ran to the Spanish chest that housed the stereo set. It was a massive carved piece built close to the floor, resting on four bun-shaped feet. Koko plumped to the floor in front of it, stretched one foreleg, and vainly tried to reach under the chest, his brown tail tensed in a scimitar curve.

Qwilleran uttered a weary moan. He knew the cat had lost his home-made mouse—a bouquet of dried mint leaves tied in the toe of an old sock. He also knew there would be no sleeping that night until the mouse was retrieved. He looked for something to poke under the chest. Broomstick? There was no broom in the kitchen closet; the maids evidently used their own sweeping equipment. . . . Fireplace poker? There were no fireplaces at the Villa Verandah. . . . Umbrella? If Noyton owned one, he had taken it to Europe. . . . Fishing rod? Golf club? Tennis racquet? The man seemed to have no active hobbies. . . . Backscratcher? Long-handled shoehorn? Clarinet? Discarded crutch?

With Koko at his heels, yowling imperious Siamese commands, Qwilleran searched the premises. He though wistfully of all the long, slender implements he could use: tree branch, fly swatter—buggy whip.

Eventually he lowered himself to the floor. Lying flat, he reached under the low chest and gingerly extracted a penny, a gold earring, an olive pit, a crumbled scrap of paper, several dustballs, and finally a familiar gray wad of indefinite shape.

Koko pounced on his mouse, sniffed it once without much interest, and gave it a casual whack with his paw. It went back under the Spanish chest, and Koko sauntered away to get a drink of water before retiring for the night.

But Qwilleran stayed up smoking his pipe and thinking about many things: Cokey and nutmeg cocktails, *Gracious Abodes* and Mrs. Middy's lace collar, buggy whips and the situation in Muggy Swamp. Once he went to the wastebasket and fished out the crumpled paper he had found beneath the Spanish chest. There was only a name on it: Arne Thorvaldson. He dropped it in the basket again. The gold earring he tossed in the desk drawer with the paper clips.

CHAPTER 10

ON THE DAY following the funeral, Qwilleran telephoned G. Verning Tait and asked if he might call and deliver the books on jade. He said he always liked to return borrowed books promptly.

Tait acquiesced in a voice that was neither cold nor cordial, and Qwilleran could imagine the crimping of the mouth that accompanied it.

"How did you get this number?" Tait asked.

Qwilleran passed a hand swiftly over his face and hoped he was saying the right thing. " I believe this is—yes, this must be the number that David Lyke gave me."

"I was merely curious. It's an unlisted number."

Qwilleran put Noyton's address book away in the desk, stroked Koko's head for luck, and drove to Muggy Swamp in a company car. It was a wild shot, but he was hoping to see or hear something that would reinforce his hunch—his vague suspicion that all was not exactly as represented on the police record.

He had planned no particular approach—just the Qwilleran Technique. In twenty-five years of newspapering around the country he had enjoyed astounding success in interviewing criminals (described as tight-lipped), old ladies (timid), politicians (cautious), and cowboys (taciturn). He asked no prying questions on these occasions. He just smoked his pipe, murmured encouraging phrases, prodded gently, and wore an expression of sympathetic concern, which was enhanced by the sober aspect of his moustache.

Tait himself, wearing his usual high color and another kind of silk sports shirt, admitted the newsman to the glittering foyer. Qwilleran looked inquiringly toward the living room, but the double doors were closed.

The collector invited him into the library. "Did you enjoy the books?" he said. "Are you beginning to feel the lure of jade? Do you think you might like to collect?"

"I'm afraid it's beyond my means at the moment," said Qwilleran, adding a small falsehood: "I'm subletting Harry Noyton's apartment at the Villa Verandah, and this little spree is keeping me broke."

The name brought no sign of recognition. Tait said: "You can start collecting in a modest way. I can give you the name of a dealer who likes to help beginners. Do you still have your jade button?"

"Carry it all the time!" Qwilleran jingled the contents of his trouser pocket. Then he asked solemnly, "Did Mrs. Tait share your enthusiasm for jade?"

The corners of Tait's mouth quivered. "Unfortunately, Mrs. Tait never warmed to the fascination of jade, but collecting it and working with it have been a joy and a comfort to me for more than fifteen years. Would you like to see my workshop?" He led the way to the rear of the house and down a flight of basement stairs.

"This is a rambling house," said Qwilleran. "I imagine an intercom system comes in handy."

"Please excuse the appearance of my shop," the collector said. "It is not as tidy as it should be. I've dismissed the housekeeper. I'm getting ready to go away."

"I suppose you'll be traveling to jade country," said Qwilleran hopefully.

His supposition got no verification.

Tait said: "Have you ever seen a lapidary shop? It's strange, but when I am down here in this hideaway, cutting and polishing, I forget everything. My back ailment gives me no discomfort, and I am a happy man." He handed the newsman a small carved dragon. "This is the piece the police found behind Paolo's bed when they searched his room. It's a fairly simple design. I've been trying to copy it."

"You must feel very bitter about that boy," Qwilleran said.

Tait averted his eyes. "Bitterness accomplishes nothing."

"Frankly, his implication came as a shock to me. He seemed an open, ingenuous young man."

"People are not always what they seem."

"Could it be that Paolo was used as a tool by the real organizers of the crime?"

"That is a possibility, of course, but it doesn't bring back my jades."

"Mr. Tait," said Qwilleran, "for what it is worth, I want you to know I have a strong feeling the stolen objects will be found."

"I wish I could share your optimism." Then the collector showed a spark of curiosity. "What makes you feel that way?"

"There's a rumor at the paper that the police are on the track of something." It was not the first time Qwilleran had spread the rumor of a rumor, and it often got results.

"Strange they have not communicated with me," said Tait. He led the way up the stairs and to the front door.

"Perhaps I shouldn't have mentioned it," Qwilleran said. Then casually he remarked, "That housekeeper of yours—would she take a temporary job while you're away? A friend of mine will need a housekeeper while his wife is in the hospital, and it's hard to get good help on a short-term basis."

"I have no doubt that Mrs. Hawkins needs work," said Tait.

"How long before you'll be needing her again?"

"I don't intend to take her back," said Tait. "Her work is satisfactory, but she has an unfortunate personality."

"If you don't mind, then, I'd like to give her phone number to my friend."

Tait stepped into his library and wrote the information on a slip of paper. "I'll also give you the name and address of that jade dealer in Chicago," he said, "just in case you change your mind."

As they passed the living room Qwilleran looked hungrily at the closed doors. "Did Paolo do any damage in opening the cases?"

"No. No damage. It's small comfort," Tait said sadly, "but I like to think the jades were taken by someone who loved them."

As Qwilleran drove away from Muggy Swamp, he felt that he had wasted a morning and two gallons of *Daily Fluxion* gas. Yet, throughout the visit, he had felt a teasing discomfort about the upper lip. He thought he sensed something false in the collector's pose. The man should have been sadder—or madder. And then there was that heart-wringing curtain line: "I like to think the jades were stolen by someone who loved them."

"Oh, brother!" Qwilleran said aloud. "What a ham!"

His morning of snooping had only whetted his curiosity, and now he headed for the place where he might get some answers to his questions. He drove to the shop called PLUG on River Street.

It was an unlikely spot for a decorating studio. PLUG looked self-consciously dapper among the dilapidated storefronts devoted to plumbing supplies and used cash registers.

The merchandise in the window was attractively arranged against a background of kitchen oilcloth in a pink kitten design. There were vases of ostrich plumes, chunks of broken concrete painted in phosphorescent colors, and bowls of eggs trimmed with sequins. The price tags were small and refined, befitting an exclusive shop: $5 each for the eggs, $15 for a chunk of concrete.

Qwilleran walked into the shop (the door handle was a gilded replica of the Statue of Liberty), and a bell announced his presence by tinkling the four notes of "How Dry I Am." Immediately, from behind a folding screen composed of old *Reader's Digest* covers, came the genial proprietor, Bob Orax, looking more fastidious than ever among the tawdry merchandise. There were paper flowers pressed under glass, trays decorated with cigar brands, and candelabra made out of steer horns, standing on crocheted doilies. One entire wall was paved with a mosaic of pop-bottle caps. Others were decorated with supermarket ads and candy-bar wrappers matted in red velvet and framed in gilt.

"So this is your racket!" said Qwilleran. "Who buys this stuff?"

"Planned Ugliness appeals to those who are bored with Beauty, tired of Taste, and fed up with Function," said Orax brightly. "People can't stand too much beauty. It's against the human grain. This new movement is a revolt of the sophisticated intellectual. The conventional middle-class customer rejects it."

"Do you design interiors around this theme?"

"Definitely! I have just done a morning room for a client, mixing Depression Overstuffed with Mail Order Modern. Very effective. I paneled one wall in corrugated metal siding from an old toolshed, in the original rust. The color scheme is Cinnamon and Parsnip with accents of Dill Weed."

Qwilleran examined a display of rattraps made into ashtrays.

"Those are little boutique items for the impulse buyer," said Orax, and he added with an arch smile, "I hope you understand that I'm not emotionally involved with this trend. True, it requires a degree of connoisseurship, but I'm in it primarily to make a buck, if I may quote Shakespeare."

Qwilleran browsed for a while and then said: "That was a good party at David's place on Monday night. I hear he's giving another one on Saturday—for Mrs. Noyton."

"I shall not be there," said Orax with regret. "Mother is giving a dinner party, and if I am not on hand to mix good stiff drinks for the guests, Mother's friends will discover how atrocious her cooking really is! Mother was not born to the apron. . . . But you will enjoy meeting Natalie Noyton. She has all the gagging appeal of a marshmallow sundae."

Qwilleran toyed with a pink plastic flamingo that lit up. "Were the Noytons and the Taits particularly friendly?" he asked.

Orax was amused. "I doubt whether they would move in the same social circles."

"Oh," said Qwilleran with an innocent expression. "I thought I had heard that Harry Noyton knew Mrs. Tait."

"Really?" The Orax eyebrows went up higher. "An unlikely pair! If it were Georgie Tait and Natalie, that might make sense. Mother says Georgie used to be quite a womanizer." He saw Qwilleran inspecting some chromium bowls. "Those are 1959 hubcaps, now very much in demand for salads and flower arrangements."

"How long had Mrs. Tait been confined to a wheelchair?"

"Mother says it happened after the scandal, and that must have been sixteen or eighteen years ago. I was away at Princeton at the time, but I understand it was quite a brouhaha, and Siggy immediately developed her indisposition."

Qwilleran patted his alerted moustache and cleared his throat before saying, "Scandal? What scandal?"

The decorator's eyes danced. "Oh, didn't you *know*? It was a juicy affair! You should look it up in your morgue. I'm sure the *Fluxion* has an extensive file on the subject." He picked up a feather duster and whisked it over a tray of tiny objects. "These are Cracker Jack prizes, circa 1930," he said. "Genuine tin, and very collectible. My knowledgeable customers are buying them as investments."

Qwilleran rushed back to the *Daily Fluxion* and asked the clerk in the library for the file on the Tait family.

Without a word she disappeared among the gray rows of head-high filing cabinets, moving with the speed of a sleepwalker. She returned empty-handed. "It's not here."

"Did someone check it out?"

"I don't know."

"Would you mind consulting whatever records you keep and telling me who signed for it?" Qwilleran said with impatience.

The clerk ambled away and returned with a yawn. "Nobody signed for it."

"Then where is it?" he yelled. "You must have a file on an important family like the Taits!"

Another clerk stood on tiptoe and called across a row of files, "Are you talking about G. Verning Tait? It's a big file. A man from the Police Department was in here looking at it. He wanted to take it to Headquarters, but we told him he couldn't take it out of the building."

"He must have sneaked it out," said Qwilleran. "Some of those cops are connivers. . . . Where's your boss?"

The first clerk said, "It's his day off."

"Well, you tell him to get hold of the Police Department and get that file back here. Can you remember that?"

"Remember what?"

"Never mind. I'll write him a memo."

CHAPTER 11

ON SATURDAY AFTERNOON Qwilleran took Alacoque Wright to the ballpark, and listened to her views on baseball.

"Of course," she said, "the game's basic appeal is erotic. All that symbolism, you know, and those sensual movements!"

She was wearing something she had made from a bedspread. "Mrs. Middy custom-ordered it for a king-size bed," she explained, "and it was delivered in queen-size, so I converted it into a costume suit."

Her converted bedspread was green corduroy with an irregular plush pile like rows of marching caterpillars.

"Very tasteful," Qwilleran remarked.

Cokey tossed her cascade of hair. "It wasn't intended to be tasteful. It was intended to be sexy."

After dinner at a chophouse (Cokey had a crab leg and some stewed plums; Qwilleran had the works), the newsman said: "We're invited to a party tonight, and I'm going to do something rash. I'm taking you to meet a young man who is apparently irresistible to women of all ages, sizes, and shapes."

"Don't worry," said Cokey, giving his hand a blithe squeeze. "I prefer older men."

"I'm not *that* much older."

"But you're so mature. That's important to a person like me."

They rode to the Villa Verandah in a taxi, holding hands. At the building entrance they were greeted with enthusiasm by the doorman, whom Qwilleran had foresightedly tipped that afternoon. It was not a large tip by Villa Verandah standards, but it commanded a dollar's worth of attention from a man dressed like a nineteenth-century Prussian general.

They walked into the lofty lobby—all white marble, plate glass, and stainless steel—and Cokey nodded approval. She had become suddenly quiet. As they ascended in the automatic elevator, Qwilleran gave her a quick private hug.

The door to David's apartment was opened by a white-coated Oriental, and there was a flash of recognition when he saw Qwilleran. No one ever forgot the newsman's moustache. Then the host surged forward, radiating charm, and Cokey slipped her hand through Qwilleran's arm. He felt her grip tighten when Lyke acknowledged the introduction with his rumbling voice and drooping eyelids.

The apartment was filled with guests—clients of David's chattering about their analysts, and fellow decorators discussing the Spanish exhibition at the museum and the new restaurant in Greektown.

"There's a simply marvelous seventeenth-century Isabellina *vargueno* in the show."

"The restaurant will remind you of that little place in Athens near the Acropolis. You know the one."

Qwilleran led Cokey to the buffet. "When I'm with decorators," he said, "I feel I'm in a never-never land. They never discuss anything serious or unpleasant."

"Decorators have only two worries: discontinued patterns and slow deliveries," Cokey said. "They have no real problems." There was scorn in the curl of her lips.

"Such disapproval can't be purely professional. I suspect you were jilted by a decorator once."

"Or twice." She smoothed her long straight hair self-consciously. "Try these little crabmeat things. They've got lots of pepper in them."

Although Qwilleran had dined recently and well, he had no difficulty in trying the lobster salad, the crusty brown potato balls flavored with garlic, the strips of ginger-spiced beef skewered on slivers of bamboo, and the hot buttered cornbread filled with ham. He had a feeling of well-being. He looked at Cokey with satisfaction. He liked her spirit, and the provocative face peeking out from that curtain of hair, and the coltish grace of her figure.

Then he glanced over her shoulder toward the living room, and suddenly Cokey looked plain. Natalie Noyton had arrived.

Harry Noyton's ex-wife was plump in all areas except for an incongru-ously small waist and tiny ankles. Her face was pretty, like a peach, and she had peach-colored hair ballooning about her head.

One of the decorators said, "How did you like the Wild West, Natalie?"

"I didn't pay any attention to it," she replied in a small shrill voice. "I just stayed in a boardinghouse in Reno and worked on my rug. I made one of those shaggy Danish rugs with a needle. Does anybody want to buy a handmade rug in Cocoa and Celery Green?"

"You've put on weight, Natalie."

"Ooh, have I ever! All I did was work on my rug and eat peanut butter. I love crunchy peanut butter."

Natalie was wearing a dress that matched her hair—a sheath of loosely woven wool with golden glints. A matching stole with long crinkly fringe was draped over her shoulders.

Cokey, who was giving Natalie an oblique inspection, said to Qwil-leran: "That fabric must be something she loomed herself, in between peanut-butter sandwiches. It would have been smarter without the metal-lic threads."

"What would an architect call that color?" he asked.

"I'd call it a yellow-pink of low saturation and medium brilliance."

"A decorator would call it Cream of Carrot," he said, "or Sweet Potato Soufflé."

After Natalie had been welcomed and teased and flattered and con-gratulated by those who knew her, David Lyke brought her to meet Qwilleran and Cokey. He told her, "The *Daily Fluxion* might want to pho-tograph your house in the Hills. What do you think?"

"Do *you* want it photographed, David?"

"It's your house, darling. You decide."

Natalie said to Qwilleran: "I'm moving out as soon as I find a studio. And then my husband—my ex-husband—is going to sell the house."

"I hear it's really something," said the newsman.

"It's super! Simply super! David has oodles of talent." She looked at the decorator adoringly.

Lyke explained: "I corrected some of the architect's mistakes and changed the window detail so we could hang draperies. Natalie wove the draperies herself. They're a work of art."

"Well, look, honey," said Natalie, "if it will do you any good, let's put the house in the paper."

"Suppose we let Mr. Qwilleran have a look at it."

"All right," she said. "How about Monday morning? I have a hair appointment in the afternoon."

Qwilleran said, "Do you have your looms at the house?"

"Ooh, yes! I have two great big looms and a small one. I'm crazy about weaving. David, honey, show them that sports coat I did for you."

Lyke hesitated for the flicker of an eyelid. "Darling, it's at the cleaner," he said. Later he remarked to Qwilleran: "I use some of her yardage out of friendship, but her work leaves a lot to be desired. She's just an amateur with no taste and no talent, so don't emphasize the hand-weaving if you publish the house."

The evening followed the usual Lyke pattern: a splendid buffet, drinks in abundance, music for dancing played a trifle too loud, and ten conversations in progress simultaneously. It had all the elements of a good party, but Qwilleran found himself feeling troubled at David Lyke's last remark. At his first opportunity he asked Natalie to dance, and said, "I hear you're going into the weaving business on the professional level."

"Yes, I'm going to do custom work for decorators," she said in her high-pitched voice that sounded vulnerable and pathetic. "David loves my weaving. He says he'll get me a lot of commissions."

She was an ample armful, and the glittering wool dress she wore was delectably soft, except for streaks of scratchiness where the fabric was shot with gold threads.

As they danced, she went on chattering, and Qwilleran's mind wandered. If this woman was banking her career on David's endorsement, she was in for a surprise. Natalie said she was hunting for a studio, and she had a cousin who was a newspaperman, and she loved smoked oysters, and the balconies at the Villa Verandah were too windy. Qwilleran said he had just moved into an apartment there, but refrained from mentioning whose. He speculated on the chances of sneaking a few tidbits from the buffet for his cat.

"Ooh, do you have a cat?" Natalie squealed. "Does he like lobster?"

"He likes anything that's expensive. I think he reads price tags."

"Why don't you go and get him? We'll give him some lobster."

Qwilleran doubted whether Koko would like the noisy crowd, but he liked to show off his handsome pet, and he went to get him. The cat was half asleep on his refrigerator cushion, and he was the picture of relaxation, sprawled on his back in a position of utter abandon, with one foreleg flung out in space and the other curled around his ears. He looked at

Qwilleran upside down with half an inch of pink tongue protruding and an insane gleam in his slanted, half-closed eyes.

"Get up," said Qwilleran, "and quit looking like an idiot. You're going to a soirée."

By the time Koko arrived at the party, sitting on Qwilleran's shoulder, he had regained his dignity. At his entrance the noise swelled to a crescendo and then stopped altogether. Koko surveyed the scene with regal condescension, like a potentate honoring his subjects with his presence. He blinked not, neither did he move a whisker. His brown points were so artistically contrasted with his light body, his fur was shaded so subtly, and his sapphire eyes had such unadorned elegance that he made David Lyke's guests look gaudily overdressed.

Then the first exclamation broke through the silence, and everyone came forward to stroke the silky fur.

"Why, it feels like ermine!"

"I'm going to throw out my mink."

Koko tolerated the attention but remained aloof until Natalie spoke to him. He stretched his neck and sniffed her extended finger.

"Ooh, can I hold him?" she asked, and to Qwilleran's surprise Koko went gladly into her arms, snuggling in her wooly stole, sniffing it with serious concentration, and purring audibly.

Cokey pulled Qwilleran away. "It makes me so mad," she said, "when I think of all the trouble I take to stay thin and get my hair straightened and improve my conversation! Then *she* comes in, babbling and looking frizzy and thirty pounds overweight, and everybody goes for her, including the cat!"

Qwilleran experienced a pang of sympathy for Cokey, mixed with something else. "I shouldn't leave Koko here too long, among all these strangers," he said. "It might upset his stomach. Let's take him back to 15-F, and you can have a look at my apartment."

"I've brought my nutmeg grater," she said. "Do you happen to have any cream and ginger ale?"

Qwilleran retrieved Koko from Natalie's stole, and led Cokey around the long curving corridor to the other wing.

When he threw open the door of his apartment, Cokey paused for one breathless moment on the threshold and then ran into the living room with her arms flung wide. "It's glorious!" she cried.

"Harry Noyton calls it Scandihoovian."

"The green chair is Danish, and so is the end-wood floor," Cokey told him, "and the dining chairs are Finnish. But the whole apartment is like a designers' Hall of Fame. Bertoia, Wegner, Aalto, Mies, Nakashima! It's too magnificent! I can't bear it!" She collapsed in the cushions of a suede sofa and put her face in her hands.

Qwilleran brought champagne glasses filled with a creamy liquid, and solemnly Cokey ground the nutmeg on the bubbling surface.

"To Cokey, my favorite girl," he said, lifting his glass. "Skinny, straight-haired, and articulate!"

"Now I feel better," she said, and she kicked off her shoes and wiggled her toes in the shaggy pile of the rug.

Qwilleran lighted his pipe and showed her the new issue of *Gracious Abodes* with the Allison living room on the cover. They discussed its challenging shades of red and pink, the buxom ship's figurehead, and the pros and cons of four-poster beds with side curtains.

Koko was sitting on the coffee table with his back turned, pointedly ignoring the conversation. The curve of his tail, with its uplifted tip, was the essence of disdain, but the angle of his ears indicated that he was secretly listening.

"Hello, Koko," said the girl. "Don't you like me?"

The cat made no move. There was not even the tremor of a whisker.

"I used to have a beautiful orange cat named Frankie," she told Qwilleran sadly. "I still carry his picture in my handbag." She extracted a wad of cards and snapshots from her wallet and sorted them on the seat of the sofa, then proudly held up a picture of a fuzzy orange blob.

"It's out of focus, and the color has faded, but it's all I have left of Frankie. He lived to be fifteen years old. His parentage was uncertain but—"

"Koko!" shouted Qwilleran. "Get away!"

The cat had silently crept up on the sofa, and he was manipulating his long pink tongue.

Qwilleran said, "He was licking that picture."

"Oh!" said Cokey, and she snatched up a small glossy photograph of a man. She slipped it into her wallet but not before Qwilleran had caught a glimpse of it. He frowned his displeasure as she went on talking about cats and grinding nutmeg into their cocktails.

"Now, tell me all about your moustache," Cokey said. "I suppose you know it's terribly glamorous."

"I raised this crop in Britain during the war," said Qwilleran, "as camouflage."

"I like it."

It pleased him that she had not said, "Which war?" as young women were inclined to do. He said: "To tell the truth, I'm afraid to shave it off. I have a strange feeling that these lip whiskers put me in touch with certain things—like subsurface truths and imminent happenings."

"How wonderful!" said Cokey. "Just like cats' whiskers."

"I don't usually confide this little fact. I wouldn't want it to get noised around."

"I can see your point."

"Lately I've been getting hunches about the theft of the Tait jades."

"Haven't they found the boy yet?"

"You mean the houseboy who allegedly stole the stuff? That's one of my hunches. I don't think he's the thief."

Cokey's eyes widened. "Do you have any evidence?"

Qwilleran frowned. "That's the trouble; I don't have a thing but these blasted hunches. The houseboy doesn't fit the role, and there's something fishy about the timing, and I have certain reservations about G. Verning Tait. Did you ever hear anything about a scandal in the Tait family?"

Cokey shook her head.

"Of course, you were too young when it happened."

Cokey looked at her watch. "It's getting late. I should be going home."

"One more drink?" Qwilleran suggested. He went to the bar with its vast liquor supply and took the cream and ginger ale from the compact refrigerator.

Cokey began walking around the room and admiring it from every angle. "Everywhere you look there's beautiful line and composition," she said with rapture on her face. "And I love the interplay of textures—velvety, sleek, wooly, shaggy. And this rug! I worship this rug!"

She threw herself down on the tumbled pile of the luxurious rug. She lay there in ecstasy with arms flung wide, and Qwilleran combed his moustache violently. She lay there, unaware that the cat was stalking her. With his tail curled down like a fishhook and his body slung low, Koko moved through the shaggy pile of the rug like a wild thing prowling through the underbrush. Then he sprang!

Cokey shrieked and sat up. "He bit me! He bit my *head*!"

Qwilleran rushed to her side. "Did he hurt you?"

Cokey ran her fingers through her hair. "No. He didn't actually bite me. He just tried to take a little nip. But he seemed so . . . *hostile*! Qwill, why would Koko do a thing like that?"

CHAPTER 12

QWILLERAN WOULD have slept until noon on Sunday, if it had not been for the Siamese Whisker Torture. When Koko decided it was time to get up, he hopped weightlessly and soundlessly onto the sleeping man's bed and lightly touched his whiskers to nose and chin. Qwilleran opened his eyelids abruptly and found himself gazing into two enormous eyes, as innocent as they were blue.

"Go 'way," he said, and went back to sleep.

Again the whiskers were applied, this time to more sensitive areas— the cheeks and forehead.

Qwilleran winced and clenched his teeth and his eyes, only to feel the cat's whiskers tickling his eyelids. He jumped to a sitting position, and Koko bounded from the bed and from the room, mission accomplished.

When Qwilleran shuffled out of the bedroom, wearing his red plaid bathrobe and looking aimlessly for his pipe, he surveyed the living room with heavy-lidded eyes. On the coffee table were last night's champagne glasses, the Sunday paper, and Koko, diligently washing himself all over.

"You were a bad cat last night," Qwilleran said. "Why did you try to nip that pleasant girl who's so fond of cats? Such bad manners!"

Koko rolled over and attended to the base of his tail with rapt concentration, and Qwilleran's attention went to the rug. There, in the flattened pile, was a full-length impression of Cokey's tall, slender body, where she had sprawled for one dizzy moment. He made a move to erase the imprint by kicking up the pile with his toe, but changed his mind.

Koko, finished with his morning chore, sat up on the coffee table, blinked at the newsman, and looked angelic.

"You devil!" said Qwilleran. "I wish I could read your mind. That photograph you licked—"

The telephone rang, and he went to answer it with pleased anticipation. He remembered the congratulatory calls of the previous Sunday. Now a new issue of *Gracious Abodes* had reached the public.

"Hello-o?" he said graciously.

"Qwill, it's Harold!" The tone was urgent, and Qwilleran cringed. "Qwill, have you heard the news?"

"No, I just got out of bed—"

"Your cover story in today's paper—your residence for professional girls—haven't you heard?"

"What's happened?" Qwilleran put a hand over his eyes. He had visions of mass murder—a houseful of innocent girls murdered in their beds, their four-poster beds with pink side curtains.

"The police raided it last night! It's a disorderly house!"

"*What!*"

"They planted one of their men, got a warrant, and knocked the place off."

Qwilleran sat down unexpectedly as his knees folded. "But the decorator told me—"

"How did this happen? Where did you get the tip on this—this *house?*"

"From the decorator. From Mrs. Middy, a nice little motherly woman. She specializes in—well—residences for girls. Dormitories, that is, and sorority houses. And this was supposed to be a high-class boardinghouse for professional girls."

"Professional is the word!" said Percy. "This is going to make us look like a pack of fools. Wait till the *Morning Rampage* plays it up."

Qwilleran gulped. "I don't know what to say."

"There's nothing we can do about it now, but you'd better get hold of that Mrs. Biddy—"

"Middy."

"—whatever she calls herself—and let her know exactly how we feel about this highly embarrassing incident. . . . It's an incredible situation per se, and on the heels of the Muggy Swamp mess it's too much!"

Percy hung up, and Qwilleran's stunned mind tried to remember how it had happened. There must be an explanation. Then he grabbed the telephone and dialed a number.

"Yes?" said a sleepy voice.

"Cokey!" said Qwilleran sternly. "Have you heard the news?"

"What news? I'm not awake yet."

"Well, wake up and listen to me! Mrs. Middy has got me in a jam. Why didn't you tip me off?"

"About what?"

"About Mrs. Allison's place."

Cokey yawned. "What about Mrs. Allison's place?"

"You mean you don't *know*?"

"What are you talking about? You don't make sense."

Qwilleran found himself with a death grip on the receiver. He took a deep breath. "I've just been notified that the police raided Mrs. Allison's so-called residence for professional girls last night. . . . It's a brothel! Did you know that?"

Cokey shrieked. "Oh, Qwill, what a hoot!"

"Did you know the nature of Mrs. Allison's house?" His voice was gruff.

"No, but I think the idea's a howl!"

"Well, I don't think it's a howl, and the *Daily Fluxion* doesn't think it's a howl. It makes us look like saps. How can I get hold of Mrs. Middy?"

Cokey's voice sobered. "You want to call her? Yourself? Now? . . . Oh, don't do that!"

"Why not?"

"That poor woman! She'll drop dead from mortification."

"Didn't she know what kind of establishment she was furnishing?" Qwilleran demanded.

"I'm sure she didn't. She's a genius at doing charming interiors, but she's rather . . ."

"Rather what?"

"Muddleheaded, you know. Please don't call her," Cokey pleaded. "Let me break the news gently. You don't want to *kill* the woman, do you?"

"I feel like killing somebody!"

Cokey burst into laughter again. "And in Early American!" she shrieked. "With all those Tom Jones beds!"

Qwilleran banged the receiver down. "Now what?" he said to Koko. He paced the floor for a few minutes and then snatched the telephone and dialed another number.

"Hi!" said a childish treble.

"Let me talk to Odd Bunsen," said Qwilleran.

"Hi!" said the little voice.

"Is Odd Bunsen there?"

"Hi!"

"Who is this? Where's your father? Go and get your father!"

"Hi!"

Qwilleran snorted and was about to slam the receiver down when his partner came on the line.

"That was our youngest," Bunsen said. "He's not much for conversation. What's on your mind this morning?"

Qwilleran broke the news and listened to an assortment of croaking noises as the photographer reacted wordlessly.

The newsman said with a sarcastic edge to his voice: "I just wanted you to know that you may get your wish. You hoped the magazine would fold! And these two incidents in succession may be enough to kill it."

"Don't blame me," said Bunsen. "I just take the pictures. I don't even get a credit line."

"Two issues of *Gracious Abodes* and two mishaps! It can't be accidental. I'm beginning to smell is rat."

"You don't mean the competition!"

"Who else?"

"The *Rampage* hasn't got the guts to try any dirty work."

"I know, but they've got a guy working for them who might try to pull something. You know that loudmouth in their Circulation Department? He played on their softball team, you told me."

"You mean Mike Bulmer?" Bunsen said. "He's a creep!"

"The first time I noticed him at the Press Club, I recognized the face, but it took me a long time to place it. I finally remembered him. He was mixed up in a circulation war in Chicago a few years back—a bloody affair. And now he's working at the *Rampage*. I'll bet he suggested the raid on the Allison house to the police, and I'll bet the Vice Squad was only too happy to act. You know how it is; every time the *Fluxion* editorial writers run out of ideas, the start sniping at the Vice Squad." Qwilleran tamped his moustache, and added, "I hate to say this, but I've got a nasty feeling that Cokey may be involved."

"Who?"

"This girl I've been dating. Works for Mrs. Middy. It was Cokey who suggested publishing Mrs. Allison's house, and now I've found out that she knows Bulmer. She said hello to him at the Press Club the other night."

"No law against that," Bunsen said.

"It was the way she said it! And the look she gave him! . . . There's something else, too," Qwilleran began with evident reluctance. "After the party at David Lyke's last night, I brought Cokey back to my apartment—"

"Ho HO! This is beginning to sound interesting."

"—and Koko tried to bite her."

"What was she doing to him?"

"She wasn't doing a thing! She was on the—she was minding her own business when Koko made a pass at her head. He's never done a thing like

that before. I'm beginning to think he was trying to tell me something."
There was silence at the other end of the line. "Are you listening?"

"I'm listening. I'm lighting a cigar."

"You get remarkably detached when you're home in Happy View Woods on Sunday. I should think you'd be more concerned about this mess."

"What mess?" Bunsen said. "I think the Allison thing is a practical joke. It's sort of funny."

"The half-million-dollar theft wasn't funny!"

"Well," Bunsen drawled, "Bulmer wouldn't go *that* far!"

"He might! Don't forget, there's a million dollars' worth of advertising involved. He might see a chance to make himself a nice bonus."

"And victimize an innocent man just to knife the competition? . . . Naw! You've seen too many old movies."

"Maybe Tait wasn't victimized," Qwilleran said slowly. "Maybe he was in on the deal."

"Brother, you're really flying high this morning."

"Goodbye," said Qwilleran. "Sorry I bothered you. Go back to your peaceful family scene."

"Peaceful!" said Bunsen. "Did you say peaceful? I'm painting the basement, and Tommy just fell in the paint bucket, and Linda threw a rag doll down the john, and Jimmy fell off the porch and blacked his eyes. You call that peaceful?"

When Qwilleran left the telephone, he wandered aimlessly through the apartment. He glanced at the shaggy rug in the living room and angrily scuffed up the pile to erase the imprint. In the kitchen he found Koko sitting on the big ragged dictionary. The cat sat tall, with forefeet pulled in close, tail curled around tightly, head cocked. Qwilleran was in no mood for games, but Koko stared at him, waiting for an affirmative.

"All right, we'll play a few innings," Qwilleran said with a sigh. He slapped the book—the starting signal—and Koko dug into the edge with the claws of his left paw.

Qwilleran flipped the pages to the spot Koko indicated—page 1102. "*Hummock* and *hungrily*," he read. "Those are easy. Find a couple of hard ones."

The cat grabbed again.

"*Feed* and *feeling*. Two more points for me."

Koko crouched in great excitement and sank his claws.

"*May queen* and *meadow mouse*," said Qwilleran, and all at once he remembered that neither he nor Koko had eaten breakfast.

As the man chopped fresh beef for the cat and warmed it in a little canned consommé, he remembered something else: In a recent game Koko had come up with the same page twice. It had happened within the last week. Twice in one game Koko had found *sacroiliac* and *sadism*. Qwilleran felt a curious tingling sensation in his moustache.

CHAPTER 13

ON MONDAY MORNING, as Qwilleran and Bunsen drove to Lost Lake Hills to inspect the Noyton house, Qwilleran was unusually quiet. He had not slept well. All night he had dreamed and waked and dreamed again—about interiors decorated in Crunchy Peanut Butter and Rice Pudding, with accents of Lobster and Blackstrap Molasses. And in the morning his mind was plagued by unfinished, unfounded, unfavorable thoughts.

He greatly feared that Cokey was involved in the "practical joke" on the *Fluxion*, and he didn't want it to be that way; he needed a friend like Cokey. He was haunted, moreover, by the possibility of Tait's complicity in the plot, although his evidence was no more concrete than a disturbance on his upper lip and a peculiar experience with the dictionary. He entertained doubts about Paolo's role in the affair; was he an innocent bystander, clever criminal, accomplice, or tool? And was Tait's love affair with his jade collection genuine or a well-rehearsed act? Had the man been as devoted to his wife as people seemed to think? Was there, by any chance, another woman in his life? Even the name of the Tait's cat was veiled in ambiguity. Was it Yu or Freya?

Then Qwilleran's thoughts turned to his own cat. Once before, when the crime was murder, Koko had flushed out more clues with his cold wet nose than the Homicide Bureau had unearthed by official investigation. Koko seemed to sense without the formality of cogitation. Instinct, it appeared, bypassed his brain and directed his claws to scratch and his nose to sniff in the right place at the right time. Or was it happenstance? Was it coincidence that Koko turned the pages of the dictionary to *hungerly* and *feed* when breakfast was behind schedule?

Several times on Sunday afternoon Qwilleran had suggested playing the word game, hoping for additional revelations, but the catchwords that Koko turned up were insignificant: *oppositional* and *optimism, cynegetic* and *cypripedium*. Qwilleran entertained little *optimism*; and *cypripedium*, which turned out to be a type of orchid also called lady's-slipper, only reminded him of Cokey's toes wiggling in the luxuriant pile of the goat-hair rug.

Still, Qwilleran's notion about Koko and the dictionary persisted. A tremor ran through Qwilleran's moustache.

Odd Bunsen, at the wheel of the car, asked: "Are you sick or something? You're sitting there shivering and not saying a word."

"It's chilly," said Qwilleran. "I should have worn a topcoat." He groped in his pocket for his pipe.

"I brought a raincoat," said Bunsen. "The way the wind's blowing from the northeast, we're going to get a storm."

The trip to Lost Lake Hills took them through the suburbs and into farm country, where the maple trees were beginning to turn yellow. From time to time the photographer gave a friendly toot of the horn and wave of his cigar to people on the side of the road. He saluted a woman cutting grass, two boys on bicycles, an old man at a rural mailbox.

"You have a wide acquaintance in this neck of the woods," Qwilleran observed.

"Me? I don't know them from Adam," said Bunsen, "but these farmers can use a little excitement. Now they'll spend the whole day figuring who they know that drives a foreign car and smokes cigars."

They turned into a country road that showed the artful hand of a landscape designer, and Qwilleran read the directions from a slip of paper. "'Follow the lakeshore, first fork to the left, turn in at the top of the hill."

"When did you make the arrangements for this boondoggle?" the photographer wanted to know.

"At Lyke's party Saturday night."

"I hope they were sober. I don't put any stock in cocktail promises, and this is a long way to drive on a wild-goose chase."

"Don't worry. Everything's okay. Natalie wants David to get some credit for decorating the house, and Harry Noyton is hoping our story will help him sell the place. The property's worth a quarter million."

"I hope his wife doesn't get a penny of it," Bunsen said. "Any woman who'll give up her kids, the way she did, is a tramp."

Qwilleran said: "I got another phone call from Denmark this morning. Noyton wants his mail forwarded to Aarhus. That's a university town. I wonder what he's doing there."

"He sounds like a decent guy. Wouldn't you know he'd get mixed up with a dame like that?"

"I don't think you should judge Natalie until you've met her," Qwilleran said. "She's sincere. Not overly bright, but sincere. And I have an idea people take advantage of her gullibility."

The house at the end of the winding drive was of complex shape, its pink-brick walls standing at odd angles and its huge roof timbers shooting off in all directions.

"It's a gasser!" said Bunsen. "How do you find the front door?"

"Lyke says the house is organic contemporary. It's integrated with the terrain, and the furnishings are integrated with the structure."

They rang the doorbell, and while they waited they studied the mosaic murals that flanked the entrance—swirling abstract designs composed of pebbles, colored glass, and copper nails.

"Crazy!" said Bunsen.

They waited a considerable time before ringing the bell again.

"See? What did I tell you?" the photographer said. "No one home."

"It's a big house," said Qwilleran. "Natalie probably needs roller skates to get from her weaving studio to the front door."

A moment later there was a click in the lock, and the door swung inward a few inches, opened with caution. A woman in a maid's uniform stood there, guarding the entrance inhospitably.

"We're from the *Daily Fluxion*," Qwilleran said.

"Yes?" said the maid, standing her ground.

"Is Mrs. Noyton home?"

"She can't see anybody today." The door began to close.

"But we have an appointment."

"She can't see anybody today."

Qwilleran frowned. "We've come a long way. She told us we could see the house. Would she mind if we took a quick look around? We expect to photograph it for the paper."

"She doesn't want anybody to take pictures of the house," the maid said. "She changed her mind."

The newsmen turned to look at each other, and the door snapped shut in their faces.

As they drove back to town, Qwilleran brooded about the rude rejection. "It doesn't sound like Natalie. What do you suppose is wrong? She was very friendly and agreeable Saturday night."

"People are different when they're drinking."

"Natalie was as sober as I was. Maybe she's ill, and the maid took it on herself to brush us off."

"If you want my opinion," said Bunsen, "I think your Natalie is off her rocker."

"Stop at the first phone booth," said Qwilleran. "I want to make a call."

From a booth at a country crossroad the newsman dialed the studio of Lyke and Starkweather and talked to David. "What's going on?" he demanded. "We drove all the way to Lost Lake Hills, and Natalie refused to see us. The maid wouldn't even let us in to look at the layout."

"Natalie's a kook," David said. "I apologize for her. I'll take you out there myself one of these days."

"Meanwhile, we're in a jam—with a Wednesday deadline and no really strong story for the cover."

"If it will help you, you can photograph my apartment," said David. "You don't have to give me a credit line. Just write about how people live at the Villa Verandah."

"All right. How about this afternoon? How about two o'clock?"

"Just give me time to buy some flowers and remove some art objects," the decorator said. "There are a few things I wouldn't want people to know I have. Just between you and me, I shouldn't even have them."

The newsmen had a leisurely lunch. When they eventually headed for the Villa Verandah, Qwilleran said, "Let's stop at the pet shop on State Street. I want to buy something."

They were battling the afternoon traffic in the downtown area. At every red light Bunsen saluted certain attractive pedestrians with the motorist's wolf whistle, touching his foot tenderly to the accelerator as they passed in front of his car. For every traffic officer he had a loud quip. They all knew the *Fluxion* photographer, and one of them halted traffic at a major intersection while the car with a press card in the windshield made an illegal left turn into State Street.

"What do you want at the pet shop?" Bunsen asked.

"A harness and a leash for Koko, so I can tie him up on the balcony."

"Just buy a harness," said the photographer. "I've got twelve feet of nylon cord you can have for a leash."

"What are you doing with twelve feet of nylon cord?"

"Last fall," Bunsen said, "when I was covering football games, I lowered my film from the press box on a rope, and a boy rushed it to the Lab. Those were the good old days! Now it's nothing but crazy decorators, ornery women, and nervous cats. I work like a dog, and I don't even get a credit line."

The newsmen spent three hours at David Lyke's apartment, photographing the silvery living room, the dining room with the Chinese rug, and the master bedroom. The bed was a low platform, a few inches high, completely covered with a tiger fur throw, and the adjoining dressing room was curtained off with strings of amber beads.

Bunsen said, "Those beads would last about five minutes at my house—with six kids playing Tarzan!"

In the living room the decorator had removed several Oriental objects, and now he was filling the gaps with bowls of flowers and large vases of glossy green leaves. He arranged them with a contemptuous flourish.

"Sorry about Natalie," he said, jabbing the stem of a chrysanthemum into a porcelain vase. "Now you know the kind of situation a decorator has to deal with all the time. One of my clients gave his wife the choice of being analyzed or having the house done over. She picked the decorating job, of course, and took out her neuroses on me. . . . *There*!" He surveyed the bouquet he had arranged, and disarranged it a little. He straightened some lampshades. He pressed a hidden switch and started the fountain bubbling and splashing in its bowl of pebbles. Then he stood back and squinted at the scene with a critical eye. "Do you know what this room needs?" he said. "It needs a Siamese cat on the sofa."

"Are you serious?" Qwilleran asked. "Want me to get Koko?"

Bunsen protested. "Oh, no! No nervous cats! Not in a wide-angle time exposure."

"Koko isn't nervous," Qwilleran told him. "He's a lot calmer than you are."

"And better looking," said David.

"And smarter," said Qwilleran.

Bunsen threw up his hands and looked grim, and within a few minutes Koko arrived to have his picture taken, his fur still striated from a fresh brushing.

Qwilleran placed the cat on the seat of the sofa, shifted him around at the direction of the photographer, folded one of the velvety brown forepaws under in an attitude of lordly ease, and arranged the silky brown tail in a photogenic curve. Throughout the proceeding Koko purred loudly.

"Will he stay like that without moving?" Bunsen asked.

"Sure. He'll stay if I say so."

Qwilleran give Koko's fur a final smoothing and stepped back, saying, "Stay! Stay there!"

And Koko calmly stood up, jumped to the floor, and walked out of the room with vertical tail expressing his indifference.

"He's calm, all right," said Bunsen. "He's the calmest cat I ever met."

While the photographer finished taking pictures, Koko played with the dangling beads in David's dressing room and sniffed the tiger bed-throw with fraternal interest. Meanwhile David was preparing something for him to eat.

"Just some leftover chicken curry," the decorator explained to Qwilleran. "Yushi came over last night and whipped up an eight-boy *rijstafel*."

"Is he the one who cooks for your parties? He's a great chef!"

"He's an artist," David said softly.

David poured ginger ale for Qwilleran and Scotch for Bunsen.

The photographer said: "Does anyone want to eat at the Press Club tonight? My wife's giving a party for a gaggle of girls, and I've been kicked out of the house until midnight."

"I'd like to join you, but I've got a date," said David. "I'll take a raincheck, though. I'd like to see the inside of that club. I hear it's got all the amenities of a medieval bastille."

THE TWO NEWSMEN went to the Press Club bar, and Bunsen switched to double martinis while Qwilleran switched to tomato juice.

"Not such a bad day after all," said Qwilleran, "although it started out bad."

"It isn't over yet," the photographer reminded him.

"That David Lyke is quite a character, isn't he?"

"I don't know what to think about that *bedroom* of his!" said Bunsen, rolling his eyes.

Qwilleran frowned. "You know, he's an agreeable joe, but there's one thing that bugs me: he makes nasty cracks about his friends. You'd think they'd get wise, but no. Everyone thinks he's the greatest."

"When you've got looks and money, you can get away with murder."

During the next round of drinks Qwilleran said, "Do you remember hearing about a scandal in the Tait family fifteen or twenty years ago?"

"Fifteen years ago I was still playing marbles."

Qwilleran huffed into his moustache. "You must have been the only marble-player with five o'clock shadow." Then he signaled the bartender. "Bruno, do you recall a scandal involving the G. Verning Tait family in Muggy Swamp?"

The bartender shook his head with authority. "No, I don't remember anything like that. If there'd been anything like that, I'd know about it. I have a memory like a giraffe."

Eventually the newsmen went to a table and ordered T-bone steaks.

"Don't eat the tail," Qwilleran said. "I'll take it home to Koko."

"Give him your own tail," said the photographer. "I'm not sharing my steak with any overfed cat. He lives better than I do."

"The leash is going to work fine. I tied him up on the balcony before I left. But I have to buckle the harness good and tight or he'll wriggle free. One fast flip and a tricky stretch—and he's out! That cat's a Houdini." There were other things Qwilleran wanted to confide about Koko's capabilities, but he knew better than to tell Bunsen.

After the steaks came apple pie à la mode, following which Qwilleran started on coffee and Bunsen started on brandy.

Qwilleran said, as he lighted his pipe, "I worry about Natalie—and why she wouldn't let us in today. That whole Noyton affair is mystifying. See what you can make out of these assorted facts: Natalie gets a divorce for reasons that are weak, to say the least, although we have only her husband's side of the story. I find an earring in the apartment that Harry Noyton is supposed to use for business entertaining. I also find out that he knows Mrs. Tait. Then she dies, and he leaves the country hurriedly. At the same time, Tait's jades are stolen, after which he also prepares to leave town. . . . What do you think?"

"I think the Yankees'll win the pennant."

"You're crocked!" Qwilleran said. "Let's go to my place for black coffee. Then maybe you'll be sober enough to drive home at midnight."

Bunsen showed no inclination to move.

"I should bring the cat in off the balcony, in case it rains," Qwilleran said. "Come on! We'll take your car, and I'll do the driving!"

"I can drive," said Bunsen. "Perfectly sober."

"Then take that salt shaker out of your breast pocket, and let's go."

Qwilleran drove, and Bunsen sang. When they reached the Villa Verandah, the photographer discovered that the elevator improved the resonance of his voice.

"'Oh, how I hate to get up in the morrr-nin'—'"

"Shut up! You'll scare the cat."

"He doesn't scare easy. He's a cool cat," said Bunsen. "A real cool cat."

Qwilleran unlocked the door of 15-F and touched a switch, flooding the living room with light.

"Where's that cool cat? I wanna see that cool cat."

"I'll let him in," Qwilleran said. "Why don't you sit down before you fall down? Try that green wing chair. It's the most comfortable thing you ever saw."

The photographer flopped into the green chair, and Qwilleran opened the balcony door. He stepped out into the night. In less than a second he was back.

"He's gone! Koko's gone!"

CHAPTER 14

A TWELVE-FOOT nylon cord was tied to the handle of the balcony door. At the end of it was a blue leather harness buckled in the last notch, with the belt and the collar making a figure eight on the concrete floor.

"Somebody stole that cool cat," said the photographer from his position of authority in the green wing chair.

"Don't kid around," Qwilleran snapped at him. "This worries me. I'm going to call the manager."

"Wait a minute," said Bunsen, hauling himself out of the chair. "Let's have a good look outside."

The two men went to the balcony. They were met by a burst of high wind, and Bunsen had to steady himself.

Qwilleran peered at the adjoining balconies. "It's only about five feet between railings. Koko could jump across, I guess."

Bunsen had other ideas. He looked down at the landscaped court, fifteen stories below.

Qwilleran shuddered. "Cats don't fall from railed balconies," he said, without conviction.

"Maybe the wind blew him over."

"Don't be silly."

They gazed blankly around the curve of the building. The wind, whistling through the balcony railings, produced vibrating chords like organ music in a weird key.

Bunsen said, "Anybody around here hate cats?"

"I don't think so. I don't know. That is, I haven't—" Qwilleran was staring across the court, squinting through the darkness. The facade of the south wing was a checkerboard of light and shadow, with many of the apartments in darkness and others with a dull glow filtering through drawn draperies. But one apartment was partially exposed to view.

Qwilleran pointed. "Do you see what I see? Look at that window over there—the one where the curtains are open."

"That's David Lyke's place!"

"I know it is. And his TV is turned on. And look who's sitting on top of it, keeping warm."

The doors of a Chinese lacquer cabinet were open and the TV screen could be seen, shimmering with abstract images. On top, in a neat bundle, sat Koko, his light breast distinct against the dark lacquer and his brown mask and ears silhouetted against the silvery wall.

"I'm going to phone Dave and see what this is all about," said Qwilleran.

He dialed the switchboard, asked for Lyke's apartment, and waited a long time before he was convinced no one was home.

"No answer," he told Bunsen.

"What now?"

"I don't know. Do you suppose Koko got lonesome and decided to go visiting?"

"He wanted some more of that curried chicken."

"He must have hopped from balcony to balcony—all the way around. Crazy cat! Lyke must have let him in and then gone out himself. He said he had a date."

"What are you going to do?" Bunsen said.

"Leave him there till morning, that's all."

"I can get him back."

"What? How could you get him back? He couldn't hear you with the door closed over there, and even if he could, how would he open the sliding door?"

"Want to bet I can't get him back?" The photographer leaped up on the side railing of the balcony and teetered there, clutching the corner post.

"No!" yelled Qwilleran. "Get down from there!" He was afraid to make a sudden move toward the man balancing on the narrow toprail. He approached Bunsen slowly, holding his breath.

"No sweat!" the photographer called out, as he leaped across the five-foot gap and grabbed the post of the next balcony. "Anything a cat can do, Odd Bunsen can do better!"

"Come back! You're out of your mind! . . . No, stay there! Don't try it again!"

"Odd Bunsen to the rescue!" yelled the photographer, as he ran the length of the balcony and negotiated the leap to the next one. But first he plucked a yellow mum from the neighbor's window box and clenched it in his teeth.

Qwilleran sat down and covered his face with his hands.

"Ya hoo!" Bunsen crowed. "Ya hoo!"

His war cries grew fainter, drowned by the whistling wind as he progressed from railing to railing around the inside curve of the Villa Verandah. Here and there a resident opened a door and looked out, without seeing the acrobatic feat being performed in the darkness.

"Ya hoo!" came a distant cry.

Qwilleran thought of the three double martinis and the two—no, three—brandies that Bunsen had consumed. He thought of the photographer's wife and six children, and his blood chilled.

There was a triumphant shout across the court, and Bunsen was waving from Lyke's balcony. He tried the sliding door; it opened. He signaled his success and then stepped into the silvery-gray living room. At his entrance Koko jumped down from his perch and scampered away.

I hope, Qwilleran told himself, that nincompoop has sense enough to bring Koko back by land and not by air.

From where the newsman stood, he could no longer see Bunsen or the cat, so he went indoors and waited for the errant pair to return. While waiting, he made two cups of instant coffee and put some cheese and crackers on a plate.

The wait was much too long, he soon decided. He went to the corridor and listened and looked down its carpeted curve. There was no sign of life—only mechanical noises from the elevator shaft and the frantic sounds of a distant TV. He returned to the balcony and scanned the south wing. There was no activity to be seen in Lyke's apartment, except for the busy images on the TV screen.

Qwilleran gulped a cup of coffee and paced the floor. Finally he went to the telephone and asked the operator to try Lyke's apartment again. The line was busy.

"What's that drunken fool doing?"

"Pardon?" said the operator.

Returning once more to the balcony, Qwilleran stared across the court in exasperation. When his telephone rang, he jumped and sprinted for it.

"Qwill," said Bunsen's voice, several tones lower than it had been all evening. "We've got trouble over here."

"Koko? What's happened?"

"The cat's okay, but your decorator friend has *had* it."

"What do you mean?"

"Looks as if Lyke's dead."

"No! . . . No!"

"He's cold, and he's white, and there's an ugly spot on the rug. I've called the police, and I've called the paper. Would you go down to the car and get my camera?"

"I gave you the car keys."

"I put them in my raincoat pocket, and I dropped my raincoat in your front hall. I think I'd better stay here with the body."

"You sound sober all of a sudden," Qwilleran said.

"I sobered up in a hurry when I saw this."

By the time Qwilleran arrived at Lyke's apartment with Bunsen's camera, the officers from the police cruiser were there. Qwilleran scanned the living room. It was just as they had photographed it in the afternoon, except that the TV in the Chinese cabinet was yakking senselessly and there was a yellow mum on the carpet, where Bunsen had dropped it.

"As soon as I came through the door," Bunsen said to Qwilleran, "Koko led me into the bedroom."

The body was on the bedroom floor, wrapped in a gray silk dressing gown. One finger wore a large star sapphire that Qwilleran had not seen before. The face was no longer handsome. It had lost the wit and animation that made it attractive. All that was left was a supercilious mask.

Qwilleran glanced about the room. The tiger skin had been removed from the bed, neatly folded, and laid on a bench. Everything else was in perfect order. The bed showed no indication of having been occupied.

Bunsen was hopping around the room looking for camera angles. "I just want to get one picture," he told the officers. "I won't disturb anything." To Qwilleran he said, "It's hard to get an interesting shot. The Picture Desk won't run gory stuff any more. They get complaints from the P.T.A., little old ladies, the American Legion, the D.A.R., vegetarians—"

"What did you do with Koko?" Qwilleran said.

"He's around here somewhere. Probably destroying the evidence."

Qwilleran found Koko in the dining room, sitting under the table as if nothing had happened. He had assumed his noncommittal pose, gathered in a comfortable bundle on the gold-and-blue Chinese rug, looking neither curious nor concerned nor guilty nor grieved.

When the detectives from the Homicide Bureau arrived, Qwilleran recognized a pair he had met before. He liked the heavy-set one called Hames, a smart detective with an off-duty personality, but he didn't care for Wojcik, whose nasal voice was well suited to sarcasm.

Wojcik gave one look at Qwilleran and said, "How'd the press get here so fast?"

The patrolman said: "The photographer was here when we arrived. He let us into the apartment. He's the one who found the body and reported it."

Wojcik turned to Bunsen. "How did you happen to be here?"

"I came in through the window."

"I see. This is the fifteenth floor. And you came in through the window."

"Sure, there are balconies out there."

Hames was ogling the sumptuous living room. "Look at this wallpaper," he said. "If my wife ever saw this—"

Wojcik went into the bedroom and after that onto the balcony. He looked at the ground fifteen stories below, and he gauged the distance between balconies. Then he cornered Bunsen. "Okay, how did you get in?"

"I told you—"

"I suppose you know you smell like a distillery."

Qwilleran said: "Bunsen's telling the truth. He jumped from balcony to balcony, all the way from my place on the other side."

"This may be a silly question," said the detective, "but do you mind if I inquire *why*?"

"Well, it's like this," said the photographer. "We went across the court—"

"He came here to get my cat," Qwilleran interrupted. "My cat was over here."

Hames said: "That must be the famous Siamese that's bucking for my job on the force. I'd like to meet him."

"He's in the dining room under the table."

"My wife's crazy about Siamese. Some day I've got to break down and buy her one."

Qwilleran followed the amiable detective into the dining room and said quietly: "There's something I ought to tell you, Hames. We were here this afternoon to photograph the apartment for *Gracious Abodes*, and David Lyke removed some valuable art objects before we took the pictures. I don't know what he did with them, but they were valuable, and I don't see them anywhere."

There was no reaction from the detective, who was now down on his knees under the table.

"As I recall," Qwilleran went on, "there was a Japanese screen in five panels, all done in gold. And a long vertical scroll with pictures of ducks and geese. And a wood sculpture of a deer, almost life-size, and very old, judging from its condition. And a big china bowl. And a gold Buddha about three feet high."

From under the table Hames said, "This guy's fur feels like mink. Are these cats very expensive?"

It was Wojcik who roused the neighbors. The apartment across the hall was occupied by an elderly woman who was hard of hearing; she said she had retired early, had heard nothing, had seen no one. The adjoining apartment to the east was vacant; the one on the other side produced a fragment of information.

"We're not acquainted with Mr. Lyke," said a man's voice, "but we see him on the elevator occasionally—him and his friends."

"And we hear his wild parties," a woman's shrill voice added.

"We didn't hear anything tonight," said the man, "except his television. That struck us as being unusual. Ordinarily he plays stereo. . . . Music, you know."

"He doesn't play it. He *blasts* it," the woman said. "Last week we complained to the manager."

"When we heard his TV," the man went on, "we decided there must be a good show, so we turned our set on. After that I didn't hear anything more from his apartment."

"No voices? No altercation of any kind?" the detective asked.

"To tell the truth, I fell asleep," said the man. "It wasn't a very good show after all."

Wojcik nodded to the woman. "And you?"

"With the TV going and my husband snoring, who could hear a bomb go off?"

When Wojcik returned, he said to Qwilleran, "How well did you know the decedent?"

"I met him for the first time a couple of weeks ago—on assignment for the *Fluxion*. Don't know much about him except that he gave big parties, and he seemed to be well liked—by both men and women."

The detective said, "He was a decorator, hmmm?"

"Yes," said Qwilleran crisply, "and a damn good one."

"When was the last time you saw him?"

"This afternoon, when we photographed the apartment. Bunsen and I invited him to dinner at the Press Club, but he said he had a date."

"Any idea who it was?"

"No, he just said he had a date."

"Did he live alone?"

"Yes. That is, I presume he lived alone."

"What do you mean by that?"

"There's only one name on his mailbox."

"Any help working here?"

"At parties he had two people working in the kitchen and serving. The building management supplies cleaning service."

"Know any of his relatives or close friends?"

"Just his partner at the decorating studio. Better try Starkweather."

By that time the coroner's man and the police photographer had arrived, and Wojcik said to the newsmen, "Why don't you two pack up and clear out?"

"I'd like to get the doctor's statement," said Qwilleran, "so I can file a complete story."

Wojcik gave him a close look. "Aren't you the *Fluxion* man who was involved in the Tait burglary?"

"I wasn't *involved* in it," said Qwilleran. "I just happened to write a story about Mr. and Mrs. Tait's house—a few days before their houseboy made off with their jades, if one can believe the statement made by the Police Department."

From the dining room Hames called out: "Have you noticed? This cat's eyes turn red in the dark."

After a while Wojcik said to the newsmen: "Death caused by a bullet wound in the chest. Fired at close range. About ten o'clock. Weapon missing. Robbery apparently no motive. . . . That's all. Now, do us a favor and go home. You probably know more than we do. I think your paper goes around setting these things up."

To retrieve Koko, Qwilleran had to crawl under the dining room table and forcibly remove the cat, who seemed to have taken root.

Hames walked the newsmen to the door. "Your Sunday supplement looks good," he said. "All those elegant homes! My wife says I should scare up a little graft so we can live like that."

"I think the magazine's a good idea," Qwilleran said, "but it's been rough going. First the Tait setback, and then—"

"Come on, clear out!" snapped Wojcik. "We've got work to do."

"Say!" said Hames. "My wife sure liked those four-poster beds you photographed on Merchant Street. Do you know where I could buy something like that?"

Qwilleran looked distressed. "That was another unfortunate coincidence! I wish I knew why the Vice Squad picked that particular weekend to raid the place."

"Well," said Hames, "I don't know how it happened, but I know the Police Widows' Fund just received a sizable donation from the Penniman Foundation. . . . Now, what did you say was missing? Five-panel gold-leaf screen? Three-foot gold Buddha? Kakemono with ducks and geese? Antique wood carving of deer? Porcelain bowl? Are you sure it was a five-panel screen? Japanese screens usually have an even number of panels."

Slowly and thoughtfully the newsmen returned to 15-F, Bunsen carrying his camera, Qwilleran carrying the cat on his shoulder.

"The Penniman Foundation!" he repeated.

"You know who the Pennimans are, don't you?" said Bunsen.

"Yes, I know who they are. They live in Muggy Swamp. And they own the *Morning Rampage*."

CHAPTER 15

QWILLERAN PHONED IN the details of David Lyke's murder to a *Flux-ion* rewrite man, and Bunsen called his wife. "Is the party over, honey? . . . Tell the girls I'll be right there to kiss 'em all good night. . . . Nothing. Not a thing. Just sat around and talked all evening. . . . Honey, you know I wouldn't do anything like that!"

The photographer left the Villa Verandah to return to Happy View Woods, and Qwilleran began to worry about Koko's prolonged tranquil-lity. Was the cat demonstrating feline sangfroid or had he gone into shock? Upon returning to the apartment, he should have prowled the premises, inspecting the kitchen for accidental leftovers, curled up on his blue cushion on top of the refrigerator. Instead, he huddled on the bare wood floor beneath the desk, with eyes wide, looking at nothing. His atti-tude suggested that he was cold. Qwilleran covered him with his old cor-duroy sports coat, arranging it like a tent over the cat, and received no acknowledgement—not even the tremor of an ear.

Qwilleran himself was exhausted after the scare of Koko's disappear-ance, Bunsen's hair-raising performance, and the discovery of Lyke's body. But when he went to bed, he could not sleep. The questions followed him from side to side as he tossed.

Question: Who would want to eliminate the easygoing, openhanded David Lyke? He was equally gracious to men and women, young and old, clients and competitors, the help in the kitchen and the guests in the living room. True, he spoke out of the other side of his mouth when their backs were turned, but still he charmed them all.

Question: Could the motive be jealousy? Lyke had everything—looks, talent, personality, success, friends. He had had a date that night. Perhaps the woman had been followed by a jealous friend or a jealous husband. Or—there was another possibility—perhaps the date had not been with a woman.

Question: Why was Lyke wearing an important ring and no other ap-parel, except a dressing gown? And why had the bedcover been removed and neatly folded in the middle of the evening? Qwilleran frowned and blew into his moustache.

Question: Why had the neighbors heard no commotion and no shot? Perhaps the audio on Lyke's television had been turned up to full volume purposely, before the shot was fired. And the neighbors had attributed everything they heard to a television program. Wonderful invention, television.

Question: Where had Koko been during the whole episode? What had he seen? What had he done? Why did he now appear to be stunned?

Qwilleran tossed from his left side to his right for the hundredth time. It was dawn before he finally fell asleep, and then he dreamed of telephone bells. Readers were phoning him with unanswered questions. *Brrrring!* "What colors do you mix to get sky-blue-pink?" *Brrrring!* "Where can I buy a Danish chair made in Japan?" And the managing editor, too. *Brrrring!* "Qwill, this is Harold! We're going to carpet the Press Room. What do you think about Bourbon Brown?"

When the ringing telephone finally dragged Qwilleran from his confused sleep, he said a mindless "Hello" into the mouthpiece.

The voice at the other end said, simply, "Starkweather," and then waited.

"Yes?" said Qwilleran, groping for words. "How are you?"

"Isn't it—isn't it terrible?" said Lyke's partner. "I haven't slept all night."

Yesterday's events came tumbling back into Qwilleran's mind. "It was a shock," he agreed. "I don't understand it."

"Is there anything—I mean—could you . . ." There was a prolonged pause.

"Can I do anything for you, Mr. Starkweather?"

"Well, I thought—if you could find out what—what they're going to say in the paper . . ."

"I reported the item myself," said Qwilleran. "I phoned it in last night—just the bare facts based on the coroner's report and the detective's statement. It'll be in the first edition this morning. If there's to be any follow-up story, the editor will probably call me in. . . . Why are you concerned?"

"Well, I wouldn't want—I wouldn't like anything to reflect—you know what I mean."

"Reflect on your studio, you mean?"

"Some of our customers, you know—they're very—"

"You're afraid the papers will make it too sensational? Is that what you're trying to say? I don't know about the *Morning Rampage*, Mr. Starkweather. But you don't need to worry about the *Fluxion*. Besides, I don't know what anyone could say that would be damaging to the studio."

"Well, you know—David and his parties—his friends. He had a lot of—you know how these young bachelors are."

Qwilleran was now fully awake. "Do you have any idea of a possible motive?"

"I can't imagine."

"Jealousy, maybe?"

"I don't know."

"Do you think it had anything to do with David's Oriental art collection?"

"I just don't know," said Starkweather in his helpless tone of voice.

Qwilleran persisted. "Do you know his collection well enough to determine if anything is missing?"

"That's what the police wanted to know last night."

"Were you able to help them?"

"I went over there right away—over to David's apartment."

"What did you find?"

"Some of his best things were locked up in a closet. I don't know why."

"I can tell you why," said Qwilleran. "Dave removed them before we took pictures yesterday."

"Oh," said Starkweather.

"Did you know we were going to take pictures of Dave's apartment?"

"Yes, he mentioned it. It slipped my mind."

"Did he tell you he was going to remove some of the art?"

"I don't think so."

"Dave told me there were certain things he didn't want the public to know he had. Were they extremely valuable?"

Starkweather hesitated. "Some of the things were—well—"

"They weren't hot, were they?"

"What?"

"Were they stolen goods?"

"Oh, no, no! He paid plenty."

"I'm sure he did," said Qwilleran, "but I'm talking about the source of the stuff. He said, 'There are some things I shouldn't even have.' What did he mean by that?"

"Well, they were—I guess you'd say—museum pieces."

"A lot of well-heeled collectors own items of museum caliber, don't they?"

"But some of David's things were—well—I guess they should never have left the country. Japan, that is."

"I see," said Qwilleran. He thought a moment. "You mean they were ostensibly protected by the government?"

"Something like that."

"National treasures?"

"I guess that's what they call them."

"Hmm . . . Did you tell the police that, Mr. Starkweather?"

"No."

"Why not?"

"They didn't ask anything like that."

Qwilleran enjoyed a moment's glee. He could picture the brusque Wojcik interrogating the laconic Starkweather. Then he thought of one more question. "Can you think of anyone who has shown particular interest in these 'protected' items?"

"No, but I wonder . . ."

"What? What do you wonder, Mr. Starkweather?"

Lyke's partner coughed. "Is the studio liable—I mean, if there's anything illegal—could they . . ."

"I doubt it. Why don't you get some sleep, Mr. Starkweather? Why don't you take a pill and try to get some sleep?"

"Oh, no! I must go to the studio. I don't know what will happen today. This is a terrible thing, you know."

When Starkweather hung up, Qwilleran felt as if he'd had all his teeth pulled. He went into the kitchen to make some coffee, and found Koko stretched out on the refrigerator cushion. The cat was lying on his side with his head thrown back and his eyes closed. Qwilleran spoke to him, and not a whisker moved. He stroked the cat, and Koko heaved a great sigh in his sleep. His hind foot trembled.

"Dreaming?" said Qwilleran. "What do you dream about? Chicken curry? People with guns that make a loud noise? I'd sure like to know what you witnessed last night."

Koko's whiskers twitched, and he threw one paw across his eyes.

The next time the telephone rang, it interrupted Qwilleran's shaving, and he answered in a mild huff. He considered shaving a spiritual rite—part ancestor worship, part reaffirmation of gender, part declaration of respectability—and it required the utmost artistry.

"This is Cokey," said a breathless voice. "I just heard the radio announcement about David Lyke. I can't believe it."

"He was murdered, all right."

"Do you have any idea who did it?"

"How would I know?"

"Are you mad at me?" Cokey said. "You're mad at me because I suggested publishing the Allison house."

"I'm not mad," said Qwilleran, letting his voice soften a little. It occurred to him that he might want to question Cokey about a few things. "I'm shaving. I've got lather all over my face."

"Sorry I called so early."

"I'll give you a ring soon, and we'll have dinner."

"How's Koko?"

"He's fine."

After saying goodbye, Qwilleran had an idea. He wiped the lather from his face, waked Koko, and placed him on the dictionary. Koko arched his back in a tense, vibrating stretch. He turned his whiskers up, rolled his eyes down, and yawned widely, showing thirty teeth, a corrugated palate, five inches of tongue, and half his gullet.

"Okay, let's play the game," Qwilleran said, after a prolonged yawn of his own.

Koko turned around three times, then rolled over and assumed a languid pose on the open pages of the dictionary.

"Game! Game! Play the game!" Qwilleran dug his fingernails into the pages to demonstrate.

Coyly Koko rolled over on his back and squirmed in a happy way.

"You loafer! What's the matter with you?"

The cat just narrowed his eyes and looked dreamy.

It was not until Qwilleran waved a sardine under Koko's nose that he agreed to cooperate. The game was uneventful, however: *maxillary* and *maypop*, *travel* and *trawlnet*, *scallion* and *Scandinavian*. Qwilleran had hoped for more pertinent catchwords. He had to admit, though, that a couple of them made sense. The sardine can said PRODUCT OF NORWAY.

Qwilleran hurried to the office and tackled the next issue of *Gracious Abodes*, but his mind was not on the magazine. He waited until he thought Starkweather would be at the studio, and then he telephoned Mrs. Starkweather at home.

She burst into tears. "Isn't it awful?" she cried. "My David! My dear David! Why would anyone want to do it?"

"It's hard to understand," said Qwilleran.

"He was so young. Only thirty-two, you know. And so full of life and talent. I don't know what Stark will do without him."

"Did David have enemies, Mrs. Starkweather?"

"I don't know. I just can't think. I'm so upset."

"Perhaps someone was jealous of David's success. Would anyone gain by his death?"

The tears tapered off into noisy sniffing. "Nobody would gain very much. David lived high, and he gave everything away. He didn't save a penny. Stark was always warning him."

"What will happen to David's half of the business?" Qwilleran asked in a tone as casual as he could manage.

"Oh, it will go to Stark, of course. That was the agreement. Stark put up all the money for the business. David contributed the talent. He had so much of that," she added with a whimper.

"Didn't Dave have any family?"

"Nobody. Not a living soul. I think that's why he gave so many parties. He wanted people around him, and he thought he had to buy their affection." Mrs. Starkweather heaved a breathy sigh. "But it wasn't true. People just naturally adored David."

Qwilleran bit his lip. He wanted to say: Yes, but wasn't he a cad? Didn't he say cutting things about the people who flocked around him? Don't you realize, Mrs. Starkweather, that David called you a middle-aged sot?

Instead he said, "I wonder what will happen to his Oriental art collection."

"I don't know. I really don't know." Her tone hardened. "I can think of three or four spongers who'd like to get their hands on it, though!"

"You don't know if the art is mentioned in David's will?"

"No, I don't." She thought for a moment. "I wouldn't be surprised if he left it to that young Japanese who cooks for him. It's just an idea."

"What makes you think that?"

"They were very close. David was the one who set Yushi up in the catering business. And Yushi was devoted to David. We were all devoted to David." The tears started again. "I'm glad you can't see me, Mr. Qwilleran. I look awful. I've been crying for hours! David made me feel young, and suddenly I feel so old."

Qwilleran's next call was to the studio called PLUG. He recognized the suave voice that answered.

"Bob, this is Qwilleran at the *Fluxion*," he said.

"Yes, indeed!" said Orax. "How the wires are buzzing this morning! The telephone company may declare an extra dividend."

"What have you heard about Dave's murder?"

"Nothing worth repeating, alas."

"I really called," said Qwilleran, "to ask about Yushi. Do you know if he's available for catering jobs? I'm giving a party for a guy who's getting married."

Orax said: "I'm sure Yushi will have plenty of time now that David has departed. He's listed in the phone book under Cuisine Internationale. . . . Are we going to see you at the Posthumous Pour?"

"What's that?"

"Oh, didn't you know?" said Orax. "When David wrote his will, he provided for one final cocktail bash for all his friends—at the Toledo! No weeping! Just laughter, dancing and booze until the money runs out. At the Toledo it runs out very fast."

"David was a real character," Qwilleran said. "I'd like to write a profile of him for the paper. Who were his best friends? Who could fill me in?"

Orax hummed on the line for a few seconds. "The Starkweathers, of course, and the Noytons, and *dear* Yushi, and quite a few unabashed free-loaders like myself."

"Any enemies?"

"Perhaps Jacques Boulanger, but these days it's hard to tell an enemy from a friend."

"How about the girls in his life?"

"Ah, yes, girls," said Orax. "There was Lois Avery, but she married and left town. And there was a creature with long straight hair who works for Mrs. Middy; I've forgotten her name."

"I think," said Qwilleran, "I know the one you mean."

CHAPTER 16

QWILLERAN TOOK a taxi to the Sorbonne Studio. He had telephoned for an appointment, and a woman with an engaging French accent had invited him to arrive *tout de suite* if he desired a *rendez-vous* with Monsieur Boulanger at the atelier.

In the taxi he thought again about Cokey. Now he knew! Koko had sensed her deception. Koko had been trying to convey that information when he nipped Cokey's head and licked the photograph from her wallet.

Qwilleran had caught only a glimpse of the picture, but he was fairly sure whose likeness the cat had licked: that arty pose, that light hair. Now he knew! Cokey—so candid, so disarming—was capable of a convincing kind of duplicity. She had allowed Qwilleran to introduce David, and the decorator had played the game with only a meager wavering of his sultry gaze. Was he playing the gentleman on a spur-of-the-moment cue? Or was there some prearranged agreement?

If Cokey had deceived Qwilleran once, she had probably deceived him twice. Had she engineered the embarrassment about the Allison house? Did she have connections at the *Morning Rampage*?

"Is this the place you want?" asked the cabdriver, rousing Qwilleran from his distasteful reverie. The taxi had stopped in front of a pretentious little building, a miniature version of the pavilions that French monarchs built for their mistresses.

The interior of the Sorbonne Studio was an awesome assemblage of creamy white marble, white carpet, white furniture, and crystal chandeliers. The carpet, thick and carved, looked like meringue. Qwilleran stepped on it cautiously.

There was an upholstered hush in the place until a dark-skinned young woman of rare beauty appeared from behind a folding screen and said, "*Bonjour, m'sieu.* May I 'elp you?"

"I have an appointment with Mr. Boulanger," said Qwilleran. "I'm from the *Daily Fluxion*."

"*Ah, oui.* Monsieur Boulanger is on the tele*phone* with a cli*ent*, but I will announce your pre*sence*."

With a sinuous walk she disappeared behind the folding screen, which was mirrored, and Qwilleran caught a reflection of himself looking smugly appreciative at her retreating figure.

In a moment a handsome Negro, wearing a goatee, came striding out from the inner regions. "Hello, there," he said with a smile and an easy manner. "I'm Jack Baker."

"I have an appointment with Mr. Boulanger," said Qwilleran.

"I'm your man," said the decorator. "Jacques Boulanger to clients, Jack Baker to my relatives and the press. Come into my office, *s'il vous plaît*."

Qwilleran followed him into a pale-blue room that was plush of carpet, velvety of wall, and dainty of chair. He glanced uneasily at the ceiling, entirely covered with pleated blue silk, gathered in a rosette in the center.

"*Man, I know what you're thinking.*" Baker laughed. "This is a real gone pad. *Mais malheureusement*, it's what the clients expect. Makes me feel like a jackass, but it's a living." His eyes were filled with merriment that began to put Qwilleran at ease. "How do you like the reception salon? We've just done it over."

"I guess it's all right if you like lots of white," said Qwilleran.

"Not white!" Baker gave an exaggerated shudder. "It's called Vichyssoise. It has an undertone of Leek Green."

The newsman asked: "Is this the kind of work you do for your customers? We'd like to photograph one of your interiors for *Gracious Abodes*. I understand you do a lot of interiors in Muggy Swamp."

The decorator hesitated. "I don't want to seem uncooperative, *vous savez*, but my clients don't go for that kind of publicity. And, to be perfectly frank, the designing I do in Muggy Swamp is not, *qu'est-ce qu'on dit*, newsworthy. I mean it! My clients are all squares. They like tired clichés. Preferably French clichés, and those are the worst! Now, if I could show you design with imagination and daring. Not so much taste, but more spirit."

"Too bad," said Qwilleran. "I was hoping we could get an important society name like Duxbury or Penniman."

"I wish I could oblige," said the decorator. "I really do. I dig the newspaper scene. It was an American newsman in Paris who introduced me to my first client—Mrs. Duxbury, as a matter of fact." He laughed joyously. "Would you like to hear the whole mad tale? *C'est formidable!*"

"Go ahead. Mind if I light my pipe?"

Baker began his story with obvious relish. "I was born right here in this town, on the wrong side of the wrong side of the tracks, if you know what I mean. Somehow I made college on a scholarship and came out with a Fine Arts degree, which entitled me—*ma foi!*—to work for a decorating studio, installing drapery hardware. So I saved my pennies and went to Paris, to the Sorbonne. *C'est bien ça.*" The decorator's face grew fond. "And that's where I was discovered by Mr. and Mrs. Duxbury, a couple of beautiful cats."

"Did they know you were from their own city?"

"*Mais non*! For kicks I was speaking English with a French accent, and I had grown this picturesque beard. The Duxbury's bought the whole exotic bit—bless them!—and commissioned me to come here and do their thirty-room house in Muggy Swamp. I did it in tones of Oyster, Pistachio, and Apricot. After that, all the important families wanted the Duxbury's Negro decorator from Paris. I had to continue the French accent, *vous savez.*"

"How long have you kept the secret?"

"It's no secret any longer, but it would embarrass too many people if we admitted the truth. So we all enjoy the harmless little *divertissement*. I pretend to be French, and they pretend they don't know I'm not. *C'est parfait!*" Baker grinned with pleasure as he related it.

The young lady with the ravishing face and figure walked into the office carrying a golden tray. On it were delicate teacups, slices of lemon, a golden teapot.

"This is my niece, Verna," said the decorator.

"Hi!" she said to Qwilleran. "Ready for your fix? Lemon or sugar?" There was no trace of a French accent. She was very American and very young, but she poured from the vermeil teapot with aristocratic grace.

Qwilleran said to Baker, "Who did the decorating in Muggy Swamp before you arrived on the scene?"

The decorator gave a twisted smile. "*Eh bien*, it was Lyke and Starkweather." He waited for Qwilleran's reaction, but the newsman was a veteran at hiding reactions behind his ample moustache.

"You mean you walked away with all their customers?"

"*C'est la vie*. Decorating clients are fickle. They are also sheep, especially in Muggy Swamp."

Baker was frank, so Qwilleran decided to be blunt. "How come you didn't get the G. Verning Tait account?"

The decorator looked at his niece, and she looked at him. Then Jack Baker smiled an ingratiating smile. "There was some feeling in the Tait family," he said, speaking carefully. "*Pourtant*, David Lyke did a good job. I would never have used that striped wallpaper in the foyer, and the lamps were out of scale, but David tried hard." His expression changed to sorrow, real or feigned. "And now I've lost my best competition. Without competition, where are the kicks in this game?"

"I'm thinking of writing a profile on David Lyke," said Qwilleran. "As a competitor of his, could you make a statement?"

"Quotable?" asked Baker with a sly look.

"How long had you known Lyke?"

"From way back. When we were both on the other side of the tracks. Before his name was Lyke."

"He changed his name?"

"It was unpronounceable and unspellable. David decided that Lyke would be more likable."

"Did you two get along?"

"*Tiens!* We were buddies in high school—a couple of esthetes in a jungle of seven-foot basketball players and teen-age goons. Secretly I felt superior to Dave because I had parents, and he was an orphan. Then I came out of college and found myself working for him—measuring windows and drilling screwholes in the woodwork so David Lyke could sell $5,000 drapery jobs and get invited to society debuts in Muggy Swamp. While I'd been grinding my brains at school and washing dishes for my keep, he'd been making it on personality and bleached hair and—who knows what else. It rankled, man; it rankled!"

Qwilleran puffed on his pipe and looked sympathetic.

"*Dites donc*, I got my revenge," Baker smiled broadly. "I came back from Paris and walked away with his Muggy Swamp clientele. And to rub it in, I moved into the same building where he lived, but in a more expensive apartment on a higher floor."

"You live at the Villa Verandah? So do I."

"Sixteenth floor, south."

"Fifteenth floor, north."

"*Alors*, we're a couple of status-seekers," said Baker.

Qwilleran had one more question. "As a competitor of David's, and a former friend, and a neighbor, do you have any educated guesses as to the motive for his murder?"

The decorator shrugged. "*Qui sait?* He was a ruthless man—in his private life as well as in business."

"I thought he was the most," said Verna.

"*Vraiment, chérie*, he had a beautiful facade, but he'd cut your throat behind your back, as the saying goes."

Qwilleran said, "I've never met anyone with more personal magnetism."

"*Eh bien!*" Baker set his jaw, and looked grim.

"Well, I'll probably see you around the mausoleum," said the newsman, as he rose to leave.

"Come up to the sixteenth floor and refuel some evening," the decorator said. "My wife's a real swinger in the kitchen."

Qwilleran went back to the office to check proofs, and he found a message to see the managing editor at once.

Percy was in a less than genial mood. "Qwill," he said abruptly, "I know you were not enthusiastic about taking the *Gracious Abodes* assignment, and I think I was wrong in pressing it on you."

"What do you mean?"

"I'm not blaming you for the succession of mishaps per se, but it does seem that the magazine has been accident-prone."

"I didn't like the idea at the beginning," said Qwilleran, "but I'm strong for it now. It's an interesting beat."

"That thing last night," said Percy, shaking his head. "That murder! Why does everything happen on your beat? Sometimes there are psychological reasons for what we call a jinx. Perhaps we should relieve you of the assignment. Anderson is retiring October first. . . ."

"Anderson!" Qwilleran said with undisguised horror! "The church editor?"

"Perhaps you could handle church news, and *Gracious Abodes* could be turned over to the Women's Department, where it belonged in the first place."

Qwilleran's moustache reared up. "If you'd let me dig into these crimes, Harold, the way I suggested, I think I could unearth some clues. There are forces working against us! I happen to know, for example, that the Police Widows' Fund got a sizable donation from the owners of the *Morning Rampage* around the same time the Vice Squad raided the Allison house."

Percy looked weary. "They're getting one from us, too. Every September both papers make a donation."

"All right, then. Maybe it wasn't a payoff, but I'll bet the timing wasn't accidental. And I suspect a plot in the Muggy Swamp incident, too."

"On what do you base your suspicions?"

Qwilleran smoothed his moustache. "I can't reveal my source at this time, but with further investigation—"

The editor slapped his hand on the desk with finality. "Let's leave it the way I've suggested, Qwill. You put next Sunday's magazine to bed, and then let Fran Unger take over."

"Wait! Give me one more week before you make a decision. I promise there'll be a surprising development."

"We've had nothing but surprising developments for the last fifteen days."

Qwilleran did not reply, and he did not move away from Percy's desk. He just stared the editor in the eye and waited for an affirmative—a trick he had learned from Koko.

"All right. One more week," said the editor. "And let's hope no one plants a bomb in the Press Room."

Qwilleran went back to the Feature Department with hope and doubt battling for position. He dialed the *Fluxion*'s extension at Police Headquarters and talked to Lodge Kendall. "Any news on the murder?"

"Not a thing," said the police reporter. "They're going through Lyke's address book. It's an extensive list."

"Did they get any interesting fingerprints?"

"Not only fingerprints, but pawprints!"

"Let me know if anything breaks," Qwilleran said. "Just between you and me, my job may depend on it."

At six o'clock, as Qwilleran was leaving for dinner, he ran into Odd Bunsen at the elevator.

"Hey, do you want those photographs of the Tait house?" Bunsen said. "They've been cluttering up my locker for a week." He went back to the Photo Lab and returned with a large envelope. "I made blowups for you, same as I made for the police. What do you want them for?"

"Thought I'd give them to Tait."

"That's what I figured. I did a careful job of printing."

Qwilleran went to the Press Club, loaded a plate at the all-you-can-eat buffet, and took it to the far end of the bar, where he could eat in solitude and contemplate the day's findings: Lyke's relationship with Cokey, his unfashionable beginnings, the boyhood friendship that went sour, the national treasures that should have stayed in Japan, and the vague status of Yushi. Once during the day Qwilleran had tried to telephone Cuisine Internationale, but Yushi's answering service had said the caterer was out of town.

While the newsman was drinking his coffee, he opened the envelope. The photographs were impressive. Bunsen had enlarged them to eleven-by-fourteen and let the edges bleed. The bartender was hovering near, wiping a spot on the bar that needed no wiping, showing curiosity.

"The Tait house," Qwilleran said. "I'm going to give them to the owner."

"He'll appreciate it. People like to have pictures of their homes, their kids, their pets—anything like that." Bruno accompanied this profound observation with a sage nod.

Qwilleran said: "Did you ever hear of a cat licking glossy photos? That's what my cat does. He also eats rubber bands."

"That's not good," said the bartender. "You better do something about it."

"You think it's bad for him?"

"It isn't normal. I think your cat is, like they say, disturbed."

"He seems perfectly happy and healthy."

Bruno shook his head wisely. "That cat needs help. You should take him to a psycatatrist."

"A psyCATatrist?" said Qwilleran. "I didn't know there was such a thing."

"I can tell you where to find a good one."

"Well, thanks," said the newsman. "If I decide to take Koko to a head-shrinker, I'll check back with you."

He went to the buffet for a second helping, wrapped a slice of turkey in a paper napkin, and took a taxi home to the Villa Verandah.

As soon as he stepped off the elevator on the fifteenth floor, he started jingling his keys. It was his signal to Koko. The cat always ran to the door and raised his shrill Siamese yowl of greeting. As part of the ritual, Qwilleran would pretend to fumble with the lock, and the longer he delayed opening the door, the more vociferous the welcome.

But tonight there was no welcoming clamor. Qwilleran opened the door and quickly glanced in Koko's three favorite haunts: the northeast corner of the middle sofa; the glass-topped coffee table, a cool surface for warm days; and the third bookshelf, between a marble bust of Sappho and a copy of *Fanny Hill*, where Koko retired if the apartment was chilly. None of the three offered any evidence of cat.

Qwilleran went to the kitchen and looked on top of the refrigerator, expecting to see a round mound of light fur curled on the blue cushion—headless, tailless, legless, and asleep. There was no Koko there. He called, and there was no answer. Systematically he searched under the bed, behind the draperies, in closets and drawers, even inside the stereo cabinet. He opened the kitchen cupboards. In a moment of panic he snatched at the refrigerator door. No Koko. He looked in the oven.

All this time Koko was watching the frantic search from the seat of the green wing chair—in plain view but invisible, as a cat can be when he is silent and motionless. Qwilleran gave a grunt of surprise and relief when he finally caught sight of the hump of fur. Then he became concerned. Koko was sitting in a hunched position with his shoulder blades up and a troubled look in his eyes.

"Are you all right?" the man said.

The cat gave a mouselike squeak without opening his mouth.

"Do you feel sick?"

Koko wriggled uncomfortably and looked in the corner of the chair seat. A few inches from his nose was a ball of fluff. Green fluff.

"What's that? Where did you get that?" Qwilleran demanded. Then his eyes traveled to the wing of the chair. Across its top a patch of upholstery fabric was missing, and the padding was bursting through.

"Koko!" yelled Qwilleran. "Have you been chewing this chair? This expensive Danish chair?"

Koko gave a little cough, and produced another wad of green wool, well chewed.

Qwilleran gasped. "What will Harry Noyton say? He'll have a fit!" Then he raised his voice to a shout, "Are you the one who's been eating my ties?"

The cat looked up at the man and purred mightily.

"Don't you dare purr! You must be crazy—to eat cloth! You're out of your mind! Lord! That's all I need—one more problem!"

Koko gave another wheezing cough, and up came a bit of green wool, very damp.

Qwilleran dashed to the telephone and dialed a number.

"Connect me with the bartender," he said, and in a moment he heard the hubbub of the Press Club bar like the roar of a hurricane. "Bruno!" he shouted. "This is Qwilleran. How do I reach that doctor? That psycatatrist?"

CHAPTER 17

THE MORNING after Koko ate a piece of the Danish chair, Qwilleran telephoned his office and told Arch Riker he had a doctor's appointment and would be late.

"Trouble?" Riker asked.

"Nothing serious," said Qwilleran. "Sort of a digestive problem."

"That's a twist! I thought you had a stomach like a billy goat."

"I have, but last night I got a big surprise."

"Better take care of it," Riker advised. "Those things can lead to something worse."

Bruno had supplied Dr. Highspight's telephone number, and when Qwilleran called, the voice of the woman who answered had to compete with the mewing and wailing of countless cats. Speaking with a folksy English accent, she told Qwilleran he could have an appointment at eleven o'clock that morning. To his surprise she said it would not be necessary to bring the patient. She gave an address on Merchant Street, and Qwilleran winced.

He prepared a tempting breakfast for Koko—jellied consommé and breast of Press Club turkey—hoping to discourage the cat's appetite for Danish furniture. He said goodbye anxiously, and took a bus to Merchant Street.

Dr. Highspight's number was two blocks from the Allison house, and it was the same type of outdated mansion. Unlike the Allison house, which was freshly painted and well landscaped, the clinic was distinctly seedy. The lawn was full of weeds. There were loose floorboards on the porch.

Qwilleran rang the doorbell with misgivings. He had never heard of a psycatatrist, and he hated the thought of being rooked by a quack. Nor did he relish being made the victim of another practical joke.

The woman who came to the door was surrounded by cats. Qwilleran counted five of them: a tiger, an orange nondescript, one chocolate brown, and two sleek black panthers. From there his glance went to the woman's runover bedroom slippers, her wrinkled stockings, the sagging hem of her housedress, and finally to her pudgy middle-aged face with its sweet smile.

"Come in, love," she said, "before the pussies run out in the road."

"My name's Qwilleran," he said. "I have an appointment with Dr. Highspight."

His nose recorded faint odors of fish and antiseptic, and his eye perused the spacious entrance hall, counting cats. They sat on the hall table, perched on several levels of stairway, and peered inquisitively through all the doorways. A Siamese kitten with an appealing little smudged face struck a businesslike pose in a flat box of sand that occupied one corner of the foyer.

"Eee! I'm no doctor, love," said the woman. "Just a cat fancier with a bit of common sense. Would you like a cuppa? Go in the front room and make yourself comfy, and I'll light the kettle."

The living room was high-ceilinged and architecturally distinguished, but the furniture had seen better days. Qwilleran selected the overstuffed chair that seemed least likely to puncture him with a broken spring. The cats had followed him and were now inspecting his shoelaces or studying him from a safe distance. He marveled at a cat's idea of a safe distance—roughly seven feet, the length of an average adult's lunge.

"Now, love, what seems to be the bother?" asked Mrs. Highspight, seating herself in a platform rocker and picking up a wild-looking apricot cat to hold on her lap. "I was expecting a young lad. You were in such a dither when you called."

"I was concerned about my Siamese," said Qwilleran. "He's a remarkable animal, with some unusual talents—and very friendly. But lately his behavior has been strange. He's crazy about gummed envelopes, masking tape, stamps—anything like that. He licks them!"

"Eee, I like to lick envelopes myself," said Mrs. Highspight, rocking her chair vigorously and stroking the apricot cat. "It's a caution how many flavors they can think up."

"But you haven't heard the worst. He's started eating cloth! Not just chewing it—swallowing it! I thought the moths were getting into my clothes, but I've found out it's the cat. He's nibbled three good wool ties, and last night he ate a chunk out of a chair."

"Now we're onto something!" said the woman. "Is it always wool that he eats?"

"I guess so. The chair is covered with some kind of woolly material."

"It won't hurt him. If he can't digest it, he'll chuck it up."

"That's comforting to know," said Qwilleran, "but it's getting to be a problem. It was a costly chair that he ate, and it doesn't even belong to me."

"Does he do it when you're at home?"

"No, always behind my back."

"The poor puss is lonesome. Siamese cats need company, they do, or they get a bit daft. Is he by himself all day?"

Qwilleran nodded.

"How long has he lived with you?"

"About six months. He belonged to my landlord, who was killed last March. Perhaps you remember the murder on Blenheim Place."

"Eee, that I do! I always read about murders, and that was a gory one, that was. They done him in with a carving knife. And this poor puss—was he very fond of the murdered man?"

"They were kindred spirits. Never separated."

"That's your answer, love. The poor puss has had a shock, like. And now he's lonesome."

Qwilleran found himself rising to his own defense. "The cat's very fond of me. We get along fine. He's affectionate, and I play with him once in a while."

Just then a large smoky-blue cat walked into the room and made a loud pronouncement.

"The kettle's boiling," said Mrs. Highspight. "Tommy always notifies me when the kettle's boiling. I'll fetch the tea things and be back in a jiff."

The company of cats kept their eyes on Qwilleran until the woman returned with cups and a fat brown teapot.

"And does he talk much, this puss of yours?" she asked.

"He's always yowling about one thing or another."

"His mother pushed him away when he was a kit. That kind always talks a blue streak and needs more affection, they do. Is he neutered?"

Qwilleran nodded. "He's what my grandmother used to call a retired gentleman cat."

"There's only one thing for it. You must get him another puss for a companion."

"Keep two cats?" Qwilleran protested.

"Two's easier than one. They keep each other entertained and help wash the places that's hard to reach. If your puss has a companion, you won't have to swab his ears with cotton and boric acid."

"I didn't know I was supposed to."

"And don't bother your head about the feed bill. Two happy cats don't eat much more than one cat that's lonesome."

Qwilleran felt a tiny breath on his neck and turned to find the pretty little Siamese he had seen in the entrance hall, now perched on the back of his chair, smelling his ear.

"Tea's ready to pour," Mrs. Highspight announced. "I like a good strong cup. There's a bit of milk in the pitcher, if you've a mind."

Qwilleran accepted a thin china cup filled with a mahogany-colored brew, and noted a cat hair floating on its surface. "Do you sell cats?" he asked.

"I breed exotics and find homes for strays," said Mrs. Highspight. "What your puss needs is a nice little Siamese ladylove—spayed, of course. Not that it makes much difference. They still know which is which, and they can be very sweet together. What's the name of your puss?"

"Koko."

"Eee! Just like Gilbert and Sullivan!" Then she sang in a remarkably good voice, "'For he's going to marry Yum *Yum*, te dum. Your anger pray bury, for all will be merry. I think you had better succumb, te dum.'"

Tommy, the big blue point, raised his head, and howled. Meanwhile, the Siamese kitten was burrowing into Qwilleran's pocket.

"Shove her off, love, if she's a bother. She's a regular hoyden. The females always take a liking to men."

Qwilleran stroked the pale fur, almost white, and the kitten purred delicately and tried to nibble his finger with four little teeth. "If I'm going to get another cat," he said, "maybe this one—"

"Eee, I couldn't let you have that one. She's special, like. But I know where there's an orphan needs a good home. Did you hear about that Mrs. Tait that died last week? There was a burglary, and it was in all the papers."

"I know a little about it," said Qwilleran.

"A sad thing, that was. Mrs. Tait had a Siamese female, and I don't fancy her husband will be keeping the poor puss."

"What makes you think so?"

"Eee, he doesn't like cats."

"How do you know all this?"

"The puss came from one of my litters, and the missus—rest her soul!—had to call on me for help. The poor puss was so nervous, wouldn't eat, wouldn't sleep. And now the poor woman's gone, and no telling what will become of the puss. . . . Let me fill your teacup, love."

She poured more of the red-black brew with its swirling garnish of tea leaves.

"And that husband of hers," she went on. "Such a one for putting on airs, but—mind this!—I had to wait a good bit for my fee. And me with all these hungry mouths to feed!"

Qwilleran's moustache was signaling to him. He said that, under the circumstances, he would consider adopting the cat. Then he tied the shoelace the cats had untied, and stood up to leave. "How much do I owe you for the consultation?"

"Would three dollars be too much for you, love?"

"I think I can swing it," he said.

"And if you want to contribute a few pennies for the cup of tea, it goes to buy a bit of a treat for the pussies. Just drop it in the marmalade crock on the hall table."

Mrs. Highspight and an entourage of waving tails accompanied Qwilleran to the door, the Siamese kitten rubbing against his ankles and touching his heart. He dropped two quarters in the marmalade jar.

"Call on me any time you need help, love," said Mrs. Highspight.

"There's one thing I forgot to mention," Qwilleran said. "A friend visited me the other evening, and Koko tried to bite her. Not a vicious attack—just a token bite. But on the head, of all places!"

"What was the lady doing?"

"Cokey wasn't doing a thing! She was minding her own business, when all of a sudden Koko sprang at her head."

"The lady's name is Cokey, is it?"

"That's what everybody calls her."

"You'll have to call her something else, love. Koko thought you were using his name. A puss is jealous of his name, he is. Very jealous."

When Qwilleran left the cattery on Merchant Street, he told himself that Mrs. Highspight's diagnosis sounded logical; the token attack on Cokey was motivated by jealously. At the first phone booth he stopped and called the Middy studio.

On the telephone he found Cokey strangely gentle and amenable. When he suggested a dinner date, she invited him to dinner at her apartment. She said it would be only a casserole and a salad, but she promised him a surprise.

Qwilleran went back to his office and did some writing. It went well. The words flowed easily, and his two typing fingers hit all the right keys. He also answered a few letters from readers who were requesting decorating advice:

"May I use a quilted *matelassé* on a small *bergére*?"

"Is it all right to place a low credenza under a high clerestory?"

In his agreeable mood Qwilleran told them all, "Yes. Sure. Why not?"

Just before he left the office at five thirty, the Library chief called to say that the Tait clipping file had been returned, and Qwilleran picked it up on his way out of the building.

He wanted to go home and shave before going to Cokey's, and he had to feed the cat. As soon as he stepped off the elevator on the fifteenth floor, he could hear paeans of greeting, and when he entered the apartment Koko began a drunken race through the rooms. He went up over the backs of chairs and down again with a thud. He zoomed up on the stereo cabinet and skated its entire length, rounded the dining table in a blur of light fur, cleared the desk top, knocked over the wastebasket—all the while alternating a falsetto howl with a baritone growl.

"That's the spirit!" said Qwilleran. "That's what I like to see," and he wondered if the cat sensed he was getting a playmate.

Qwilleran chopped some chicken livers for Koko and sautéed them in butter, and he crumbled a small side order of Roquefort cheese. Hurriedly he cleaned up and put on his other suit and his good plaid tie. Then it was six thirty, and time to leave. For a few seconds he hesitated over the Tait file from the Library—a bulky envelope of old society notes, obsolete business news, and obituaries. His moustache pricked up, but his stomach decided the Tait file could wait until later.

CHAPTER 18

COKEY LIVED on the top floor of an old town house, and Qwilleran, after climbing three flights of stairs, was breathing hard when he arrived at her apartment. She opened the door, and he lost what little breath he had left.

The girl who greeted him was a stranger. She had cheekbones, temples, a jawline, and ears. Her hair, that had formerly encased her head and most of her visage like a helmet of chain mail, was now a swirling frame for her face. Qwilleran was fascinated by Cokey's long neck and graceful chinline.

"It's great!" he said. His eyes followed her as she moved about the apartment doing domestic and unnecessary little tasks.

The furnishings were spare, with an understated Bohemian smartness; black canvas chairs, burlap curtains in the honest color of potato sacks, and painted boards supported by clay plant pots to make a bookcase. Cokey had created a festive atmosphere with lighted candles and music. There were even two white carnations leaning out of a former vinegar bottle.

Her economies registered favorably with Qwilleran. There was something about the room that looked sad and brave to a resident of the Villa Verandah. It touched him in a vulnerable spot, and for one brief moment he had a delirious urge to support this girl for life, but it passed quickly. He pressed a handkerchief to his brow and remarked about the music coming from a portable record player.

"Schubert," she said sweetly. "I've given up Hindemith. He doesn't go with my new hairdo."

For dinner she served a mixture of fish and brown rice in a sauce flecked with green. The salad was crunchy and required a great deal of chewing, retarding conversation. Later came ice cream made of yogurt and figs, sprinkled with sunflower seeds.

After dinner Cokey poured cups of herb tea (she said it was her own blend of alfalfa and bladder wrack) and urged her guest to take the most comfortable chair and prop his feet on a hassock that she had made from a beer crate, upholstering it with shaggy carpet samples. While he lighted his pipe, she curled up on the couch—an awning-striped mattress on legs—and started knitting something pink.

"What's that?" Qwilleran gasped, and almost inhaled the match he intended to blow out.

"A sweater," she said. "I knit all my own sweaters. Do you like the color? Pink is going to be part of my new image, since I had no luck with the old image."

Qwilleran smoked his pipe and marveled at the omnipotence of hairdressers. Billions are spent for neurophysiological research to control human behavior, he reflected. Beauty shops would be cheaper.

For a while he watched the angular grace of Cokey's hands as she manipulated the knitting needles, and suddenly he said: "Tell me honestly,

Cokey. Did you know the nature of the Allison house when you suggested publishing it?"

"Honestly, I didn't," she said.

"Did you happen to mention it to that fellow from the *Morning Rampage*?"

"What fellow?"

"Mike Bulmer in their Circulation Department. You seem to know him. You spoke to him at the Press Club."

"Oh, *that* one! I don't really know him. He bought some lamps from Mrs. Middy last spring and gave her a bad check; that's why I remembered him."

Qwilleran felt relieved. "I thought you were keeping secrets from me."

Cokey stopped knitting. She sighed. "There's one secret I'd better confess, because you'll find out sooner or later. You're so snoopy!"

"Occupational disease," said Qwilleran. He lighted his pipe again, and Cokey watched intently as he knocked it on the ashtray, drew on it, peered into it, filled it, tamped it, and applied a match.

"Well," said Cokey, when that was done, "it's about David Lyke. When you took me to his party and introduced him, I pretended we had never met."

"But you had," said Qwilleran. "In fact, you carry his picture in your handbag."

"How did you know?"

"You spilled everything on my sofa Saturday night, and Koko selected Lyke's picture and started licking it."

"You and your psychic cat are a good team!"

"Then it's true?"

She shrugged helplessly. "I was one of the hordes of women who fell for that man. Those bedroom eyes! And that voice like a roll of drums! . . . Of course, it never amounted to anything. David charmed everyone and loved no one."

"But you still carry his picture."

Cokey pressed her lips together, and her eyelashes fluttered. "I tore it up—a few days ago." Then all at once it became necessary for her to repair her lipstick, change the records, snuff the candles on the dinner table, put the butter in the refrigerator. When she had finished her frantic activity, she sat down again with her knitting. "Let's talk about you," she said to Qwilleran. "Why do you always wear red plaid ties?"

He fingered his neckwear tenderly. "I like them. This one is a Mackin-tosh tartan. I had a Bruce and a MacGregor, too, but Koko ate them."

"*Ate* them!"

"I was blaming the moths, but Koko was the culprit. I'm glad he didn't get this one. It's my favorite. My mother was a Mackintosh."

"I never heard of a cat eating ties."

"Wool-eating is a neurotic symptom," Qwilleran said with authority. "The question is: Why didn't he touch the Mackintosh? He had plenty of opportunity. He ruined all the others. Why did he spare my favorite tie?"

"He must be a very considerate cat. Has he eaten anything else?"

Qwilleran nodded gloomily. "You know that Danish Modern chair in my apartment? He ate a piece of that, too."

"It's wool," Cokey said. "Animal matter. Maybe it tastes good to neu-rotic cats."

"The whole apartment is full of animal matter: vicuña chairs, suede sofas, goat-hair rug! But Koko had to pick Harry Noyton's favorite chair. How much will I have to pay to get it reupholstered?"

"Mrs. Middy will do it at cost," said Cokey, "but we'll have to order the fabric from Denmark. And how can you be sure Koko won't nibble it again?"

Qwilleran told her about Mrs. Highspight and the plan to adopt the Tait cat. "She told me Tait is unfond of cats. She also said he's slow to pay his bills."

"The richer they are, the harder it is to collect," said Cokey.

"But is Tait as rich as people think? David hinted that the decorating bill was unpaid. And when we discussed the possibility of publishing the Tait house, David said he thought he could use persuasion; it sounded as if he had some kind of leverage he could employ. Actually, Tait agreed quite readily. Why? Because he was really broke and inclined to cooperate with his creditor? Or for some other obscure reason?" Qwilleran touched his moustache. "Sometimes I think the Muggy Swamp episode is a frame-up. And I still think the police theory about the houseboy is all wet."

"Then what's happened to him?"

"Either he's in Mexico," said Qwilleran, "or he's been murdered. And if he's in Mexico, either he went of his own accord or he was sent there by the conspirators. And if he was sent, either he has the jades with him or he's clean. And if he has the jades, I'll bet you ten to one that Tait is plan-ning a trip to Mexico in the near future. He's going away for a rest. If he heads west, he'll probably wind up in Mexico."

"You can also go west by heading east," said Cokey.

Qwilleran reached over and patted her hand. "Smart girl."

"Do you think he'd trust the houseboy with the jades?"

"You've got a point. Maybe Paolo didn't take the loot. Maybe he was dispatched to Mexico as a decoy. If that's the case, where are the jades hidden?"

The answer was a large silence filling the room. Qwilleran clicked his pipe on his teeth. Cokey clicked her knitting needles. The record player clicked as another disc dropped on the turntable. Now it was Brahms.

Finally Qwilleran said, "You know that game Koko and I play with the dictionary?" He proceeded with circumspection. "Lately Koko's been turning up some words that have significance. . . . I shouldn't talk about it. It's too incredible."

"You know how I feel about cats," said Cokey. "I'll believe anything."

"The first time I noticed it was last Sunday morning. I had forgotten to fix his breakfast, and when we played the dictionary game he turned up *hungerly*."

Cokey clapped her hands. "How clever!"

"On the next try he turned up *feed*, but I didn't catch on until he produced *meadow mouse*. Apparently he was getting desperate. I don't think he really cares for mice."

"Why, that's like a Ouija board!"

"It gives me the creeps," said Qwilleran. "Ever since the mystery in Muggy Swamp, he's been flushing out words that point to G. Verning Tait, like *bald* and *sacroiliac*. He picked *sacroiliac* twice in one game, and that's quite a coincidence in a dictionary with three thousand pages."

"Is Mr. Tait bald?"

"Not a hair on his head. He also suffers from a back ailment. . . . Do you know what a koolokamba is?"

Cokey shook her head.

"It's an ape with a bald head and black hands. Koko dredged that one up, too."

"Black hands! That's poetic symbolism," Cokey said. "Can you think of any more?"

"Not every word pertains to the situation. Sometimes it's *visceri-pericardial* or *calorifacient*. But one day he found two significant words on one page: *rubeola* and *ruddiness*. Tait has a florid complexion, I might add."

"Oh, Qwill, that cat's really tuned in!" Cokey said. "I'm sure he's on the right track. Can you do anything about it?"

"Hardly." Qwilleran looked dejected. "I can't go to the police and tell them my cat suspects the scion of a fine old family. . . . Still, there's another possibility. . . ."

"What's that?"

"It may be," said Qwilleran, "that the police suspect Tait, too, and they're publishing the houseboy theory as a cover-up."

CHAPTER 19

QWILLERAN ARRIVED HOME from Cokey's apartment earlier than he had expected. Cokey had chased him out. She said they both had to work the next day, and she had to fix her hair and iron a blouse.

When he arrived at the Villa Verandah, Koko greeted him with a table-hopping routine that ended on the desk. The red light on the telephone was glowing. The phone had been ringing, Koko seemed to be saying, and no one had been there to answer.

Qwilleran dialed the switchboard.

"Mr. Bunsen called you at nine o'clock," the operator told him. "He said to call him at home if you came in before one A.M."

Qwilleran consulted his watch. It was not yet midnight, and he started to dial Bunsen's number. Then he changed his mind. He decided Cokey was right about the importance of image. He decided it would not hurt to enhance his own image—the enviable one of a bachelor carousing until the small hours of the morning.

Qwilleran emptied his coat pockets, draped his coat on a chairback, and sat down at the desk to browse through the Tait file of newspaper clippings. Koko watched, lounging on the desk top in a classic pose known to lions and tigers, curving his tail around a Swedish crystal paperweight.

The newsprint was in varying shades of yellow and brown, depending on the age of the news item. Each was rubber-stamped with the date of publication. It was hardly necessary to read the stamp; outmoded typefaces, as well as mellowed paper, gave a clue to the date.

First Qwilleran shuffled through the clippings hastily, hoping to spot a lurid headline. Finding none in a cursory search, he started to read systematically: three generations of Tait history in chronological disorder.

Five years ago Tait had given a talk at a meeting of the Lapidary Society. Eleven years ago his father had died. There was a lengthy feature on the Tait Manufacturing Company, apparently one of a series on family-owned firms of long standing; organized in 1883 for the manufacture of buggy whips, the company was now producing car radio antennas. Old society clippings showed the elder Taits at the opera or charity functions. Three years ago G. Verning Tait announced his intention of manufacturing antennas that looked like buggy whips. A year later a news item stated that the Tait plant had closed and bankruptcy proceedings were being instituted.

Then there was the wedding announcement of twenty-four years ago. Mr. George Verning Tait, the son of Mr. and Mrs. Verning H. Tait of Muggy Swamp, was taking a bride. The entire Tait family had gone to Europe for the ceremony. The nuptials had been celebrated at the home of the bride's parents, the Victor Thorvaldsons of—

Qwilleran's eyes popped when he read it. "The Victor Thorvaldsons of Aarhus, Denmark."

He leaned back in his chair and exhaled into his moustache.

"Koko," he said, "what do you suppose Harry Noyton is pulling off in Aarhus?"

The cat opened his mouth to reply, but there was not enough breath behind his comment to make it audible.

Qwilleran's watch said one o'clock, and he hurried through the rest of the clippings until he found what he was looking for. Then he dialed Odd Bunsen's number excitedly.

"Hope I didn't get you out of bed," he said to the photographer.

"How was your date, you old tomcat?" Bunsen demanded.

"Not bad. Not bad."

"What were you doing on Merchant Street this morning?"

"How do you know I was on Merchant Street?"

"Aha! I saw you waiting for a bus on the southwest corner of Merchant and State at eleven fifty-five."

"You don't miss a thing, do you?" Qwilleran said. "Why didn't you stop and give me a lift?"

"I was going in the other direction. Brother! You were getting an early start. It wasn't even lunchtime."

"I had a doctor's appointment."

"On Merchant Street? Ho ho HO! Ho ho HO!"

"Is that all you called about? You're a nosy old woman."

"Nope. I've got some information for you."

"I've got some news for you, too," said Qwilleran. "I've found the skeleton in the Tait closet."

"What is it?"

"A court trial. G. Verning Tait was involved in a paternity suit!"

"Ho ho HO! That old goat! Who was the gal?"

"One of the Taits' servants. She got a settlement, too. According to these old clippings it must have been a sensational trial."

"A thing like that can be a rough experience."

"You'd think a family with the Taits' money and position would settle out of court—at any cost," Qwilleran said. "I covered a paternity trial in Chicago several years ago, and the testimony got plenty raw. . . . Now, what's on *your* mind? What's this information you've got for me?"

"Nothing much," said Bunsen, "but if you're going to send those photographs to Tait, you'd better make it snappy. He's leaving the country in a couple of days."

"How do you know?"

"I ran into Lodge Kendall at the Press Club. Tait's leaving Saturday morning."

"For Mexico?" asked Qwilleran as his moustache sprang to attention.

"Nope. Nothing as obvious as that! You'd like it if he was heading for Mexico, wouldn't you?" the photographed teased.

"Well, where is he going?"

"Denmark!"

QWILLERAN WAKED EASILY the next morning after a night of silly dreams that he was glad to terminate. In one episode he dreamed he was flying to Aarhus to be best man at the high-society wedding of two neutered cats.

Before leaving for the office, he telephoned Tait and offered to deliver the photographs of the jade the next day. He also inquired about the female cat and was appalled to hear that Tait had put her out of the house to fend for herself.

"Can you get her back?" Qwilleran asked, controlling his temper. He had a particular loathing for people who mistreated animals.

"She's still on the grounds," Tait said. "She howled all night. I'll let her come back in the house. . . . How many photos do you have for me?"

• • •

QWILLERAN WORKED HARD and fast at the office that day, while the clerk in the Feature Department intercepted all phone calls and uninvited visitors with the simple explanation that permits no appeal, no argument, no exceptions. "Sorry, he's on deadline."

Only once did he take time out, and that was to telephone the Taits' former housekeeper.

"Mrs. Hawkins," he said, taming his voice to an aloof drawl, "this is an acquaintance of Mr. Tait in Muggy Swamp. I am being married shortly, and my wife and I will need a housekeeper. Mr. Tait recommends you highly—"

"Oh, he does, does he?" said a musical voice with impudence in the inflection.

"Could you come for an interview this evening at the Villa Verandah?"

"Who'll be there? Just you? Or will the lady be there?"

"My fiancée is unfortunately in Tokyo at the moment, and it will be up to me to make the arrangements."

"Okey doke. I'll come. What time?"

Qwilleran set the appointment for eight o'clock. He was glad he was not in need of a housekeeper. He wondered if Mrs. Hawkins was an example of Tait's ill-advised economies.

By the time Mrs. Hawkins presented herself for the interview, the rain had started, and she arrived with dripping umbrella and a dripping raincoat over a gaudy pink and green dress. Qwilleran noted that the dress had the kind of neckline that slips off the shoulder at the slightest encouragement, and there was a slit in the side seam. The woman had sassy eyes, and she flirted her shoulders when she walked. He liked sassy, flirtatious females if they were young and attractive, but Mrs. Hawkins was neither.

With exaggerated decorum he offered her a glass of sherry "against the weather," and poured a deep amber potion from Harry Noyton's well-stocked bar. He poured an exceptionally large glass, and by the time the routine matters had been covered—experience, references, salary—Mrs. Hawkins had relaxed in the cushions of a suede sofa and was ready for a chatty evening.

"You're one of the newspaper fellows that came to the house to take pictures," she announced at this point, with her eyes dancing at him. "I remember your moustache." She waved an arm at the appointments of the room. "I didn't know reporters made so much money."

"Let me fill your glass," said Qwilleran.

"Aren't you drinking?"

"Ulcers," he said with a look of self-pity.

"Lordy, I know all about *them*!" said Mrs. Hawkins. "I cooked for two people with ulcers in Muggy Swamp. Sometimes, when Mr. Tait wasn't around, *she* would have me fix her a big plate of French fried onion rings, and if there's anything that doesn't go with ulcers, it's French fried onion rings, but I never argued. Nobody dared argue with her. Everybody went around on tippy-toe, and when she rang that bell, everybody dropped everything and rushed to see what she wanted. But I didn't mind, be-cause—if I have my druthers—I druther cook for a couple of invalids than a houseful of hungry brats. And I had help out there. Paulie was a big help. He was a sweet boy, and it's too bad he turned out to be no good, but that's the way it is with foreigners. I don't understand foreigners. *She* was a for-eigner, too, although it was a long time ago that she came over here, and it wasn't until near the end that she started screaming at all of us in a foreign language. Screaming at her husband, too. Lordy, that man had the pa-tience of a saint! Of course, he had his workshop to keep him happy. He was crazy about those rocks! He bought a whole mountain once—some place in South America. It was supposed to be chock-full of jade, but I guess it didn't pan out. Once he offered me a big jade brooch, but I wouldn't take it. I wasn't having any of *that*!" Mrs. Hawkins rolled her eyes suggestively. "He was all excited when you came to take pictures of his knickknacks, which surprised me because of the way he felt about the *Daily Fluxion*." She paused to drain her glass. "This is good! One more lit-tle slug? And then I'll be staggering home."

"How did Mr. Tait feel about the *Fluxion*?" Qwilleran asked casually, as he refilled Mrs. Hawkin's glass.

"Oh, he was dead set against it! Wouldn't have it in the house. And that was a crying shame, because everybody knows the *Fluxion* has the best comics, but . . . that's the way he was! I guess we all have our pecu—peculiarities. . . . Whee! I guess I'm feeling these drinks."

Eventually she lapsed into a discourse on her former husband and her recent surgery for varicose veins. At that point Qwilleran said he would let her know about the housekeeping position, and he marched her to a taxi and gave her a five-dollar bill to cover the fare.

He returned to the apartment just as Koko emerged from some secret hiding place. The cat was stepping carefully and looking around with cau-tious eye and incredulous ears.

"I feel the same way," Qwilleran said. "Let's play the game and see if you can come up with something useful."

They went to the dictionary, and Koko played brilliantly. Inning after inning he had Qwilleran stumped with *ebionitism* and *echidna*, *cytodiagnosis* and *czestochowa*, *onychophore* and *opalinid.*

Just as Qwilleran was about to throw in the sponge, his luck changed. Koko sank his claws into the front of the book, and the page opened to *arene* and *argue.* On the very next try it was *quality* and *quarreled.* Qwilleran felt a significant vibration in his moustache.

CHAPTER 20

THE MORNING AFTER Mrs. Hawkin's visit and Koko's stellar performance with the dictionary, Qwilleran waked before the alarm clock rang, and bounded out of bed. The pieces of the puzzle were starting to fall into place.

Tait must have had a grudge against the *Fluxion* ever since coverage of the paternity trial. The family had probably tried to hush it up, but the *Fluxion* would naturally insist that the public has a right to know. None of the agonizing details had been spared. Perhaps the *Rampage* had dealt more kindly with the Taits; it was owned by the Pennimans, who were part of the Muggy Swamp clique.

For eighteen years Tait had lived with his grudge, letting it grow into an obsession. Despite his subdued exterior, he was a man of strong passions. He probably hated the *Fluxion* as fervently as he loved jade. His ulcers were evidence of inner turmoil. And when the *Fluxion* offered to publish his house, he saw an opportunity for revenge; he could fake a theft, hide the jades, and let them be recovered after the newspaper had simmered in its embarrassment.

What would be a safe hiding place for a teapot as thin as a rose petal? Qwilleran asked himself as he prepared Koko's breakfast.

But would Tait go to such lengths for the meager satisfaction of revenge? He would need a stronger motive. Perhaps he was not so rich as his position indicated. He had lost the manufacturing plant; he had gambled on a jade expedition that failed to produce; he owed a large decorating bill. Had he devised a scheme to collect insurance? Had he and his wife argued about it? Had they quarreled on the night of the alleged theft? Had the quarrel been violent enough to cause a fatal heart attack?

Qwilleran placed Koko's breakfast on the kitchen floor, slipped into his suit coat, and started filling his pockets. Here and there around the apartment he collected his pipe, tobacco pouch, matches, card case, a comb, some loose silver, his bill clip, and a clean handkerchief, but he could not find the green jade button that usually rattled around in his change pocket. He remembered leaving it on the desk top.

"Koko, did you steal my lucky piece?" Qwilleran said.

"YARGLE!" came the reply from the kitchen, a yowl gargled with a throatful of veal kidneys in cream.

Once more Qwilleran opened the envelope of photographs he was going to deliver to Tait. He spread them on the desk: wide-angle pictures of beautiful rooms, medium shots of expensive furniture groupings, and close-ups of the jades. There was a perfect shot of the rare white teapot as well as one of the bird perched on the back of a lion. There were the black writing desk, ebony and black marble heavily ornamented with gilded bronze; the table supported by a sphinx; the white silk chairs that did not look comfortable.

Koko rubbed against Qwilleran's ankles.

"What's on your mind?" the man said. "I made your breakfast. Go and finish it. You've hardly touched that food!"

The cat arched his back, curved his tail into a question mark, and walked back and forth over the newsman's shoes.

"You're getting your playmate today," Qwilleran said. "A little cross-eyed lady cat. Maybe I should take you along. Would you like to put on your harness and go for a ride?"

Koko pranced in figure eights with long-legged grace.

"First I've got to punch another hole in your harness."

The kitchen offered no tools for punching holes in leather straps: no awl, no icepick, no sixpenny nails, not even an old-fashioned can opener. Qwilleran managed the operation with the point of a nail file.

"There!" he said, as he went to look for Koko. "I defy you to slip out of it again! . . . Now, where the devil did you go?"

There was a wet, slurping, scratching sound, and Qwilleran wheeled around. Koko was on the desk. He was licking a photograph.

"Hey!" yelled Qwilleran, and Koko jumped to the floor and bounded away like a rabbit.

The newsman examined the prints. Only one of them was damaged. "Bad cat!" he said. "You've blistered this beautiful photo."

Koko sat under the coffee table, hunched in a small bundle.

It was the Biedermeier armoire he had licked with his sandpaper tongue. The surface of the photograph was still sticky. From one angle the damage was hardly noticeable. Only when the light hit the picture in a certain way could the dull and faintly blistered patch be noticed.

Qwilleran examined it closely and marveled at the detail in Bunsen's photo. The grain of the wood stood out clearly, and whatever lighting the photographer had used gave the furniture a three-dimensional quality. The chased metal around the tiny keyhole was in bold relief. A fine line of shadow accentuated the edge of the drawer across the bottom.

There was another thin dark line down the side panel of the armoire that Qwilleran had not noticed before. It sliced through the grain of the wood. It hardly made sense in the design or construction of the cabinet.

Qwilleran felt a prickling in his moustache, and stroked it hurriedly. Then he grabbed Koko and trussed him in his harness.

"Let's go," he said. "You've licked something that gives me ideas!"

It was a long and expensive taxi ride to Muggy Swamp. Qwilleran listened to the click of the meter and wondered if he could put this trip on his expense account. The cat sat on the seat close to the man's thigh, but as soon as the taxi turned into the Tait driveway, Koko was alerted. He rose on his hind legs, placed his front paws on the window and scolded the landscape.

Qwilleran told the driver, "I want you to wait and take me back to town. I'll probably be a half hour."

"Okay if I go to the railway station and get some breakfast?" the man asked. "I'll stop the meter."

Qwilleran tucked the cat under his left arm, coiled the leash in his left hand, and rang the doorbell of the Spanish mansion. As he stood waiting, he detected a note of neglect about the premises. The grass was badly in need of cutting. Curled yellow leaves, the first of the season to fall, were swirling around the courtyard. The windows were muddied.

When the door opened, it was a changed man who stood there. Tait, despite his high color, looked strained and tired. The old clothes and tennis shoes he wore were in absurd contrast to the black-and-white marble elegance of the foyer. Muddied footprints had dried on the white marble squares.

"Come in," said Tait. "I was just packing some things away." He made an apologetic gesture toward his garb.

"I brought Koko along," said Qwilleran coolly. "I thought he might help in finding the other cat." And he thought, Something's gone wrong, or he's scared or the police have been questioning him. Have they linked the murder of his decorator with the theft of his jades?

Tait said, "The other cat's here. It's locked up in the laundry room."

Koko squirmed, and was transferred to Qwilleran's shoulder, where he could survey the scene. The cat's body was taut, and Qwilleran could feel a vibration like a low-voltage electric current.

He handed the envelope of photographs to Tait and accepted an off-hand invitation into the living room. It had changed considerably. The white silk chairs were shrouded with dust covers. The draperies were drawn across the windows. And the jade cases were dark and empty.

One lamp was lighted in the shadowy room—a lamp on the writing desk, where Tait had apparently been working. A ledger lay open there, and his collection of utilitarian jades was scattered over the desk—the primitive scrapers, chisels, and ax heads.

Tait yanked a dust cover off a deskside chair and motioned Qwilleran to sit down, while he himself stood behind the desk and opened the envelope. The newsman glanced at the ledger upside down; it was a catalog of the jade collection, written in a precise, slanted hand.

While the jade collector studied the photographs, Qwilleran studied the man's face. This is not the look of grief, he thought; this is exhaustion. The man has not been sleeping well. His plan is not working out.

Tait shuffled through the photographs, crimping the corners of his mouth and breathing heavily.

"Pretty good photography, isn't it?" said Qwilleran.

"Yes," Tait murmured.

"Surprising detail."

"I didn't realize he had taken so many pictures."

"We always take more than we know we can use."

Qwilleran cast a side-glance at the armoire. There was no fine dark line down the side of the cabinet—at least, none that could be discerned from where he sat.

Tait said, "This desk photographed well."

"It has a lot of contrast. Too bad there's no picture of the Biedermeier wardrobe." He watched Tait closely. "I don't know what happened. I was sure Bunsen had photographed the wardrobe."

Tait maneuvered the corners of his mouth. "It's a fine piece. It belonged to my grandfather."

Koko squirmed again and voiced a small protest, and the newsman stood up, strolled back and forth and patted the silky back. He said: "This is the first time this cat has gone visiting. I'm surprised he's so well behaved." He walked close to the armoire, and still he could see no fine dark line.

"Thank you for the pictures," Tait said. "I'll go and get the other cat."

When the collector left the room, Qwilleran's curiosity came to a boil. He walked to the armoire and examined the side panel. There was indeed a crack running vertically from top to bottom, but it was virtually invisible. Qwilleran ran his finger along the line. It was easier to feel than to see. Only the camera with its uncanny vision had observed clearly the hairline joining.

Koko was struggling now, and Qwilleran placed him on the floor, keeping the leash in his hand. Experimentally he ran his free hand up and down the crevise. He thought, It *must* be a concealed compartment. It's got to be! But how does it open? There was no visible hardware of any kind.

He glanced toward the foyer, listened for approaching footsteps, then applied himself to the puzzle. Was it a touch latch? Did they have touch latches in the old days? The cabinet was over a hundred years old.

He pressed the side panel and thought that it had a slight amount of give, as if it were less than solid. He pressed again, and it responded with a tiny cracking noise like the sound of old, dry wood. He pressed the panel hard along the edge of the crack—first at shoulder level, then higher, then lower. He reached up and pressed it at the top, and the side of the armoire slowly opened with a labored groan.

It opened only an inch or two. Cautiously Qwilleran increased the opening enough to see what was inside. His lips formed a silent exclamation. For a moment he was transfixed. He felt a prickle in his blood, and he forgot to listen for footsteps. Koko's ears were pivoting in alarm. Tennis shoes were coming noiselessly down the corridor, but Qwilleran didn't hear. He didn't see Tait enter the room . . . stop abruptly . . . move swiftly. He heard only the piercing soprano scream, and then it was too late.

The scene blurred in front of his eyes. But he saw the spike. He heard the snarls and blood-chilling shrieks. There was a shock of white lightning. The lamp crashed. In the darkness he saw the uplifted spike . . . saw the spiraling white blur . . . felt the tug at his hand . . . heard the great wrenching thud . . . felt the sharp pain . . . felt the trickle of blood . . . and heard a sound like escaping steam. Then all else was still.

Qwilleran leaned against the armoire and looked down. Blood was dripping from his fingertips. The leash was cutting into his other palm, and twelve feet of nylon cord were wound tightly around the legs of G. Verning Tait, who lay gasping on the floor. Koko, anchored at the other end of the leash, was squirming to slip out of his harness. The room was silent except for the hard breathing of the prisoner and the hissing of a female cat on top of the Biedermeier armoire.

CHAPTER 21

THE NURSE in the First Air room at the *Fluxion* bandaged the slash on Qwilleran's hand.

"I'm afraid you'll live," she said cheerfully. "It's only a scratch."

"It bled a lot," he said. "That spike was razor-sharp and a foot long! It was actually a jade harpoon used for spearing walrus in the Arctic."

"How appropriate—under the circumstances," said the nurse with an affectionate side-glance at Qwilleran's moustache.

"Lucky I didn't get it in the stomach!"

"The wound looks clean," said the nurse, "but if it gives you any trouble, see a doctor."

"You can skip the commercial," Qwilleran said. "I know it by heart."

She patted the final strip of adhesive tape, and admired her handiwork.

The nurse had made a good show of the bandage. It did nothing for Qwilleran's typing efficiency, but it enhanced his story when he faced his audience at the Press Club that evening. An unusually large number of *Fluxion* staffers developed a thirst at five thirty, and the crowd formed around Qwilleran at the bar. His published account had appeared in the afternoon edition, but his fellow staffers knew that the best details of any story never get into print.

Qwilleran said, with barely suppressed pride: "It was Koko who alerted me to the hoax. He licked one of Bunsen's photos and drew attention to the secret compartment."

"I used sidelighting," Bunsen explained. "I put a light to the left of the camera at a ninety-degree angle, and it showed up the tiny crack. The camera caught it, but the eye would never know it was there."

"When I discovered the swing-out compartment packed full of jade," said Qwilleran, "I was so fascinated that I didn't hear Tait coming. First thing I knew, a cat shrieked, and there was that guy coming at me with an Eskimo harpoon, a spike *this long*!" He measured an exaggerated twelve inches with his hands. "Koko was snarling. The other cat was flying around, screaming. And there was that maniac, coming at me with a spike! Everything went out of focus. Then—crash! Tait fell flat on his face." Qwilleran displayed his bandaged hand. "He must have hurled the spike as he fell."

Arch Riker said, "Tell them how your cat tripped him up."

Qwilleran took time to light his pipe, while his audience waited for the inside story: "Koko was on a long leash, and he flew around in circles so fast—all I could see was a smoke ring in midair. And when Tait crashed to the floor, his legs were neatly trussed up in twelve feet of cord."

"Crazy!" said the photographer. "Wish I'd been there with a movie camera."

"I picked up the jade spike and kept Tait down on the floor while I called the police on that gold-plated French phone."

"When you go, you go first class," Bunsen said.

Then Lodge Kendall arrived from Headquarters. "Qwill was right all along," he told everyone. "The houseboy was innocent. Tait has told the police that he staked Paolo to a one-way fare to Mexico, then transferred the jade to the wardrobe cabinet and threw one piece behind Paolo's bed. And you remember the missing luggage? He'd given it to the boy himself."

"Was it the insurance money he was after?"

"Chiefly. Tait wasn't an astute businessman. He'd lost the family fortune, and he needed a large sum of cash to invest in another harebrained scheme. . . . But there was something else, too. He hates the *Fluxion*. Ever since they played up his role in a paternity case."

"I'd like to know why he didn't settle that claim out of court," Qwilleran said.

"He tried, but he was up against dirty politics, he claims. It seems there was another Tait, a cousin of George Verning, who was running for Congress that year, and the paternity claim was timed accordingly. Somebody figured the voters wouldn't know one Tait from another, and apparently it was true. They guy lost the election."

Qwilleran said, "Did Tait tell the police anything about his proposed trip to Denmark?"

"Nobody mentioned it at Headquarters."

"Well," said Riker, "I'll tune in tomorrow for the next installment. I'm going home to dinner."

"I'm going home to feed Koko a filet mignon," said Qwilleran. "After all, he saved my neck."

"Don't kid yourself," Bunsen said. "He was chasing that female cat."

"I dropped her off at the pet hospital," Qwilleran said. "She had an infected wound in her side. That guy probably gave her a kick when he threw her out."

Qwilleran had floated high on excitement all afternoon, but when he arrived home he succumbed to exhaustion. Koko reacted the same way. The cat lay on his side, legs stiffly extended, one ear bent under his head— to all appearances a dead cat except for a thoughtful look in half-open eyes. He ignored his dinner.

Qwilleran went to bed early, and his dreams were pertinent and convincing. He dreamed that Percy was saying, "Qwill, you and Koko have done such a good job on the Tait case, we want you to find David Lyke's murderer," and Qwilleran said, "The investigation may take us to Japan, Chief," and Percy said, "Go right ahead! You can have an unlimited expense account." Qwilleran's moustache twitched in his sleep. So did the cat's whiskers. Koko was dreaming, too.

Early Saturday morning, while Qwilleran was snoring gently and his subconscious was wrestling with the Lyke mystery, the telephone began ringing insistently. When it succeeded in shaking him awake, he reached groggily toward the bedside table, found the receiver, and heard the operator say: "This is Aarhus, Denmark. I have a call for Mr. James Qwilleran."

"Speaking," Qwilleran croaked in his early-morning voice.

"Qwill, this is Harry," came a transatlantic shout. "We just heard the news."

"You did? In Denmark?"

"It came over the radio."

"It's a big shame. He was a nice guy."

"I don't know about *him*," said Noyton. "I only knew her. He must have cracked up."

"Who cracked up?"

"What's the matter? Aren't you awake yet?"

"I'm awake," said Qwilleran. "What are you talking about?"

"Is this Qwill? This *is* Qwilleran, isn't it?"

"I think so. I'm a little groggy. Are you talking about the murder?"

"Murder!" shouted Noyton. "What murder?"

Qwilleran paused. "Aren't you talking about David Lyke?"

"I'm talking about G. Verning Tait! What's happened to David?"

"He's dead. He was shot last Monday night."

"David dead! My God! Who did it?"

"They don't know. It happened in his apartment. In the middle of the evening."

"Somebody break in?"

"It doesn't appear so."

"Why would anyone want to kill David? He was a fantastic guy!"

"What was it you heard on the radio over there?" Qwilleran asked.

"About Tait's arrest. Mrs. Tait's family couldn't believe it when they heard the news."

Qwilleran sat up straight. "You know her family?"

"Just met them. Fine people. Her brother's working with me on the hush-hush deal I told you about. Don't forget: I promised you the *Fluxion* will get the scoop!"

"What's the nature of it?"

"I'm financing a fantastic manufacturing process. Qwill, I'm going to be the richest man in the world!"

"Is it a new invention?"

"A scientific discovery," Noyton said. "While the rest of the world is fooling around with outer space, the Danes are doing something for mankind here and now."

"Sounds great!"

"Until I got over here, I didn't know what it was all about. I just took her word that it was something world-shaking."

"Whose word?"

"Mrs. Tait's."

"She tipped you off to her brother's discovery?"

"Well, you see, Dr. Thorvaldson needed financing, and she knew her husband couldn't swing it. She'd heard about me and thought I could handle it. Of course, she wanted a kickback—under the table, so to speak." Noyton paused. "This is all off-the-record, of course."

Qwilleran said: "Tait was heading for Denmark. He probably expected to invest the insurance money."

There was some interference on the line.

"Are you still there?" Qwilleran said.

Noyton's voice had faded. "Listen, I'll call you tomorrow—can you hear me?—as soon as everything's sewed up legally. . . . This is a lousy connection. . . . Hope they nab David's killer. So long! Call you within twenty-four hours."

It was Saturday, but Qwilleran went into the office to work ahead on the next issue of *Gracious Abodes*. He was determined, now, that Fran Unger should not get the magazine away from him. He hoped also to see Percy and say "I told you so," but the managing editor was attending a publishers' conference in New York. During the day Qwilleran made two important phone calls—one to the hospital to inquire about the cat, and one to the Middy Studio to make a dinner date with Cokey.

When he went home in the late afternoon to feed Koko, he found a scene of frantic activity. Koko was careening drunkenly around the apartment. He was playing with his homemade mouse—a game related to hockey, basketball, and tennis, with elements of wrestling. The cat skidded the small gray thing over the polished floor, pounced on it, tossed it in the air, batted it across the room, pursued it, made a flying tackle, clutched it in his forepaws, and rolled back and forth in ecstasy until the mouse slipped from his grasp, and the chase began again. With an audience Koko was inclined to vaunt his prowess. As Qwilleran watched, the cat dribbled the mouse the length of the living room, gave it a well-aimed whack, and scored a goal—directly under the old Spanish chest. Then he trotted after it, peered under the low chest, and raised his head in a long, demanding howl.

"No problem," said Qwilleran. "This time I'm equipped."

From the hall closet he brought the umbrella that Mrs. Hawkins had so conveniently forgotten. The first sweep under the chest produced nothing but dust, and Koko increased the volume of his demands. Qwilleran got down on the floor and poked the finial into far dark corners, fishing out the jade button that had disappeared a few days before. Koko's clamor was loud and increasing.

The next sweep of the umbrella brought forth something pink!

Not exactly pink, Qwilleran told himself, but almost pink . . . and it looked vaguely familiar. He had an idea what it was. And he knew very well how it had managed to get there.

"Koko!" he said sternly. "What do you know about this?"

Before the cat could answer with a gutteral sound and a wrestling match with an invisible enemy, Qwilleran went to the telephone and rapidly dialed a number.

"Cokey," he said, "I'm going to be late picking you up. Why don't you take a cab to the Press Club and meet me there? . . . No, just a little business emergency I've got to handle . . . All right. See you shortly. And I may have some news for you!"

Qwilleran turned back to the cat. "Koko, when did you eat this pink stuff? Where did you find it?"

WHEN QWILLERAN arrived at the Press Club, Cokey was waiting in the lobby, sitting in one of the worn leather sofas.

"There's trouble," she said. "I can read it in your face."

"Wait till we get a table, and I'll explain," he said. "Let's sit in the cocktail lounge. I'm expecting a phone call."

They went to a table with a red-checked tablecloth, well patched and darned.

"There's been an unexpected development in connection with David's murder," Qwilleran began, "and Koko's involved. He was in David's apartment when the fatal shot was fired, and he apparently ate some wool. When I brought him home that night, he looked odd. I thought he'd had a fright. Now I'm inclined to think it was a stomachache. I suppose cats get stomachaches."

"He couldn't digest the wool?" Cokey said.

"He might have managed the wool, but there was something else in the cloth. After he came home, he must have upchucked the whole thing and hidden it under the Spanish chest. I found it an hour ago."

Cokey clapped her hands to her face. "And you recognized it? Don't tell me you actually *recognized* it!"

"Yes, and I think it would have looked familiar to you, too. It was a yellowish-pink wool with gold metallic threads."

"Natalie Noyton! That handwoven dress she wore to the party!"

Qwilleran nodded. "It appears that Natalie was in Dave's apartment Monday night, and she may have been there when he was shot. At any rate, it was something that had to be reported to the police, so I took the peach-colored wool over to Headquarters. That's why I was late."

"What did they say?"

"When I left, they were hustling out to Lost Lake Hills. Our police reporter promised to call me here if anything develops."

"I wonder why Natalie didn't come forward and volunteer some information to the police?"

"That's what worries me," said Qwilleran. "If she had information to give, and the killer knew it, he might try to silence her."

The domed ceiling of the club multiplied the voices of the Saturday-night crowd into a roar, but above it came an amplified announcement on the public-address system: "Telephone for Mr. Qwilleran."

"That's our night man at Police Headquarters. I'll be right back." He hurried to the phone booth.

When he returned, his eyes had acquired a darkness.

"What's wrong, Qwill? Is it something terrible?"

"The police were too late."

"Too late?"

"Too late to find Natalie alive."

"Murdered!"

"No. She took her own life," said Qwilleran.

"Evidently a heavy dose of alcohol and then sleeping pills."

A sad wail came from Cokey. "But why? Why?"

"Apparently it was explained in her diary. She was hopelessly in love with her decorator, and he wasn't one to discourage an affair."

"That I know!"

"Natalie thought Dave was ready to marry her the moment she got a divorce, and she wanted him so desperately that she agreed to her husband's terms: no financial settlement and no request for child custody. Then last weekend it dawned on her that Dave would never marry her—or anyone else. When Odd Bunsen and I turned up at her house Monday morning and she refused to see us, she must have been out of her mind with disappointment and remorse and a kind of hopeless panic."

"I'd be blind with fury!" said Cokey.

"She was blind enough to think she could set things right by killing David."

"Then it was Natalie—"

"It was Natalie. . . . Afterward, she went home, dismissed the maid, and lived through twenty-four hours of hell before ending it. She's been dead since Tuesday night."

There was a long silence at the table.

After a while Qwilleran said, "The police found the peach-colored dress in her closet. The shawl had quite a lot of fringe missing."

Then the menus came, and Cokey said: "I'm not hungry. Let's go for a walk—and talk about other things."

They walked, and talked about Koko and the new cat whose name was Yu or Freya.

"I hope they'll be happy together," said Cokey.

"I think we're all going to be happy together," said Qwilleran. "I'm going to change her name to Yum Yum. I've got to change your name, too."

The girl looked at him dreamily.

"You see," said Qwilleran, "Koko doesn't like it when I call you Cokey. It's too close to his own name."

"Just call me Al," said Alacoque Wright with a wistful droop in her voice and a resigned lift to her eyebrows.

IT WAS MONDAY when the news of Harry Noyton's Danish enterprise appeared on the front page of the *Daily Fluxion* under Qwilleran's by-line. In the first edition a typographical error had substituted "devious" for "diverse," but it was a mistake so customary that the item would have been disappointing without it:

"Harry Noyton, financier and promoter of devious business interests," said the bulletin, "has acquired the worldwide franchise for a Danish scientist's unique contribution to human welfare—calorie-free beer with Vitamin C added."

On the same day, in a small ceremony at the Press Club, Qwilleran was presented with an honorary press card for his cat. On it was pasted Koko's identification photo, with eyes wide, ears alert, whiskers bristling.

"I took his picture," said Odd Bunsen, "that night in David Lyke's apartment."

And Lodge Kendall said, "Don't think I had an easy time getting the police chief and fire commissioner to sign it!"

WHEN QWILLERAN returned to the Villa Verandah that evening, he entered the apartment with his fingers crossed. He had brought Yum Yum home from the hospital at noon, and the two cats had had several hours in which to sniff each other, circle warily, and make their peace.

All was silent in the living room. On the green Danish chair sat Yum Yum, looking dainty and sweet. Her face was a poignant triangle of brown, and her eyes were enormous circles of violet-blue, slightly crossed. Her brown ears were cocked at a flirtatious angle. And where the silky hairs of her pelt grew in conflicting directions on her white breast, there was a cowlick of fur softer than down.

Koko sat on the coffee table, tall and masterful, with a ruff of fur brushed around his neck.

"You devil!" said Qwilleran. "There's nothing neurotic about you, and there never was! You knew what you were doing all the time!"

With a grunt Koko jumped down from the table and ambled over to join Yum Yum. They sat side by side in identical positions, like bookends, with both tails curled to the right, both pairs of ears worn like coronets, both pairs of eyes ignoring Qwilleran with pointed unconcern. Then Koko gave Yum Yum's face two affectionate licks and lowered his head, arching his neck gracefully. He narrowed his eyes, and they became slits of catly ecstasy as the little female recognized her cue and washed inside his ears with her long pink tongue.

The Cat
Who Turned
On and Off

CHAPTER 1

IN DECEMBER the weather declared war. First it bombarded the city with ice storms, then strafed it with freezing winds. Now it was snowing belligerently. A blizzard whipped down Canard Street, past the Press Club, as if it had a particular grudge against newspapermen. With malicious accuracy the largest flakes zeroed in to make cold wet landings on the neck of the man who was hailing a taxi in front of the club.

He turned up the collar of his tweed overcoat—awkwardly, with one hand—and tried to jam his porkpie hat closer to his ears. His left hand was plunged deep in his coat pocket and held stiffly there. Otherwise there was nothing remarkable about the man except the luxuriance of his moustache—and his sobriety. It was after midnight; it was nine days before Christmas; and the man coming out of the Press Club bar was sober.

When a cab pulled to the curb, he eased himself carefully into the back seat, keeping his left hand in his pocket, and gave the driver the name of a third-rate hotel.

"Medford Manor? Let's see, I can take Zwinger Street and the expressway," the cabbie said hopefully as he threw the flag on the meter, "or I can take Center Boulevard."

"Zwinger," said the passenger. He usually took the Boulevard route, which was cheaper, but Zwinger was faster.

"You a newspaperman?" the driver asked, turning and giving his fare a knowing grin.

The passenger mumbled an affirmative.

"I figured. I knew you couldn't be one of them publicity types that hang around the Press Club. I mean, I can tell by the way you dress. I don't mean newspapermen are slobs or anything like that, but they're— well *you* know! I pick 'em up in front of the Press Club all the time. Not very big tippers, but good guys, and you never know when you're gonna need a friend at the paper. Right?" He turned and flashed a conspiratorial grin at the back seat.

"Watch it!" snapped the passenger as the cab veered toward a drunk staggering across Zwinger Street.

"You with the *Daily Fluxion* or the *Morning Rampage*?"

"*Fluxion.*"

The cab stopped for a red light, and the driver stared at his passenger. "I've seen your picture in the paper. The moustache, I mean. You get a by-line?"

The man in the back seat nodded.

They were in a blighted area now. Cheap lodgings and bars occupied old town houses that had once been the homes of the city's elite.

"Lock your door," the driver advised. "You wouldn't believe the scum that drifts around this street after dark. Drunks, hopheads, cruisers, you-name-it. Used to be a ritzy neighborhood. Now they call it Junktown."

"Junktown?" repeated the passenger with his first show of interest in the conversation.

"You a newspaper guy and you never heard of Junktown?"

"I'm a—I'm fairly new in the city." The passenger smoothed his moustache with his right hand.

His left was still in his pocket when he got out of the cab on the other side of town. Entering the deserted lobby of the Medford Manor, he walked hurriedly past the registration desk, where the elderly clerk sat dozing at the switchboard. In the elevator he found an aged bellhop slumped on a stool, snoring softly. The man flicked a switch and pressed a lever, taking the car and its sleeping occupant to the sixth floor.

Then he strode down the corridor to room 606. With his right hand he found a key in his trouser pocket, unlocked the door, and stepped inside the room. He closed the door gently before switching on the light. Then he stood and listened. He moved his head slowly from side to side, examining the room: the double bed, the armchair, the cluttered dresser, the closet door standing ajar.

"All right, you guys," he said. "Come on out!"

Slowly and cautiously he withdrew his left hand from his pocket.

"I know you're here. Come on out!"

There was a creaking of bedsprings and a grunt, followed by a sharp ripping sound and two soft thuds on the floor. Between the limp fringes of the cotton bedspread there appeared two heads.

"You crazy nuts! You were inside the bedsprings again!"

They squeezed out from under the bed—two Siamese cats. First there were two brown heads, one more wedge-shaped than the other; then two pale fawn bodies, one daintier than the other; then two brown silky tails, one with a kink in the tip.

The man held out his left hand, exhibiting a soggy mass in a paper napkin. "See what I brought you? Turkey from the Press Club."

Two black velvet noses sniffed the air, two sets of whiskers twitched, and both cats howled in unison.

"Shhh! The old gal next door will have you arrested."

The man started cutting up the turkey with a pocket knife, while they paced the room in ecstatic figure eights, waving their tails and howling a discordant duet.

"Quiet!"

They howled louder.

"I don't know why I do this for you heathens. It's against the rules—sneaking takeouts from the Press Club buffet. Not to mention the mess! I've got a pocketful of gravy."

They drowned out his voice with their clamor.

"Will you guys shut up?"

The telephone rang.

"See? I told you so!"

The man hurriedly placed a glass ashtray full of turkey on the floor and went to the telephone.

"Mr. Qwilleran," said the quavering voice of the desk clerk, "sorry to call you again, but Mrs. Mason in 604 says your cats—"

"Sorry. They were hungry. They're quiet now."

"If—if—if you don't mind taking an inside room, 619 is vacant, and you could ask the day clerk tomorrow—"

"It won't be necessary. We're moving out as soon as I find an apartment."

"I hope you're not offended, Mr. Qwilleran. The manager—"

"No offense, Mr. McIldoony. A hotel room is no place for cats. We'll be out before Christmas . . . I hope," he added softly, surveying the bleak room.

He had lived in better places when he was young and successful and well-known and married. Much had happened since his days as a crime reporter in New York. Now, considering his backlog and debts and the wage scale on a Midwestern newspaper, the Medford Manor was the best he could afford. Qwilleran's only luxury was a pair of roommates whose expensive tastes he was inclined to indulge.

The cats were quiet now. The larger one was gobbling turkey with head down and tail up, its tip waving in the slow rhythm of rapture. The little female, sitting a few inches apart, was respectfully waiting her turn.

Qwilleran took off his coat and tie and crawled under the bed to thumbtack the torn ticking to the wooden frame of the box spring. There had been a small rip when he moved into the hotel two weeks ago, and it had steadily enlarged. He had composed a pseudoserious essay on the subject for the feature page of the *Daily Fluxion*.

"Any small aperture is challenging to the feline sensibility," he had written. "For a cat it is a matter of honor to enlarge the opening and squeeze through."

After repairing the spring, Qwilleran groped in his coat pocket for his pipe and tobacco and withdrew a handful of envelopes. The first, postmarked Connecticut, was still sealed and unread, but he knew what it contained—another graceless hint for money.

The second—a note written in brown ink with feminine flourishes— he had read several times. Regretfully she was canceling their date for Christmas Eve. With tact so delicate that it was painful she was explaining that this other man—this engineer—it was all so sudden—Qwill would understand.

Qwilleran twisted the note into a bowknot before dropping it in the wastebasket. He had half expected this news. She was young, and the Qwilleran moustache and temples were graying noticeably. It was a disappointment, nevertheless. Now he had no date for the Christmas Eve party at the Press Club—the only Christmas celebration he expected to have.

The third communication was a memo from the managing editor, reminding staffers of the annual writing competition. Besides $3,000 in cash prizes there would be twenty-five frozen turkeys for honorable mentions, donated by Cybernetic Poultry Farms, Inc.

"Who will expect to be loved, cherished, and publicized by *Fluxion* writers till death do us part," said Qwilleran, aloud.

"Yow," said Koko between licks, as he washed his face.

The little female was now taking her turn at the turkey; Koko always left half the food for her—or a good 40 percent.

Qwilleran stroked Koko's fur, soft as ermine, and marveled at its shading—from pale fawn to seal brown—one of nature's more spectacular successes. Then he lighted his pipe and slouched in the armchair with his feet on the bed. He could use one of those cash prizes. He could send a couple of hundred to Connecticut and then start buying furniture. If he had his own furniture, it would be easier to find lodgings that accepted pets.

There was still time to write something prizeworthy and get it published before the December 31 deadline, and the feature editor was desperate for Christmas material. Arch Riker had called a meeting of the feature staff, saying, "Can't you guys come up with some ideas?" Without much hope he had searched the faces of the assembled staffers: the paunchy columnists, the cadaverous critics, Qwilleran on general assignment, and the specialist who handled travel, hobbies, aviation, real estate, and gardening. They had all stared back at the editor with the blank gaze of veterans who had reported on too many Yuletides.

Qwilleran noticed Koko watching him closely. "To win a prize," he told the cat, "you've got to have a gimmick."

"Yow," said Koko. He jumped to the bed and looked at the man with sympathetically blinking eyes. They were sapphire blue in bright light, but in the lamplit hotel room they were large circles of black onyx with flashes of diamond or ruby.

"What I need is an idea that's spectacular but not cheap." Qwilleran was frowning and jabbing his moustache with his pipestem. He was thinking irritably about the *Fluxion*'s Jack Jaunti, a young smart-aleck in the Sunday Department who had taken a job as Percival Duxbury's valet, incognito, in order to write an inside story on the richest man in town. The stunt had won no friends among the city's First Families, but it had increased circulation for two weeks, and the rumor was that Jaunti would walk off with first prize. Qwilleran resented juveniles who substituted nerve for ability.

"Why, that guy can't even spell," he said to his attentive audience of one.

Koko went on blinking. He looked sleepy.

The female cat was on the prowl, searching for playthings. She rose on her hind legs to examine the contents of the wastebasket and hauled out a twist of paper about the size of a mouse. She brought it to Qwilleran in her teeth and dropped it—the letter written in brown ink—on his lap.

"Thanks, but I've read it," he said. "Don't rub it in." He groped in the drawer of the nightstand, found a rubber mouse and tossed it across the room. She bounded after it, sniffed it, arched her back and returned to the wastebasket, this time extracting a crumpled paper handkerchief, which she presented to the man in the armchair.

"Why do you fool around with junk?" he said. "You've got nice toys."

Junk! Qwilleran experienced a prickling sensation in the roots of his moustache, and a warmth spread over his face.

"Junktown!" he said to Koko. "Christmas in Junktown! I could write a heartbreaker." He came out of his slouch and slapped the arms of the chair. "And it might get me out of this damned rut!"

His job in the Feature Department was considered a comfortable berth for a man over forty-five, but interviewing artists, interior decorators and Japanese flower arrangers was not Qwilleran's idea of newspapering. He longed to be writing about con men, jewel thieves, and dope peddlers.

Christmas in Junktown! He had done Skid Row assignments in the past, and he knew how to proceed: quit shaving—pick up some ratty clothes—get to know the people in the dives and on the street—and then listen. The trick would be to make the series compassionate, relating the personal tragedies behind society's outcasts, plucking the heartstrings.

"Koko," he said, "by Christmas Eve there won't be a dry eye in town!"

Koko was watching Qwilleran's face and blinking. The cat spoke in a low voice, but with a sense of urgency.

"What's on your mind?" Qwilleran asked. He knew the water dish was freshly filled. He knew the sandbox in the bathroom was clean.

Koko stood up and walked across the bed. He rubbed the side of his jaw against the footboard, then looked at Qwilleran over his shoulder. He rubbed the other side of his jaw, and his fangs clicked against the metal finial of the bedpost.

"You want something? What is it you want?"

The cat gave a sleepy yowl and jumped to the top edge of the footboard, balancing like a tightrope walker. He walked its length and then, with forepaws against the wall, stretched his neck and scraped his jaw against the light switch. It clicked, and the light went out. Murmuring little noises of satisfaction, Koko made himself a nest on the bed and curled up for sleep.

CHAPTER 2

"CHRISTMAS IN JUNKTOWN!" Qwilleran said to the feature editor. "How does that grab you?'

Arch Riker was sitting at his desk, browsing through the Friday morning mail and tossing most of it over his shoulder in the direction of a large wire bin.

Qwilleran perched on the corner of the editor's desk and waited for his old friend's reaction, knowing there would be no visible clue. Riker's face had the composure of a seasoned deskman, registering no surprise, no enthusiasm, no rejection.

"Junktown?" Riker murmured. "It might have possibilities. How would you approach it?"

"Hang around Zwinger Street, mix with the characters there, get them to talk."

The editor leaned back in his chair and clasped his hands behind his head. "Okay, go ahead."

"It's a hot subject, and I can give it a lot of heart."

Heart was the current password at the *Daily Fluxion*. In frequent memos from the managing editor, staff writers were reminded to put heart into everything including the weather report.

Riker nodded. "That'll make the boss happy. And it should get a lot of readership. My wife will like it. She's a junker."

He said it calmly, and Qwilleran was shocked. "Rosie? You mean—"

Riker was rocking contentedly in his swivel chair. "She got hooked a couple of years ago, and it's been keeping me poor ever since."

Qwilleran stroked his moustache to hide his dismay. He had known Rosie years ago when he and Arch were cub reporters in Chicago. Gently he asked, "When—how did this happen, Arch?"

"She went to Junktown with some gal friends one day and got involved. I'm beginning to get interested myself. Just paid twenty-eight dollars for an old tea canister in painted tin. Tin is what I go for—tin boxes, tin lanterns—"

Qwilleran stammered, "What—what—what are you talking about?"

"Junk. Antiques. What are *you* talking about?"

"Hell, I'm talking about narcotics!"

"I said we were junkers, not junkies!" Arch said. "Junktown, for your information, is the place with all the antique shops."

"The cabdriver said it was a hangout for hopheads."

"Well, you know how cabdrivers are. Sure, it's a declining neighborhood, and the riffraff may come out after dark, but during the day it's full of respectable junkpickers like Rosie and her friends. Didn't your ex-wife ever take you junking?"

"She dragged me to an antique show in New York once, but I hate antiques."

"Too bad," said Arch. "Christmas in Junktown sounds like a good idea, but you'd have to stick to antiques. The boss would never go for the narcotics angle."

"Why not? It would make a poignant Christmas story."

Riker shook his head. "The advertisers would object. Readers spend less freely when their complacency is disturbed."

Qwilleran snorted his disdain.

"Why don't you go ahead, Qwill, and do a Christmas series on antiquing?"

"I hate antiques, I told you."

"You'll change your mind when you get to Junktown. You'll be hooked like the rest of us."

"Want to bet?"

Arch took out his wallet and extracted a small yellow card. "Here's a directory of the Junktown dealers. Let me have it back."

Qwilleran glanced at some of the names: Ann's 'Tiques, Sorta Camp, The Three Weird Sisters, the Junque Trunque. His stomach rebelled. "Look, Arch, I wanted to write something for the contest—something with guts! What can I do with antiques? I'd be lucky if I tied for the twenty-fifth frozen turkey."

"You might be surprised! Junktown is full of kooks, and there's an auction this afternoon."

"I can't stand auctions."

"This should be a good one. The dealer was killed a couple of months ago, and they're liquidating his entire stock."

"Auctions are the world's biggest bore, if you want my opinion."

"A lot of the dealers in Junktown are single girls—divorcees—widows.

That's something you should appreciate. Look, you donkey, why do I have to give you a big selling on this boondoggle? It's an assignment. Get busy."

Qwilleran gritted his teeth. "All right. Give me a taxi voucher. Round trip!"

He took time to have his hair trimmed and his moustache pruned—his standard procedure before tackling a new beat, although he had intended to postpone this nicety until Christmas. Then he hailed a cab and rode out Zwinger Street, not without misgivings.

Downtown it was a boulevard of new office buildings, medical clinics, and fashionable apartment houses. Then it ran through a snow-covered wasteland where a former slum had been cleared. Farther out there were several blocks of old buildings with boarded windows, awaiting demolition. Beyond that was Junktown.

In daylight the street was even worse than it had appeared the night before. For the most part the rows of old town houses and Victorian mansions were neglected and forlorn. Some had been made into rooming houses, while others were disfigured with added storefronts. The gutters were choked with an alloy of trash and gray ice, and refuse cans stood frozen to the unshoveled sidewalks.

"This neighborhood's an eyesore," the cab driver remarked. "The city should tear it down."

"Don't worry. They will!" Qwilleran said with optimism.

As soon as he spotted antique shops, he stopped the cab and got out without enthusiasm. He surveyed the gloomy street. So this was Christmas in Junktown! Unlike other shopping areas in the city, Zwinger Street was devoid of holiday decorations. No festoons spanned the wide thoroughfare; no glittering angels trumpeted from the light poles. Pedestrians were few, and cars barreled past with whining snow tires, in a hurry to be elsewhere.

A wintry blast from the northeast sent Qwilleran hurrying toward the first store that professed to sell antiques. It was dark within, and the door was locked, but he cupped his hands to his temples and looked through the glass. What he saw was a gigantic wood carving of a gnarled tree with five lifesize monkeys swinging from its branches. One monkey held a hatrack. One monkey held a lamp. One monkey held a mirror. One monkey held a clock. One monkey held an umbrella stand.

Qwilleran backed away.

Nearby was the shop called The Three Weird Sisters. The store was closed, although a card in the window insisted it was open.

The newsman turned up his coat collar and covered his ears with gloved hands, wishing he had not had his hair trimmed. He next tried the Junque Trunque—closed—and a basement shop called Tech-Tiques, which looked as if it had never been open. Between the antique shops there were commercial establishments with dirty windows, and in one of these—a hole in the wall labeled Popopopoulos' Fruit, Cigars, Work Gloves and Sundries—he bought a pouch of tobacco and found it to be stale.

With growing disaffection for his assignment he walked past a dilapidated barbershop and a third-class nursing home until he reached a large antique shop on the corner. Its door was padlocked, and its windows were plastered with notices of an auction. Qwilleran, looking through the glass door, saw dusty furniture, clocks, mirrors, a bugle made into a lamp, and marble statues of Greek maidens in coy poses.

He also saw the reflection of another man approaching the store. The figure came up behind him with a faltering step, and a thick voice said amiably, "You like 'at slop?"

Qwilleran turned and faced an early-morning drunk, red-eyed and drooling but amiable. He was wearing a coat obviously made from a well-used horse blanket.

"Know what it is? Slop!" the man repeated with a moist grin as he peered through the door at the antiques. Relishing the wetness of the word, he turned to Qwilleran and said it again with embellishments. "Sssssloppp!"

The newsman moved away in disgust and wiped his face with a handkerchief, but the intruder was determined to be friendly.

"You can't get in," he explained helpfully. "Door locked. Locked it after the murder." Perhaps he caught a flicker of interest in Qwilleran's face, because he added, "Stabbed! Sssstabbed!" It was another juicy word, and he illustrated it by plunging an imaginary dagger into the newsman's stomach.

"Get lost!" Qwilleran muttered and strode away.

Nearby there was a carriage house converted into a refinishing shop. Qwilleran tried that door, too, knowing it would not open, and he was right.

He was beginning to have an uneasy feeling about this street, as if the antique shops were fakes—stage props. Where were the proprietors? Where were the collectors who paid twenty-eight dollars for an old tin box? The only people in sight were two children in shabby snowsuits, a workman with a lunchpail, an old lady in black, who was plodding along with a shopping bag, and the good-natured drunk, now sitting on the frozen sidewalk.

At the moment Qwilleran looked up and saw movement in a curved bay window—a clean, sparkling window in a narrow town house painted dark gray with fresh black trim and a fine brass knocker on the door. The building had a residential look, but there was a discreet sign: The Blue Dragon—Antiques.

Slowly he mounted the flight of eight stone steps and tried the door, fearing it would be locked, but to his surprise it opened, and he stepped into an entrance hall of great elegance and formality. There was an Oriental rug on the waxed floor and delicate Chinese paper on the walls. A gilded mirror crowned with three carved plumes hung over a well-polished table that held chrysanthemums in a porcelain bowl. There was a fragrance of exotic wood. There was also the hush of death, except for the ticking of a clock.

Qwilleran, standing there in amazement, suddenly felt he was being watched, and he turned on his heel, but it was only a blackamoor, a lifesize ebony carving of a Nubian slave with turbaned head and an evil glint in his jeweled eyes.

Now the newsman was convinced that Junktown was something less than real. This was the enchanted palace in the depths of the dark forest.

A blue velvet rope barred the stairway, but the parlor doors stood open invitingly, and Qwilleran advanced with caution into a high-ceilinged room filled with furniture, paintings, silver, and blue and white china. A silver chandelier hung from the sculptured plaster ceiling.

His footsteps made the floor creak, and he coughed self-consciously. Then he caught a glimpse of something blue in the window—a large blue porcelain dragon—and he was moving toward it when he almost fell over a foot. It looked like a human foot in an embroidered slipper. He sucked in his breath sharply and stepped back. A lifesize female figure in a long blue satin kimono was seated in a carved Oriental chair. One elbow rested on the arm of the chair, and the slender hand held a cigarette holder. The face seemed to be made of porcelain—blue-white porcelain—and the wig was blue-black.

Qwilleran started to breathe again, thankful he had not knocked the thing over, and then he noticed smoke curling from the tip of the cigarette. It—or she—was alive.

"Are you looking for anything in particular?" she asked coolly. Only the lips moved in her masklike face. Her large dark eyes, heavily rimmed with black pencil, fixed themselves on the newsman without expression.

"No. Just looking," said Qwilleran with a gulp.

"There are two more rooms in the rear, and eighteenth century oils and engravings in the basement." She spoke with a cultivated accent.

The newsman studied her face, making mental notes for the story he would write: wide cheekbones, hollow cheeks, flawless complexion, blue-black hair worn Oriental style, haunting eyes, earrings of jade. She was about thirty, he guessed—an age to which he was partial. He relaxed.

"I'm from the *Daily Fluxion*," he said in his most agreeable voice, "and I'm about to write a series on Junktown."

"I prefer to have no publicity," she said with a frozen stare.

Only three times in his twenty-five years of newspapering had he heard anyone decline to be mentioned in print, and all three had been fugitives—from the law, from blackmail, from a nagging wife. But here was something incomprehensible: the operator of a business enterprise refusing publicity. *Free* publicity.

"All the other shops seem to be closed," he said.

"They should open at eleven, but antique dealers are seldom punctual."

Qwilleran looked around aimlessly and said, "How much for the blue dragon in the window?"

"It's not for sale." She moved the cigarette holder to her lips and drew on it exquisitely. "Are you interested in Oriental porcelains? I have a blue and white stemmed cup from the Hsuan Te period."

"No, I'm just digging for stories. Know anything about the auction sale down at the corner?"

She coughed on the cigarette smoke, and for the first time her poise wavered. "It's at one thirty today," she said.

"I know. I saw the sign. Who was this dealer who was killed?"

Her voice dropped to a lower pitch. "Andrew Glanz. A highly respected authority on antiques."

"When did it happen?"

"The sixteenth of October."

"Was it a holdup? I don't remember reading about a murder in Junktown, and I usually follow the crime news carefully."

"What makes you think it was—murder?" she said with a wary glint in her unblinking eyes.

"I heard someone say—and in this kind of neighborhood, you know . . ."

"He was killed in an accident."

"Traffic accident?"

"He fell from a ladder." She crushed her cigarette. "I would rather not talk about it. It was too—too—"

"He was a friend of yours?" Qwilleran asked in the sympathetic tone that had won him the confidence of maidens and murderers in the past.

"Yes. But, if you don't mind, Mr.—Mr.—"

"Qwilleran."

"The name is Irish?" She was deliberately changing the subject.

"No, Scottish. Spelled with a Qw. And your name?"

"Duckworth."

"Miss or Mrs.?"

She drew a breath. "Miss. . . . I have quite a few antiques from Scotland in the other room. Would you like to see them?"

She rose and led the way. She was tall and slender, and the kimono, a long shaft of blue, moved with silky grace among the mahogany sideboards and walnut tables.

"These andirons are Scottish," she said, "and so is this brass salver. Do you like brass? Most men like brass."

Qwilleran was squinting at something leaning against the wall in a far corner. "What's that?" he demanded. He pointed to a wrought-iron coat of arms, a yard in diameter. It was a shield surrounded by three snarling cats.

"An ornament from an iron gate, I think. It may have come from the arch over the gate of a castle."

"It's the Mackintosh coat of arms!" said Qwilleran. "I know the inscription: *Touch not the catt bot a glove.* My mother was a Mackintosh." He patted his moustache with satisfaction.

"You ought to buy it," Miss Duckworth said.

"What would I do with it? I don't even have an apartment. How much is it?"

"I've been asking two hundred dollars, but if you like it, you can have it for one hundred twenty-five dollars. That's actually what I paid for it." She lifted the weighty piece out from the wall to show it off to better advantage. "You'll never find a better buy, and you can always sell it for what you paid—or more. That's the nice thing about antiques. It would be wonderful over a fireplace—against a chimney wall. See, it has remnants of a lovely old red and blue decoration."

As she warmed to her sales talk, she grew animated and her dark-rimmed eyes glistened. Qwilleran began to feel mellow. He began to regard this blue-white porcelain creature as a possible prospect for Christmas Eve at the Press Club.

"I'll think about it," he said, turning away from the coat of arms with reluctance. "Meanwhile, I'm going to cover the auction this afternoon. Do you happen to know where I could get a picture of Andrew Glanz to use with my story?"

Her reserved manner returned. "What—what kind of story are you going to write?"

"I'll just describe the auction and give suitable recognition to the deceased."

She hesitated, glancing at the ceiling.

"If it's true what you say, Miss Duckworth—that he was a highly respected authority—"

"I have a few pictures in my apartment upstairs. Would you like to look at them?"

She unhooked the velvet rope that barred the stairs. "Let me go first and restrain the dog."

At the top of the stairs a large German police dog was waiting with unfriendly growl and quivering jaws. Miss Duckworth penned him in another room and then led the newsman down a long hallway, its walls covered with framed photographs. Qwilleran thought he recognized some rather important people in those frames. Of the deceased dealer there were three pictures: Glanz on a lecture platform, Glanz with the director of the historical museum, and then a studio portrait—a photograph of a young man with a square jaw, firm mouth, and intelligent eyes—a good face, an honest face.

Qwilleran glanced at Miss Duckworth, who was clasping and unclasping her hands, and said, "May I borrow this studio shot? I'll have it copied and return it."

She nodded sadly.

"You have a beautiful apartment," he said, glancing into a living room that was all gold velvet, blue silk, and polished wood. "I had no idea there was anything like this in Junktown."

"I wish other responsible people would buy some of the old houses and preserve them," she said. "So far the only ones who have shown any inclination to do so are the Cobbs. They have the mansion on this block. Antiques on the first floor and apartments upstairs."

"Apartments? Do you know if they have one for rent?"

"Yes," the girl said, lowering her eyes. "There's one vacant in the rear."

"I might inquire about it. I need a place to live."

"Mrs. Cobb is a very pleasant woman. Don't let her husband upset you."

"I don't upset easily. What's wrong with her husband?"

Miss Duckworth turned her attention to the downstairs hall. Customers had walked into the house and were chattering and exclaiming. "You go down," she instructed Qwilleran, "and I'll let the dog out of the kitchen before I follow you."

Downstairs two women were wandering among the treasures—women with the air and facial characteristics of suburban housewives; the newsman had met hundreds of them at flower shows and amateur art exhibits. But the garb of these women was out of character. One wore a man's leather trench coat and a woolly mop of a hat studded with seashells, while the other was bundled up in an Eskimo parka over black-and-white checkerboard trousers stuffed into hunting boots with plaid laces.

"Oh, what a lovely shop," said the parka.

"Oh, she's got some old Steuben," said the trench coat.

"Oh, Freda, look at this decanter! My grandmother had one just like it. Wonder what she wants for it."

"She's high, but she has good things. Don't act too enthusiastic, and she'll come down a few dollars," the trench coat advised, adding in a low voice, "Did you know she was Andy's girlfriend?"

"You mean—Andy, the one who . . . ?"

The trench coat nodded. "You know how he was killed, don't you?"

The other one shuddered and made a grimace of distaste.

"Here she comes."

As Miss Duckworth glided into the room, looking cool, poised, fragile as bone china—Qwilleran went to the rear of the shop to have one more look at the Mackintosh coat of arms. It was massive and crudely made. He felt a need to touch it, and his flesh tingled as his hand made contact with the iron. Then he hefted it—with an involuntary grunt. It felt like a hundred-pound weight.

And yet, he remembered afterwards, the delicate Miss Duckworth had lifted it with apparent ease.

CHAPTER 3

BY NOON Zwinger Street showed signs of coming to life. A halfhearted winter sunshine had broken through the gloom, adding no real joy to the scene—only a sickly smile. The sidewalks were now populated with women and quite a few men in their antiquing clothes—deliberately outlandish, mismatched, or shabby. They moved from shop to shop while waiting for the auction at one thirty.

Qwilleran decided there was time for a quick lunch and found a diner, where he gulped a leathery hot dog on a spongy roll, a beverage claiming to be coffee and a piece of synthetic pie with crust made of papier-mâché. He also telephoned the feature editor and asked for a photographer.

"About this auction," he told Arch Riker. "We should get some candids of the crowd. Their getups are incredible."

"I told you Junktown was colorful," Riker reminded him.

"Don't send me Tiny Spooner. He's a clumsy oaf, and there are lots of breakables here."

"At this short notice we'll have to take any man we can get. Have you bought any antiques yet?"

"NO!" Qwilleran bellowed into the mouthpiece, at the same time thinking warmly of the Mackintosh coat of arms.

By one o'clock the scene of the auction was crowded. Andrew Glanz had done business in a large building, probably dating from the 1920s when the neighborhood had begun to go commercial. The high ceiling was hung with ladderback chair, copper pots, birdcages, sleds, and chandeliers of every description. The floor was crowded with furniture in a disorganized jumble, pushed back to make room for rows of folding chairs. A narrow stairway led to a balcony, and from its railings hung Oriental rugs and faded tapestries. Everywhere there were signs reminding customers, "If you break it, you've bought it."

The auctiongoers were circulating, examining the merchandise with studious frowns, looking at the underside of plates, ringing crystal with a flick of a finger.

Qwilleran pushed through the crowd, making mental notes of the conversation around him.

"Look at this rocking horse! I had one exactly like it in the attic, and my husband burned it in the fireplace!"

"If it has a little man with a parasol on the bridge, it's Canton china, but if he's sitting in the teahouse, it's Nanking . . . or maybe it's the other way around."

"What's this thing? It would make a wonderful punch bowl!"

"I don't see the finial anywhere, thank God!"

"There's Andy's stepladder."

"My grandmother had a Meissen ewer, but hers was blue."

"Do you think they'll put up the finial?"

As the auction hour approached, people began to take seats facing the platform, and Qwilleran found a chair at the end of a row where he could watch for the *Fluxion* photographer to arrive. There were all kinds, all ages in the audience. One man in a Hudson Bay blanket coat carried a small dog dressed to match. Another was wearing a Santa Claus cap and a rainbow-striped muffler that hung down to the floor.

Next to Qwilleran sat a plump woman with two pairs of glasses hanging from ribbons around her neck.

"This is my first auction," he said to her. "Do you have any advice for a greenhorn?"

The woman had been designed with a compass: large round pupils in round eyes in a round face. She gave him a half-circular smile. "Don't scratch your ear, or you'll find you've bought that pier mirror." She pointed to a narrow mirror in an ornate frame that towered a good fourteen feet high and leaned against the balcony rail. "I was afraid I'd miss the auction. I had to go to the eye doctor, and he kept me waiting. He put drops in my eyes, and I can't see a thing."

"What's the finial that everyone's talking about?"

She shivered. "Don't you know about Andy's accident?"

"I heard he fell off a ladder."

"Worse than that!" She made a pained face. "Let's skip the details. It makes me sick to my stomach. . . . At first I thought you were an out-of-town dealer."

"I'm from the *Daily Fluxion*."

"Really?" She smoothed her ash-colored hair and turned adoring pupils in his direction. "Are you going to write up the auction? I'm Iris Cobb. My husband runs The Junkery down the street."

"You must be the people with the apartment to rent."

"Are you interested? You'd love it? It's furnished with antiques." The woman kept glancing toward the door. "Wonder if my husband is here yet. I can't see a thing."

"What does he look like?"

"Tall and nice-looking and probably needs a shave. He'll be wearing a red flannel shirt."

"He's standing at the back, next to a grandfather's clock."

The woman settled back in her chair. "I'm glad he got here. He'll do the bidding, and I won't have to worry about it."

"He's talking to a character in a Santa Claus cap."

"That must be Ben Nicholas. Ben rents one of our apartments and runs a shop called Bit o' Junk." With an affectionate smile she added, "He's an idiot!"

"Anyone else I should know? There's a blond guy on crutches, all dressed in white."

"Russell Patch, the refinisher. He never wears anything but white." She lowered her voice. "In front of us—the thin man—he's Hollis Prantz. He has a new shop called Tech-Tiques. The man with the briefcase is Robert Maus, attorney for the estate."

Qwilleran was impressed. The firm of Teahandle, Burris, Hansblow, Maus and Castle was the most prestigious in the city.

"Mr. Maus has a personal interest in Junktown," Mrs. Cobb explained. "Otherwise—"

The rapping of a gavel interrupted the conversation in the audience, and the auctioneer opened the sale. He wore a dark business suit with a plaid shirt, string tie, and Texas boots.

"We have a lot of good goods here today," he said, "and some smart cookies in the audience, so bid fast if you want to buy. Please refrain from unnecessary yakking so I can hear spoken bids. Let's go!" He struck the lectern with an ivory hammer. "We'll start with a Bennington hound-handle pitcher—collector's dream—slight chip but what's the difference? Who'll give me five? Five is bid—now six? Six is bid—do I hear seven? Seven over here. Eight over there—anybody give nine?—eight I've got—sold for eight!"

There were protests from the audience.

"Too fast for you clods, eh? If you want to buy, keep on your toes," the auctioneer said crisply. "We've got a lot of stuff to move this afternoon."

"He's good," Mrs. Cobb whispered to Qwilleran. "Wait till he really gets wound up!"

Every sixty seconds another item went down under the hammer—a silver inkwell, pewter goblets, a pair of bisque figures, a prayer rug, an ivory snuffbox. Three assistants were kept busy up and down the aisles, while porters carried items to and from the platform.

"And now we have a fine, fat, cast-iron stove," said the auctioneer, raising his voice. "We won't lug it to the platform, because you eagle eyes can see it on the stair landing. Who'll give me fifty?"

All heads turned to look at a sculptured black monster with a bloated silhouette and bowlegged stance.

"Fifty I have—who'll say seventy-five?—it's a beauty. . . . Seventy-five is bid—do I hear a hundred?—you're getting it cheap. . . . I have a hundred—what do I hear? . . . Hundred and ten—it's worth twice the price. . . . Hundred-twenty is bid. . . . Hundred-thirty back there—don't lose this prize—a nice big stove—big enough to hide a body. . . . Hundred-forty is bid—make it a hundred fifty. . . . *Sold* for a hundred-fifty." The auctioneer turned to the assistant who recorded sales. "Sold to C.C. Cobb."

Mrs. Cobb gasped. "That fool!" she said. "We'll never get our money out of it! I'll bet Ben Nicholas was bidding against him. The bids were going up too fast. Ben didn't want that stove. He was bidding just to be funny. He does it all the time. He knew C.C. wouldn't let him have it." She turned around and glared with unseeing eyes in the direction of the red flannel shirt and the Santa Claus cap.

The auctioneer was saying, "And now before we take an intermission, we'll unload a few items of office equipment."

There were reference books, a filing cabinet, a portable tape recorder, a typewriter—mundane items that had little interest for the crowd of junkers. Mrs. Cobb made a hesitant bid on the tape recorder and got it for a pittance.

"And here we have a portable typewriter—sold as is—one letter missing—who'll give me fifty?—do I hear fifty? I'll take forty—I think it's the Z that's missing—I'm waiting for forty—thirty, then—who'll say thirty?"

"Twenty," said Qwilleran, to his own surprise.

"Sold to the astute gentleman with the big moustache for twenty smackers and now we'll take a fifteen-minute break."

Qwilleran was stunned by his windfall. He had not expected to do any bidding.

"Let's stretch our legs," Mrs. Cobb said, pulling at his sleeve in a familiar way.

As they stood up they were confronted by the man in the red flannel shirt. "Why'd you buy that stupid tape recorder?" he demanded of his wife.

"You wait and see!" she said with a saucy shake of her head. "This is a reporter from the *Daily Fluxion*. He's interested in our vacant apartment."

"It's not for rent. I don't like reporters," Cobb growled and walked away with his hands in his trouser pockets.

"My husband is the most obnoxious dealer in Junktown," Mrs. Cobb said with pride. "Don't you think he's good-looking?"

Qwilleran was trying to think of a tactful reply when there was a crash near the front door, followed by exclamations and groans. The *Fluxion* photographer was standing at the entrance.

Tiny Spooner was six-feet-three and weighed close to four hundred pounds, including the photographic equipment draped about his person. Added to his obesity were cameras, lens cases, meters, lights, film kits, and folding tripods dangling from straps and connected by trailing cords.

Mrs. Cobb said, "What a shame! Must have been the Sèvres vase on the Empire pedestal."

"Was it valuable?"

"Worth about eight hundred dollars, I guess."

"Save my seat for me," Qwilleran said. "I'll be right back."

Tiny Spooner was standing near the door, looking uncomfortable. "So help me, I'm innocent," he told Qwilleran. "I was nowhere near the silly thing." He shifted the equipment that hung around his neck and over both shoulders, and his tripod whacked a bust of Marie Antoinette. Qwilleran flung his arms around the white marble.

"Oops," said Tiny.

The auctioneer was looking at the remains of the Sèvres vase, instructing the porter to gather the shattered fragments carefully, and Qwilleran thought it was time to introduce himself.

"We want to get a few candid shots during the bidding," he told the auctioneer. "You can proceed normally. Don't pay any attention to the photographer."

Spooner said, "I'd like to get some elevation and shoot down. Do you have a stepladder?"

There was an awkward pause. Someone laughed nervously.

"Skip it," said the photographer. "I see there's a balcony. I'll shoot from the stairway."

"Take it easy," Qwilleran cautioned him. "If you break it, you've bought it."

Spooner surveyed the scene with scorn. "Do you want form or content? I don't know what I can do with this rubbish. Too many dynamic lines and no chiarascuro." He waddled toward the stairway, his photo equipment swinging, and the wagging tripod narrowly missed the crown glass doors of a breakfront.

Back in his seat, Qwilleran explained to Mrs. Cobb, "He's the only press photographer I know with a Ph.D. in mathematics, but he's inclined to be clumsy."

"My goodness!" she said. "If he's so smart, why is he working for a newspaper?"

The gavel rapped, and the second half of the auction began, bringing out the most desirable items: an English bookcase, a Boule commode, a seventeenth century Greek icon, a small collection of Benin bronzes.

Occasionally there was a flash from the photographer's lights, and women in the audience touched their hair and assumed bright, intelligent expressions.

"And now," said the auctioneer, "we have this beautiful pair of French chairs in the original—"

There was a shriek!

A shout: "Look out!"

A porter lunged forward with arms outstretched, barely in time to steady a teetering mirror—the pier mirror that almost reached the ceiling. In another second the towering glass would have crashed on the audience.

The spectators gasped, and Qwilleran said, "Whew!" At the same time he scanned the crowd for Spooner.

The photographer was leaning over the balcony railing. He caught the newsman's eye and shrugged.

Mrs. Cobb said, "I've never seen so many accidents at an auction! It gives me the creeps. Do you believe in ghosts?"

The audience was nervous and noisy. The auctioneer raised his voice and increased the tempo of his spiel. Waving his hand, jabbing his finger at bidders, jerking his thumb over his shoulder when each item was sold, he whipped the spectators into a frenzy.

"Do you want this or don't you?—Five hundred I've got—Do I hear

six hundred?—What's the matter with you?—it's two hundred years old!—
I want seven—I want seven—I'll buy it myself for seven—going, going—
take it away!" The thumb jerked, the gavel crashed on the lectern, and the
excitement in the audience reached a crescendo.

The two-hundred-year-old desk was removed, and the spectators
waited eagerly for the next item.

At this point there was a significant pause in the action, as the auctioneer spoke to the attorney. It was a pantomime of indecision. Then they
both nodded and beckoned to a porter. A moment later a hush fell on the
crowd. The porter had placed a curious object on the platform—a tall,
slender ornament about three feet high. It had a square base topped by a
brass ball, and then a shaft of black metal tapering up to a swordlike point.

"That's it!" someone whispered behind Qwilleran. "That's the finial!"

Beside him, Mrs. Cobb was shaking her head and covering her face
with her hands. "They shouldn't have done it!"

"We have here," said the auctioneer in slow, deliberate tones, "the
finial from a rooftop—probably an ornament from an old house in the
Zwinger reclamation area. The ball is solid brass. Needs a little polishing.
What am I offered?"

The people seated around Qwilleran were shocked.

"Makes my blood run cold," one whispered.

"I didn't think they'd have the nerve to put it up."

"Who's bidding? Can you see who's bidding?"

"Very bad taste! Very bad!" someone said.

"Did Andy actually fall on it?"

"Didn't you know? He was impaled!"

"Sold!" snapped the auctioneer. "Sold to C.C. Cobb."

"No!" cried Mrs. Cobb.

At that moment there was a spine-chilling crash. A bronze chandelier
let loose from the ceiling and crashed on the floor, narrowly missing Mr.
Maus, the attorney.

CHAPTER 4

IT HAD BEEN a splendid Victorian mansion in its day—a stately red brick with white columns framing the entrance, a flight of broad steps, and a railing of ornamental ironwork. Now the painted trim was peeling, and the steps were cracked and crumbling.

This was the building that housed the Cobbs' antique shop, The Junkery, and the bay windows on either side of the entrance were filled with colored glass and bric-a-brac.

After the auction Qwilleran accompanied Mrs. Cobb to the mansion, and she left him in the tacky entrance hall.

"Have a look at our shop," she said, "while I go upstairs and see if the apartment is presentable. We've been selling out of it for two months, and it's probably a mess.

"It's been vacant two months?" Qwilleran asked, counting back to October. "Who was your last tenant?"

Mrs. Cobb looked apologetic. "Andy Glanz lived up there. You don't mind, do you? Some people are squeamish."

She hurried upstairs, and Qwilleran inspected the hallway. Although shabby, it was graciously wide, with carved woodwork and elaborate gaslight fixtures converted for electricity. The rooms opening off the hall were filled with miscellany in various stages of decrepitude. One room was crowded with fragments of old buildings—porch posts, fireplaces, slabs of discolored marble, stained-glass windows, an iron gate and sections of stair railing. Customers who had drifted in after the auction were poking among the debris, appraising with narrowed eyes, exhibiting a lack of enthusiasm. They were veteran junkers.

Eventually Qwilleran found himself in a room filled with cradles, brass beds, trunks, churns, weather vanes, flatirons, old books, engravings of Abraham Lincoln, and a primitive block and tackle made into a lamp. There was also a mahogany bar with brass rail, evidently salvaged from a turn-of-the-century saloon, and behind it stood a red-shirted man, unshaven, and handsome in a brutal way. He watched Qwilleran with a hostile glare.

The newsman ignored him and picked up a book from one of the tables. It was bound in leather, and the cracking spine was lettered in gold that had worn away with age. He opened the book to find the title page.

"*Don't* open that book," came a surly command, "unless you're buying it."

Qwilleran's moustache bristled. "How do I know whether I want it till I read the title?"

"To hell with the title!" said the proprietor. "If you like the looks of it, buy it. If you don't, keep your sweatin' hands in your pockets. How long do you think those books will last if every jerk that comes in here has to paw the bindings?"

"How much do you want for it?" Qwilleran demanded.

"I don't think I want to sell it. Not to you, anyway."

The other customers had stopped browsing and were looking mildly amused at Qwilleran's discomfiture. He sensed the encouragement in their glances and rose to the occasion.

"Discrimination! That's what this is," he roared. "I should report this and have you put out of business! This place is a rat's nest anyway. The city should condemn it. . . . Now, how much do you want for this crummy piece of junk?"

"Four bucks, just to shut your loud mouth!"

"I'll give you three." Qwilleran threw some bills on the bar.

Cobb scooped them up and filed them in his billfold. "Well, there's more than one way to skin a sucker," he said with a leer at the other customers.

Qwilleran opened the book he had bought. It was *The Works of the Reverend Dr. Ishmael Higginbotham, Being a Collection of Interesting Tracts Explaining Several Important Points of the Divine Doctrine, Set Forth with Diligence and Extreme Brevity.*

Mrs. Cobb burst into the room. "Did you let that dirty old man bully you into buying something?"

"Shut up, old lady," said her husband.

She had put on a pink dress, fixed her hair, and applied make-up, and she looked plumply pretty. "Come upstairs with me," she said sweetly, putting a friendly hand on Qwilleran's arm. "We'll have a cozy cup of coffee and let Cornball Cobb fume with jealousy."

Mrs. Cobb started up the creaking staircase, her round hips bobbling from side to side and the backs of her fat knees bulging in a horizontal grin. Qwilleran was neither titillated nor repelled by the sight, but rather saddened that every woman was not blessed with a perfect figure.

"Don't pay any attention to C.C.," she said over her shoulder. "He's a great kidder."

The spacious upstairs hall was a forest of old chairs, tables, desks, and chests. Several doors stood open, revealing dingy living quarters.

"Our apartment is on that side," said Mrs. Cobb, indicating an open door through which came a loud radio commercial, "and on this side we have two smaller apartments. Ben Nicholas rents the front, but the rear is nicer because it has a view of the backyard."

Qwilleran looked out the hall window and saw two station wagons backed in from the alley, an iron bed, a grindstone, the fender from a car, some wagon wheels, an old refrigerator with no door, and a wooden washing machine with attached clothes wringer—most of them frozen together in a drift of dirty ice and snow.

"Then how come Nicholas lives in the front?" he asked.

"His apartment has a bay window, and he can keep an eye on the entrance to his shop, next door."

She led the way into the rear apartment—a large square room with four tall windows and a frightening collection of furniture. Qwilleran's gaze went first to an old parlor organ in jaundiced oak—then a pair of high-backed gilded chairs with seats supported by gargoyles—then a round table, not quite level, draped with an embroidered shawl and holding an oil lamp, its two globes painted with pink roses—then a patterned rug suffering from age and melancholy—then a crude rocking chair made of bent twigs and treebark, probably full of termites.

"You *do* like antiques, don't you?" Mrs. Cobb asked anxiously.

"Not especially," Qwilleran replied in a burst of honesty. "And what is that supposed to be?" He pointed to a chair with tortured iron frame, elevated on a pedestal and equipped with headrest and footrest.

"An old dentist's chair—really quite comfortable for reading. You can pump it up and down with your foot. And the painting over the fireplace is a very good primitive."

With a remarkably controlled expression on his face, Qwilleran studied the lifesize portrait of someone's great-great-grandmother, dressed in black—square-jawed, thin-lipped, steely-eyed, and disapproving all she surveyed.

"You haven't said a word about the daybed," said Mrs. Cobb with enthusiasm. "It's really unique. It came from New Jersey."

The newsman turned around and winced. The daybed, placed against one wall, was built like a swan boat, with one end carved in the shape of a long-necked bad-tempered bird and the other end culminating in a tail.

"Sybaritic," he said drily, and the landlady went into spasms of laughter.

A second room, toward the front of the house, had been subdivided into kitchenette, dressing room, and bath.

Mrs. Cobb said, "C.C. installed the kitchen himself. He's handy with tools. Do you like to cook?"

"No, I take most of my meals at the Press Club."

"The fireplace works, if you want to haul wood upstairs. Do you like the place? I usually get one hundred and ten dollars a month, but if you like it, you can have it for eighty-five dollars."

Qwilleran looked at the furniture again and groomed his moustache thoughtfully. The furnishings gave him a chill, but the rent suited his economic position admirably. "I'd need a desk and a good reading light and a place to put my books."

"We've got anything you want. Just ask for it."

He bounced on the daybed and found it sufficiently firm. Being built down to the floor, it would offer no temptations to burrowing cats. "I forgot to tell you," he said. "I have pets. A couple of Siamese cats."

"Fine! They'll get rid of our mice. They can have a feast."

"I don't think they like meat on the hoof. They prefer it well-aged and served medium rare with pan juices."

Mrs. Cobb laughed heartily—too heartily—at his humor. "What do you call your cats?"

"Koko and Yum Yum."

"Oh, excuse me a minute!" She rushed from the room and returned to explain that she had a pie in the oven. An aroma of apples and spices was wafting across the hall, and Qwilleran's moustache twitched.

While Mrs. Cobb straightened pictures and tested surfaces for dust, Qwilleran examined the facilities. The bathroom had an archaic tub with clawed feet, snarling faucets, and a maze of exposed pipes. The refrigerator was new, however, and the large dressing room had a feature that interested him; one wall was a solid bank of built-in bookshelves filled with volumes in old leather bindings.

"If you want to use the shelves for something else, we'll move the books out," Mrs. Cobb said. "We found them in the attic. They belonged to the man who built this house over a hundred years ago. He was a newspaper editor. Very prominent in the abolitionist movement. This house is quite historic."

Qwilleran noticed Dostoyevski, Chesterfield, Emerson. "You don't need to move the books, Mrs. Cobb. I might like to browse through them."

"Then you'll take the apartment?" Her round eyes were shining. "Have a cup of coffee and a piece of pie, and then you can decide."

Soon Qwilleran was sitting in a gilded chair at the lopsided table, plunging a fork into bubbling hot pie with sharp cheese melted over the top. Mrs. Cobb watched with pleasure as her prospective tenant devoured every crumb of flaky crust and every dribble of spiced juice.

"Have some more?"

"I shouldn't." Qwilleran pulled in his waistline. "But it's very good."

"Oh, come on! You don't have to worry about weight. You have a very nice physique."

The newsman tackled his second wedge of pie, and Mrs. Cobb described the joys of living in an old house.

"We have a ghost," she announced cheerfully. "A blind woman who used to live here fell down the stairs and was killed. C.C. says her ghost is fascinated by my glasses. When I go to bed, I put them on the night table, and in the morning they're on the window sill. Or if I put them in the dresser drawer, they're moved to the night table. . . . More coffee?"

"Thanks. Do the glasses move around every night?"

"Only when the moon is full." The landlady grew thoughtful. "Do you realize how many strange things happened at the auction today? The Sèvres vase, and the chandelier that fell, and the pier mirror that started to topple. . . . It makes me wonder."

"Wonder what?"

"It's almost as if Andy's spirit was *protesting*."

"Do you believe in that kind of thing?"

"I don't know. I do and I don't."

"What do you think Andy might have been trying to say?" Qwilleran wore a sincere expression. He had a talent for sincerity that had drawn confidences from the most reticent persons.

Mrs. Cobb chuckled. "Probably that the auctioneer was letting things go too cheap. There were some terrific buys."

"All the junkers call Andy's death an accident, but I met someone on the street who said he was murdered."

"No, it was an accident. The police said so. And yet . . ." Her voice trailed away.

"What were you going to say?"

"Well . . . it seems strange that Andy would be careless enough to slip and fall on that thing. He was a very . . . a very *prudent* young man, you know."

Qwilleran smoothed his moustache hurriedly. "I'd like to hear more about Andy," he said. "Why don't I go and get my luggage and the cats . . . ?"

"You'll take the apartment?" Mrs. Cobb clapped her hands. "I'm so glad! It will be nice to have a professional writer in the house. It will give us *class*, if you know what I mean."

She gave him a key to the downstairs door and accepted a month's rent.

"We don't bother to lock our doors up here," he said, "but if you want a key, I'll find you one."

"Don't worry about it. Nothing that I own is worth locking up."

She gave him a mischievous look. "Mathilda walks right through doors, anyway."

"Who?"

"Mathilda. Our ghost."

Qwilleran went back to his hotel and made one telephone call before packing his suitcases. He called the Photo Lab at the *Daily Fluxion* and asked for Tiny Spooner.

"How'd the pictures turn out, Tiny?"

"Fair. They're on the dryer. Can't say they're graphically articulate. Too many incongruous shapes."

"Leave them in the Feature slot, and I'll pick them up Monday. And Tiny," Qwilleran said, "I want to ask you one question. Give me the truth. Did you or didn't you—"

"I was nowhere near that blasted crockery. I swear! I looked at it, that's all, and it started to jiggle."

"And how about the chandelier and the big mirror?"

"Don't try to pin those on me, either! So help me, I was twenty feet away when they let loose!"

CHAPTER 5

THE CATS KNEW something was afoot. When Qwilleran returned to Medford Manor, both were huddled in wary anticipation.

"Come on, you guys. We're moving out of Medicare Manor," Qwilleran said.

From the closet he brought the soup carton with airholes punched in the side. Koko had been through this routine twice before, and he consented to hop in, but Yum Yum was having none of it.

"Come on, sweetheart."

Yum Yum responded by turning into a lump of lead, her underside fused to the carpet and anchored by twenty efficient little hooks. Only when Qwilleran produced a can opener and a small can with a blue label did she loosen her grip. With a sensuous gurgle in her throat, she leaped onto the dresser.

"All right, sister," the man said as he grabbed her. "It was a dirty trick, but I had to do it. We'll open the chicken when we get to Junktown."

When Qwilleran and his two suitcases, four cartons of books, and one carton of cats arrived at the Cobb mansion, he hardly recognized his apartment. The dentist's chair and parlor organ were gone, and the pot-bellied stove from the auction was standing in one corner. Two lamps had been added: a reading lamp sprouting out of a small brass cash register, and a floor lamp that had once been a musket. The elderly battle-ax over the fireplace still glowered at him, and the depressing rug was still grieving on the floor, but there were certain improvements: a roll-top desk, a large open cupboard for books, and an old-fashioned Morris chair—a big, square contraption with reclining back, soft black leather cushions, and ottoman to match.

As soon as Qwilleran opened the soup carton, Yum Yum leaped out, dashed insanely in several directions, and ended on top of the tall cupboard. Koko emerged slowly, with circumspection. He explored the apartment systematically and thoroughly, approved the red-cushioned seats of the two gilt chairs, circled the pot-bellied stove three times and discovered no earthly use for it, leaped to the mantel and sniffed the primitive portrait, afterwards rubbing his jaw on the corner of the frame and tilting the picture askew. Then he arranged himself attractively between two brass candlesticks on the mantelshelf.

"Oh, isn't he lovely!" exclaimed Mrs. Cobb, appearing with a stack of clean towels and a cake of soap. "Is that Koko? Hello, Koko. Do you like it here, Koko?" She looked at him in a near-sighted way, waggling a finger at his nose and speaking in the falsetto voice with which cats are often addressed—an approach that always offended Koko. He sneezed in her face, enveloping her in a gossamer mist.

"The cats will like it here," she said, straightening the picture that Koko had nudged. "They can watch the pigeons in the backyard."

She bustled into the bathroom with the towels, and as soon as she turned her back, Koko scraped his jaw with vengeance on the corner of the picture frame, pitching it into a forty-five-degree list.

Qwilleran cleared his throat. "I see you've made a few changes, Mrs. Cobb."

"Right after you left, a customer wanted that dentist's chair, so we sold it. Hope you don't mind. I've given you the pot-bellied stove to fill up the empty corner. How do you like your roll-top desk?"

"My grandfather—"

"The tavern table will be nice for your typewriter. And what do you usually do about your personal laundry? I'll be glad to put it through the automatic washer for you."

"Oh, no, Mrs. Cobb! That's too much trouble."

"Not at all. And please call me Iris." She drew the draperies across the windows—velvet draperies in streaked and faded gold. "I made these out of an old stage curtain. C.C. got it from a theatre that's being torn down."

"Did you do the wall behind the bed?"

"No. That was Andy's idea." The wall was papered with the yellowed pages of old books, set in quaint typefaces. "Andy was quite a bookworm."

"As soon as I unpack and feed the cats," Qwilleran said. "I'd like to talk to you about Andy."

"Why don't you come across the hall when you're settled? I'll be doing my ironing." And then she added, "C.C. has gone to look at a Jacobean dining room set that someone wants to sell."

Qwilleran emptied his suitcases, lined up his books in the open cupboard, put the cats' blue cushion on top of the refrigerator—their favorite perch—and drew their attention to the new location of the unabridged dictionary which served as their new scratching pad. Then he walked across the hall to the Cobbs' apartment. The first thing he noticed was Mrs. Cobb ironing in the big kitchen, and she invited him to sit on a rush-seated chair (A-522-001) at a battered pine table (D-573-091).

"Do you sell out of your apartment?" he asked.

"Constantly! Last Tuesday we had breakfast at a round oak table, lunch at a cherry dropleaf, and dinner at that pine trestle table."

"Must be hard work, moving the stuff around, up and down stairs."

"You get used to it. Right now I'm not supposed to lift anything. I wrenched my back a couple of months ago."

"How did you get my apartment rearranged so fast?"

"C.C. got Mike to help him. He's the grocer's son. A nice boy, but he thinks antique dealers are batty. We are, of course," she added with a sly glance at her guest.

"Mrs. Cobb—"

"Please call me Iris. Mind if I call you Jim?"

"People call me Qwill."

"Oh, that's nice. I like that." She smiled at the pajamas she was pressing.

"Iris, I wish you'd tell me more about Andy. It might help me write my story about the auction."

She set the electric iron on its heel and gazed into space. "He was a fine young man! Nice personality, honest, intelligent. He was a writer—like you. I admire writers. You'd never guess it, but I was an English major myself."

"What did Andy write?"

"Mostly articles for antique magazines, but he liked to play around with fiction. Some day I should write a book myself! The people you meet in this business!"

"How much do you know about the accident? When did it happen?"

"One evening in October." Iris coughed. "He'd been having dinner with the Dragon at her apartment—"

"You mean Miss Duckworth?"

"We call her the Dragon. She frightens people with that hoity-toity manner, you know. Well, anyway, Andy had dinner with her and then went to his shop for something, and when he didn't return, she went looking for him. She found him in a pool of *blood*!"

"Did she call the police?"

"No. She came flying over here in hysterics, and C.C. called the police. They decided Andy had fallen off the stepladder while getting a chandelier down from the ceiling. They found the light fixture on the floor smashed. It was all crystal. Five long curving crystal arms and a lot of crystal prisms."

"Is it true that he fell on that sharp finial?"

She nodded. "That's one thing that doesn't make sense. Andy was always so careful! In fact, he was a fussbudget. I don't think he would leave that finial standing around where it would be a hazard. Antique dealers are always spraining their backs or rupturing something, but nothing ever happened to Andy. He was very cautious."

"Maybe he had a couple of drinks with Miss Duckworth and got reckless."

"He didn't drink. She probably had a drink or two, but Andy didn't have any bad habits. He was kind of straitlaced. I always thought he'd make a good minister of the gospel if he hadn't gone into the junk business. He was really dedicated. It's a calling, you know. It gets to be your whole life."

"Could it have been suicide?"

"Oh, no! Andy wasn't the type."

"You never know what goes on in people's heads—or what kind of trouble—"

"I couldn't believe it. Not about Andy."

Qwilleran drew his pipe and tobacco pouch from the pocket of his tweed sports coat. "Mind if I smoke?"

"Go right ahead. Would you like a can of C.C.'s beer?"

"No, thanks. I'm on the wagon."

With fascination Iris watched the sucking in of cheeks and soft oompah-oompah of pipe lighting. "I wish C.C. smoked a pipe. It smells so good!"

The newsman said, "Do you suppose Andy might have been killed by a prowler?"

"I don't know."

"Can you think of a motive for murder?"

Iris pressed down on the iron while she thought about it. "I don't know . . . but I'll tell you something if you'll promise not to tell C.C. He would kid me about it. . . . It was Andy's horoscope. I just happened to read it in the paper. The *Daily Fluxion* has the best horoscopes, but we get the *Morning Rampage* because it has more pages, and we need lots of paper for wrapping china and glass."

"And what did the *Morning Rampage* have to say about Andy?"

"His sign was Aquarius. It said he should beware of trickery." She gave Qwilleran a questioning glance. "I didn't read it till the day after he was killed."

The newsman puffed on his pipe with sober mien. "Not what you would call substantial evidence. . . . Was Andy engaged to the Duckworth girl?"

"Not officially, but there was a lot of running back and forth," Iris said with raised eyebrows.

"She's very attractive," Qwilleran remarked, thinking about the Dragon's eyes. "How did she react after Andy was killed?"

"She was all broken up. My, she was broken up! And that surprised me, because she had always been such a cool cucumber. C.C. said Andy probably got her in a family way before he died, but I don't believe it. Andy was too honorable."

"Maybe Andy was more human than you think."

"Well, he died before Halloween, and this is almost Christmas, and the Dragon's still as skinny as a rake handle. . . . But she's changed. She's very moody and withdrawn."

"What will happen to Andy's estate?"

"I don't know. Mr. Maus is handling it. Andy's parents live upstate somewhere."

"How did the other dealers feel about Andy? Was he well liked?"

Iris reflected before she answered. "Everyone *respected* Andy—for his ability—but some people thought he was too much of a goody."

"What do you mean?"

"How shall I explain? . . . In this business you have to grab every advantage you can. You work hard without letup and don't make any money. Some months we can hardly make the payments on this house, because C.C. has tied up his cash in something crazy—like the pot-bellied stove—that we won't be able to sell." She wiped her damp forehead on her sleeve. "So if you see a chance to make a good profit, you grab it. . . . But Andy was always leaning over backwards to be *ethical*, and he condemned people who were trying to make an extra dollar or two. I don't say he was wrong, but he carried it too far. That's the only thing I had against him. . . . Don't say that in the paper. On the whole he was a wonderful person. So considerate in unexpected ways!"

"In what ways?"

"Well, for one thing, he was always so nice to Papa Popopopoulos, the fruit man. The rest of us just ignore the lonely old fellow. . . . And then there was Ann Peabody. When the antique dealers had a neighborhood meeting, Andy always made sure that Ann attended, even if he had to carry her. She's ninety years old and still runs a shop, although she hasn't sold so much as a salt dip in four years." The iron was making light passes over a red and grey striped sport shirt. "One good thing about being in this business—you don't have to iron white shirts."

"Was Andy successful—financially?"

"He made a go of it, I guess. He also sold articles to magazines and taught an evening class in antiques at the Y.W.C.A. In this business everybody has to have some kind of job on the side—or else a rich uncle. C.C. is a professional picket. He was on the picket line this morning in that bitter cold."

"What was he picketing?"

"I don't know. He goes wherever the agency sends him. He likes the work, and it pays time and a half in bad weather."

"Does Miss Duckworth have a sideline?"

"I doubt whether she needs one. I think she has money. She sells very fine things—to a select clientele. She has a Sheraton card table over there that I'd commit murder to own! It's priced way out of my class."

"I was surprised to find such an expensive shop in Junktown."

"I suppose she wanted to be near her boyfriend. In this business, location is unimportant; customers will go anywhere to find what they're looking for."

"But isn't there some risk in having valuable things in a neighborhood like this?" Qwilleran asked.

Iris frowned at him. "You're just like everyone else! You think an old neighborhood that's run down is a hotbed of crime. It's not true! We don't have any trouble." She fell silent as she concentrated on the collar of a blouse.

The newsman stood up. "Well, I'd better get back to work—try out the new typewriter—and see if I can write something about the auction."

"By the way," said Iris, "there's a box of old keys on that Empire chest. See if one of them fits your lock."

He glanced in the box and saw nothing but old-fashioned keys, four inches long. "I don't need to lock my door," he said.

Returning to his apartment, Qwilleran opened the door and reached in for the wall switch that activated three sources of light: the reading light near the Morris chair, the floor lamp standing at the desk, and the hand-painted relic on the tilted table. Then he looked for the cats, as he always did upon coming home.

There they were—sitting on the two gilt chairs like two reigning heads of state on their thrones—with brown paws tucked fastidiously under white breasts and brown ears worn like two little crowns.

"You guys look pretty contented," Qwilleran remarked. "Didn't take you long to feel at home."

Koko squeezed his eyes and said, "Yow," and Yum Yum, whose eyes were slightly crossed, peered at Qwilleran with her perpetual I-don't-know-what-you're-talking-about look and murmured something. Her normal speaking voice was a soprano shriek, but in her softer moments she uttered a high-pitched "Mmmm" with her mouth closed.

The newsman went to work. He opened the typewriter case, hit a few keys on his newly acquired machine and thought, Andy may have been prudent, ethical, intelligent, and good-looking, but he kept a scruffy type-writer. It was filled with eraser crumbs, and the ribbon had been hammered to shreds. Furthermore, the missing letter was not the expendable Z but the ubiquitous E. Qwilleran began to write:

"Th* spirit of th* lat* Andr*w Glanz hov*r*d ov*r Junktown wh*n th* tr*asur*s of this highly r*sp*ct*d d*al*r w*r* sold at auction to th* cr*am of th* city's junk*rs."

He described the cream: their purposely raffish clothes, their wacky conversations, the calculated expressions on their faces. He had made no notes during the day; after twenty-five years of newspapering, his mind was a video tape recorder.

It was slow work, however. The tavern table was rickety. The lack of an E was frustrating, and the asterisks—inserted for the benefit of the typesetter—dazzled his eyes. Between paragraphs, moreover, a pair of piercing eyes kept boring into his consciousness. He knew that kind of stare. It indicated one of two things. The elegant Miss Duckworth was either myopic—or frightened.

At one point Qwilleran was alerted by a low rumble coming from Koko's throat, and soon afterward he heard footsteps slowly mounting the stairs and entering the front apartment. Some minutes later he heard a telephone ring in the adjoining rooms. Then the heavy footsteps started down the hall again.

Qwilleran's curiosity sent him hurrying to the door for a close-up of the man who wore a Santa Claus cap. He saw instead a Napoleonic bicorne perched squarely above a round face that lacked eyebrows.

The man threw up his hands in exaggerated surprise. His small bloodshot eyes stretched wide in astonishment. "Sir! You startled us!" he said in an overly dramatic voice.

"Sorry. Didn't mean to. I just moved in here. My name's Qwilleran."

"Welcome to our humble abode," said the man with a sweeping gesture. He suddenly looked down. "And what have we here?"

Koko had followed Qwilleran into the hall and was rubbing against the stranger's rubber boots in an affectionate way.

"I've never seen him do that before," Qwilleran said. "Koko usually doesn't warm up to strangers right away."

"They know! They know! Ben Nicholas is the friend of bird and beast!"

"You have a shop next door, I understand. I'm with the *Daily Fluxion*, and I'm writing a series on Junktown."

"Pray visit us and write a few kind words. We need the publicity."

"Tomorrow," Qwilleran promised.

"Till then!" With an airy wave of the hand the dealer started downstairs, his ridiculously long scarf dragging on the carpeted treads behind him. "A customer awaits us," he explained. "We must be off."

Mrs. Cobb was right, Qwilleran thought. Ben Nicholas was an idiot, but Koko evidently approved.

Again all was quiet in the hall beyond Qwilleran's door. Recklessly the newsman wrote about things he did not understand (a M*iss*n armorial sucri*r, *arly Am*rican tr**n and A Qu*zal compot* in quincunx d*sign), making frequent trips to the dictionary.

After a while, as he sat there pounding out copy with the two long fingers of each hand, he thought he saw—out of the corner of his eye—something moving. He turned his head and looked over his roll-top desk just in time to see the door slowly opening inward. It opened a few inches and stopped.

"Yes? Who is it?" Qwilleran demanded.

There was no answer. He jumped up and went to the door, opening it wide. No one was there, but at the end of the hall, in a jumble of furniture, there was a flicker of movement. Qwilleran pressed his weary eyeballs with his fingers and then stared at the confusion of mahogany, pine, and walnut—legs, lids, drawers, seats, and backs. He saw it again—behind a low blanket chest. It was the tip of a brown tail.

"Koko!" he said sharply.

There was no reply from the cat.

"Koko, come back here!" He knew it was Koko; there was no kink in the tail tip.

The cat ignored him, as he customarily did when concentrating on important business of his own.

Qwilleran strode down the hall and saw Koko disappear behind the parlor organ. The man could guess how the cat had managed to get out. Old houses had loosely fitting doors with weak latches, or else they had swollen doors, thick with paint, that refused to close at all. Koko had pulled the door open with his claws. He was clever about doors; he knew when to pull and when to push.

The man leaned over a marble-topped commode and peered behind the parlor organ. "Get out of there, Koko! It's none of your business."

The cat had leaped to a piano stool. He was sniffing intently. With whiskers back, he moved his nose like a delicate instrument up and down the length of a sharp metal object with a brass ball at its base.

Qwilleran's moustache bristled. The cat had walked out of the apartment and had gone directly to the finial. He was sniffing it with mouth open and fangs bared, a sign of repugnance.

Qwilleran reached behind the organ and grabbed Koko around the middle. The cat squawked as if he were being strangled.

"Mrs. Cobb!" the man called through the open door of his landlady's apartment. "I've changed my mind. I want a key."

While she rummaged through the keybox, he touched his moustache gingerly. There was an odd feeling in the roots of it—a tingling sensation he had experienced several times before. It always happened when there was murder in the air.

CHAPTER 6

LATE THAT EVENING Qwilleran sampled the abolitionist's library and became fascinated by a volume of bound copies of *The Liberator*, and it was after midnight when he realized he had nothing in the apartment for breakfast. He had noticed an all-night grocery on the corner, so he put on his overcoat and the latest acquisition in his wardrobe, a porkpie hat in black and white checked tweed with a rakish red feather. It was the reddest red feather he had ever seen, and he liked red.

He locked the door with a four-inch key and went down the squeaking stairs. Snow had begun to fall—in a kindly way this time, without malice—and Qwilleran stood on the front steps to enjoy the scene. Traffic was sparse, and with the dimness of the outdated streetlights and the quaintness of the buildings and the blessing of the snow, Junktown had an old-time charm. The snow sugared the carved lintels of doors and windows, voluted iron railings, tops of parked cars, and lids of trash cans.

At the nearby intersection there was a glow on the whitened sidewalks, spilling out from the grocery, the drugstore, and the bar called The Lion's Tail. A man came out of the bar, walking with uncertain dignity and clutching for a handrail that did not exist. A girl in tight trousers and spotted fur jacket sauntered past the Cobb mansion, staring at passing cars. Catching sight of Qwilleran, she slithered in his direction. He shook his head. Ben Nicholas emerged from his shop next door and walked toward the bar, slowly and solemnly, moving his lips and paying no attention to the newsman on the steps.

Turning up his coat collar, Qwilleran went to Lombardo's grocery. It was an old-fashioned market with $4.95 Christmas trees heaped on the sidewalk and, inside, a smell of pickles, sausage, and strong cheese. He bought instant coffee and a sweet roll for his breakfast and some round steak and canned consommé for the cats. He also selected some cheese—Cheddar for himself, cream cheese for Yum Yum, and a small wedge of blue for Koko, wondering if the domestic product would be acceptable; Koko was used to genuine Roquefort.

Just as the newsman was leaving the store, the eyes that had been haunting his thoughts all evening materialized in front of him. The blue-white porcelain complexion was wet with snow, and the lashes were spangled with snowflakes. The girl stared and said nothing.

"Well, as you can see, I'm still hanging around the neighborhood," he said to break the silence. "I've moved into the Cobb mansion."

"You have? You really have?" Miss Duckworth's expression brightened, as if living in Junktown constituted an endorsement of character. She pushed her fur hood back from her blue-black hair, now piled in a ballerina's topknot.

"The auction was an interesting experience. A lot of dealers were there, but I didn't see you."

She shook her head wistfully. "I thought of going, but I lacked the courage."

"Miss Duckworth," said Qwilleran, coming boldly to the point, "I'd like to write a tribute to Andy Glanz, but I need more information. I wish you'd fill me in." He could see her shrinking from the suggestion. "I know it's a painful subject for you, but Andy deserves the best we can give him."

She hesitated. "You wouldn't quote me directly, would you?"

"Word of honor!"

"Very well," she said in a small voice, searching Qwilleran's face for reassurance. "When?"

"Sooner the better."

"Would you like to come over to my place tonight?"

"If it isn't too late for you."

"I always stay up half the night." She said it wearily.

"I'll take my groceries home and be right over."

A few minutes later Qwilleran went striding through the snow to The Blue Dragon with an elation that was only partly connected with the Andy Glanz story, and he soon found himself sitting on a stiff velvet sofa in the gold and blue living room and enjoying the aroma of sandalwood furniture wax. The belligerent dog had been penned up in the kitchen.

The girl explained, "My family disapproves of this neighborhood, and they insist I keep Hepplewhite for protection. Sometimes he takes his job too seriously."

"There seems to be a sharp division of opinion about Junktown," said Qwilleran. "Is it really a bad neighborhood?"

"We have no trouble," Miss Duckworth said. "Of course, I observe certain precautions, as any woman should if she lives alone."

She brought a silver coffeepot on a silver tray, and Qwilleran watched her silky movements with admiration. She had the long-legged grace he admired in Koko and Yum Yum. What a sensation she would make at the Press Club on Christmas Eve! he told himself. She was wearing slim, well-fitted trousers in a delectable shade of blue, and a cashmere sweater dyed to match, probably at great expense.

"Have you ever done any fashion modeling?" he asked.

"No." She smiled patiently, as if she had been asked a thousand times before. "But I did a great deal of Modern Dance at Bennington."

She poured one cup of coffee. Then, to Qwilleran's surprise, she reached for a crystal decanter with a silver label and poured Scotch for herself.

He said, "Well, I rented Mrs. Cobb's apartment this afternoon and moved in immediately—with my two roommates, a pair of Siamese cats."

"Really? You hardly look like a man who would keep cats."

Qwilleran eyed her defensively. "They were orphans. I adopted them—first the male and then, some months later, the female."

"I'd like to have a cat," she said. "Cats seem to go with antiques. They're so gentle."

"You don't know Siamese! When they start flying around, you think you've been hit by a Caribbean hurricane."

"Now that you have an apartment, you ought to buy the Mackintosh coat of arms. It would be perfect over your fireplace. Would you like to take it home on approval?"

"It's rather heavy to be lugging back and forth. In fact," Qwilleran said, "I was surprised to see you handle it with so much ease this morning."

"I'm strong. In this business you have to be strong."

"What do you do for recreation? Lift weights?"

She gave a small laugh. "I read about antiques, attend antiques lectures, and go to exhibits at the historical museum."

"You've got it bad, haven't you?"

She looked at him engagingly. "There's something mystic about antiques. It's more than intrinsic value or beauty or age. An object that has been owned and cherished by other human beings for centuries develops a personality of its own that reaches out to you. It's like an old friend. Do you understand? I wish I could make people understand."

"You explain it very well, Miss Duckworth."

"Mary," she said.

"Mary, then. But if you feel so strongly about antiques, why don't you want to share your interest with our readers? Why don't you let me quote you?"

She hesitated. "I'll tell you why," she said suddenly. "It's because of my family. They don't approve of what I'm doing, living on Zwinger Street and peddling—junk!"

"What's their objection?"

"Father is a banker, and bankers are rather stuffy. He's also English. The combination is deadly. He subsidizes my business venture on condition that I don't embarrass the family. That's why I must decline any publicity."

She refilled Qwilleran's coffee cup and poured herself another Scotch.

In a teasing tone he said, "Do you always serve your guests coffee while you drink pedigreed Scotch?"

"Only when they are total abstainers," she replied with a smug smile.

"How did you know I'm on the wagon?"

She buried her nose in her glass for a few seconds. "Because I called my father this afternoon and had him check your credentials. I found out that you've been a crime reporter in New York, Los Angeles, and elsewhere, and that you once wrote an important book on urban crime, and that you've won any number of national journalism awards." She folded her arms and looked triumphant.

Warily Qwilleran said, "What else did you find out?"

"That you had some lean years as a result of an unhappy marriage and a case of alcoholism, but you made a successful recovery, and the *Daily Fluxion* employed you last February, and you have been doing splendidly ever since."

Qwilleran flushed. He was used to prying into the lives of others; it was disconcerting to have his own secrets exposed. "I should be flattered that you're interested," he said with chagrin. "Who is your father? What's his bank?"

The girl was enjoying her moment of oneupmanship. She was also enjoying her drink. She slid down in her chair and crossed her long legs. "Can I trust you?"

"Like a tombstone."

"He's Percival Duxbury. Midwest National."

"Duxbury! Then Duckworth isn't your real name?"

"It's a name I've taken for professional purposes."

Qwilleran's hopes for Christmas Eve soared; a Duxbury would make an impressive date at the Press Club. They immediately crashed; a Duxbury would probably never accept the invitation.

"A Duxbury in Junktown!" he said softly. "That would really make headlines."

"You promised," she reminded him, snapping out of her casual pose.

"I'll keep my promise," he said. "But tell me: why are you doing business on Zwinger Street? A nice shop like this belongs downtown—or in Lost Lake Hills."

"I fell in love," she said with a helpless gesture. "I fell in love with these wonderful old houses. They have so much character and such potential for restoration. At first I was attracted to the idea of a proud old neighborhood resisting modernization, but after I had been here for a few months, I fell in love with the people."

"The antique dealers?"

"Not exactly. The dealers are dedicated and plucky, and I admire them—with certain reservations—but I'm talking about the people on the street. My heart goes out to them—the working class, the old people, the lonely ones, foreigners, illiterates, even the shady characters. Are you shocked?"

"No. Surprised. Pleasantly surprised. I think I know what you mean. They're earthy; they get to you."

"They're genuine, and they're unabashed individualists. They have made my former life seem so superficial and useless. I wish I could do something for the neighborhood, but I don't know what it would be. I have no money of my own, and Father made me promise not to mix."

Qwilleran regarded her with a wishful wonder that she misinterpreted.

"Are you hungry?" she asked. "I think I'll find us something to eat."

When she returned with crackers and caviar and smoked salmon, he said, "You were going to tell me about Andy Glanz. What kind of man was he? How did the junkers feel about him?"

The Scotch had relaxed her. She put her head back, gazed at the ceiling and collected her thoughts, her posture and trousered legs jarringly out of tune with the prim eighteenth century room.

"Andy did a great deal for Junktown," she began, "because of his scholarly approach to antiques. He gave talks to women's clubs. He convinced the museum curators and the serious collectors to venture into Zwinger Street."

"Could I call him the major-domo of Junktown?"

"I'd avoid saying that, if I were you. C.C. Cobb considers himself the neighborhood leader. He opened the first shop and promoted the idea of Junktown."

"How would you describe Andy as to character?"

"Honest—scrupulously honest! Most of us have a little larceny in our hearts, but not Andy! And he had a great sense of responsibility. I saw him make a citizen's arrest one night. We were driving past an abandoned house in the reclamation area, and we saw a light inside. Andy went in and caught a man stripping the plumbing fixtures."

"That's illegal, I assume."

"Condemned houses are city property. Yes, it's technically illegal. Anyone else would have looked the other way, but Andy was never afraid to get involved."

Qwilleran shifted his position on the stiff sofa. "Did the other dealers share your admiration for Andy's integrity?"

"Yes-s-s . . . and no," Mary said. "There's always jealousy among deal-ers, even though they appear to be the best of friends."

"Did Andy have any other friends I could interview?"

"There's Mrs. McGuffey. She's a retired schoolteacher, and Andy helped her start her antique shop. He was magnanimous in many ways."

"Where would I find the lady?"

"At The Piggin, Noggin and Firkin in the next block."

"Did Andy get along with Cobb?"

She drew a deep breath. "Andy was a diplomat. He knew how to han-dle C.C."

"Mrs. Cobb was evidently very fond of Andy."

"All women adored him. Men were not so enthusiastic, perhaps. It usually happens that way, doesn't it?"

"How about Ben Nicholas? Did they hit it off?"

"Their relations were amicable, although Andy thought Ben spent too much time at The Lion's Tail."

"Is Ben a heavy drinker?"

"He likes his brandy, but he never gets out of line. He used to be an actor. Every city has one antique dealer who used to be on the stage and one who makes it a point to be obnoxious."

"What do you know about the blond fellow on crutches?"

"Russell Patch used to work for Andy, and they were great friends. Then suddenly they parted company, and Russ opened his own shop. I'm not sure what caused the rift."

"But you were Andy's closest friend?" Qwilleran asked with a search-ing look.

Abruptly Mary Duckworth stood up and wandered around the room hunting for her cigarette holder. She found it and sat on the sofa and let Qwilleran offer her a light. After one deep inhalation she laid the cigarette down and curled up as if in pain, hugging her knees. "I miss Andy so much," she whispered.

Qwilleran had a desire to reach out and comfort her, but he restrained himself. He said, "You've had a shock, and you've been living with your grief. You shouldn't bottle it up. Why don't you tell me about it? I mean, everything that happened on that night. It might do you some good."

The warmth of his tone brought a wetness to her dark eyes. After a while she said, "The terrible thing is that we quarreled on our last eve-ning together. I was feeling peevish. Andy had . . . done something . . .

that irritated me. He was trying to make amends, but I kept goading him during dinner."

"Where did you have dinner?"

"Here. I made beef Bordelaise, and it was a failure. The beef was tough, and we had this personal argument, and at nine o'clock he went back to his shop. He said someone was coming to look at a light fixture. Some woman from the suburbs was bringing her husband to look at a chandelier."

"Did he say he would return?"

"No. He was rather cool when he left. But after he'd gone, I felt miserable, and I decided to go to his shop and apologize. That's when I found him—"

"Was his shop open?"

"The back door was unlocked. I went in the back way—from the alley. Don't ask me to describe what I saw!"

"What did you do?"

"I don't remember. Iris says I ran to the mansion, and C.C. called the police. She says she brought me home and put me to bed. I don't remember."

Intent on their conversation, neither of them heard the low growl in the kitchen—at first no more than a rattle in the dog's throat.

"I shouldn't be telling you this," Mary said.

"It's good to get it off your mind."

"You won't mention it, will you?"

"I won't mention it."

Mary sighed deeply and was quiet, while Qwilleran smoked his pipe and admired her large dark-rimmed eyes. They had mellowed during the evening, and now they were beautiful.

"You were right," she said. "I feel better now. For weeks after it happened, I had a horrible dream, night after night. It was so vivid that I began to think it was true. I almost lost my mind! I thought—"

It was then that the dog barked—in a voice full of alarm.

"Something's wrong," Mary said, jumping to her feet, and her eyes widened to their unblinking stare.

"Let me go and see," Qwilleran said.

Hepplewhite was barking at the rear window.

"There's a police car at the end of the alley," the newsman said. "You stay here. I'll see what it's all about. Is there a rear exit?"

He went down the narrow back stairs and out through a walled garden, but the gate to the alley was padlocked, and he had to return for a key.

By the time he reached the scene, the morgue wagon had arrived, and the revolving roof lights on the two police vehicles made blue flashes across the snow and the faces of a few onlookers and a figure lying on the ground.

Qwilleran stepped up to one of the officers and said, "I'm from the *Daily Fluxion*. What's happened here?"

"Routine lush," said the man in uniform with a smirk. "Drank too much antifreeze."

"Know who he is?"

"Oh, sure. He's got a pocketful of credit cards and a diamond-studded platinum ID bracelet."

Qwilleran moved closer as the body was loaded on a stretcher, and he saw the man's coat. He had seen that coat before.

Mary was waiting for him in the walled garden, and although she was warmly wrapped, she was shaking. "Wh-what was the matter?"

"Just a drunk," he told her. "You'd better get indoors before you catch cold. You're shivering."

They went upstairs, and Qwilleran prescribed hot drinks for both of them.

As Mary warmed her hands on her coffee cup, he studied her face. "You were telling me—just before the dog barked—about your recurrent dream."

She shuddered. "It was a nightmare! I suppose I was feeling guilty because I had been unpleasant to Andy."

"What did you dream?"

"I dreamed . . . I kept dreaming that I had *pushed* Andy to his death on that finial!"

Qwilleran paused before making his comment. "There may be an element of fact in your dream."

"What do you mean?"

"I have a hunch that Andy's death was not an accidental fall from a ladder." As he said it, he again felt the telltale prickling in his moustache.

Mary became defensive. "The police called it an accident."

"Did they investigate? Did they come to see you? They must have inquired who found the body."

She shook her head.

"Did they interview people in the neighborhood?"

"It was not necessary. It was obviously a mishap. Where did you get the idea that it might have been . . . anything else?"

"One of your talkative neighbors—this morning—"

"Nonsense."

"I assumed he must have some reason for calling it murder."

"Just an irresponsible remark. Why would anyone say such a thing?"

"I don't know." Then Qwilleran watched Mary's eyes grow wide as he added, "But by a strange coincidence, the man who told me is now on his way to the morgue."

Whether it was that statement or the startling sound of the telephone bell, he could not tell, but Mary froze in her chair. It rang several times.

"Want me to answer?" Qwilleran offered, glancing at his watch.

She hesitated, then nodded slowly.

He found the phone in the library across the hall. "Hello? . . . Hello? . . . Hello? . . . They hung up," he reported when he returned to the living room. Then noticing Mary's pallor, she asked, "Have you had this kind of call before? Have you been getting crank calls? Is that why you stay up late?"

"No, I've always been a night owl," she said, shaking off her trance. "My friends know it, and someone was probably phoning to—discuss the late movie on TV. They often do that. Whoever it was undoubtedly hung up because of hearing a man's voice. It would appear that I had company, or it might have seemed to be a wrong number."

She talked too fast and explained too much. Qwilleran was unconvinced.

CHAPTER 7

QWILLERAN WENT HOME through snow that was ankle-deep, its hush accentuating the isolated sounds of the night: a blast of jukebox music from The Lion's Tail, the whine of an electric motor somewhere, the idle bark of a dog. But first he stopped at the all-night drugstore on the corner

and telephoned the *Fluxion*'s night man in the Press Room at Police Headquarters and asked him to check two Dead on Arrivals from the Junktown
area.

"One came in tonight and one October sixteenth," Qwilleran said.
"Call me back at this number, will you?"

While he was waiting, he ordered a ham sandwich and considered the
evidence. The death of the man in a horse-blanket coat might have no significance, but the fear in Mary's eyes was real and incontrovertible, and her
emphatic insistence that Andy's death was an accident left plenty of room
for conjecture. If it was murder, there had to be motive, and Qwilleran had
an increasing curiosity about the young man of superior integrity who
made citizen's arrests. He knew the type. On the surface they looked good,
but they could be troublemakers.

The phone call came in from the police reporter. "That October DOA
was filed as accidental death," he said, "but I couldn't get any dope on the
other one. Why don't you try again in the morning?"

Qwilleran went home, tiptoed up the protesting stairs of the Cobb
mansion, unlocked his door with the big key, and searched for the cats.
They were asleep on their blue cushion on top of the refrigerator, curled
together in a single mound of fur with one nose, one tail and three ears.
One eye opened and looked at him, and Qwilleran could not resist stroking the pair. Their fur was incredibly silky when they were relaxed, and it
always appeared darker when they were asleep.

Soon after, he settled in his own bed, hoping that his mates at the
Press Club never found out he was sleeping in a swan boat.

It was then that he heard the odd sound—like soft moaning. It was the
purring of cats, but louder. It was the cooing of pigeons, but more gut-
tural. It had a mechanical regularity, and it seemed to be coming from the
partition behind his bed—the wall that was papered with book leaves. He
listened—keenly at first, then drowsily, and the monotony of the sound
soon lulled him to sleep.

He slept well that first night in the Cobb mansion, dreaming pleasantly of the Mackintosh coat of arms with its three snarling cats and its
weathered blues and reds. His pleasurable dreams were always in color;
others were in sepia, like old-time rotogravure.

On Saturday morning, as he began to emerge from slumber, he felt a
great weight pressing on his chest. In the first stages of waking, before his
eyes were open and before his mind was clear, he had a vision of the
iron coat of arms, crushing him, pinning him to the bed. He struggled to

regain his senses, and as he succeeded in opening his eyelids, he found himself staring into two violet-blue eyes, slightly crossed. Little Yum Yum was sitting on his chest in a compact and featherweight bundle. He took a deep breath of relief, and the heaving of his chest pleased her. She purred. She reached out one velvety paw and touched his moustache tenderly. She used the stubble on his chin to scratch the top of her head.

Then, from somewhere overhead, came an imperious command. Koko was sitting on the tail of the swan, making pronouncements in a loud voice. Either he was ordering breakfast, or he was deploring Yum Yum's familiarity with the man of the house. Koko seemed to have strong ideas about priorities.

The steam was hissing and clanking in the radiators, and when the heat came on in this old house, the whole building smelled of baked potatoes. Qwilleran got up and diced some round steak for the cats and heated it in a spoonful of consommé, while Koko supervised and Yum Yum streaked around the apartment, chased by an imaginary pursuer. For his own breakfast the newsman was contemplating the sugary bun that had become unappetizingly gummy during the night.

As he arranged the diced meat on one of the antique blue and white plates that came with the apartment, he heard a knock on the door. Iris Cobb was standing there, beaming at him.

"I'm sorry. Did I get you out of bed?" she asked when she saw the red plaid bathrobe. "I heard you talking to the cats and thought you were up. Here's a fresh shower curtain for your bathtub. Did you sleep well?"

"Yes, it's a good bed." Qwilleran protruded his lower lip and blew into his moustache, dislodging a cat hair that was waving under his nose.

"I had a terrible night. C.C. snored like a foghorn, and I didn't get a wink of sleep. Is there anything you need? Is everything all right?"

"Everything's fine, except that my toothbrush has disappeared. I put it in a tumbler last night, and this morning it's gone."

Iris rolled her eyes. "It's Mathilda! She's hidden it somewhere. Just hunt around and you'll find it. Would you like a few antique accessories to make your apartment more homey? Some colored glass? Some figurines?"

"No, thanks, but I'd like to get a telephone installed in a hurry."

"You can call the phone company from our apartment. And why don't you let me fix you a bite of breakfast? I made corn muffins for C.C. before he went picketing, and there's half a panful left."

Qwilleran remembered the sticky breakfast roll glued to its limp paper wrapper—and accepted.

Later, while he was eating bacon and eggs and buttering hot corn muffins, Iris talked to him of the antiques business. "You know the dentist's chair that was in your apartment?" she said. "C.C. originally found it in the basement of a clinic that was being torn down, and Ben Nicholas bought it from him for fifty dollars. Then Ben sold it to Andy for sixty dollars. After that, Russ gave Andy seventy-five for it and put new leather on the seat. When C.C. saw it, he wanted it back, so Russ let it go for a hundred and twenty-five, and yesterday we sold it for two hundred and twenty dollars."

"Cozy arrangement," said Qwilleran.

"Don't put that in the paper, though."

"Do all the dealers get along well?"

"Oh, yes. Occasionally there's a flare-up, like the time Andy fired Russ for drinking on the job, but it was soon forgotten. Russ is the one with the gorgeous blond hair. I used to have lovely blond hair myself, but it turned ashen overnight when I lost my first husband. I suppose I should have something done to it."

After breakfast Qwilleran called the telephone company and asked to have an instrument connected at 6331 Zwinger.

"There will be a fif-ty dol-lar de-pos-it, sir," said the singsong female voice on the line.

"Fifty! In advance! I never heard of such a thing!"

"Sor-ry. You are in zone thir-teen. There is a fif-ty dol-lar de-pos-it."

"What's the zone got to do with it?" Qwilleran shouted into the mouthpiece. "I need that phone immediately, and I'm not going to pay your outrageous deposit! I'm a staff writer for the *Daily Fluxion*, and I'm going to report this to the managing editor."

"One mo-ment, please."

He turned to the landlady. "Of all the high-handed nerve! They want eight months' payment in advance."

"We get that kind of treatment all the time in Junktown," Iris said with a meek shrug.

The voice returned to the line. "Ser-vice will be sup-plied at once, sir. Sor-ry, sir."

Qwilleran was still simmering with indignation when he left the house to cover his beat. He was also unhappy about the loss of his red feather. He was sure it had been in his hatband the night before, but now it was gone, and without it the tweed porkpie lost much of its éclat. A search of the apartment and staircase produced nothing but a cat's hairball and a red gum wrapper.

On Zwinger Street the weather growled at him, and he was in a mood to growl back. All was gray—the sky, the snow, the people. At that moment a white Jaguar sleeked down the street and turned into the carriage house on the block. Qwilleran regarded it as a finger of fate and followed it.

Russell Patch's refinishing shop had been a two-carriage carriage house in its heyday. Now it was half garage and half showroom. The Jaguar shared the space with items of furniture in the last stages of despair—peeling, mildewed, crazed, waterstained, or merely gray with dirt and age—and the premises smelled high of turpentine and lacquer.

Qwilleran heard a scuffing and thumping sound in the back room, and a moment later a husky young man appeared, swinging ably across the rough floor on metal crutches. He was dressed completely in white—white ducks, white open-necked shirt, white socks, white tennis shoes.

Qwilleran introduced himself.

"Yes, I know," said Patch with a smile. "I saw you at the auction, and word got around who you were."

The newsman glanced about the shop. "This is what I call genuine junk-type junk. Do people really buy it?"

"They sure do. It's having a big thing right now. Everything you see here is in the rough; I refinish it to the customer's specifications. See that sideboard? I'll cut off the legs, paint the whole thing mauve, stripe it in magenta, spatter it with umber, and give it a glaze of Venetian bronze. It's going into a two-hundred-thousand-dollar house in Lost Lake Hills."

"How long have you been doing this kind of work?"

"Just six months for myself. Before that, I worked for Andy Glanz for four years. Want to see how it's done?"

He led the way into the workshop, where he put on a long white coat like a butcher's, daubed with red and brown.

"This rocker," he said, "was sitting out in a barnyard for years. I tightened it up, gave it a red undercoat, and now—watch this." He drew on a pair of plastic gloves and started brushing a muddy substance on the chair seat.

"Did Andy teach you how to do this?"

"No, I picked it up myself," said Patch, with a trace of touchiness.

"From what I hear," Qwilleran said, "he was a great guy. Not only knowledgeable but generous and civic-minded."

"Yeah," the young man said with restraint.

"Everyone speaks highly of him."

Patch made no comment as he concentrated on making parallel brush-strokes, but Qwilleran noticed the muscles of his jaw working.

"His death must have been a great loss to Junktown," the newsman persisted. "Sorry I never had the opportunity to meet—"

"Maybe I shouldn't say this," the refinisher interrupted, "but he was a hard joe to work for."

"How do you mean?"

"Nobody could be good enough to suit Andy."

"He was a perfectionist?"

"He was a professional saint, and he expected everybody to operate the same way. I'm just explaining this because people around here will tell you Andy fired me for drinking on the job, and that's a lie. I quit because I couldn't stand his attitude." Patch gave the red chair a final brown swipe and dropped the brush into a tomato can.

"He was sanctimonious?"

"I guess that's the word. I didn't let it get under my skin, you understand. I'm just telling you to keep the record straight. Everybody's always saying how honest Andy was. Well, there's such a thing as being too honest."

"How do you figure that?" Qwilleran asked.

"Okay, I'll explain. Suppose you're driving out in the country, and you see an old brass bed leaning against a barn. It's black, and it's a mess. You knock on the farmhouse door and offer two bucks for it, and most likely they're tickled to have you cart it away. You're in luck, because you can clean it up and make two thousand percent profit. . . . But not Andy! Oh, no, not Andy! If he thought he could peddle the bed for two hundred dollars, he'd offer the farmer a hundred. Operating like that, he was spoiling it for the rest of us." The refinisher's frown changed to a grin. "One time, though, we were out in the country together, and I had the laugh on Andy. The farmer was a real sharpie. He said if Andy was offering a hundred dollars, it must be worth a thousand, and he refused to sell. . . . You want another example? Take scrounging. Everybody scrounges, don't they?"

"What do you mean?"

"You know these old houses that are being torn down? After a house is condemned, you can go in and find salable things like fireplaces and paneling. So you salvage them before the demolition crew comes along with the wrecking ball."

"Is that legal?"

"Not technically, but you're saving good stuff for someone who can use it. The city doesn't want it, and the wreckers don't give a damn. So we all scrounge once in a while—some more than others. But not Andy! He said a condemned house was city property, and he wouldn't touch it. He wouldn't mind his own business, either, and when he squealed on Cobb, that's when I quit. I thought that was a stinkin' thing to do!"

Qwilleran patted his moustache. "You mean Andy reported Cobb to the authorities?"

Patch nodded. "Cobb got a stiff fine that he couldn't pay, and he would have gone to jail if Iris hadn't borrowed the money. C.C.'s a loud-mouth, but he's not a bad guy, and I thought that was a lousy trick to pull on him. I got a few drinks under my belt and told Andy off."

"Does Cobb know it was Andy who reported him?"

"I don't think anybody knows it was a tip-off. Cobb was prying a stair-case out of the Pringle house—he told us all he was going to do it—and the cops came along in a prowl car and nabbed him. It looked like a coinci-dence, but I happened to hear Andy phoning in an anonymous tip." The refinisher reached for a wad of steel wool and started streaking the sticky glaze on the chair seat. "I have to comb this now—before it sets up too hard," he explained.

"How about Andy's private life?" Qwilleran asked. "Did he have the same lofty standards?"

Russell Patch laughed. "You better ask the Dragon. . . . About this other thing—don't get me wrong. I didn't have any hard feelings against Andy personally, you understand. Some people carry grudges. I don't carry a grudge. I may blow my stack, but then I forget it. You know what I mean?"

After Qwilleran left the carriage house, he made a telephone call from the corner drugstore, where he went to buy a new toothbrush. He called the feature editor at his home.

"Arch," he said, "I've run into an interesting situation in Junktown. You know the dealer who was killed in an accident a couple of months ago—"

"Yes. He's the one who sold me my Pennsylvania tin coffeepot."

"He allegedly fell off a stepladder and allegedly stabbed himself on a sharp object, and I'm beginning to doubt the whole story."

"Qwill, let's not turn this quaint, nostalgic Christmas series into a criminal investigation," the editor said. "The boss wants us to emphasize peace-on-earth and goodwill toward advertisers until the Christmas shop-ping season is over."

"Just the same, there's something going on in this quaint, nostalgic neighborhood that bears questioning."

"How do you know?"

"Private hunch—and something that happened yesterday. One of the Junktown regulars stopped me on the street and spilled it—that Andy had been murdered."

"Who was he? Who told you that?" Riker demanded.

"Just a neighborhood barfly, but great truths are spoken while under the influence. He seemed to know something, and twelve hours after he talked to me, he was found dead in the alley."

"Drunks are always being found dead in alleys. You should know that."

"There's something else. Andy's girlfriend is obviously living in fear. Of what, I can't find out."

"Look, Qwill, why don't you concentrate on writing the antique series and getting yourself a decent place to live?"

"I've got an apartment. I've moved into a haunted house on Zwinger Street—over the Cobb Junkery."

"That's where we bought our dining room chandelier," said Riker. "Now why don't you just relax and enjoy the holidays and—say!—be sure to visit The Three Weird Sisters. You'll flip! When will you have your first piece of copy?"

"Monday morning."

"Keep it happy," Riker advised. "And listen, you donkey! Don't waste any time trying to turn an innocent accident into a Federal case!"

That directive was all the encouragement Qwilleran needed. It was not for nothing that his old friend called him a donkey.

CHAPTER 8

WITH A STUBBORN determination to unearth the truth about the death of Andy Glanz, Qwilleran continued his tour of Zwinger Street. He walked past the Bit o' Junk antique shop (closed)—past The Blue Dragon—past a paint store (out of business)—past a bookstore (pornographic)—until he reached a place called Ann's 'Tiques, a subterranean shop smelling of moldy rugs and rotted wood.

The little old white-haired woman seated in a rocking chair resembled a dandelion gone to seed. She looked at Qwilleran blankly and kept on rocking.

"I'm Jim Qwilleran from the *Daily Fluxion*," the newsman said in his courtliest manner.

"Nope, I haven't had one o' them for years," she replied in a reedy voice. "People like the kind with china handles and a double lid."

Qwilleran inspected the litter of indescribable knick-knacks and raised his voice. "What's your specialty, Miss Peabody?"

"No sir! No discounts! If you don't like my prices, leave the things be. Somebody else'll buy 'em."

Qwilleran bowed and left the shop. He walked past a billiard hall (windows boarded up)—past a chili parlor with a ventilator exhausting hot breath across the sidewalk (rancid grease, fried onions, sour mop)—until he reached the fruit and tobacco shack of Papa Popopopoulos. There was an aroma of overripe banana and overheated oil stove in the shack. The proprietor sat on an orange crate, reading a newspaper in his native language and chewing a tobacco-stained moustache of great flamboyance.

Qwilleran stamped his feet and clapped his gloved hands together. "Pretty cold out there," he said.

The man listened attentively. "Tobac?" he said.

Qwilleran shook his head. "No, I just stopped in for a chat. Frankly, that last pouch I bought was somewhat past its prime."

Popopopoulos rose and came forward graciously. "Fruit? Nize fruit?"

"I don't think so. Cozy little place you've got here. How long have you been doing business in Junktown?"

"Pomegranate? Nize pomegranate?" The shopkeeper held up a shriveled specimen with faded red skin.

"Not today," said Qwilleran, looking toward the door.

"Pomegranate make babies!"

Qwilleran made a hasty exit. There was nothing to be learned, he decided, from Andy's two protégés.

It was then that he spotted the shop of The Three Weird Sisters, its window filled with washbowl and pitcher sets, spittoons, and the inevitable spinning wheel. Arch Riker might flip over this junk, but Qwilleran had no intention of flipping. He squared his shoulders and marched into the shop. As soon as he opened the door, his nose lifted. He could smell—was it or wasn't it? Yes, it was—clam chowder!

Three women wearing orange smocks stopped what they were doing and turned to regard the man with a bushy moustache. Qwilleran returned their gaze. For a moment he was speechless.

The woman sitting at a table addressing Christmas cards was a brunette with luscious blue eyes and dimples. The one polishing a brass samovar was a voluptuous orange-redhead with green eyes and a dazzling smile. The young girl standing on a stepladder hanging ropes of Christmas greens was a tiny blonde with upturned nose and pretty legs.

Qwilleran's face was radiant as he finally managed to say, "I'm from the *Daily Fluxion*."

"Yes, we know!" they chorused, and the redhead added in a husky voice, "We saw you at the auction and *adored* your moustache. Sexiest one we've ever seen in Junktown!" She hobbled toward him with one foot in a walking cast and gave his hand a warm grasp. "Pardon my broken metatarsal. I'm Cluthra. Godawful name, isn't it?"

"And I'm Amberina," the brunette said.

"I'm Ivrene," said a chirping voice from the top of the stepladder. "I'm the drudge around here."

The redhead sniffed, "Ivy, the soup's scorching!"

The little blonde jumped down from the ladder and ran into the back room.

Flashing her dimples, the brunette said to Qwilleran, "Would you have a bowl of chowder with us? And some cheese and crackers?"

If they had offered hardtack and goose grease, he would have accepted.

"Let me take your overcoat," said the redhead. "It's awfully warm in here." She threw her smock back over her shoulders, revealing a low-cut neckline and basic architecture of an ample nature.

"Sit here, Mr. Qwilleran." The brunette moved some wire carpet beaters from the seat of a Victorian settee.

"Cigarette?" offered the redhead.

"I'll get you an ashtray," said the brunette.

"I smoke a pipe," Qwilleran told the sisters, groping in his pocket and thinking, If only the guys in the Feature Department could see me now! As he filled his pipe and listened to two simultaneous conversations, he glanced around the shop and saw lead soldiers, cast-iron cherubs, chamber pots, and a tableful of tin boxes that had once held tobacco, crackers, coffee, and the like. The old stenciled labels were half obliterated by rust and scuffmarks, and Qwilleran had an idea. Arch Riker said he collected tin; this was the chance to buy him a crazy Christmas present.

"Do you really sell those old tobacco tins?" he asked. "How much for the little one that's all beat up?"

"We're asking ten," they said, "but if it's for yourself, you can have it for five."

"I'll take it," he said and threw down a nickel, without noticing the expression that passed among them.

The youngest one served the soup in antique shaving mugs. "The Dragon just phoned," she told Qwilleran. "She wants to see you this afternoon." She seemed unduly pleased to give him the message.

"How did she know I was here?"

"Everybody knows everything on this street," the redhead said.

"The Dragon has this place bugged," the young one whispered.

"Ivy, don't talk silly."

The sisters continued the conversation in three-part harmony—Cluthra in her husky voice, Amberina with a musical intonation, and Ivrene piping grace notes from her perch. Eventually Qwilleran brought up the subject of Andy Glanz.

"He was a real guy!" the redhead said with lifted eyebrows, and her rasping voice showed a trace of tenderness.

"He had quite an intellect, I understand," Qwilleran said.

"Cluthra wouldn't know anything about that," said the young one on the ladder. "She brings out the beast in men."

"Ivy!" came the sharp reprimand.

"It's true, isn't it? You said so yourself."

The brunette hastily remarked, "People don't believe we're sisters. The truth is, we had the same mother but different fathers."

"Does this business support the three of you?"

"Heavens, no! I have a husband, and I do this just for fun. Ivy's still in school—art school—and—"

"And Cluthra lives on her alimony," chipped in the youngest, earning pointed glares from her elders.

"Business has been terrible this month," said the brunette. "Sylvia's the only one who's doing any business around here."

"Who's Sylvia?" Qwilleran asked.

"A rich widow," came the prompt reply from the top of the ladder.

"Sylvia sells camp," the redhead explained.

"That's not what you called it yesterday!" Ivy reminded her.

"Where's her shop?" asked the newsman. "What's her full name?"

"Sylvia Katzenhide. She calls her place Sorta Camp. It's in the next block."

"Cluthra calls her the Cat's Backside," Ivy said, ignoring the exasperated sighs from her sisters.

"If you go to see Sylvia, wear earmuffs," the redhead advised.

"Sylvia's quite a talker," said the brunette.

"She's got verbal diarrhea," said the blonde.

"Ivy!"

"Well, that's what you *said*!"

When Qwilleran left The Three Weird Sisters, he was walking with a light step. He had heard little Ivy say, as he walked out the door, "Isn't he groovy?"

He preened his moustache, undecided whether to answer Mary Duckworth's summons or visit the loquacious Sylvia Katzenhide. Mrs. McGuffey was also on his list, and sooner or later he would like to talk to the outspoken Ivy again—alone. She was a brat, but brats could be useful, and she was an engaging brat, as brats went.

On Zwinger Street a hostile sun had penetrated the winter haze—not to warm the hearts and frozen nosetips of Junktown residents, but to convert the lovely snow into a greasy slush for the skidding of cars and splashing of pedestrians, and Qwilleran's mind went to Koko and Yum Yum—lucky cats, asleep on their cushions, warm and well-fed, with no weather to weather, no deadlines to meet, no decisions to make. It had been a long time since he had consulted Koko, and now he decided to give it a try.

There was a game they played with the unabridged dictionary. The cat dug his claws into the book, and Qwilleran opened to the page indicated, where the catchwords at the top of the columns usually offered some useful clue. Incredible? Yes. But it had worked in the past. A few months before, Qwilleran had been credited with finding a stolen jade collection, but the credit belonged chiefly to Koko and Noah Webster. Perhaps the time had come to play the game again.

He went home and unlocked his apartment door, but neither cat was anywhere in sight. Someone had been in the apartment, though. Qwilleran noticed a slight rearrangement and the addition of several useless gimcracks. The brass candlesticks on the mantel, which he liked, had gone, and in their place stood a pottery pig with a surly sneer.

He called the cats by name and go no answer. He searched the apartment, opening all doors and drawers. He got down on his knees at the fireplace and looked up the chimney. It was an unlikely possibility, but one could never tell about cats!

While he was posed on all fours with his head in the fireplace and his neck twisted in an awkward position, Qwilleran sensed movement in the room behind him. He withdrew his head just in time to see the missing pair walk nonchalantly across the carpet, Koko a few paces ahead of Yum Yum as usual. They had come from nowhere, as cats have a way of doing, holding aloft their exclamatory tails. This unpredictable pair could walk on little cat feet, silent as fog, or they could thump across the floor like clodhoppers.

"You rascals!" Qwilleran said.

"Yow?" said Koko with an interrogative inflection that seemed to imply, "Were you calling us? What's for lunch?"

"I searched all over! Where the devil were you hiding?"

They had come, it seemed, from the direction of the bathroom. They were blinking. Their eyes were intensely blue. And Yum Yum was carrying a toothbrush in her tiny V-shaped jaws. She dropped it in front of him.

"Good girl! Where did you find it?"

She looked at him with eyes bright, crossed, and uncomprehending.

"Did you find it under the tub, sweetheart?"

Yum Yum sat down and looked pleased with herself, and Qwilleran stroked her tiny head without noticing the faraway expression in Koko's slanted eyes.

"Come on, Koko, old boy!" he said. "Let's play the game." He slapped the cover of the dictionary—the starting signal—and Koko hopped on the big book and industriously sharpened his claws on its tattered binding. Then he hopped down and went to the window to watch pigeons.

"The game! Remember the game? Play the game!" Qwilleran urged, opening the book and demonstrating the procedure with his fingernails. Koko ignored the invitation; he was too busy observing the action outdoors.

The newsman grabbed him about the middle and placed him on the open pages. "Now dig, you little monkey!" But Koko stood there with his back rigidly arched and gave Qwilleran a look that could only be described as insulting.

"All right, skip it!" the man said with disappointment. "You're not the cat you used to be. Go back to your lousy pigeons," and Koko returned his attention to the yard below where Ben Nicholas was scattering crusts of bread.

Qwilleran left the apartment to continue his rounds, and as he went downstairs, Iris Cobb came flying out of the Junkery.

"Are you having fun in Junktown?" she asked gaily.

"I'm unearthing some interesting information," he replied, "and I'm beginning to wonder why the police never investigated Andy's death. Didn't the detectives ever come around asking questions?"

She was shaking her head vaguely when a man's gruff voice from within the shop shouted, "I'll tell you why they didn't. Junktown's a slum, and who cares what happens in a slum?"

Mrs. Cobb explained in a low voice, "My husband is rabid on the subject. He's always feuding with City Hall. Of course, he's probably right. The police would be glad to label it an accident and close the case. They can't be bothered with Junktown." Then her expression perked up; she had the face of a woman who relishes gossip. "Why were you asking about the detectives? Do you have any *suspicions*?"

"Nothing definite, but it was almost too freakish to dismiss as an accident."

"Maybe you're right. Maybe there was something going on that nobody knows about." She shivered. "The idea gives me goosebumps . . . By the way, I sold the brass candlesticks from your apartment, but I've given you a Sussex pig—very rare. The head comes off, and you can drink out of it."

"Thanks," said Qwilleran.

He started down the front steps and halted abruptly. That toothbrush that Yum Yum had brought him! It had a blue handle, and the handle of his old toothbrush, he seemed to recall, was green. . . . Or was it?

CHAPTER 9

QWILLERAN WALKED TO The Blue Dragon with a long stride, remembering the vulnerable Mary of the night before, but he was greeted by another Mary—the original one—aloof and inscrutable in her Japanese kimono. She was alone in the shop. She sat in her carved teakwood chair, as tall and straight as the wisp of smoke ascending from her cigarette.

"I got your message," he said, somewhat dismayed at the chilly reception. "You *did* say you wanted to see me, didn't you?"

"Yes. I am very much disturbed." She laid down the long cigarette holder and faced him formally.

"What's the trouble?"

"I used poor judgment last night. I am afraid," she said in her precise way, "that I talked too much."

"You were delightful company. I enjoyed every minute."

"That's not what I mean. I should never have revealed my family situation."

"You have nothing to be afraid of. I gave you my word."

"I should have remembered the trick your Jack Jaunti played on my father, but unfortunately the Scotch I was drinking—"

"You were completely relaxed. It was good for you. Believe me, I would never take advantage of your confidence."

Mary Duckworth gave him a penetrating look. There was something about the man's moustache that convinced people of his sincerity. Other moustaches might be villainous or supercilious or pathetic, but the outcropping on Qwilleran's upper lip inspired trust.

Mary took a deep breath and softened slightly. "I believe you. Against my will I believe you. It's merely that—"

"Now may I sit down?"

"I'm sorry. How rude of me. Please make yourself comfortable. May I offer you a cup of coffee?"

"No, thanks. I've just had soup at The Three Weird Sisters."

"Clam chowder, I suppose," said Mary with a slight curl of the lip. "The shop always reminds me of a fish market."

"It was very good chowder."

"Canned, of course."

Qwilleran sensed rivalry and was inwardly pleased. "Any bad dreams last night?" he asked.

"No. For the first time in months I was able to sleep well. You were quite right. I needed to talk to someone." She paused and looked in his eyes warmly, and her words were heartfelt. "I'm grateful, Qwill."

"Now that you're feeling better," he said, "would you do something for me? Just to satisfy my curiosity?"

"What do you want?" She was momentarily wary.

"Would you give me a few more details about the night of the accident? It's not morbid interest, I assure you. Purely intellectual curiosity."

She bit her lip. "What else can I tell you? I've given you the whole story."

"Would you draw me a diagram of the room where you discovered the body?" He handed her a ball-point pen and a scrap of paper from his pocket—the folded sheet of newsprint that was his standard equipment. Then he knocked his pipe on an ashtray and went through the process of filling and lighting.

Mary gave him a skeptical glance and started to sketch slowly. "It was in the workroom—at the rear of Andy's shop. The back door is here," she said. "To the right is a long workbench with pigeonholes and hangers for tools. Around the edge of the room Andy had furniture or other items, waiting to be glued or refinished or polished."

"Including chandeliers?"

"They were hanging overhead—perhaps a dozen of them. Lighting fixtures were Andy's specialty."

"And where was the stepladder?"

"In the middle of the room there was a cleared space—about fifteen feet across. The stepladder was off to one side of this area." She marked the spot with an X. "And the crystal chandelier was on the floor nearby—completely demolished."

"To the right or left of the ladder?"

"To the right." She made another X.

"And the position of the body?"

"Just to the left of the stepladder."

"Face down?"

She nodded.

Qwilleran drew long and slowly on his pipe. "Was Andy right-handed or left-handed?"

Mary stiffened with suspicion. "Are you sure the newspaper didn't send you to pry into this incident?"

"The *Fluxion* couldn't care less. All my paper wants is an entertaining series on the antiquing scene. I guess I spent too many years on the crime beat. I've got a compulsion to check everything out."

The girl studied his sober gaze and the downcurve of the ample moustache, and her voice became tender. "You miss your former work, don't you, Qwill? I suppose antiques seem rather mild after the excitement you've been accustomed to."

"It's an assignment," he said with a shrug. "A newsman covers the story without weighing the psychic rewards."

Her eyes flickered downward. "Andy was right-handed," she said after a moment's pause. "Does it make any difference?"

Qwilleran studied her sketch. "The stepladder was here . . . and the broken chandelier was over here. And the finial, where he fell, was . . . to the left of the ladder?"

"Yes."

"In the middle of the floor? That was a strange place for a lethal object like that."

"Well, it was—toward the edge of the open space—with the other items that had been pushed back around the walls."

"Had you seen it there before?"

"Not exactly in that location. The finial, like everything else, moved about frequently. The day before the accident it was on the workbench. Andy was polishing the brass ball."

"Was it generally known that he owned the finial?"

"Oh, yes. Everyone assured him he had bought a white elephant. Andy quipped that some fun-type suburbanite would think it was a fun thing for serving pretzels."

"How did he acquire it in the first place? The auctioneer said it came from an old house that had been torn down."

"Andy bought it from Russell Patch. Russ is a great scrounger. In fact, that's how he fractured his leg. He and Cobb were stripping an empty house, and Russ slipped off the roof."

"Let me get this straight," Qwilleran said. "Andy didn't believe in scrounging, and yet he was willing to buy from scroungers? Technically that finial was hot merchandise."

Mary's shrug was half apology for Andy and half rebuke for Qwilleran. He smoked his pipe in silence and wondered about this girl who was disarmingly candid one moment and wary the next—lithe as a willow and strong as an oak—masquerading under an assumed name—absolutely sure of certain details and completely blank about others—alternately compassionate and aloof.

After a while he said, "Are you perfectly satisfied that Andy's death was accidental?"

There was no response from the girl—merely an unfathomable stare.

"It might have been suicide."

"No!"

"It might have been attempted robbery."

"Why don't you leave well enough alone?" Mary said, fixing Qwilleran with her wide-eyed gaze. "If rumors start circulating, Junktown is bound to suffer. Do you realize this is the only neighborhood in town that's been able to keep down crime? Customers still feel safe here, and I want to keep it that way." Then her tone turned bitter. "I'm a fool, of course, for thinking we have a future. The city wants to tear all of this down and build sterile high-rise apartments. Meanwhile, we're designated as a slum, and the banks refuse to lend money to property owners for improvements."

"How about your father?" Qwilleran asked. "Does he subscribe to this official policy?"

"He considers it entirely reasonable. You see, no one thinks of Junktown as a community of living people—merely a column of statistics. If they would ring doorbells, they would find respectable foreign families, old couples with no desire to move to the suburbs, small businessmen like Mr. Lombardo—all nationalities, all races, all ages, all types—including a certain trashy element that does no harm. That's the way a city should be—one big hearty stew. But politicians have an à la carte mentality. They refuse to mix the onions and carrots with the tenderloin tips."

"Has anyone tried to fight it?"

"C.C. has made a few attempts, but what can one man accomplish?"

"With your name and your influence, Mary, you could get something done."

"Dad would never hear of it! Not for a minute! Do you know how I am classified at the Licensing Bureau? As a junk dealer! The newspapers would have a field day with *that* item. . . . Do you see that Chippendale chair near the fireplace? It's priced two thousand dollars! But I'm licensed as a Class C junk dealer."

"Someone should organize this whole community," Qwilleran said.

"You're undoubtedly right. Junktown has no voice at City Hall." She walked to the bay window. "Look at those refuse receptacles! In every other part of town the rubbish is collected in the rear, but Junktown's alleys are too narrow for the comfort of the city's 'disposal engineers,' and they require us to put those ugly containers on the sidewalk. Thursday is collection day; this is Saturday, and the rubbish is still there."

"The weather has fouled everything up," Qwilleran said.

"You talk like a bureaucrat. Excuses! That's all we hear."

Qwilleran had followed her to the window. The street was indeed a sorry sight. "Are you sure Junktown has a low crime rate?" he asked.

"The antique dealers never have any trouble. And I'm not afraid to go out at night, because there are always people of one sort or another walking up and down the street. Some of my rich customers in the suburbs are afraid to drive into their own garages!"

The newsman looked at Mary with new respect. Abruptly he said, "Are you free for dinner tonight, by any chance?"

"I'm dining with my family," she said with regret. "Mother's birthday. But I appreciate your invitation." Then she took a small silvery object from the drawer of a secretary-desk and slipped it into Qwilleran's hand. "Souvenir of Junktown," she said. "A tape measure. I give them to my customers because they always want to know the height, width, depth, length, diameter, circumference, and thickness of everything they see."

Qwilleran glanced toward the rear of the shop. "I notice nobody's bought the Mackintosh coat of arms." He refrained from mentioning that he had dreamed about it.

"It's still there, pining for you. I think you were made for each other. When the right customer meets the right antique, something electric happens—like falling in love. I can see sparks between you and that piece of iron."

He gave her a quick glance; she was quite serious. He tugged at his moustache, reflecting that one hundred twenty-five dollars would buy him two suits of clothes.

She said, "You don't need to pay for it until after Christmas. Why don't you take it home and enjoy it over the holidays? It's just gathering dust here."

"All right!" he said with sudden resolve. "I'll give you a twenty-dollar deposit."

He rolled the hoop-shaped coat of arms to the front door.

"Can you manage it alone? Why don't you ask C.C. to help you carry it up to your apartment?" she suggested. "And don't drop it on your toe," she called out, as Qwilleran struggled down the front steps with his burden.

When he and his acquisition reached the foyer of the Cobb mansion, he stopped to catch his breath, and he heard the ranting voice of C.C. coming from The Junkery.

"You don't know a piece of black walnut from a hole in your head!" Cobb was saying. "Why don't you admit it?"

"If that's black walnut, I'll eat my crutch. You're the biggest fake in the business! I'll give you twenty bucks—no more!"

Qwilleran wrestled the ironwork up the staircase alone.

The cats were asleep in the Morris chair, curled up like Yin and Yang, and Qwilleran did not disturb them. He leaned the coat of arms against the wall and left the apartment, hoping to make three more stops before calling it a day. He had promised to visit Ben's shop, but first he wanted to meet the talkative Sylvia Katzenhide. He liked garrulous subjects; they made his job so easy.

Arriving at The Sorta Camp shop, he held the door open for a well-dressed man who was leaving with a large purchase wrapped in newspaper, black tubes protruding from the wrappings. Inside the shop a woman customer was haggling over the price of a chair made out of automobile tires.

"My dear," Sylvia was telling her, "age and intrinsic value are unimportant. Camp is all wit and whimsy, plus a gentle thumbing of the nose. Either you dig it or you don't, as my son would say."

Mrs. Katzenhide was a handsome, well-groomed, self-assured woman who looked forty and was undoubtedly fifty-five. Qwilleran had seen hundreds like her in the women's auxiliary at the art museum, all identical in their well-cut tweed suits, jersey blouses, gold chains, and alligator shoes. This one had added black cotton stockings as a touch of eccentricity that seemed to be necessary in Junktown.

Qwilleran introduced himself and said, "Was I seeing things, or did a man leave this store with a stuffed—"

"You're right! A stuffed octopus," said Mrs. Katzenhide. "Hideous thing! I was glad to get rid of it. That was Judge Bennett from Municipal Court. Do you know the judge? He bought the octopus for his wife's Christmas present. She's mad about crawly things."

"How come you're dealing in—"

"In camp? It was my son's idea. He said I needed a project to keep my mind off myself." She lighted a cigarette. "Did you know my late husband? He was corporation counsel for the city. My son is in law school. . . . Excuse me, would you like a cigarette?"

Qwilleran declined. "But why camp? Why not something more—"

"More genteel? that's what all my friends say. But you have to *know something* to deal in genuine antiques. Besides, my son insists that camp is what the public wants. If anything is unattractive, poorly made, and secondhand, it sells like hot cakes. I really don't understand it."

"Then I suppose you didn't buy anything at—"

"At the auction yesterday?" The woman had a phenomenal knack of reading minds. "Just a small chandelier for my own apartment. When my husband passed away, I gave up the big house in Lost Lake Hills and moved to Skyline Towers. I have a lovely apartment, and it's not furnished in camp, believe me!"

"How do the Junktown dealers regard your specialty? Have you—"

"Developed a rapport? Definitely! I go to their association meetings, and we get along beautifully. When I first opened the shop, Andy Glanz took me under his wing and gave me a lot of valuable advice." She heaved a great sigh. "It was a shock to lose that boy. Did you know Andy?"

"No, I never met him. Was he—?"

"Well, I'll tell you. He always gave the impression of wearing a white tie and tails, even when he was in dungarees and scraping down a piece of furniture. And he was so good-looking—and intelligent. I always thought it was a pity he never married. What a waste!"

"Wasn't he more or less engaged to—"

"The Dragon? Not in the formal sense, but they would have made a perfect couple. Too bad he had to get mixed up with that other woman."

"You mean . . ." said Qwilleran with an encouraging pause.

"Here I am, prattling again! My son says I've become an incorrigible gossip since coming to Junktown. And he's right. I'm not going to say another word."

And she didn't.

There were obvious disadvantages to Qwilleran's position. He was trying to investigate an incident that no one wanted him to investigate, and he was not even sure what he was investigating. Any sensible man would have dropped the matter.

Stroking his moustache thoughtfully, Qwilleran took the next step in his noninvestigation of a questionable crime; he visited the shop called Bit o' Junk, a choice that he later regretted.

CHAPTER 10

BIT O' JUNK was next door to the Cobb Junkery, sharing the block with The Blue Dragon, Russell Patch's carriage house, Andy's place on the corner, and a variety store that catered to the needs of the community with embroidered prayer books and black panties trimmed with red fringe. Ben had his shop on the main floor of a town house that was similar in design to the Cobb mansion, but only half as wide and twice as dilapidated. The upper floors were devoted to sleeping rooms for men only, according to a weather-stained sign on the building.

Qwilleran climbed the icy stone steps and entered a drab foyer. Through the glass panes of the parlor doors he could see a hodge-podge of cast-offs: dusty furniture, unpolished brass and copper, cloudy glass, and other dreary oddments. The only thing that attracted him was the kitten curled up on a cushion with chin on paw. It was in the center of a table full of breakables, and Qwilleran could imagine with what velvet-footed care the small animal had tiptoed between the goblets and teacups. He went in.

At the sight of the bushy moustache, the proprietor rose from a couch and extended his arms in melodramatic welcome. Ben was wearing a bulky ski sweater that emphasized his rotund figure, and with it he sported a tall silk hat. He swept off the hat and bowed low.

"How's business? Slow?" Qwilleran asked as he appraised the unappealing shop.

"Weary, stale, flat, and unprofitable," said the dealer, returning the hat to cover his thinning hair.

Qwilleran picked up a World War I gas mask.

"An historic treasure," Nicholas informed him. "Came over on the *Mayflower*." He padded after the newsman in white stockinged feet.

"I hear you used to be in the theatre," the newsman remarked.

The tubby little dealer drew himself up from five-feet-four to five-feet-five. "Our Friar Laurence on Broadway was acclaimed by critics. Our Dogberry was superb. Our Bottom was unforgettable. . . . How now? You tremble and look pale!"

Qwilleran was staring at the kitten on its cushion. "That—that cat!" he sputtered. "It's dead!"

"An admirable example of the taxidermist's art. You like it not?"

"I like it not," said Qwilleran, and he blew into his moustache. "What's your specialty, anyway? Do you have a specialty?"

"I am a merry wanderer of the night."

"Come off it. You don't have to put on a performance for me. If you want any publicity, give me some straight answers. Do you specialize in anything?"

Ben Nicholas pondered. "Anything that will turn a profit."

"How long have you been operating in Junktown?"

"Too long."

"Did you know Andy Glanz very well?"

The dealer folded his hands and rolled his eyes upward. "Noble, wise, valiant, and honest," he intoned. "It was a sad day for Junktown when Saint Andrew met his untimely end." Then he hitched his trousers and said roguishly, "How about a tankard of sack at the local pub?"

"No, thanks. Not today," said Qwilleran. "What's this? A folding bookrack?" He had picked up a hinged contraption in brassbound ebony. "How much do you want for it?"

"Take it—take it—with the compliments of jolly old St. Nicholas."

"No, I'll buy it if it isn't too expensive."

"We have been asking fifteen, but allow us to extend the favor of a clergyman's discount. Eight simoleons."

At this point another customer, who had entered the shop and had been thoroughly ignored, said impatiently, "Got any horse brasses?"

"Begone, begone!" said the dealer, waving the man away. "This gentlemen is from the press, and we are being interviewed."

"I'm through. I'm leaving," said the newsman. "I'll send a photographer Monday to get a picture of you and your shop," and he paid for the bookrack.

"I humbly thank you, sir."

Nicholas doffed his silk topper and held it over his heart, and that was when Qwilleran noticed the small red feather stuck in the hat. It was *his feather*! There was no doubt about it; it had a perforation near the quill. In a playful moment two weeks before, he had plucked it from his hatband to tickle Koko's nose, but the cat's jaws were faster than the man's hand, and Koko had punctured the feather with the snap of a fang.

Qwilleran walked slowly from the shop. He stood at the top of the stone steps, wondering how that feather had made its way to Ben's topper.

As he stood there, frowning, Qwilleran was suddenly struck down. All creation descended on him, and he fell to his knees on the stone stoop. There was a rush and a roar and a crash, and he was down on hands and knees in snow and ice.

In a matter of seconds Ben Nicholas came rushing to his aid. "A bloody avalanche!" he cried, helping the newsman to his feet. "From the roof of this benighted establishment! We shall sue the landlord."

Qwilleran brushed the snow from his clothes. "Lucky I was wearing a hat," he said.

"Come back and sit down and have a wee drop of brandy."

"No, I'm okay. Thanks just the same."

He picked up his bookrack and started down the stone steps, favoring his left knee.

When Qwilleran reached his apartment, having ascended the stairs with difficulty, he was greeted by a rampaging Koko. While Yum Yum sat on the bookcase with her shoulder blades up, looking like a frightened grasshopper, Koko raced from the door to the desk, then up on the daybed and back to the roll-top desk.

"So! Those monkeys installed my phone!" Qwilleran said. "I hope you bit the phone company's representative on the ankle."

Koko watched with interest and wigwagging ears while Qwilleran dialed the *Fluxion* Photo Lab and requisitioned a photographer for Monday morning. Then the cat led the way into the kitchen with exalted tail and starched gait to supervise the preparation of his dinner. With his whiskers curved down in anticipation, he sat on the drainboard and watched the chopping of chicken livers, the slow cooking in butter, the addition of cream, and the dash of curry powder.

"Koko, I've joined the club," the man told him. "The landlady has a wrenched back, Russ Patch has a broken leg, the redhead's in a cast, and now I've got a busted knee! I won't be cutting any rugs at the Press Club tonight."

"Yow," said Koko in a consoling tone.

Qwilleran always spent Saturday evenings at the Press Club, most recently in the company of a young woman who wrote with brown ink, but she was out of the picture now. On a bold chance he looked up The Three Weird Sisters in the phone book and dialed their number. Most women, he was aware, jumped at the chance to dine at the Press Club. Unfortunately, there was no answer at the antique shop.

He then called a girl who worked in the Women's Department at the *Fluxion*—one of the society writers.

"Wish I could," she said, "but I've got to address Christmas cards tonight if I want them to be delivered before New Year's."

"While I have you on the line," he said, "tell me what you know about the Duxbury family."

"They do their bit socially, but they avoid publicity. Why?"

"Do they have any daughters?"

"Five—all named after English queens. All married except one. She came out ten years ago and . . . "

"And what?"

"Went right back in, I guess. You never see her—or hear of her."

"What's her name?"

"Mary. She's the oddball of the family."

"Thanks," said Qwilleran. He went to the Press Club alone.

The club occupied the only old building in the downtown area that had escaped the wrecking ball. A former county jail, it was built like a medieval fortress with turrets, crenelated battlements, and arrow slots. Whenever the city proposed to condemn it for an expressway of civic mall, a scream of outrage went up from the *Daily Fluxion* and the *Morning Rampage*, and no elected or appointed official had dared to campaign against the wrath of the united press.

As Qwilleran limped up the steps of the dismal old building, he met Lodge Kendall, a police reporter, on his way out.

"Come on back, and I'll buy you a drink," Qwilleran said.

"Can't, Qwill. Promised my wife we'd shop for a Christmas tree tonight. If you don't pick one out early, you're out of luck. I hate a lopsided tree."

"Just one question, then. What section of town has the highest crime rate?"

"It's a tossup between the Strip and Sunshine Gardens. Skyline Park is getting to be a problem, too."

"How about Zwinger Street?"

"I don't hear much about Zwinger Street."

"I've taken an apartment there."

"You must be out of your mind! That's a slum."

"Actually it's not a bad place to live."

"Well, don't unpack all your gear—because the city's going to tear it down," Kendall said cheerfully as he departed.

Qwilleran filled a dinner plate at the buffet and carried it to the bar, which was surprisingly vacant. "Where's everybody?" he asked Bruno, the bartender.

"Christmas shopping. Stores are staying open till nine."

"Ever do any junking, Bruno? Are you a collector?" the newsman asked. The bartender was known for his wide range of interests.

"Oh, sure! I collect swizzle sticks from bars all over the country. I've got about ten thousand."

"That's not what I mean. I'm talking about antiques. I just bought part of an iron gate from a castle in Scotland. It's probably been around for three centuries."

Bruno shook his head. "That's what I don't like about antiques. Everything's so *old.*"

Qwilleran finished eating and was glad to go home to Junktown, where there were more vital interests than lopsided Christmas trees and swizzle sticks. No one at the Press Club had even noticed he was limping.

On the steps of the Cobb mansion he looked up at the mansard roof punctuated by attic windows. Its slope still held its load of snow. So did the roof of Mary's house. Only Ben's building, though of identical style, had produced an avalanche.

In his apartment Qwilleran found the cats presiding on their gilded thrones with a nice understanding of protocol; Yum Yum as always on Koko's left. The man cut up the slice of ham he had brought them from the Press Club buffet, then went to the typewriter and worked on the Junktown series. After a while Koko jumped on the tavern table and watched the new mechanical contraption in operation—the type flying up to hit the paper, the carriage jerking across the machine. And when Qwilleran stopped to allow a thought to jell, Koko rubbed his jaw against a certain button and reset the margin.

There were two other distractions that evening. There was an occasional thumping and scraping overhead, and there were tantalizing smells drifting across the hall—first anise, then a rich buttery aroma, then chocolate.

Eventually he heard his name called outside his door, and he found the landlady standing there, holding a large brass tray.

"I heard you typing and thought you might like a snack," she said. "I've been doing my Christmas baking." On her tray were chocolate brownies, a china coffee service, and two cups.

Qwilleran was irked at the interruption, but mesmerized by the sight of the frosted chocolate squares topped with walnut halves, and before he could reply, Mrs. Cobb had bustled into the room.

"I've spent the whole evening over a hot stove," she announced. "All the dealers are upstairs making plans for the Christmas Block Party. C.C. has the third floor fixed up kind of cute for meetings. He calls it Hernia Heaven. You know, antique dealers are always—Oh, my! You're limping! What happened?"

"Bumped my knee."

"You must be careful! Knees are pesky things," she warned him. "You sit in the Morris chair and put your leg up on the ottoman, and I'll put the goodies on the tea table between us." She plopped her plumpness into the rocking chair made of bent twigs, unaware that Koko was watching critically from the mantelshelf.

For someone who had spent several hours slaving in the kitchen, Iris Cobb was rather festively attired. Her hair was carefully coifed. She wore a bright pink dress, embroidered with a few sad glass beads, and her two dangling pairs of eyeglasses, one of which was studded with rhinestones.

Qwilleran bit into a rich, dark chocolate square—soft and still warm from the oven and filled with walnut meats—while Mrs. Cobb rocked industriously in the twiggy rocking chair.

"I wanted to talk to you about something," she said. "What I said about Andy's horoscope—I really wasn't serious. I mean I never actually thought there was anything in it. I wouldn't want to stir up any trouble."

"What kind of trouble?"

"Well, I just heard that you're a crime reporter, and I thought you might be here to—"

"That's ancient history," Qwilleran assured her. "Who told you?"

"The Dragon. I went over to borrow some beeswax, and she told me you were a famous crime reporter in New York or somewhere, and I thought you might be here to snoop around. I honestly never thought Andy's fall was anything but a misstep on that ladder, and I was afraid you might get the wrong idea."

"I see," said Qwilleran. "Well, don't worry about it. I haven't had an assignment on the crime beat in a dog's age."

"That's a load off my mind," she said, and she relaxed and began to survey the apartment with a proprietary air.

"Do you care for that papered wall?" she asked with a critical squint. "It would drive me crazy to lie in bed and look at all those printed pages from books. They're applied with peelable paste, so you can pull them off it you object—"

"To tell the truth, I rather like that wall," Qwilleran said as he helped himself to a second chocolate brownie. "It's *Don Quixote* mixed with Samuel Pepys."

"Well, everyone to his own taste. Are you going away for Christmas? I'll be glad to look after the cats."

"No. No plans."

"Do you have a Christmas party at the office?"

"Just a Christmas Eve affair at the Press Club."

"You must have a very interesting job!" She stopped rocking and looked at him with frank admiration.

"Koko!" Qwilleran shouted. "Stop tormenting Yum Yum." Then he added to Mrs. Cobb, "They're both neutered, but Koko sometimes behaves in a suspicious way."

The landlady giggled and poured another cup of coffee for him. "If you're going to be alone for Christmas," she said, "you must celebrate with us. C.C. trims a big tree, and my son comes here from St. Louis. He's sort of an architect. His father—my first husband—was a schoolteacher. I'm an English major myself, although you'd never guess it. I never read any more. In this business you don't have time for anything. We've had this house four years, and there's always something—"

She prattled on, and Qwilleran wondered about this fatuous little woman. As a newsman, he was used to being cajoled and plied with food—the latter being one of the fringe benefits of the profession—but he would have preferred a landlady who was a degree less chummy, and he hoped she would leave before the dealers came down from Hernia Heaven.

Her overtures were innocent enough, he was sure. Her exuberance was simply a lack of taste. She was not amply endowed with gray matter, and her attempt to reverse herself about Andy's accident was pathetically transparent. Had she guessed that her husband might be implicated, if it proved to be murder?

"He died of food poisoning—a rare botulism," Mrs. Cobb was saying.

"Who?" asked Qwilleran.

"My first husband. I knew something tragic was going to happen. I'd seen it in his hand. I used to read palms—just as a hobby, you know. Would you like me to read your palm?"

"I don't have much faith in palmistry," Qwilleran said, beginning to edge out of the deep-cushioned Morris chair.

"Oh, be a sport! Let me read your future. I won't tell you if it's anything really bad. You don't have to move an inch. You sit right where you are, and I'll perch on the ottoman."

She plumped her round hips down beside his propped foot and gave his leg a cordial pat, then reached for his hand. "Your right hand, please." She held it in a warm moist grasp and stroked the palm a few times to straighten the curled and uncooperative fingers.

Trapped in the big chair, he wriggled uncomfortably and tried to devise a tactful escape.

"A very interesting palm," she said, putting on one pair of glasses.

She was stroking his hand and bending her head close to study the lines when the room exploded in a frenzy of snarling and soprano screams. Koko had pounced on Yum Yum with a savage growl. Yum Yum shrieked and fought back. They rolled over and over, locked in a double stranglehold.

Mrs. Cobb jumped up. "Heavens! They'll kill each other!"

Qwilleran yelled, smacked his hands at them, struggled to his feet and whacked the nearest cat's rump. Koko gave a nasty growl, and Yum Yum broke away. Immediately Koko gave chase. The little female went up over the desk, round the Morris chair, under the tea table—with Koko in pursuit. Round and round the room they went, with Qwilleran shouting and Mrs. Cobb squealing. On the fourth lap of the flying circus, Yum Yum ducked under the tea table and Koko sailed over it. Qwilleran made a lucky grab for the coffee pot, but Koko skidded on the tray and sent the cream and sugar flying.

"The rug!" the landlady cried. "Get a towel, quick! I'll get a sponge."

She ran from the apartment just as the dealers came hurrying down from Hernia Heaven.

"What's the uproar?" they said. "Who's getting murdered?"

"Only a family quarrel," Qwilleran explained, jerking his head toward the cats.

Koko and Yum Yum were sitting quietly in the Morris chair together. She was looking sweet and contented, and Koko was licking her face with affection.

CHAPTER 11

COBB SNORED again that night. Qwilleran, waked at three o'clock by the pain in his knee, took some aspirin and then listened to the muffled snorts coming through the wall. He wished he had an ice pack. He wished he had never moved to Junktown. The whole community was accident prone, and it seemed to be contagious. Why had he paid a month's rent in advance? No matter; he could stay long enough to complete the Junktown series and then move out, chalking it up to experience: Beware of prospective landladies who give you homemade apple pie. Yes, that was the smart thing to do—concentrate on writing a good series and quit snooping into the activities of a deceased junk dealer.

Then Qwilleran felt a familiar tingling sensation in the roots of his moustache, and he began to argue with himself.

—*But you've got to admit there's something dubious about the setup in Andy's workroom.*

—So he was murdered. So it was a prowler. Attempted robbery.

—*A prowler would whack him on the head and then run. No, the whole incident looked staged. Staged, I said. Did you hear that?*

—If you're thinking about the retired actor, forget it. He's a harmless old codger who likes animals. Koko took to him right away.

—*Don't forget how that avalanche slid off the roof at the appropriate moment. One of those icicles could have brained you. As for Koko, he can be remarkably subjective. He rejected Mrs. Cobb simply because she squeaked at him.*

—Still, it would be interesting to know how she wrenched her back two months ago.

—*Now you're grabbing at straws. She doesn't have the temperament for murder. It takes someone like Mary Duckworth—ice cold, single-minded, extremely capable.*

—You're wrong about her. She can be warm and compassionate. Besides, she would have no motive.

—*Oh, no? She had quarreled with Andy. Who knows how serious it might have been?*

—Undoubtedly they quarreled about the other woman in his life—still no motive for murder, if she loved him.

—*Perhaps he was threatening to do something that would hurt her more deeply than that.*

—But Mary insists he was kind and thoughtful.

—*He was also dogmatic and intolerant. He might be "doing his duty" again. That kind of person is a classic heel.*

—I wish you'd shut up and let me go to sleep.

Eventually Qwilleran slept, and in the morning he was waked by two hungry cats, playing hopscotch on his bed and miraculously missing his sore knee. Cats had a sixth sense, he noted, that prevented them from hurting the people they liked. He gave them a good breakfast of canned crabmeat.

Later he was applying cold wet towels to his knee when he heard a knock. He took a deep breath of exasperation and moved painfully to open the door.

Iris Cobb was standing there, wearing her hat and coat and holding a plate of coffeecake. "I'm on my way to church," she said. "Would you like some cranberry twists? I got up early and made them. I couldn't sleep."

"Thanks," said Qwilleran, "but I'm afraid you're trying to fatten me up."

"How does the rug look this morning? Did the cream leave a spot?"

"Not bad, but if you want to send it out and have it cleaned, I'll pay for it."

"How's your knee? Any better?"

"These injuries are always worse in the morning. I'm trying cold compresses."

"Why don't you have dinner with us around seven o'clock, and then you won't have to go out of the house. . . . C.C. can tell you some interesting stories about Junktown," she added when Qwilleran hesitated. "We're having pot roast and mashed potatoes—nothing fancy. Just potatoes whipped with sour cream and dill. And a salad with Roquefort dressing. And coconut cake for dessert."

"I'll be there," said Qwilleran.

As soon as he was dressed, he limped to the drugstore, being unable to survive Sunday without the Sunday papers. At the lunch counter he choked down two hard-boiled eggs that were supposed to be soft-boiled and gave himself indigestion by reading Jack Jaunti's new column. Jaunti, who was half Qwilleran's age, now had the gall to write a column of wit and wisdom from the Delphic heights of his adolescent ignorance.

The newsman spent the rest of the day nursing his crippled knee and pecking at his crippled typewriter, and his ailment activated the Florence Nightingale instinct that is common to cats. Every time he sat down, Yum Yum hopped on his lap, while Koko hovered nearby, looking concerned, spoke softly, and purred whenever Qwilleran glanced in his direction.

When seven o'clock arrived, whiffs of beef simmering with garlic and celery tops beckoned the newsman across the hall to the Cobbs' apartment. C.C., shirtless and shoeless, sat with one leg thrown over the arm of his chair and a can of beer in his hand. He grunted at the arriving guest—a welcome more cordial than Qwilleran had expected—and Mrs. Cobb turned joyous eyes on her tenant and ushered him to a stately wing chair.

"It's Charles II," she said. "Best thing we own." She pointed out other treasures, which he admired with reserve: a stuffed owl, a wood carving of an adenoidal eagle, an oil portrait of an infant with a bloated forty-year-old face, and an apothecary desk with two dozen tiny drawers of no use to anyone but an apothecary. A radio on the desk top pounded out a senseless, ceaseless beat.

Mrs. Cobb, playing the fussy hostess, passed a platter of tiny meat turnovers and served small glasses of cranberry juice cocktail on plates with lace paper doilies.

C.C. said, "Who you trying to impress with this fancy grub?"

"Our new tenant, of course. I wouldn't slave over *piroshki* for a slob like you," she said sweetly.

C.C. turned an unshaven but handsome face to Qwilleran. "If she starts buttering you up with her goodies, watch out, mister. She might poison you, like she did her first husband." His tone was belligerent, but Qwilleran caught a glint in the man's eye that was surprisingly affectionate.

"If I poison anybody," his wife said, "it will be Cornball Cobb. . . . Would you all like to hear something interesting?" She reached under a small table and brought a portable tape recorder from its lower shelf. She rewound the reel, touched a green push button and said, "Now listen to this."

As the tape started to unwind, the little machine gave forth an unearthly concert of gurgles, wheezes, whistles, hoots, honks, and snorts.

"Shut that damn thing off!" Cobb yelled, more in sport than in anger.

She laughed. "Now you know how you snore. You wouldn't believe me, would you? You sound like a calliope."

"Did you spend my good money just for that?" He got up and hit the red push button with a fist, silencing the recital, but he wore a peculiar look of satisfaction.

"I'm going to use this for evidence when I sue for divorce." Mrs. Cobb winked at Qwilleran, and he squirmed in his chair. This display of thinly veiled sexuality between husband and wife made him feel like a Peeping Tom.

C.C. said, "When do we eat?"

"He hates my cooking," Iris Cobb said, "but you should see him put it away."

"I can eat anything," her husband grumbled with good humor. "What kind of slop have we got today?"

When they sat down at the big kitchen table, he applied himself to his food and became remarkably genial. Qwilleran tried to visualize C.C. with a shave, a white shirt, and a tie. He could be a successful salesman, a middle-aged matinee idol, a lady-killer, a confidence man. Why had he chosen this grubby role in Junktown?

The newsman ventured to remark, "I met the Three Weird Sisters yesterday," and waited for a reaction.

"How d'you like the redhead?" Cobb asked, leering at his plate. "If she didn't have her foot in a cast, she'd chase you down the street."

"And what do you think of our other tenant?" Mrs. Cobb asked. "Isn't he a funny little man?"

"He puts on a pretty good show," Qwilleran said. "He tells me he was a Broadway actor."

C.C. snorted. "Nearest he ever got to Broadway was Macy's toy department."

His wife said, "Ben loves to play Santa Claus. Every Christmas he puts on a red suit and beard and goes to children's hospital wards."

"They must pay him for it," said C.C. "He wouldn't do it for free."

"One day," she went on, "there was an injured pigeon in the middle of Zwinger Street—with dozens of other pigeons fluttering around to protect it from traffic, and I saw Ben go out with a shoebox and rescue the bird."

Qwilleran said, "He has a repulsive thing in his shop—a stuffed cat on a dusty velvet pillow."

"That's a pincushion. They were all the rage in the Gay Nineties."

"Can he make a living from that dismal collection of junk? Or does he have a sideline, too?"

"Ben's got a bundle salted away," C.C. said. "He used to make big money in his day—before taxes got so high." Mrs. Cobb gave her husband a startled look.

The man finished eating and pushed his dessert plate away. "I'm gonna scrounge tonight. Anybody want to come?"

"Where do you go?" Qwilleran asked.

"Demolition area. The old Ellsworth house is full of black walnut paneling if I can beat the other vultures to it. Russ says they've already grabbed the stained-glass windows."

"I wish you wouldn't go," his wife said. "It's so cold, and the ice is treacherous, and you know it isn't legal."

"Everybody does it just the same. Where do you think the Dragon got that Russian silver chandelier? She makes like she's so high class, but you should see her with a crowbar!"

Mrs. Cobb said to Qwilleran. "C.C. got caught once and had to pay a heavy fine. You'd think he would have learned his lesson."

"Aw, hell! It won't happen twice," her husband said. "Somebody tipped off the police the other time, and I know who it was. It won't happen again."

"Let's take coffee in the living room," Mrs. Cobb suggested.

Cobb lighted his cigar and Qwilleran lighted his pipe and said, "I understand Junktown doesn't get much cooperation from the city government."

"Mister, you'd think we were some kind of disease that's got to be wiped out," Cobb said. "We asked for better street lights, and the city said no, because Junktown's due to be torn down within the next ten years. *Ten years!* So we tried to put in old-fashioned gaslights at our own expense, but the city said no dice. All light poles gotta be forty feet high."

"C.C. has spent days at City Hall," said Mrs. Cobb, "when he could have been earning good money on the picket line."

"We used to have big elm trees on this street," her husband went on, "and the city cut 'em down to widen the street. So we planted saplings on the curb, and guess what! Chop chop! They widened the street another two feet."

"Tell Qwill about the signs, C.C."

"Yeah, the signs. We all made old-time signs out of wormy wood, and the city made us take 'em down. Unsafe, they said. Then Russ put hand-split cedar shingles on the front of his carriage house, and the city yanked 'em off. Know why? They projected a *half-inch* over the sidewalk! Mister, the city *wants* this neighborhood to decline so the land-grabbers can get it and the grafters can get their cut!"

"Now we're planning a Christmas Block Party to bring in a little business," said Mrs. Cobb, "but there's so much red tape."

"You gotta get permission to decorate the street. And if you want to play Christmas music outdoors, you get a permit from the Noise Abatement Commission. If you want to give door prizes, you get fingerprinted by the Gambling Commission. If you want to serve refreshments, you get a blood test at the Board of Health. *Nuts!*"

"Maybe the *Daily Fluxion* could expedite matters," Qwilleran suggested. "We have some pull at City Hall."

"Well, I don't care one way or the other. I'm gonna go scrounging."

"I'd go with you," said the newsman, "if I didn't have this bum knee."

Mrs. Cobb said to her husband, "Don't go alone! Can't you get Ben to go with you?"

"That lazy bugger? He wouldn't even carry the flashlight."

"Then ask Mike. He'll go if you give him a couple of dollars." She looked out the window. "It's starting to snow again. I wish you'd stay home."

Without any formal goodbyes, Cobb left the apartment, bundled up in a heavy coat, boots and knitted cap, and after another cup of coffee Qwilleran rose and thanked his hostess for the excellent dinner.

"Do you think the *Fluxion* could do something about our Block Party?" she asked as she accompanied him to the door and gave him a snack for the cats. "It means a lot to C.C. He's like a little boy about Christmas, and I hate to see his heart broken."

"I'll work on it tomorrow."

"Isn't he wonderful when he gets wound up about City Hall?" Her eyes were shining. "I'll never forget the time I went with him to the City Council meetings. He was making things hot for them and the mayor told him to sit down and keep quiet. C.C. said, 'Look buddy, don't tell *me* to pipe down. I pay your salary!' I was so proud of my husband that tears came to my eyes."

Qwilleran went across the hall, unlocked the door, and peeked in. The cats jumped down from their gilded thrones, knowing that the waxed paper package he carried contained pot roast. Yum Yum rubbed against his ankles, while Koko made loud demands.

The man leaned over to rub Koko's head, and that was when he saw it—on the floor near the desk: a dollar bill! It was folded lengthwise. He knew it was not his own. He never folded his money that way.

"Where did this come from?" he asked the cats. "Has anybody been in here?"

It had to be someone with a key, and he knew it was neither of the Cobbs. He inspected the typed sheets on his desk and the half-finished page in his typewriter. Had someone been curious about what he was writing? It could hardly be anyone but the other tenant in the house. Perhaps Ben doubted that he was a writer—it had happened before—and sneaked in to see for himself, dropping the dollar bill when he pulled something out of his pocket—glasses, or a handkerchief, perhaps. The incident was not really important, but it irritated Qwilleran, and he went back to the Cobb apartment.

"Someone's been snooping around my place," he told Mrs. Cobb. "Would it be Ben? Does he have a key?"

"Goodness, no! Why would he have a key to your apartment?"

"Well, who else could get in?"

An expression of delight began to spread over the landlady's round face.

"Don't say it! I know!" said Qwilleran with a frown. "She walks through doors."

CHAPTER 12

EARLY MONDAY MORNING, Qwilleran opened his eyes suddenly, not knowing what had waked him. Pain in his knee reminded him where he was—in Junktown, city of sore limbs.

Then the sound that had waked him came again—a knock at the door—not an urgent rapping, not a cheery tattoo, but a slow pounding on the door panel, as ominous as it was strange. Wincing a little, he slid his legs out of bed, put on his robe and answered the summons.

Iris Cobb was standing there, her round face strained, her eyes swollen. She was wearing a heavy coat and a woolen scarf over her head.

"I'm sorry," she said in a shaken voice. "I've got trouble. C.C. hasn't come home."

"What time is it?"

"Five o'clock. He's never been later than two."

Qwilleran blinked and shook his head and ran his fingers through his hair, as he tried to recall the events of the previous evening. "Do you think the police might have picked him up again?"

"If they had, they'd let him phone me. They did last time."

"What about the boy who was going with him?"

"I've just been around the corner to Mike's house. His mother says he didn't go with C.C. last night. He went to a movie."

"Want me to call the police?"

"No! I don't want them to know he's been scrounging again. I have a feeling he might have fallen and hurt himself."

"Want me to go and see if I can find him?"

"Would you? Oh, would you please? I'll go with you."

"It'll take me a couple of minutes to get dressed."

"I'm sorry to bother you. I'd wake Ben, but he was out drinking half the night."

"That's all right."

"Dress warm. Wear boots." Her voice, normally musical, had flattened out to a gloomy monotone. "I'll call a taxi. C.C. took the station wagon."

"Do you have a flashlight?"

"A small one. C.C. took the big lantern."

As Qwilleran, trying not to limp, took the woman's arm and escorted her down the snow-covered steps to the taxi, he said, "This is going to look peculiar, going to a deserted house at this hour. I'll tell the driver to drop us at the corner. It'll still look odd, but . . ."

The cabdriver said, "Fifteenth and Zwinger? There's nothing there! It's a ghost town."

"We're being met there by another car," Qwilleran said. "My brother—driving in from downriver. A family emergency."

The driver gave an exaggerated shrug and drove them down Zwinger Street. Iris Cobb rode in silence, shivering visibly, and Qwilleran gripped her arm with a steadying hand.

Once she spoke. "I saw something so strange when I was coming home from church yesterday morning. Hundreds of pigeons circling over

Junktown—flying round and round and round—a big black cloud. Their wings were like thunder."

At the corner of Fifteenth, Qwilleran gave the driver the folded dollar he had found in his apartment and helped Mrs. Cobb out of the cab. It was a dark night. Other parts of the sky reflected a glow from city lighting, but the street lights in the demolition area were no longer operating.

They waited until the cab was out of sight. Then Qwilleran grasped the woman's arm, and they picked their way across icy ruts where the sidewalk had been cracked by heavy trucks hauling away debris. Several houses had already been leveled, but toward the end of the block stood a large, square, solid house built of stone.

"That's it. That's the one," she said. "It used to have a high iron fence. Some scrounger must have taken it."

There was a carriage entrance at the side. The driveway ran under this porte-cochère, and there was evidence of tire tracks, partially filled with snow. How recent they were, it was impossible to tell.

"I suppose he'd park around back, out of sight," Qwilleran said.

They moved cautiously up the driveway.

"Yes, there's the wagon!" she cried. "He must be here. . . . Can you hear anything?"

They stood still. There was dead silence, except for the lonely whine of tires from the expressway across the open fields.

They went in the back door. "I can hardly walk up the steps," Iris said. "My knees are like jelly. I have a terrible feeling—"

"Take it easy." Qwilleran guided her with a firm hand. "There's a loose board here."

The back door showed signs of having been wrenched open violently. It led into a dusty porch and then into a room that had been a large kitchen. Only the upper wall cabinets remained. Lying in the middle of the floor, waiting to be moved out, were a pink marble fireplace and a tarnished brass light fixture.

They paused again and listened. There was no sound. The rooms were dank and icy.

Flashing the light ahead, Qwilleran led the way through a butler's pantry and then a dining room. Gaping holes indicated that the mantel and chandelier had come from this room. Beyond was the parlor, with a large fireplace still intact. A wide archway equipped with sliding doors opened into the front hall, and one of them stood ajar.

Qwilleran went through first, and the woman crowded behind him.

The hall was a shambles. He flashed his light over lengths of stair rail, sections of paneling leaning against the wall, pieces of carved molding, and there—at the foot of the stairs . . .

She screamed. "There he is!" She rushed forward. A large section of paneling lay on top of the sprawled body. "Oh, my God! Is he—Is he—?"

"Maybe he's unconscious. You stay here," Qwilleran said. "Let me have a look."

The slab of black walnut that lay on top of the fallen man was enormously heavy. With difficulty Qwilleran eased it up and tilted it against the wall.

Mrs. Cobb was sobbing. "I'm afraid. Oh, I'm afraid."

Then he beamed the light on the face—white under the gray stubble.

She tugged at Qwilleran's coat. "Can you tell? Is he breathing?"

"It doesn't look good."

"Maybe he's just frozen. Maybe he fell and knocked himself out, and he's been lying here in the cold." She took her husband's icy hand. She leaned over and flooded warm breath over his nose and mouth.

Neither of them heard the footsteps coming through the house. Suddenly the hall was alight, and the glare of a powerful flashlight blinded them. Someone was standing in the doorway that led from the parlor.

"This is the police," said an official voice behind the light. "What are you doing here?"

Mrs. Cobb burst into tears. "My husband is hurt. Quick! Get him to a hospital."

"What are you doing here?"

"There's no time! No time!" she cried hysterically. "Call an ambulance—call an ambulance before it's too late!"

One of the officers stepped into the beam of light and bent over the body. He shook his head.

"No! No!" she cried wildly. "They can save him! They can do something, I know! Hurry . . . hurry!"

"Too late, lady." Then he said to his partner, "Tell dispatch we've got a body."

Mrs. Cobb uttered a long heartbroken wail.

"You'll have to make a statement at headquarters," the officer said.

Qwilleran showed his police card. "I'm with the *Daily Fluxion*."

The officer nodded and relaxed his brusque manner. "Do you mind coming downtown? The detectives will want a statement. Just routine."

The newsman put an arm around his landlady to support her. "How did you fellows happen to find us?" he asked.

"A cabbie reported two fares dropped at Zwinger and Fifteenth. . . . What happened to this man? Did he fall downstairs?"

"Looks like it. When he failed to come home, we—"

Iris Cobb wailed wretchedly. "He was carrying that panel. He must have slipped—missed his step. . . . I told him not to come. I told him!" She turned a contorted face to Qwilleran. "What will I do? . . . What will I do? . . . I loved that wonderful man!"

CHAPTER 13

AFTER QWILLERAN had brought Iris Cobb home from Police Head-quarters and had called Mary Duckworth to come and stand by, he went to the office. With a bleak expression on his face, accentuated by the down-curve of his moustache, he threw ten pages of triple-spaced copy on Arch Riker's desk.

"What's the matter?" Arch said.

"Rough morning! I've been up since five," Qwilleran told him. "My landlord was killed. Fell down a flight of stairs."

"You mean Cobb?

"He was stripping one of the condemned houses, and when he didn't come home, I went out with Mrs. Cobb to look for him. We found him dead at the foot of the stairs. Then the police took us in for questioning. Mrs. Cobb is a wreck."

"Too bad. Sorry to hear that."

"It was the Ellsworth house on Fifteenth Street."

"I know the place," Riker said. "A big stone mausoleum. Hector Ellsworth was mayor of this town forty years ago."

"He was?" Qwilleran laughed without mirth. "Then Cobb lost his last battle with City Hall. They finally got him! I'm beginning to believe in the spirit world."

"How are you going to write this up?"

"It's a trifle awkward. Cobb was trespassing."

"Scrounging? All the junkers do that. Even Rosie! She never goes out without a crowbar in her car."

"Tell your wife she's guilty of looting city property. Cobb was caught once. They arrested him and gave him a heavy fine—and a warning, which he disregarded."

"Doesn't sound like the kind of jolly Christmas story the boss wants."

"There's one thing we could do," said Qwilleran. "Cobb was organizing a Christmas celebration for Junktown—a Block Party—and the city was giving him a hard time. Wouldn't let him decorate the street, play Christmas music, or serve refreshments. All kinds of red tape. Why don't we talk to City Hall and railroad this thing through for Wednesday afternoon? It's the least we can do. It's not much, but it might make the widow fell a little better."

"I'll ask the boss to get the mayor on the phone."

"The way I see it, there are five city bureaus giving Junktown the runaround. If they could just get someone from the mayor's office to cut through the whole mess . . ."

"All right. And why don't you write a plug for the Block Party? We'll run it in tomorrow's paper. We'll get every junker in town to turn out. And write something about Cobb—something with heart."

Qwilleran nodded. The phrases were already forming in his mind. He'd write about the man who tried to make people hate him, but in the topsy-turvy world of the junker, everyone loved his perversity.

Qwilleran stopped in the *Fluxion* library to look up the clips on Hector Ellsworth and at the payroll cage to pick up his check, and then he returned to Junktown.

Mary Duckworth, handsomely trousered, met him at the door of the Cobb apartment. He was aware of a subtle elation in her manner.

"How's Iris?" he asked.

"I gave her a sedative, and she's sleeping. The funeral will be in Cleveland, and I've made a plane reservation for her."

"Anything I can do? Perhaps I should pick up the station wagon. It's still behind the Ellsworth house. Then I can drive her to the airport."

"Would you? I'm packing a bag for her."

"When she wakes," Qwilleran said, "tell her that Junktown is going to have everything C.C. wanted for the Christmas party."

"I know," said Mary. "The mayor's office has already called. His representative is coming here to speak to the dealers this afternoon, and then we'll have a meeting upstairs tonight."

"In Hernia Heaven? I'd like to attend."

"The dealers would be delighted to have you."

"Come across the hall," Qwilleran said. "I have something to report."

As he unlocked the door of his apartment, the cats—who had been curled together in a sleeping pillow of fur in the Morris chair—immediately raised their heads. Yum Yum scampered from the room, but Koko stood his ground, arching his back and bushing his tail as he glared at the stranger. His reaction was not hostile—only unflattering.

"Do I look like an ogre?" Mary wanted to know.

"Koko can sense Hepplewhite," Qwilleran said. "He knows you've got a big dog. Cats are psychic."

He threw his overcoat on the daybed and placed his hat on the desk, and when he did so, he saw a small dark object lying near his typewriter. He approached it gingerly. It looked like the decomposed remains of a small bird.

"What's this?" he said. "What the devil is this?"

Mary examined the small brown fragment. "Why, it's a piece of hair jewelry. A brooch!"

He combed his moustache with his fingertips. "Some uncanny things have been happening on these premises. Yesterday some benevolent spirit left me a dollar bill!" He examined the birdlike form woven of twisted brown strands. "You mean this is real hair?'"

"Human hair. It's memorial jewelry. They used to make necklaces, bracelets, all sorts of things from the hair of someone who had died."

"Who would want to keep such stuff?"

"Iris has an extensive collection. She even wears it occasionally."

Qwilleran dropped the brooch with distaste. "Sit down," he said, "and let me tell you what I discovered about the Ellsworth house in the *Fluxion* clip file." He offered her a gilded chair, flipping the red cushion to the side that was not furred with cat hair. "Did you know that Ellsworth was a former mayor?"

"Yes, I've heard about him."

"He died at the age of ninety-two, having achieved a reputation for eccentricity. He was a compulsive collector—never threw anything away. He had a twenty-year accumulation of old newspapers, string, and vinegar bottles. And he was supposed to be worth quite a sum of money, but a large chunk of his holdings was never found. . . . Does that suggest anything to you?"

Mary shook her head.

"Suppose someone was looking for buried treasure in the old house last night . . . and suppose C.C. arrived with his crowbar, looking for black walnut paneling . . . and suppose they thought he was after the strongbox?"

"Don't you think that's rather far-fetched?"

"Maybe he accidentally found the loot when he ripped open the paneling . . . and maybe another scrounger came along and pushed him downstairs. I admit it's far-fetched, but it's a possibility."

The girl looked at Qwilleran with sudden curiosity. "Is it true what my father says about you? That you've solved two murder cases since joining the *Fluxion*?"

"Well, I was instrumental—that is, I didn't do it alone. I had help." He touched his moustache tentatively and threw a glance in Koko's direction. Koko was watching, and he was all ears.

"Do you really think that Cobb might have been murdered?"

"Murder shouldn't be ruled out too quickly—although the police accepted it as an accident. A man with Cobb's personality must have had enemies."

"His churlishness was a pose—for business reasons. Everyone knew that. Many junkers think prices go up if a dealer is friendly, and if his shop is clean."

"Whether it was an act or not, I don't suppose anyone hated him enough to kill him. Competition for the Ellsworth treasure would make a better motive."

Mary stood up and looked out the back window for a while. "I don't know whether this will have any bearing on the case," she said finally, "but . . . when C.C. went scrounging late at night, he didn't always go to a condemned building."

"You think he was playing around?"

"I know he was."

"Anybody we know?"

Mary hesitated and then said, "One of The Three Weird Sisters."

Qwilleran gave a dry chuckle. "I can guess which one."

"She's a nymphomaniac," said Mary with her cool porcelain look.

"Did Iris suspect?"

"I don't think so. She's near-sighted in more ways than one."

"How did you know this was going on?"

"Mrs. Katzenhide lives in the same apartment building. Several times she saw Cobb paying late evening calls, and you know very well he was not there to discuss the hallmarks on English silver."

Qwilleran studied Mary's face. Her eyes were sparkling, and her personality had a new buoyancy.

"What's happened to you, Mary?" he asked. "You've changed."

She smiled joyously. "I feel as if I've been living under a cloud, and the sun has just broken through!"

"Can you tell me about it?"

"Not now. Later. I'd better go back to Iris. She'll wake and think she's deserted."

After she had left, Qwilleran took another look at the hair brooch—and a good hard look at the cats. The male was graciously allowing the female to wash his ears.

"Okay, Koko, the game's up," he said. "Where are you getting this loot?"

Koko sat very tall and squeezed his eyes innocently.

"You feline Fagin! I'll bet you find the stuff, and you make Yum Yum steal it. Where's your secret cache?"

Koko unfolded his rear half and with dignity walked from the room. Qwilleran followed him—into the bathroom.

"You're finding them under the tub?"

"Yow," said Koko with a noncommittal inflection.

Qwilleran started to go down on all fours, but a twinge in his bad knee discouraged the effort. "I'll bet no one's cleaned under that monster for fifty years," he told the cat, who was now sitting in his sandbox with a soulful look in his eyes and paying no attention to anyone.

Shortly after, when Qwilleran returned to the Ellsworth house to pick up the Cobb car, he did some treasure hunting of his own. He looked for footprints and tire tracks in the snow and telltale marks in the dust of the stripped rooms.

White plaster dust had settled everywhere. Large objects had been dragged through it, leaving dark trails, and footprints had piled on footprints, but here and there a mark could be distinguished. Qwilleran noticed the patterned tread of boots, the imprint of a claw hammer, some regularly spaced dots (made by crutches?), and even the pawprints of a large animal, and a series of feathery arabesques in the dust, perhaps caused by the switching of a tail. Evidently every dealer in Junktown had been through the Ellsworth house at one time or another; recent prints were lightly filmed over and the older ones were almost covered.

Qwilleran dug Cobb's flashlight out of a pile of rubble and retrieved his crowbar. Then he went upstairs. Everything on the stair treads had been obliterated, but on the landing there was evidence of three kinds of footwear, and although it was impossible to guess whether all three had been there at the same time, they were sharp enough to be recent.

The newsman copied the tread marks on the folded sheet of newsprint that was always in his pocket. One print was a network of diamond shapes, another was a series of closely spaced dots, and the third was crossbarred. His own galoshes left a pattern of small circles.

The tire tracks in the yard contributed nothing to Qwilleran's investigation. There was no telling how many junkers had been in and out of the driveway. Tire tracks had crisscrossed and frozen and melted and frozen again, and snow had frosted the unreadable hieroglyphics.

Qwilleran backed the tan station wagon out of its hiding place in the backyard, and as he pulled away, he noticed that the vehicle left a rectangle of gray in the field of white snow. He also noticed another such rectangle nearby. Two cars had parked there on the dirty ice Sunday night, after which a light snow had fallen. Qwilleran jumped out of the wagon, thanked fate and Mary Duckworth for the tape line in his pocket, and measured the length and breadth of the second rectangle. It was shorter than the imprint left by Cobb's wagon, and it was not quite square at one corner, the snow having drifted in from the northwest.

Qwilleran's findings did not amount to much, he had to admit. Even if the owner of the second car were known, there was no proof that he had engineered Cobb's fatal fall. Nevertheless, the mere routine of investigation was exhilarating to Qwilleran, and he drove from the scene with a feeling of accomplishment. On second impulse he drove back into the Ellsworth yard, entered the house, and salvaged two items for the Cobb Junkery: a marble mantel and a chandelier of blackened brass.

Later he drove Mrs. Cobb to the airport.

"I don't have anything black to wear," she said wearily. "C.C. always liked me to wear bright colors. Pink especially." She huddled on the car seat in her cheap coat with imitation fur lining, her pink crocheted church-going hat, and her two pairs of glasses hanging from ribbons.

"You can pick up something in Cleveland," Qwilleran said, "if you think it's necessary. Who's going to meet you there?"

"My brother-in-law—and Dennis, if he gets in from St. Louis."

"Is that your son?"

"Yes."

"What's he doing in St. Louis?"

"He finished school last June and just started his first job."

"Does he like antiques?"

"Oh, dear, no! He's an architect!"

Keep her talking, Qwilleran thought. "How old is he?"

"Twenty-two."

"Single?"

"Engaged. She's a nice girl. I wanted to give them some antique silver for Christmas, but Dennis doesn't approve of anything old. . . . Oh, dear! I forgot the presents for the mailman and the milkman. There are two envelopes behind the clock in the kitchen—with a card and a little money in them. Will you see that they get them—in case I don't come home right away? I wrapped up a little Christmas treat for Koko and Yum Yum, too. It's in the top drawer of the Empire chest. And tell Ben that I'll make his bourbon cake when I get back from the—from Cleveland."

"How do you make bourbon cake?" Keep her talking.

"With eggs and flour and walnuts and raisins and a cup of bourbon."

"Nothing could beat that coconut cake you made yesterday."

"Coconut was C.C.'s favorite," she said, and then she fell silent, staring straight ahead but seeing nothing beyond the windshield.

CHAPTER 14

WHEN QWILLERAN RETURNED from the airport in the Cobb station wagon, he saw a fifth of a ton of *Fluxion* photographer squeezing into a Volkswagen at the curb.

"Tiny!" he hailed him. "Did you get everything?"

"I went to five places," Tiny said. "Shot six rolls."

"I've got another idea. Do you have a wide angle lens? How about shooting a picture of my apartment? To show how people live in Junk-town?"

The staircase groaned when the photographer followed Qwilleran up-stairs, and Yum Yum gave one look at the outsize stranger decked with strange apparatus and promptly took flight. Koko observed the proceed-ings with aplomb.

Tiny cast a bilious glance around the room. "How can you live with these crazy anachronisms?"

"They grow on you," Qwilleran said smugly.

"Is that a bed? Looks like a funeral barge on the Nile. And who's your embalmed friend over the fireplace? You know, these junk dealers are a bunch of graverobbers. One guy wanted me to photograph a dead cat, and those three dames with all that rusty tin were swooning over some burial jewelry from an Inca tomb."

"You're not tuned in," Qwilleran said with the casual air of authority that comes easily to a newsman after three days on a new beat. "Antiques have character—a sense of history. See this bookrack? You wonder where it's been—who owned it—what books it's held—who polished the brass. An English butler? A Massachusetts poet? An Ohio schoolteacher?"

"You're a bunch of necrophiles," said Tiny. "My God! Even the cat!" He stared at Yum Yum, trudging into the room with a small dead mouse.

"Drop that dirty thing!" Qwilleran shouted, stamping his foot.

She dropped it and streaked out of sight. He scooped up the gray morsel on a sheet of paper, rushed it into the bathroom and flushed it down the toilet.

After Tiny had left, Qwilleran sat at his typewriter, aware of an un-common silence in the house. The cats were snoozing, the Cobb radio was quiet, Ben was about his business elsewhere, and The Junkery was closed. When the doorbell rang, it startled him.

There was a man waiting on the stoop—an ordinary-looking man in an ordinary-looking gray car coat.

"Sorry to bother you," he said. "I'm Hollis Prantz. I have a shop down the street. Just heard the bad news about brother Cobb."

Qwilleran nodded with the appropriate amount of gloom.

"Rotten time of year to have it happen," said Prantz. "I hear Mrs. Cobb has left town."

"She went to Cleveland for the funeral."

"Well, tell you why I came. Cobb was saving some old radios for me, and I could probably unload them in my shop during the shindig tomorrow. Mrs. Cobb would appreciate it, I'm sure. Every little bit helps at a time like this."

Qwilleran waved toward The Junkery. "Want to go in and have a look?"

"Oh, they wouldn't be in their shop. Cobb had put them aside in his apartment, he said."

The newsman took time to pat his moustache before saying, "Okay, go on upstairs," and he added, "I'll help you look."

"Don't trouble yourself. I'll find them." The dealer bounded up the stairs, two at a time.

"No trouble," Qwilleran insisted, following as quickly as he could and trying to catch a glimpse of the man's boot soles. He stayed close behind as Prantz opened a coat closet, the window seat, the armoire.

"Look, friend, I hate to take up your time. I know you must be busy. You're writing that series for the paper, they tell me."

"No problem," said Qwilleran. "Glad to stretch my legs." He watched the dealer's eyes as they roved around the apartment and returned repeatedly to the desk—the apothecary desk with its tall bank of miniature drawers. Crowded on top of the lofty superstructure were some pewter candlesticks, the stuffed owl, a tin box, a handful of envelopes, and the Cobbs' overworked radio.

"What I'm interested in," said Prantz, "is equipment from the early days—crystal sets and old beehive radios. Not so easy to come by. . . . Well, sorry to trouble you."

"I'll be in to see your shop," Qwilleran said, ushering him out of the apartment.

"Sure! It's a little unusual, and you might get a bang out of it."

The newsman looked at the dealer's footwear. "Say, did you buy those boots around here? I need a pair like that."

"No, these are old," said Prantz. "I don't even remember where I bought them, but they're just ordinary boots."

"Do the soles have a good grip?"

"Good enough, although the treads are beginning to wear slick."

The dealer left without offering Qwilleran a view of his soles, and the newsman telephoned Mary Duckworth at once. "What do you know about Hollis Prantz?" he asked.

"Not much. He's new on the street. He sells techtiques, whatever they might be."

"I noticed his shop the first day I was here. Looks like a TV repair shop."

"He has some preposterous theories."

"About what?"

"About 'artificially accelerated antiquity.' Frankly, I haven't decided whether he's a prophetic genius or a psychopath."

"Has he been friendly with the Cobbs?"

"He tries to be friendly with everyone. Really *too* friendly. Why are you interested?"

"Prantz was just over here. Invited me to see his shop," the newsman said. "By the way, have you ever been to the Ellsworth house?"

"No, I haven't, but I know which one it is. The Italianate sandstone of Fifteenth Street."

"When you go scrounging, do you ever take Hepplewhite?"

"Scrounging! I never go scrounging! I handle nothing but eighteenth century English."

After his conversation with Mary, Qwilleran looked for Koko. "Come on, old boy," he said to the room at large. "I've got an assignment for you."

There was no response from Koko, but Yum Yum was staring at the third shelf of the book cupboard, and that meant he was snuggling behind the biographies. That's where Qwilleran had first met Koko—on a shelf between the lives of Van Gogh and Leonardo da Vinci.

He pulled the cat out and showed him a tangle of blue leather straps and white cord. "Do you know what this is?"

Koko had not worn the harness since the day in early autumn when he had saved Qwilleran's life. On that occasion he had performed some sleight-of-paw with the four yards of nylon cord that served as a leash. Now he allowed the halter to be slipped over his head and the belt to be buckled under his soft white underside. His body pulsed with a rasping purr of anticipation.

"We'll leave Yum Yum here to mind the house," Qwilleran told him, "and we'll go and play bloodhound."

As soon as the apartment door was opened, Koko bounded like a rabbit toward the furniture stacked at the front end of the hall, and before Qwilleran could haul in the cord, the cat had squeezed between the spindles of a chair, scuttled under a chest of drawers, circled the leg of a spinning wheel, and effectively tangled the leash, leaving himself free to sniff the finial hidden in the jumble.

"You think you're smart, don't you?" Qwilleran said, as he worked to free the cord and extricate the cat. Some minutes later, he lugged the protesting Koko, squirming and squawking, to the door of the Cobb apartment. "I have news for you. This is where we're going to explore."

Koko sniffed the corner of the worn Oriental rug before setting foot on it. Then, to Qwilleran's delight he walked directly to the apothecary desk, stopping only to scratch his back on a copper coalhod filled with magazines. At the desk Koko hopped to the chair seat and then to the writing surface, where he moved his nose from right to left across an envelope that had come in the mail.

"Find anything interesting?" Qwilleran inquired, but it was only a telephone bill.

Next Koko reared on his haunches and regarded the bank of small drawers—twenty-four of them with white porcelain knobs—and selected one on which to rub his jaw. His white fangs clicked on the white ceramic, and Qwilleran gingerly opened drawer he indicated. It contained a set of false teeth made of wood. Guiltily the newsman opened other drawers and found battered silver spoons, primitive eyeglasses, tarnished jewelry, and a few bracelets made of hair. Most of the drawers were empty.

While Qwilleran was thus occupied, a feather floated past his nose. Koko had stealthily risen to the top of the drawer deck and was nuzzling the stuffed owl.

"I might have known!" Qwilleran said in disgust. "Get down! Get away from that bird!"

Koko sailed to the floor and stalked haughtily from the apartment, leading the newsman behind him on a slack leash.

"I'm disappointed in you," the man told him. "You used to be good at this sort of thing. Let's try the attic."

The attic room had been romantically remodeled to resemble a barn, the walls paneled with silvery weathered planks and hung with milking stools, oil lanterns, and old farm implements. A papier-mâché steer, relic of a nineteenth century butcher shop, glared out of a corner stall, and a white leghorn brooded on a nest of straw.

In the center of the room, chairs were arranged in a circle, and Qwilleran was fascinated by their decrepitude. He noted an ice cream parlor chair of wire construction, badly bent; a Windsor with two spindles missing; a porch rocker with one arm, and other seating pieces in various stages of collapse. While he was viewing these derelicts, Koko was stalking the white feathered biddy on her nest.

The man yanked the leash. "I don't know what's happened to you," he said. "Pigeons—owls—hens! I think I'm feeding you too much poultry. Come on. Let's go."

Koko rushed downstairs and clamored to get into his apartment, where Yum Yum was calling him with high, pitched mews.

"Oh, no, you don't! We have one more investigation to make. And this time try to be objective."

In Ben's apartment furniture was herded together without plan, and every surface was piled high with items of little worth. Ben's long knitted muffler was draped incongruously over the chandelier, dangling its soiled tassels, and his many hats—including the silk topper and the Santa Claus cap—were to be seen on tables, hatracks, chair seats and lamp chimneys.

Qwilleran found the apartment layout similar to his own, with the addition of a large bay window in the front. With one ear tuned to the sound of a downstairs door opening, he stepped cautiously into each room, finding dirty dishes in the kitchen sink and a ring in the bathtub, as he had expected. In the dressing room, jammed to the ceiling with bundles and boxes, he looked for boots, but Ben, wherever he was, had them on his feet.

"No clues here," Qwilleran said, starting toward the door and casually lifting his red feather from Ben's silk topper. He yanked the leash. "And you're no help any more. It was a mistake to get you a companion. You've lost your talent."

He had not noticed Koko, sitting up like a squirrel, batting the tassels of Ben's long scarf.

CHAPTER 15

WHEN THE TIME came for meeting in Hernia Heaven, Qwilleran climbed to the third floor with some discomfort. His bad knee, although it had improved during the day, tightened up at nightfall, and he arrived at the meeting with a noticeable limp.

The dealers sat in a circle, and Qwilleran looked at their feet before he looked at their faces. They had tramped upstairs in their outdoor togs, and he saw velvet boots, a single brown suede teamed with a walking cast, some man-sized boots in immaculate white, and assorted rubbers and galoshes.

He took the nearest vacant seat—on a church pew with threadbare cushions—and found himself sitting between Cluthra's cast and Russ Patch's crutches.

"Looks like the bus stop for Lourdes," said the redhead with a fraternal lean in Qwilleran's direction. "What happened to you?"

"I was felled by an avalanche."

"I wouldn't have struggled up all those stairs, one sloggin' foot at a time, only I heard you were going to be here." She gave him a wink and a friendly nudge.

"How did the picture-taking go?" he asked

"That photographer you sent is a big hunk of a man."

"Did he break anything?"

"Only a small Toby jug."

"Newspapers always assign bulls to china shops," Qwilleran explained. He was trying to see the soles of the footwear around him, but every pair of feet remained firmly planted on the floor. He turned to Russell Patch and said, "Good-looking boots you're wearing. Where did you manage to find white ones?"

"Had to have them custom-made," said the young man, stretching out his good leg for advantageous display.

"Even the soles are white!" Qwilleran said, staring at the ridged bottoms and patting his moustache with satisfaction. "I suppose those crutches cramp your style when it comes to scrounging."

"I still get around, and I won't have to use them much longer."

"Get anything out of the Ellsworth house?"

"No, I skipped that one. The kitchen cabinets were grabbed off before I could get there, and that's all I'm interested in."

They lie, Qwilleran thought. All these dealers lie. They're all actors, unable to tell reality from fantasy. Aloud he said, "What do you do with kitchen cabinets?"

"The real old ones make good built-ins for stereo installation, if you give them a provincial finish. I've got a whole wall of them myself, with about twenty thousand dollars worth of electronic equipment. Thirty-six speakers. You like music? I've got everything on tapes. Operas, symphonies, chamber music, classic jazz—"

"You must have quite an investment there," Qwilleran said, alerted to the apparent wealth of this young man.

"Priceless! Come up and have a listen some night. I live right over my shop, you know."

"Do you own the building?"

"Well, it's like this. I rented it for a while and built in so many improvements—me and my roommate, that is—that I had to buy it to protect my investment."

Qwilleran forgot to pry any further, because Mary Duckworth arrived. Wearing a short blue plaid skirt, she sat on a kitchen chair of the Warren Harding period and crossed her long elegant legs. For the first time Qwilleran saw her knees. He considered himself a connoisseur of knees, and these had all the correct points. They were slender, shapely, and eminently designed for their function—with the kind of vertical indentations on either side of the kneecap that caused a stir in the roots of his moustache.

"My Gawd! *She's* here!" said a husky voice in his ear. "Keep her away from me, will you? She might try to break the other one." The redhead's ample bosom heaved with anger. "You know, she deliberately dropped a cast-iron garden urn on my foot."

"Mary did?"

"*That woman*," she said between clenched teeth, "is capable of *anything*! I wish she'd get out of Junktown! Her shop doesn't belong here. That high-priced pedigreed stuff spoils it for the rest of us."

There was a sudden round of applause as Ben Nicholas, who had been acting as doorman down below, made a grandiose entrance in an admiral's cocked hat, and then the meeting began.

Sylvia Katzenhide reviewed the plans for the Block Party on Wednesday. "The city is going to rope off four blocks," she said, "and decorate the utility poles with plastic angels. They've run out of Christmas angels, but they have some nice lavender ones left over from last Easter. Carol singers will be supplied by the Sanitation Department Glee Club."

Qwilleran added, "Could we keep The Junkery open during the party? I hate to see Mrs. Cobb lose that extra business. I'd be willing to mind the store for a couple of hours myself."

Cluthra squeezed his arm and said, "You're a honey! We'll help, too—my sisters and I. We'll take turns."

Then someone suggested sending flowers to the Cobb funeral, and just as they were taking up a collection, they were stunned by a blast of noise from the floor below. It was a torrent of popular music—raucous, bouncy, loud. They listened in open-mouthed astonishment for a few seconds, then all talked at once.

"What's that?"

"A radio?"

"Who's down there?"

"Nobody!"

"Where's it coming from?"

"Somebody's downstairs!"

"Who could it be?"

"How could they get in?"

"The front door's locked, isn't it?"

Qwilleran was the first one on his feet. "Let's go down and see." He grabbed a wooden sledge hammer that was hanging on the wall and started down the narrow stairs, left foot first on each step. The only other men at the meeting followed—Russ on his crutches and Ben lumbering after them with a pitchfork in his hand.

The noise was coming from the Cobb apartment. The door stood open. The apartment was in darkness.

Qwilleran reached in, groped for a wall switch and flooded the room with light. "Who's there?" he shouted in a voice of authority.

There was no answer. The music poured out of the small radio on the apothecary desk.

The three men searched the apartment, Ben bringing up a delayed rear.

"No one here," Qwilleran announced.

"Maybe it has an automatic timer," Russ said.

"The thing doesn't have a timer," Qwilleran said as he turned off the offensive little radio. He frowned at the writing surface of the desk. Papers were scattered. A pencil cup was knocked over. From the floor he picked up a telephone bill and an address book—and a gray feather.

As the men emerged from the Cobb apartment, the women were beginning to venture down from the attic.

"Is it safe?" they asked.

Cluthra said, "If it was a man, which way did he go?"

"What was it? Does anyone know what it was?"

"That crazy radio," Russ said. "It turned on all by itself."

"How could it do that?"

"I don't know," said Qwilleran . . . but he did.

After the dealers had straggled out the front door and Ben had departed for an evening at The Lion's Tail, Qwilleran unlocked his apartment door and looked for the cats. Yum Yum was sitting on top of the refrigerator with eyes bright and ears alert—eyes and ears a trifle too large for her tiny wedge-shaped face. Koko was lapping up a drink of water, his tail lying straight on the floor as it did when he was especially thirsty.

"Okay, Koko," said Qwilleran. "How did you do it? Have you teamed up with Mathilda?"

The tip of Koko's tail tapped the floor lightly, as he went on drinking.

Qwilleran wandered through his suite of rooms and speculated on each one. He knew Koko could turn a radio dial by scraping it with his hard little jaw, but how was this feline Houdini getting out of the apartment? Qwilleran moved the swan bed away from the wall and looked for a vent in the baseboard. He examined the bathroom for trap doors (turn-of-the-century plumbers had been fond of trap doors), but there was nothing of the sort. The kitchenette had a high transom window cut through to the hall, presumably for ventilation, and it would be easily accessible from the top of the refrigerator, but it was closed and latched.

The telephone rang.

"Qwill," said Mary's pleasing voice, "are you doing anything about your knee? You looked as if you were in pain tonight."

"I used cold compresses until the swelling went down."

"What you need now is a heat lamp. May I offer you mine?"

"I'd appreciate it," he said. "Yes, I'd appreciate it very much."

In preparation for his session with the heat lamp, Qwilleran put on a pair of sporty walking shorts that had survived a country weekend the previous summer and admired himself in the long mirror on the dressing room door, at the same time pulling in his waistline and expanding his chest. He had always thought he would look admirable in Scottish kilts. His legs were straight, solid, muscular and moderately haired—just enough to look virile, not enough to look zoological. The puffiness around the left knee that had destroyed its perfection had now subsided, he was glad to note.

He told the cats, "I'm having a guest, and I want you guys to use some discretion. No noisy squabbles! No flying around and disturbing the status quo!"

Koko squeezed his eyes and tilted his whiskers in what looked like a knowing smile. Yum Yum exhibited indifference by laundering the snow-white cowlick where her fur grew in two directions on her breast.

When Mary arrived, carrying a basket, Koko looked her over from an unfriendly distance.

"He's not overwhelmed with joy," she said, "but at least he's civil this time."

"He'll get used to you," Qwilleran assured her.

In her basket she had homemade fruitcake and an espresso maker, as well as a heat lamp. She plugged in the little silver coffee machine and positioned the infrared lamp over Qwilleran's knee and then sat in the twiggy rocker. Immediately the country bumpkin of a rocking chair looked gracefully linear and organically elegant, and Qwilleran wondered why he had ever thought it was ugly.

"Do you have any idea what caused the outburst in the Cobb apartment?" she asked.

"Just another of the cockeyed things that happen in this house. . . . By the way, I wonder why Hollis Prantz didn't attend the meeting."

"Half the dealers stayed away. They probably knew we'd collect money for flowers."

"Prantz was here this afternoon, looking for some antique radios the Cobbs were supposed to be saving for him—or so he said. Does that make sense?"

"Oh, certainly. Dealers make most of their money by selling to each other. . . . How does the heat feel? Is the lamp too close?"

Soon a rushing, bubbling roar in the kitchen announced that the espresso was ready. It alarmed Yum Yum, who ran in the opposite direction, but Koko made it his business to march into the kitchen and investigate.

With a mixture of pride and apology Qwilleran said, "Koko's a self-assured fellow, but Yum Yum's as nervous as a cat; when in doubt, she exits. She's what you might call a pussycat's pussycat. She sits on laps and catches mice—all the things cats are supposed to do."

"I've never owned a cat," Mary said as she poured the coffee in small cups and added a twist of lemon peel. "But I used to study them for their grace of movement when I was dancing."

"No one ever owns a cat," he corrected her. "You share a common habitation on a basis of equal rights and mutual respect . . . although somehow the cat always comes out ahead of the deal. Siamese particularly have a way of getting the upper hand."

"Some animals are almost human. . . . Please try this fruitcake, Qwill."

He accepted a dark, moist, mysterious, aromatic wedge of cake. "Koko is more than human. He has a sixth sense. He seems to have access to information that a human couldn't collect without laborious investigation." Qwilleran heard himself saying it, and he hoped it was still true, but deep in his heart he was beginning to wonder.

Mary turned to look at the remarkable animal. Koko was sitting on his spine with one leg in midair as he washed the base of his tail. He paused with pink tongue extended and returned her admiring gaze with an insolent stare. Then, having finished his ablutions, he went on to the ritual of sharpening his claws. He jumped on the daybed, stood on his hind legs and scratched the papered wall where the book pages overlapped and corners were beginning to curl up tantalizingly.

"No! Down! Scram! Beat it!" Qwilleran scolded. Koko obeyed, but not until he had finished the sharpening job and taken his time about it.

The man explained to his guest. "Koko was given a dictionary for a scratching pad, and now he thinks he can use any printed page for a pedicure. Sometimes I'm convinced he can read. He once exposed a series of art forgeries that way."

"Are you serious?"

"Absolutely. . . . Tell me, is there much fakery in antiques?"

"Not in this country. An unscrupulous dealer may sell a nineteenth century Chippendale reproduction as an eighteenth century piece, or an artist may do crude paintings on old canvas and call them early American primitives, but there's no large-scale faking to my knowledge. . . . How do you like the fruitcake? One of my customers made it. Robert Maus."

"The attorney?"

"Do you know him? He's a superb cook."

"Wasn't he Andy's lawyer? Quite an important attorney for a little operation in Junktown," Qwilleran remarked.

"Robert is an avid collector and friend of mine. He represented Andy as a courtesy."

"Did his legal mind ever do any questioning about Andy's so-called accident?"

Mary gave him an anxious glance. "Are you still pursuing that?"

Qwilleran decided to be candid. He was tired of hearing about Andy's superlative qualities from all the women in Junktown. "Are you aware," he said, "that it was Andy who tipped off the police to Cobb's scrounging?"

"No, I can't believe—"

"Why did he squeal on Cobb and not on Russ or some of the other scroungers? Did he have a grudge against Cobb?"

"I don't—"

"It may be that Andy also threatened Cobb—threatened to tell Iris about his philandering. I hate to say this, Mary, but your friend Andy was a meddler—or else he had an ax to grind. Perhaps he considered that Cobb was trespassing on his own territory when he visited Cluthra."

Mary flushed. "So you found out about *that*, too!"

"I'm sorry," said Qwilleran. "I didn't want to embarrass you."

She shrugged, and she was attractive when she shrugged. "I knew that Andy was seeing Cluthra. That's why we quarreled the night he was killed. Andy and I weren't really committed. We had an understanding. Not even an understanding—just an arrangement. But I'm afraid I was beginning to feel possessive." She reached over and clicked off the heat lamp. "That knee has broiled long enough. How does it feel?"

"Better. Much better." Qwilleran started to fill his pipe. "After Andy left your house that night—to meet the prospective customers—what route did he take?"

"He went out my back door, through the alley and into the back of his shop."

"And when you followed, you went the same way? Did you see anyone else in the alley?"

Mary gave Qwilleran a swift glance. "I don't think so. There might have been one of those invisible men from the rooming house. They slink around like ghosts."

"How much time had elapsed when you followed Andy?"

She hesitated. "Oh . . . about an hour . . . More fruitcake, Qwill?"

"Thanks. During that time the customers may have come, found the front door locked, and gone away—unaware that Andy lay dead in the back room. Before they arrived, someone else could have followed Andy into his shop through the back door—someone who had seen him enter. . . . Let's see, how many buildings stand between your house and Andy's store?"

"Russ's carriage house, then the variety store, then this house, then the rooming house where Ben has his shop."

"That building and your own place are duplicates of this house, aren't they?" Qwilleran asked. "Only narrower."

"You're very observant. The three houses were built by the same family."

"I know Russ lives upstairs over his workshop. Who's his roommate? Is he in the antique business?"

"No. Stanley is a hairdresser."

"I wonder where Russ gets all his dough. He owns the carriage house, wears custom-made boots, has twenty thousand dollars worth of sound equipment, stables a white Jaguar. . . . Is he on the up-and-up? Did Andy think he was simon-pure? Maybe Andy was getting ready to put the finger on him. Where *does* Russ get his dough? Does he have a sideline?"

"I only know that he's a hard worker. Sometimes I hear his power tools at three o'clock in the morning."

"I wonder—" Qwilleran stopped to light his pipe. "I wonder why Russ lied to me tonight. I asked him if he'd been scrounging at the Ellsworth house, and he denied it. Yet I could swear that those crutches and those white boots had been through that house."

"Dealers are sensitive about their sources of supply," Mary said. "It's considered bad form to ask a dealer where he acquires his antiques, and if he answers you at all, he never feels bound to state the truth. It's also bad form to tell a dealer about your grandmother's attic treasures."

"Really? Who decrees these niceties of etiquette?"

Mary smiled in a lofty way that Qwilleran found charming. "The same authority who gives newspapers the right to invade everyone's privacy."

"Touché!"

"Did I tell you about finding the twenty dollar bill?" she asked after they had gazed at each other appreciatively for a few seconds.

"Some people get all the breaks," he said. "Where did you find it?"

"In the pocket of my sweater—the one I was wearing on the night of Andy's accident. The sweater dipped in his blood, and I rolled it up in a ball and stuffed it on a closet shelf. My cleaning woman found it this weekend, and that's when the twenty dollar bill came to light."

"Where did it come from?"

"I picked it up in Andy's workroom."

"You mean you found money at the scene of the accident? And you picked it up? Didn't you realize it might be an important clue?"

Mary shrugged and looked appealingly guilty. "Banker's child," she explained.

"Was it folded?"

She nodded.

"How was it folded?"

"Lengthwise—and then in half."

"Did Andy fold his money that way?"

"No. He used a billfold."

Qwilleran turned his head suddenly. "Koko! Get away from that lamp!"

The cat had crept onto the table and was rubbing his jaw against the wick regulator of the lamp decorated with pink roses. At the same moment Qwilleran felt a flicker of awareness in the same old place, and he smoothed his moustache with the stem of his pipe.

"Mary," he said, "who were the people who were coming to look at the light fixture?"

"I don't know. Andy merely said a woman from the suburbs was bringing her husband to approve it before she bought it."

Qwilleran leaned forward in his Morris chair. "Mary, if Andy was getting the chandelier down from the ceiling when he fell, it means that the customers had already okayed it! Andy was getting the thing down so they could take it with them! Don't you see? If the accident was genuine, it means the suburban couple were in the store when it happened. Why didn't they call the police? Who were they? Were they there at all? And if not, who *was* there?"

Mary looked guilty again. "I guess it's all right to tell you—now. . . . When I went to Andy's shop to apologize, I went twice. The first time I peeked in and saw him talking with someone, so I made a hasty retreat and tried again later."

"Did you recognize the person?"

"Yes, but I was afraid to let anyone know I had seen anything."

"What did you see, Mary?"

"I saw them arguing—Andy and C.C. And I was afraid C.C. might have seen *me*. You have no idea how relieved I was when I heard about his accident this morning. That's a terrible thing to say, I know."

"And you've been living in fear of that guy! Did he give you any reason to be?"

"Not actually, but . . . that's when the mysterious phone calls started."

"I knew it!" Qwilleran said. "I knew there was something fishy about that call the other night. How often—?"

"About once a week—always the same voice—obviously disguised. It sounded like a stage whisper—raspy—asthmatic."

"What was said?"

"Always something stupid and melodramatic. Vague hints about Andy's death. Vague predictions of danger. Now that C.C. is gone, I have a feeling the calls will stop."

"Don't be too sure," Qwilleran said. "There was a third person in Andy's shop that night—the owner of that twenty dollar bill. C.C. used a billfold and filed his currency flat. Someone else . . . I wonder how Ben Nicholas folds his money?"

"Qwill—"

"Would a woman ever fold a bill lengthwise?"

"Qwill," she said earnestly, "you're not serious about this, are you? I don't want any official interest to be revived in Andy's death." She said it bluntly and confronted him squarely.

"Why do you say that?"

Her eyes wavered. "Suppose you continued to investigate . . . and suppose you found an answer that pointed to murder . . . you would report it, wouldn't you?"

"Of course."

"And there would be a trial."

Qwilleran nodded.

"And because I found the body, I would have to testify, wouldn't I? And then my position would be exposed!" She slid out of the rocking chair and knelt on the floor at his side. "Qwill, that would be the end of everything I live for! The publicity—my father—you know what would happen!"

He put aside his pipe, and it fell on the floor. He studied her face.

"It's the newspapers I'm afraid of!" she said. "You know how they are about *names*. Anything for a *name*! Leave matters the way they are," she begged. "Andy's gone. Nothing will bring him back. Don't make any more inquiries. Qwill. Please!" She reached for his hands and stared at him with eyes wide and pleading. "Please do it for me." She bent her head and rubbed her smooth cheek against the back of his hand, and Qwilleran quickly raised her face to his.

"Please, Qwill, tell me you'll drop the whole matter."

"Mary, I don't . . ."

"Qwill, please promise." Her lips were very close.

There was a breathless moment. Time stood still.

Then they heard: "*Grrrowrrr . . . yeowww!*"

Then a hissing: "*Hhhhhhh!*"

"*Grrrowrrr! Owf!*"

"KOKO!" shouted the man.

"*Ak-ak-ak-ak-ak!*"

"Yum Yum!"
"*GRRRRR!*"
"Koko, *quit* that!"

CHAPTER 16

QWILLERAN DREAMED ABOUT Niagara Falls that night, and when the tumult of the cataract succeeded in waking him, he glanced about wildly in his darkened room. There was a roar of water—a rushing, raging torrent. Then, with a gasp and a choking groan, it stopped.

He sat up in his swan bed and listened. In a moment it started again, somewhat less deafening than in his dream—a gushing, swishing whirlpool, followed by a snort, a shuddering groan, a few final sobs, and silence.

Gradually the source of the noise penetrated his sleep-drugged mind. Plumbing! The aged plumbing of an old house! But why was it flushing in the night? Qwilleran swung his legs out of bed and staggered to the bathroom.

He switched on the light. There, balancing on the edge of the baroque bathtub, was Koko, with one paw on the porcelain lever of the old-fashioned toilet, watching the swirling water with an intent, near-sighted gaze. Yum Yum was sitting in the marble washbowl, blinking her eyes at the sudden brightness. Once more Koko stepped on the lever and stared in fascination as the water cascaded, churned, gurgled, and disappeared.

"You monkey!" Qwilleran said. "How did you discover that gadget?" He was unsure whether to be peeved at the interruption of his sleep or proud of the cat's mechanical aptitude. He lugged Koko, squalling and writhing, from the bathroom and tossed him on the cushions of the Morris chair. "What were you trying to do? Resurrect Yum Yum's mouse?"

Koko licked his rumpled fur as if it had been contaminated by something indescribably offensive.

Daylight in a menacing yellow-gray began to creep over the winter sky, devising new atrocities in the form of weather. While opening a can of minced clams for the cats, Qwilleran planned his day. For one thing, he wanted to find out how Ben Nicholas folded his money. He also wished he knew how that red feather had transferred from a tweed porkpie to a silk tophat. He had asked Koko about it, and Koko had merely squeezed one eye. As for the avalanche, Qwilleran had discussed it with Mary, and she had a glib explanation: "Well, you see, the attic in Ben's building is used for sleeping rooms, and it's heated."

He had not exactly promised Mary that he would drop his unofficial investigation. He had been on the verge of promising when Koko created that commotion. Afterwards, Qwilleran had simply said, "Trust me, Mary. I won't do anything to hurt you," and she had become nicely emotional, and altogether it had been a gratifying evening. She had even accepted his Christmas Eve invitation. She said she would go to the Press Club as Mary Duxbury—not Mary Duckworth, junk dealer—because the society writers would recognize her.

Qwilleran still faced a dilemma, however. To drop his investigation was to shirk his own idea of responsibility; to pursue it was to hurt Junktown, and this neglected stepchild of City Hall needed a champion, not another antagonist.

By the time the junk shops opened and Qwilleran started his rounds, the weather had devised another form of discomfort: a clammy cold that chilled the bones and hovered over Junktown like a musty dishrag.

He went first to Bit o' Junk, but Ben's shop was closed.

Then he tried the store that sold tech-tiques, and for the first time since Qwilleran had arrived in Junktown, the place was open. When he walked in, Hollis Prantz came loping from the stockroom in the rear, wearing something somber and carrying a paintbrush.

"Just varnishing some display cabinets," he explained. "Getting ready for the big day tomorrow."

"Don't let me interrupt you," Qwilleran said, as he perused the shop in mystification. He saw tubes from fifteen-year-old television sets, early hand-wired circuits, prehistoric radio parts, and old-fashioned generator cutouts from 1935 automobiles. "Just tell me one thing," he said. "Do you expect to make a living from this stuff?"

"Nobody makes a living in this business," said Prantz. "We all need another source of income."

"Or extreme monastic tastes," Qwilleran added.

"I happen to have a little rental property, and I'm semi-retired. I had a heart attack last year, and I'm taking it easy."

"You're young to have a thing like that happen." Qwilleran guessed the dealer was in his early forties.

"You're lucky if you get a warning early in life. It's my theory that Cobb had a heart attack when he was tearing that building apart; that's heavy work for a man of his age."

"What kind of work did you do—before this?"

"I was in paint and wallpaper." The dealer said it almost apologetically. "Not much excitement in the paint business, but I get a real charge out of this new shop of mine."

"What gave you the idea for tech-tiques?"

"Wait till I get rid of this varnish brush." In a second Prantz was back with an old straight-back office chair. "Here. Have a seat."

Qwilleran studied the disassembled innards of a primitive typewriter. "You'll have to talk fast to convince me this junk is going to catch on."

The dealer smiled. "Well, I'll tell you. People will collect anything today, because there aren't enough good antiques to go around. They make lamps out of worm-eaten fence posts. They frame twenty-year-old burlesque posters. Why not preserve the fragments of the early automotive and electronics industry?" Prantz shifted to a confidential tone. "I've got a promotion I'm working on, based on a phenomenon of our times—the acceleration of obsolescence. My idea is to accelerate antiquity. The sooner an item goes out of style, the quicker it makes its comeback as a collector's piece. It used to be a hundred years before discards made the grade as collectibles. Now it's thirty. I intend to speed it up to twenty or even fifteen. . . . Don't write this up," the dealer added hastily. "It's still in the thinking stage. Protect me, like a good fellow."

Qwilleran shrank into his overcoat when he left Hollis Prantz. The dealer had changed a five for him—with dollar bills folded crosswise—but there was something about Prantz that did not ring true.

"Mr. Qwilleran! Mr. Qwilleran!"

Running footsteps came up behind him, and he turned to catch an armful of brown corduroy, opossum fur, notebooks, and flying blond hair.

Ivy, the youngest of the three sisters, was out of breath. "Just got off the bus," she panted. "Had a life class this morning. Are you on your way to our shop?"

"No, I'm heading for Mrs. McGuffey's."

"Don't go there! 'Mrs. McGuffey is too damn stuffy!' That's what Cluthra says."

"Business is business, Ivy. Are you all ready for Christmas?"

"Guess what! I'm getting an easel for Christmas! A real painter's easel."

"I'm glad I ran into you," Qwilleran said. "I'd like to decorate my apartment for the holidays, but I don't have your artistic touch. Besides, this tricky knee—"

"I'd love to help you. Do you want an old-fashioned Christmas tree or something swinging?"

"A tree would last about three minutes at my place. I have a couple of cats, and they're airborne most of the time. But I thought I could get some ropes of greens at Lombardo's—"

"I've got a staple gun at the shop. I can do it right now."

When Ivy arrived at Qwilleran's apartment, the cedar garlands—ten dollars' worth—were heaped in the middle of the floor, being circled warily by Koko and Yum Yum. The latter left for parts unknown at the sight of the blond visitor, but Koko sat tall and watched her carefully as if she were not to be trusted.

Qwilleran offered Ivy a Coke before she started decorating, and she sat in the rocking chair made of twigs, her straight blond hair falling like a cape over her shoulders. As she talked, her little-girl mouth pouted and pursed and broke into winning smiles.

Qwilleran asked, "Where did you three sisters get such unusual names?"

"Don't you know? They're different kinds of art glass. My mother was madly Art Nouveau. I'd rather be called Kim or Leslie. When I'm eighteen I'm going to change my name and move to Paris to study art. I mean, when I get the money my mother left me—if my sisters haven't used it all up," she added with a frown. "They're my legal guardians."

"You seem to have a lot of fun together in that shop."

Ivy hesitated. "Not really. They're kind of mean to me. Cluthra won't let me go steady . . . and Amberina is trying to suppress my talent. She wants me to study bookkeeping or nursing or something *grim* like that."

"Who's giving you the magnificent Christmas present?"

"What?"

"The easel."

"Oh! Well . . . I'm getting that from Tom. He's Amberina's husband. He's real neat. I think he's secretly in love with me, but don't *say* anything to anybody."

"Of course not. I'm flattered," said Qwilleran, "that you feel you can confide in me. What do you think about all the mishaps in Junktown? Are they as accidental as they appear?"

"Cluthra says the Dragon dropped that thing on her foot on purpose. Cluthra may decide to sue her for an enormous amount of money. *Five thousand dollars!*"

"An astronomical figure," Qwilleran agreed. "But what about the two recent deaths in Junktown?"

"Poor C.C.! He was a creep, but I felt sorry for him. His wife wasn't nice to him at all. Did you know she murdered her first husband? Of course, nobody could ever prove it."

"And Andy. Did you know Andy?"

"He was dreamy. I was mad about Andy. Wasn't that a horrible way to die?"

"Do you think he might have been murdered?"

Ivy's eyes grew wide with delight at the possibility. "Maybe the Dragon—"

"But Mary Duckworth was in love with Andy. She wouldn't do a thing like that."

The girl thought about it for a few seconds. "She couldn't be in love with him," she announced. "She's a witch! Cluthra says so! And everybody knows witches can't fall in love."

"I must say you have a colorful collection of characters in Junktown. What do you know about Russell Patch?"

"I used to like him before he bleached his hair. I kind of think he's mixed up in some kind of racket, like—I don't know . . ."

"Who's his roommate?"

"Stan's a hairdresser at Skyline Towers. You know all those rich widows and kept women that live there? They tell Stan all their secrets and give him fabulous presents. He does Cluthra's hair. She pretends it's natural, but you should see how *gray* it is when it starts to grow out."

"Sylvia Katzenhide lives in the same building, doesn't she?"

The girl nodded and reflected. "Cluthra says she'd be a brilliant success at blackmail. Sylvia's got something on everybody."

"Including Ben Nicholas and Hollis Prantz?"

"I don't know." Ivy sipped her Coke while she toyed with the possibilities. "But I think Ben's a dope addict. I haven't decided about the other one. He may be some kind of pervert."

Later, when the garlands were festooned on the fireplace wall and Ivy had departed with her staple gun, Qwilleran said to Koko: "Out of the mouths of babes come the damnedest fabrications!" Furthermore, the experiment had cost him ten dollars, and the decorations only served to enshrine the bad-dispositioned old lady hanging over the fireplace. He determined to substitute the Mackintosh coat of arms as soon as he could get some assistance in hoisting it to the mantel.

Before going downtown to hand in his copy, he made two phone calls and wangled some invitations. He told Cluthra he wanted to see how antique dealers live, what they collect, how they furnish their apartments. He told Russell Patch he had a Siamese cat who was crazy about music. And he told Ben he wanted to have the firsthand experience of scrounging. He also asked him to change a five-dollar bill.

"Alas," said Ben, "if we could change a fin, we would retire from this wretched business."

At the *Daily Fluxion* that afternoon Qwilleran walked into the Feature Department with its even rows of modern metal desks that had always looked so orderly and serene, and suddenly he found the scene cold, sterile, monotonous, and without character.

Arch Riker said, "Did you see how we handled the auction story in today's paper? The boss liked your copy."

"The whole back page! That was more than I expected," Qwilleran said, tossing some triple-spaced sheets on the desk. "Here's the second installment, and I'll have more tomorrow. This morning I interviewed a man who sells some absurd junk called tech-tiques."

"Rosie told me about him. He's new in Junktown."

"He's either out of his mind or pulling a hoax. In fact, I think Hollis Prantz is a fraud. He claims to have a weak heart, but you should have seen him running up stairs two at a time! I'm discovering all kinds of monkeyshines in Junktown."

"Don't get sidetracked," Riker advised him. "Bear down on the writing."

"But, Arch! I've unearthed some good clues in the Andy Glanz case! I also have my suspicions about Cobb's death."

"For Pete's sake, Qwill, the police called them accidents. Let's leave it that way."

"That's one reason I'm suspicious. Everyone in Junktown is busy explaining that the two deaths were accidents. They protest too much."

"I can understand their position," Riker told him. "If Junktown gets a reputation as a high-crime neighborhood, the junkers will stay away in droves. . . . Look here, I've got five pages to lay out. I can't argue with you all day."

"If there's been a crime committed, it should be exposed," Qwilleran persisted.

"All right," said Riker. "If you want to investigate, go ahead. But do it on your time and wait until after Christmas. The way your antique series is shaping up, you've got a good chance to win first prize."

By the time Qwilleran returned to Junktown, Ivy had spread the word that he was a private detective operating with two evil-eyed Siamese cats who were trained to attack.

"Is it true?" asked the young man in sideburns and dark glasses at the Junque Trunque.

"Is it true?" asked the woman who ran the shop called Nuthin' But Chairs.

"I wish it were," Qwilleran said. "I'm just a newspaperman, doing a job that isn't very glamorous."

She half closed her eyes. "I see you as a Yorkshire Windsor. Everyone resembles some kind of chair. That dainty little Sheraton is a ballet dancer. That English Chippendale looks just like my landlord. You're a Yorkshire Windsor. . . . Think about it for a while, and all your friends will turn into chairs."

After listening to this woman's conversation and Ivy's speculation and Hollis Prantz's dubious theories, Qwilleran was relieved to meet Mrs. McGuffey. She seemed to be a sensible sort.

He asked about the name of her shop, and she explained, "They're all wooden containers. The noggin has a handle like a cup. The piggin has a stave, and it's used as a dipper. The firkin is for storage."

"Where do you get your information?"

"From books. When I have no customers, I sit here and read. Nice work for a retired schoolteacher. If there's any book on American history or antiques that you'd like to borrow, just ask."

"Do you have anything on the history of Junktown? I'm especially curious about the Cobb mansion."

"Most important house on our street! Built by William Towne Spencer, the famous abolitionist, in 1855. He had two younger brothers, James and Philip, who built smaller replicas next door. Also a spinster sister, Mathilda, blind from birth and killed at the age of thirty-two when she fell down the stairs of her brother's house." She spoke with an authority that Qwilleran welcomed. He had had his fill of hearsay and addled theories.

"I've noticed that Junktown residents are prone to fall and kill themselves," he said. "Strange that it started way back when."

The dealer shook her head mournfully. "Poor Mrs. Cobb! I wonder if she'll be able to continue running the shop without her husband."

"He was the sparkplug of Junktown, they tell me."

"Probably true . . . but confidentially, I abhorred the man. He had no manners! You don't act that way in a civilized society. In my opinion the real loss to the community was Andrew Glanz. A fine young man, with great promise, and a real scholar! I say this with pride, because it was I who taught him to read—twenty-five years ago, up north in Boyerville. My, he was a smart boy! And a good speller. I knew he would turn out to be a writer." The lines in her face were radiant.

"He wrote features on antiques?"

"Yes, but he was also writing a novel, about which I have mixed emotions. He gave me the first ten chapters to read. I refrained from discouraging him, naturally, but . . . I'm afraid I do not approve of today's sordid fiction. And yet that is what sells, they say."

"What was the setting of Andy's novel?"

"The setting was authentic—a community of antique dealers similar to ours—but the story involved all sorts of unsavory characters: alcoholics, gamblers, homosexuals, prostitutes, dope peddlers, adulterers!" Mrs. McGuffey shuddered. "Oh, dear! If our street were anything like that book, I believe I would close up shop tomorrow!"

Qwilleran stroked his moustache. "You don't think there's anything like that going on in Junktown?"

"Oh, no! Nothing at all! Except . . ." She lowered her voice and glanced toward a customer who had wandered into the store. "I wouldn't want you to repeat this, but . . . they say that the little old man at the fruit stand is a bookkeeper."

"You mean a bookmaker? He takes bets?"

"That's what they *say*. Please don't put it in the paper. This is a respectable neighborhood."

The customer interrupted. "Excuse me. Do you have any butter molds?"

"Just one moment," the dealer said with a gracious smile, "and I'll be glad to help you."

"What happened to Andy's manuscript?" Qwilleran asked as he headed for the door.

"I believe he gave it to his friend, Miss Duckworth. She was begging to see it, *but*," Mrs. McGuffey concluded triumphantly, "he wanted his old schoolmarm to read it first."

CHAPTER 17

WITH SAVAGE GLEE the humidity decided to turn into a cold ugly rain. Qwilleran hurried to The Blue Dragon as fast as his knee would permit.

"I'm going to do some illegal scrounging tonight," he announced to Mary Duckworth. "Ben Nicholas is going to show me the ropes."

"Where is he taking you?"

"To an old theatre on Zwinger Street. He said it's boarded up, but he knows how to get through the stage door. All I want is the experience, so I can write a piece about the preservationists who risk arrest to salvage historical architectural fragments. I think the practice should be publicized with a view to having it sanctioned."

Mary beamed her admiration for him. "Qwill, you're talking like a confirmed junker! You've been converted!"

"I know a good story when I see one, that's all. Meanwhile, would you mind lending me the manuscript of Andy's novel? Mrs. McGuffey was telling me about it, and since it's all about Junktown—"

"Manuscript? I have no manuscript."

"Mrs. McGuffey said—"

"Andy allowed me to read the first chapter, that was all."

"What happened to it, then?"

"I have no idea. Robert Maus would know."

"Will you phone him?"

"Now?"

Qwilleran nodded impatiently.

She glanced at the tall-case clock. "This is an inconvenient time to call. He'll be preparing dinner. Is it really so urgent?"

Nevertheless, she dialed the number.

"William," she said, "may I speak with Mr. Maus? . . . Please tell him it's Mary Duxbury. . . . That's what I was afraid of. Just a moment." She turned to Qwilleran. "The houseboy says Bob is making hollandaise for the kohlrabi and can't be interrupted."

"Tell him the *Daily Fluxion* is about to print a vile rumor about one of his clients."

The attorney came to the telephone (Qwilleran could visualize him, wearing an apron, holding a dripping spoon) and said he knew nothing about a manuscript; nothing had turned up among the papers of the Andrew Glanz estate.

"Then where is it?" Qwilleran asked Mary. "Do you suppose it was destroyed—by someone who had reason to want it suppressed? What was in the chapter that you read?"

"It was about a woman who was plotting to poison her husband. It immediately captured one's interest."

"Why didn't Andy let you read more?"

"He was quite secretive about his novel. Don't you think most writers are sensitive about their work before it's published?"

"Perhaps all the characters were drawn from life. Mrs. McGuffey seemed to think they were wildly imaginary, but I doubt whether she's in a position to know. She's lived a sheltered life. Perhaps Andy's story exposed a few Junktown secrets that would prove embarrassing—or incriminating."

"He wouldn't have done anything like that! Andy was so considerate—"

Qwilleran clenched his teeth. So considerate, so honest, so clever, so intelligent. He knew it by heart. "Perhaps you were in the story, too," he told Mary. "Perhaps that's why Andy wouldn't let you read farther. You may have been so transparently disguised that your position would be revealed and your family would crack down on you."

Mary's eyes flashed. "No! Andy would never have been so unkind."

"Well, we'll never know now!" Qwilleran started to leave and then turned back. "You know this Hollis Prantz. He says he used to be in the paint and wallpaper business and he retired because of a weak heart, and yet he's as agile as a fox. He was varnishing display cases when I was there today—"

"Varnishing?" Mary asked.

"He said he was getting ready for the Block Party tomorrow, and yet he has very little merchandise to offer."

"Varnishing on a day like this? It will never dry! If you varnish in damp weather, it remains sticky forever."

"Are you sure?"

"It's a fact. You may think it's dry, but whenever the humidity is high, the surface becomes tacky again."

Qwilleran huffed into his moustache. "Strange mistake to make, isn't it?"

"For someone who claims he's been in the paint business," Mary said, "it's an incredible mistake!"

Later, the rain turned to a treacherous wet snow as fine as fog, and Qwilleran went to a cheap clothing store in the neighborhood to buy a red hunting cap with earflaps. He also borrowed the Cobb flashlight and crowbar in preparation for his scrounging debut.

But first he had an invitation to drop in on Russell Patch at the cocktail hour to hear the twenty thousand dollar sound system. He went home and trussed Koko in the blue harness. The leash had unaccountably disappeared, but it was not necessary for a social call. The harness alone made Koko look trim and professional, and it afforded a good grip while Qwilleran was carrying the cat down the street.

"This trip," he explained to his purring accomplice, "is not purely in the pursuit of culture. I want you to nose around and see if you can turn up anything significant."

The carriage house was two doors away, and Qwilleran tucked Koko inside his overcoat to keep him dry. They entered through the refinishing shop, and their host led them up a narrow staircase to a dazzling apartment. The floor was a checkerboard of large black and white tiles, and a dozen white marble statues on white pedestals were silhouetted against the walls, some of which were painted dull black, some shiny red.

Russell introduced his roommate, a sallow young man who was either shy or furtive and who wore on his finger a diamond of spectacular brilliance, and Qwilleran introduced Koko, who was now riding on his shoulder. Koko regarded the two strangers briefly and dismissed them at once by turning and staring in the opposite direction.

The music that filled the room was the busy kind of fiddling and tootling that made Qwilleran nervous. It came at him from all directions.

"Do you like baroque music?" Russ asked. "Or would you prefer another type?"

"Koko prefers something more soothing," Qwilleran replied.

"Stan, put on that Schubert sonata."

The sound system occupied a bank of old kitchen cabinets transformed into an Italian Renaissance breakfront, and Koko immediately checked it out.

"Stan, make us a drink," Russell ordered. "Say, that cat isn't vicious at all. I heard he was a wild one!"

"If you also heard that I'm a private eye, it's a lie," said Qwilleran.

"Glad of that. I'd hate to see anyone loafing around Junktown digging up dirt. We've worked hard to build a good image here."

"I dug up an interesting fact, however. I learned your friend Andy was writing a novel about Junktown."

"Oh, sure," said Russ. "I told him he was wasting his time. Unless you dish out a lot of sex, who buys novels?"

"Maybe he did just that. Had you read the manuscript?"

Russ laughed. "No, but I can guess what it was like. Andy was a prune, a real prune."

"The funny thing is that the manuscript has disappeared."

"He probably scrapped it. I told you how he was—a perfectionist."

Qwilleran accepted the ginger ale he had requested and said to Stan, "Are you in the antique business?"

"I'm a hairdresser," Stan said quietly.

"A lucrative field, I hear."

"I do all right."

Russ volunteered, "If you want to know what really keeps him in Jaguars and diamonds, he plays the stock market."

"Are you interested in the market?" Stan asked the newsman.

"To tell the truth, I've never had anything to invest, so I've never made a study of it."

"You don't have to know much," Stan said. "You can go in for no-load mutuals or do like me. I have a discretionary account, and my broker doubles my money every year."

"You mean that?" Qwilleran lighted his pipe thoughtfully. He was making a computation. If he won one of the *Fluxion*'s top prizes, he could run it up to . . . two, four, eight, sixteen, thirty-two thousand in five years. Perhaps, after all, he was wasting his time trying to make murders out of molehills.

As for Koko, he had checked the place out and was now lounging near a heat register, ignoring the Schubert.

"Say, I'd like to try something," Russ said. "I've got some electronic music that hits the high frequencies—white noise, computer music, synthesized sound, and all that. Let's see if the cat reacts. Animals can hear things beyond the human range."

"Okay with me," Qwilleran said.

The Schubert came to an end, and then the thirty-six speakers gave out a concert of whines and whinnies, blats and beeps, flutterings and tweeterings that baffled the eardrums. At the first squawk Koko pricked up his ears, and in a moment he was on his feet. He looked bewildered. He ran across the room, changed course and dashed back erratically.

"He doesn't like it," Qwilleran protested.

The music slid into a series of hollow whispers and echoes, with pulsing vibrations. Koko raced across the room and threw himself against the wall.

"You'd better turn it off!"

"This is great!" Russ said. "Stan, did you ever see anything like this?"

From the speakers came an unearthly screech. Koko rose in the air, faster than the eye could register, and landed on top of the stereo cabinets.

"Turn it off!" Qwilleran shouted above the din.

It was too late. Koko had swooped down again, landing on Russ Patch's head, digging in with his claws, until the bellow that came from the man's throat sent him flying through space.

Russ touched his hand to his temple and found blood.

"Serves your right," said Stan quietly, as he flipped the switch on the stereo.

Moments later, when Qwilleran took Koko home, the cat was outwardly calm, but the man could feel him trembling.

"Sorry, old boy," he said. "That was a dirty trick."

He carried Koko back to his apartment and set him gently on the floor. Yum Yum came running to touch noses, but Koko ignored her. He had a long drink of water, then stood on his hind legs and clawed Qwilleran's trousers. The man picked him up and walked the floor with him until it was time to leave for his next appointment.

Locking the cats in the apartment, he started for the stairway, but the long forlorn howl behind the closed door tore at his heart. As he went slowly down the stairs, the cries became louder and more piteous, and all Qwilleran's regrets about Koko's self-sufficiency vanished. The cat needed him. Inwardly elated, Qwilleran returned and gathered up his eager friend and took him to call on Cluthra.

CHAPTER 18

WITH ENTICING interrogatives in her voice Cluthra had invited Qwilleran to come later (?) in the evening (?) when they could both relax (?). But he had pleaded another engagement and had played dumb to her innuendoes.

Now at the discreet hour of seven thirty he and Koko took a taxi to Skyline Towers and a swift elevator to the seventeenth floor. Koko did not object to elevators that ascended—only the kind that sank beneath him.

Cluthra met them in a swirling cloud of pale green chiffon and ostrich feathers. "I didn't know you were bringing a friend," she said with her husky laugh.

"Koko has had a bad experience this evening, and he didn't want me to leave him." Qwilleran told her about Russell's cruel experiment with electronic music.

"Beware of young men dressed in white!" she said. "They've got something they're hiding."

She ushered him into the cozy living room, which was done entirely in matching paisley—paisley fabric on the walls, paisley draperies, paisley slipcovers—all in warm tones of beige, brown and gold. The fabric gave the room the stifling hush of a closed coffin. Music was playing softly—something passionate, with violins. Cluthra's perfume was overpowering.

Qwilleran looked around him at the polliwogs that characterized the paisley pattern and tried to estimate their number. Ten thousand? A hundred thousand? Half a million?

"Will you have a drinkie?" Cluthra extended the invitation with a conspiratorial gleam in her green eyes.

"Just a club soda. No liquor. Heavy on the ice."

"Honey, I can do better than that for my favorite newspaper reporter," she said, and when the drink came, it was pink, sparkling, and heavily aromatic.

Qwilleran sniffed it and frowned.

"Homemade chokecherry syrup," she explained. "Men like it because it's bitter."

He took a cautious sip. The taste was not bad. Pleasant, in fact. "Did you make it?"

"Lordy, no! One of my kooky customers. She's made a study of medicinal weeds, and she does this stuff with juniper, lovage, mullein, and I don't know what else. Mullein puts hair on your chest, lover," Cluthra added with a wink.

Qwilleran had taken a seat in a stiff pull-up chair, with Koko huddled on his lap.

"You've picked the only backbreaking chair in the place," she protested. She herself was now seductively arranged on the paisley sofa surrounded by paisley pillows, carefully concealing her walking cast with the folds of her chiffon gown. Yards of ostrich fluff framed her shoulders, cascaded down her hilly slopes and circled the hem.

She patted the sofa cushions. "Why don't you sit over here and be comfy?"

"With this cranky knee I'm better off on a straight chair," Qwilleran said, and it was more or less true.

Cluthra regarded him with fond accusation. "You've been kidding us," she said. "You're not really a newspaper reporter. But we like you just the same."

"If your kid sister has been spreading stories, forget it," he said. "I'm just an underpaid, overworked feature writer for the *Fluxion*, with a private curiosity about sudden deaths. Ivy has a wild imagination."

"It's just a phase she's going through."

"By the way, did you know Andy was writing a novel about Junktown?"

"When Andy came over here," she said, relishing the memory, "we did very little talking about literature."

"Do you know Hollis Prantz very well?"

Cluthra rolled her eyes. "Preserve me from men who wear gray button-front sweaters!"

Qwilleran gulped his iced drink. The apartment was warm, and Koko was like a fur lap robe. But as they talked, the cat relaxed and eventually slid to the floor, much to the man's relief. Soon Koko disappeared against the protective coloration of the beige and brown paisley. Qwilleran mopped his brow. He was beginning to suffocate. The temperature seemed to be in the nineties, and the polliwogs dazzled his eyes. He could look down at the plain beige carpet and see polliwogs; he could look up at the white ceiling and see polliwogs. He closed his eyes.

"Do you feel all right, honey?"

"Yes, I feel fine. My eyes are tired, that's all. And it's a trifle warm in here."

"Would you like to lie down? You look kind of groggy. Come and lie down on the sofa."

Qwilleran contemplated the inviting picture before him—the deep-cushioned sofa, the soft pillows. He also caught a glimpse of movement behind Cluthra's halo of red hair. Koko had risen silently and almost invisibly to the back of the sofa.

"Take off your coat and lie down and make yourself comfy," his hostess was urging. "You don't have to mind your manners with Cousin Cluthra." She gave his moustache and shoulders an appreciative appraisal and batted her lashes.

Qwilleran wished he had not come. He liked women who were more subtle. He hated paisley. His eyes had been bothering him lately (maybe he needed glasses) and the allover pattern was making him dizzy. Or was it the drink? He wondered about that cherry syrup. Juniper, mullein, *lovage*. What the devil was lovage?

Then without warning Cluthra sneezed. "Oh! Excuse me!"

Qwilleran took the opportunity to change the subject. "They'll be burying old C.C. tomorrow," he said with an attempt at animation, although he had an overwhelming desire to close his eyes.

"He was a real man," Cluthra said with narrowed eyes. "You don't find many of them any more, believe me!" She sneezed again. "Excuse me! I don't know what's the matter with me."

Qwilleran could guess. Koko had his nose buried in her ostrich feathers. "Iris is taking it very hard," he said.

Cluthra pulled a chiffon handkerchief from some hidden place and touched her eyes, which were reddening and beginning to stream. "Iris wod't have ady bore ghostly problebs with her glasses," she said. "C.C. used to get up id the dight to play tricks with theb."

"That's what I call devotion," Qwilleran said. "Look here! Are you by any chance allergic to cat hair?"

The visit ended abruptly, and it was with a great sense of escape that Qwilleran got out in the cold air and shook the polliwogs from his vision.

Cluthra called after him. "You bust visit be without your buddy dext tibe."

He took Koko home and got into his scrounging clothes for his next appointment. But first he looked up a word in the dictionary. "Lovage—a domestic remedy." For what ailment or deficiency, the book did not say. Qwilleran also opened a can of shrimp and gave Koko a treat, and he spent a certain amount of time thinking about Cluthra's voice. Whiskey voice, they used to call it.

At the appointed hour he found Ben waiting at the curb in a gray station wagon that was a masterpiece of rust, with a wire coat hanger serving as a radio antenna and with the curbside headlight, anchored by a single screw, staring glumly at the gutter. The driver was bundled up in a mackinaw, early aviator's helmet, and long striped muffler.

The motor coughed a few times, the car shuddered and lurched away from the curb, sucking up blasts of icy cold and dampness through a gaping hole under the dashboard. Fortunately it was a short drive to the Garrick Theatre in the demolition area. It stood proudly among other abandoned buildings, looking like a relic of fifteenth century Venice.

"Alas, poor Garrick! We knew it well," said Ben morosely. "The great and glorious names of the theatre once played here. Then . . . vaudeville. Then silent pictures. Then talkies. Then double features. Then Italian films. Then horror movies. Then nothing. And now—only Benjamin X. Nicholas, playing to a ghostly audience and applauded by pigeons."

Qwilleran carried the crowbar. They both carried flashlights, and Ben directed the newsman in wrenching the boarding from the stage door. The boards came away easily, as if accustomed to cooperating, and the two men entered the dark, silent, empty building.

Ben led the way down a narrow hall, past the doorkeeper's cubicle, past the skeleton of an iron staircase, and onto the stage. The auditorium was a hollow shell, dangling with dead wires, coated with dust, and raw in patches where decorations had been pried from the sidewalls and the two tiers of boxes. Qwilleran beamed his light at the ceiling; all that remained of the Garrick's grandeur were the frescoes in the dome—floating images of Romeo and Juliet, Antony and Cleopatra. If there was nothing left to scrounge, why had Ben brought him here? Soon Qwilleran guessed the answer. The old actor had taken center stage, and an eerie performance began.

"Friends, Romans, countrymen—" Ben declaimed in passionate tones.

"*Friends, Romans*—" came a distant reverberating voice.

"Lend me your ears!" said Ben.

"*Countrymen—friends, Romans—lend me—countrymen—ears—lend me*," whispered the ghosts of old actors.

"Alas," said Ben when he had spoken the speech and Qwilleran had applauded with gloved thumps and a bravo or two. "Alas, we were born too late. . . . But let us to work! What does our heart desire? A bit of carving? A crumb of marble! Not much choice; the wretches have raped the place. But here!" He kicked a heating grille. "A bronze bauble for your pleasure!"

The moldings crumbled, and the newsman easily pried the blackened grillwork loose. The dust rose. Both men coughed and choked. There was a whirring of wings in the darkness overhead, and Qwilleran thought of bats.

"Let's get out of here," he said.

"But stay! One more treasure!" said Ben, flashing his light around the tiers of boxes. All but one of them had been denuded of embellishment. The first box on the left still bore its sculptured crest supported by cherubs blowing trumpets and wearing garlands of flowers. "It would bring a pretty penny."

"How much?"

"A hundred dollars from any dealer. Two hundred from a smart collector. Three hundred from some bloody fool."

"How would we get it off?"

"Others have succeeded. Let us be bold!"

Ben led the way to the mezzanine level and into the box.

"You hold both lights," Qwilleran told him, "and I'll see what I can do with the crowbar."

The newsman leaned over the railing and pried at the carving. The floor of the box creaked.

"Lay on, Macduff!" cried Ben.

"Shine the light over the railing," Qwilleran instructed. "I'm working in shadow." Then he paused with crowbar in midair. He had seen something in the dust on the floor. He turned to look at Ben and was blinded by two flashlights. A shudder in his moustache made him plunge to the rear of the box. There was a wrenching of timbers and a crash and a cloud of choking dust rising from the floor below. Two beams of light danced crazily on the walls and ceiling.

"What the hell happened?" gasped Qwilleran. "The railing let loose!"

The railing was gone, and the sagging floor of the box sloped off into blackness.

"The saints were with us!" cried Ben, choked with emotion or dust.

"Give me a light and let's get out of here," said the newsman.

They drove back to Junktown with the brass grille in the back seat, Qwilleran silent as he recalled his narrow escape and what he had seen in the dust.

"Our performance lacked fire this evening," Ben apologized. An icicle glistened on the tip of his nose. "We were frozen to the bone. But come to the pub and witness a performance that will gladden your heart. Come join us in a brandy."

The Lion's Tail had been a neighborhood bank in the 1920s—a miniature Roman temple, now desecrated by a neon sign and panels of glass blocks in the arched windows. Inside, it was lofty, undecorated, smoke-filled, and noisy. An assortment of patrons stood at the bar and filled half the tables—men in work clothes, and raggle-taggle members of Junktown's after-dark set.

As Ben made his entrance, he was greeted by cheering, stamping feet, and pounding of tables. He acknowledged the acclaim graciously and held up his hand for silence.

"Tonight," he said, "a brief scene from *King Richard III*, and then drinks for the entire house!"

With magnificent poise he moved through the crowd, his muffler hanging down to his heels, and disappeared. A moment later he emerged on a small balcony.

"Now is the winter of our discontent. . ." he began.

The man had a ringing delivery, and the audience was quiet if not wholly attentive.

"He capers nimbly in a lady's chamber," came the voice from the balcony, and there was riotous laughter down below.

Ben concluded with a melodramatic leer: "I am determined to prove a villain and hate the idle pleasures of these days!"

The applause was deafening, the actor bowed humbly, and the bartender went to work filling glasses.

When Ben came down from the balcony, he threw a wad of folded bills on the bar—bills folded lengthwise. "King Richard or Charley's aunt, what matter?" he said to Qwilleran with a gloomy countenance. "The day of the true artist is gone forever. The baggy-pants comic is an 'artist.' So is the bullfighter, tightrope walker and long-haired guitar player. Next it will be baseball players and bricklayers! Sir, the time is out of joint."

The thirsty audience soon demanded an encore.

"Pardon us," Ben said to Qwilleran. "We must oblige," and he moved once more toward the balcony.

The newsman quietly left The Lion's Tail, wondering where Ben acquired the cash to buy the applause that he craved—and whether he had known that the box at the Garrick was a booby trap.

Qwilleran went home. He found the cats asleep on their cushions, which bent their whiskers into half-smiles, and he retired to his own bed, his mind swimming with questions. What was Ben's racket? Was the actor as nutty as he appeared? Was his sudden affluence connected with the Ellsworth house? Ben had been there, Qwilleran was sure. He had seen the evidence in the dust—feathery arabesques made by the tassels of his muffler. Still, Ben's reception at The Lion's Tail indicated that his audience was accustomed to his largess.

The newsman remembered something Cobb had said. "The nearest Ben ever got to Broadway was Macy's toy department." Then a few minutes later Cobb had contradicted himself. "Ben's got a bundle. He used to make big money." And at this remark Iris had glanced at her husband in surprise.

Did Ben have a shady sideline that supplied him with the money to bribe his audience into attention and applause? Did Cobb know about it? Qwilleran's answers were only guesses, as unprovable as they were improbable, and the questions kept him awake.

Deliberately he turned his mind to a more agreeable subject: Christmas Eve at the Press Club. He could picture the society writers—and Jack Jaunti—doing a double take when he walked in with Mary, and he could see the newshounds being outwardly casual but secretly impressed by the magic name of Duxbury. Qwilleran realized he ought to cap the evening with a Christmas gift for Mary, but what could he buy for the daughter of a millionaire?

Before he fell asleep, the answer spread over his consciousness like a warm blanket. It was a brilliant idea—so brilliant that he sat up in bed. And if the *Daily Fluxion* would cooperate, it would save Junktown.

Qwilleran made a mental note to call the managing editor the first thing in the morning, and then he slept, the pillow turning up one end of his moustache in a half-smile.

CHAPTER 19

WAKING ON WEDNESDAY morning, Qwilleran was vaguely aware of a lump in his armpit. It was Yum Yum, hiding under the blankets in the safest spot she could find. But while she had run for cover, Koko was investigating the shattering noise that alarmed her. With his hind feet on a chair and his forepaws on the window sill, he was watching the pellets of ice that bounced off the panes of glass.

"Hailstorm!" Qwilleran groaned. "That's all we need to ruin the Block Party!"

Koko left the window and routed Yum Yum out of bed.

The hail sheathed the city in ice, but by eleven o'clock that morning, the weather developed a conscience and the sun broke through. Junktown sparkled like a jewel. Buildings became crystal palaces. Utility wires, street signs, and traffic lights wore a glistening fringe of icicles, and even the trash cans were beautiful. It was the only decent gesture the weather had made all winter.

By noon the junkers were flocking into Zwinger Street. Angels flew from the lampposts, carolers were caroling, and Ben Nicholas in white beard and Santa Claus pantaloons held audience on the stoop in front of his shop. Tiny Spooner was there, taking pictures, and even the *Morning Rampage* had sent a photographer.

Qwilleran mixed with the crowd and eavesdropped in the shops, until it was time to return to the Junkery to take his turn at tending the shop. He found Cluthra on duty.

"This chair is *very* old," she was telling a customer. "It has the original milk paint. You'd better grab it. At twenty-seven fifty Mrs. Cobb isn't making a penny on it, I can guarantee. Why, on Cape Cod, you'd have to pay sixty-five dollars!"

The customer capitulated, wrote a check, and left the shop in high glee, carrying a potty chair with sawed-off legs.

Cluthra turned the cashbox over to Qwilleran and explained the price tags. "Do you understand the code, hon?" she asked. "You read the numbers backwards to get the asking price, and then you can go up or down a few dollars, depending on the customer. Be careful of that banister-back chair; it has a loose leg. And don't forget, you're entitled to strangle every third customer who tells you about her grandmother."

The traffic in and out of the shop was heavy, but the buyers were less plentiful than the lookers and askers. Qwilleran decided to keep a log for Mrs. Cobb's benefit:

—Sold two blue glass things out of window, $18.50.

—Woman asked for Sheffield candlesticks.

—Man asked for horse brasses.

—Sold spool chest, $30.

—Kissed female customer and sold tin knife box, $35.

The customer in question had rushed at Qwilleran with a gay little shriek. "Qwill! What are you doing here?"

"Rosie Riker! How are you? You're looking great!" Actually she was looking matronly and somewhat ludicrous in her antiquing clothes.

"How've you been, Qwill? I keep telling Arch to bring you home to dinner. Mind if I sit down? I've been walking around for three hours."

"Not in the banister-back, Rosie. The leg's loose."

"I wish they'd turn those carol singers off for five minutes. How've you been, Qwill? What are you doing here?"

"Keeping shop while Mrs. Cobb's at her husband's funeral."

"You're looking fine. I'm glad you've still got that romantic moustache! Do you ever hear from Miriam?"

"Not directly, but my ex-mother-in-law puts the bite on me once in a while. Miriam's in that Connecticut sanitarium again."

"Don't let those vultures take advantage of you, Qwill. They're plenty well off."

"Well, how've you been, Rosie? Are you buying anything?"

"I'm looking for a Christmas present for Arch. How are your cats?"

"They're great! Koko's getting smarter all the time. He opens doors, turns lights on and off, and he's learning to type."

"You're kidding."

"He rubs his jaw against the levers and flips the carriage or resets margins—not always at the most opportune time."

"He's cleaning his teeth," Rosie explained. "Our vet says that's how cats try to clean their teeth. You should take Koko to the dentist. Our gray tabby just had a dental prophylaxis. . . . Say, have you got any tin? I want to buy something for Arch."

She found a tin knife box, and Qwilleran—torn between two loyalties—guiltily knocked two dollars off Mrs. Cobb's asking price.

Rosie said, "I thought your story on the auction was great!"

"The story behind the story is better."

"What's that? Arch didn't tell me. He never tells me anything."

Qwilleran reconstructed the night of Andy's accident. "I can't believe," he said, "that Andy simply missed his footing and fell. He'd have to have been an acrobat to land on the finial the way he did. There were customers coming to look at a chandelier that night. If he was in the process of getting it down off the ceiling, it would mean they had already okayed it; in other words, they were there when he fell! . . . It doesn't click. I don't think they ever got in the store. I think the whole accident was staged, and Andy was dead when the customers arrived."

As he talked, Rosie's eyes had been growing wider and wider. "Qwill, I think Arch and I . . . I think we might have been the customers! When did it happen?"

"Middle of October. The sixteenth, to be exact."

"We wanted to get this chandelier installed before our Halloween party, but I didn't want to buy it without Arch seeing it. He came home to dinner, and then we drove back to Junktown. Andy was going to open up especially for us. But when we got there, the store was locked up, and no one was in sight. In the meantime I noticed a chandelier in the Cobbs' window that looked good, so we bought that one instead."

"Were the Cobbs open at that late hour?"

"No, but we saw someone going up the steps and asked him if the Cobbs would mind coming down to show us the fixture. He went upstairs and got Mrs. Cobb, and we bought it. It was a couple of weeks later that one of my junking friends told me about Andy's accident, and I never connected—"

"Who was the man who was going up the Cobbs' front steps?"

"He's a dealer himself. He has the Bit o' Junk shop. It really worked out better for us, because the fixture we bought from Mrs. Cobb was painted tin, and I realized afterwards that Andy's brass chandelier would have been too formal for our dining room."

"Did you say brass?"

"Yes. Sort of Williamsburg."

"Not glass? Not a chandelier with five crystal arms?"

"Oh, no! Crystal would be much too dressy for our house."

That was when Qwilleran kissed Rosie Riker.

Later in the afternoon he made a few additional entries in the log:

—Sold turkey platter, $75.

—Customer broke goblet. Collected $4.50. Showed no mercy.

—Sold apple peeler to make into a lamp, $12.

—Sold bronze grille from Garrick Theatre, $45.

—Photographer sat in banister-back chair. *Fluxion* will pay for damage.

—SOLD ROLL-TOP DESK, $750!

The woman who came bursting into the shop, asking for a roll-top desk, was not an experienced junker. Qwilleran could tell that by her enthusiasm and her smart clothes.

"The man next door told me you have a roll-up desk," she announced breathlessly, "and I must have one before Christmas."

"The one we have is in use," said Qwilleran, "and the user would be extremely reluctant to part with it."

"I don't care what it costs," she said. "I've got to have it for my husband's Christmas gift. I'll write you a check, and my driver will pick it up in the morning."

Qwilleran felt pleased with himself that evening. He had personally taken in almost $1,000 for Mrs. Cobb. He had gleaned information from Rosie Riker that reinforced his theory about the finial incident. And he had broached an idea to the managing editor of the *Daily Fluxion* that had made a big impression; if it proved to be workable—and the boss felt that it might—it would solve a lot of problems for a lot of people.

After dinner Qwilleran was removing his belongings from the pigeonholes of the roll-top desk when he heard a heavy tread coming up the stairs. He opened his door and hailed his neighbor. Ben was still wearing his Santa Claus disguise.

"Ben, what's a roll-top desk worth?" Qwilleran asked. "There's no price tag on the one I'm using, and I sold it for seven hundred and fifty, chair included."

"Oh, excellent swindle!" said the dealer. "Sir, you should be in the business." He trudged toward his apartment, then turned around and resolutely trudged back. "Will you join me in a drop of brandy and a crumb of rare cheese?"

"I'll go for some of that cheese," Qwilleran said. He had just finished an unsatisfactory dinner of canned stew.

His host moved a copper wash boiler from the seat of a Victorian sofa, leaving an oval silhouette in the dust on the black horsehair, and the news-man sat on the clean spot and surveyed the appointments of the room: a bust of Hiawatha, a wooden plane propellor, empty picture frames, a wicker baby carriage, a leather pail labeled FIRE, a wooden washboard, a wigless doll.

Ben brought Qwilleran some cheese and crackers on a plate decorated with an advertisement for an 1870 patent medicine that relieved itching. Then he lowered himself with a groan into a creaking chair of mildewed wicker. "We are faint," he said. "Our gashes cry for help." He drank fastidiously from a cracked teacup.

Ben had removed his white beard, and now he looked absurd with rouged nose and cheeks, pale jowls, and powdered artificial eyebrows.

Qwilleran said, "I've been in Junktown a week now, and frankly I don't know how you dealers make a living."

"We muddle through. We muddle through."

"Where do you acquire your goods? Where does it all come from?"

Ben waved a hand at the sculptured head of an angel, minus nose. "Behold! A repulsive little gem from the façade of the Garrick Theatre. Genuine stone, with the original bird droppings." He waved toward a discolored washbowl and pitcher. "A treasure from Mount Vernon, with the original soap scum."

For half an hour Qwilleran plied his host with questions, receiving flowery answers with no information whatever. At last he prepared to leave, and as he glanced at a few stray cracker crumbs on the seat of the black horsehair sofa, he saw something else that alerted him—a stiff blond hair. He casually picked it up.

Back in his own apartment he examined the hair under a lamp. There was no doubt what it was—three inches long, slightly curved, tapering at one end.

He went to the telephone and dialed a number.

"Mary," he said, "I've made a discovery. Do you want to see something interesting? Put on your coat and run over here."

Then he turned to the cats, who were lounging contentedly on their gilded chairs.

"Okay, you guys!" he said. "What do you know about this?"

Koko scratched his left ear with his hind foot, and Yum Yum licked her right shoulder.

CHAPTER 20

QWILLERAN HEARD Ben Nicholas leave his house, and shortly afterward the downstairs buzzer sounded, and Mary Duckworth arrived with a fur parka thrown over a skyblue corduroy jumpsuit.

She examined the stiff blond hair.

"Know what it is?" Qwilleran asked.

"A bristle. From some kind of brush."

"It's a whisker," he corrected her, "from some kind of cat. I found it on Ben's living room sofa. Either my two rascals have found a way to get into the apartment next door, or the spirit of Mathilda Spencer is getting pretty cheeky."

Mary examined the cat whisker. "It's mottled—white and gray."

"It obviously belongs to Yum Yum. Koko's are pure white."

"Have you any idea how they could get through the wall?"

Qwilleran beckoned her to follow as he led the way to the dressing room. "I've checked out the bathroom. The wall is solid tile. The only other possibility is in here—behind these bookshelves."

Koko followed them into the dressing room and rubbed his jaw ardently against the books on the lower shelf.

"Beautiful bindings!" Mary said. "Mrs. Cobb could sell these to decorators for several dollars apiece."

There was a yowl from Koko, but it was a muffled yowl, and Qwilleran looked down in time to see a tail tip disappearing between two volumes—in precisely the spot where he had removed the bound copies of *The Liberator*.

"Koko, come out!" he ordered. "It's dusty back there."

"Yow!" came the faint reply.

Mary said, "He sounds as if he's down a deep well."

The man attacked the bookshelf with both hands, pulling out volumes and tossing them on the floor. "Bring the flashlight, Mary. It's on the desk."

He flashed the light toward the back wall, and its beam picked up an expanse of paneling similar to the fireplace wall in the living room—narrow planks with beveled edges.

"Solid," said Qwilleran. "Let's clear more shelves . . . Ouch!"

"Careful! Don't twist your knee, Qwill. Let me do it."

Mary got down on her hands and knees and peered under a low shelf. "Qwill, there's an opening in the wall, sure enough."

"How big?"

"It looks as if a single board is missing."

"Can you see what's beyond? Take the flashlight."

"There's another wall—about two feet back. It makes a narrow compartment."

"Mary, do you think . . . ?"

"Qwill, could this be . . . ?"

The idea occurred to them both, simultaneously.

"An Underground Railway station," Qwilleran said.

"Exactly!" she said. "William Towne Spencer built this house."

"Many abolitionists—"

"Built secret rooms—yes!"

"To hide runaway slaves."

Mary ducked her head under the shelf again. "It slides!" she called over her shoulder. "The whole panel is a sliding door. There's a robe in here." She pulled out twelve feet of white cord. "And a toothbrush!"

"Yow!" said Koko, making a sudden appearance in the beam of the flashlight. He stepped out from his hideaway and staggered a little as he gave a delicate shudder.

"Close the panel," Qwilleran directed. "Can you close it?"

"All but half an inch. It seems to be warped."

"I'll bet Koko opened the panel with his claws, and Yum Yum followed him through. She's the one who did the fetching and carrying. . . . Well, that solves one mystery. How about a cup of coffee?"

"Thanks, no. I must go home. I'm wrapping Christmas presents." Mary stopped short. "You've been emptying your desk! Are you moving out?"

"Only the desk is moving. I sold it this afternoon for seven hundred and fifty dollars."

"Qwill, you didn't! It's worth two hundred dollars at most."

He showed her the log of his afternoon session in The Junkery. "Not bad for a greenhorn, is it?"

"Who is this woman who wanted Sheffield candlesticks?" Mary asked, as she scanned the report. "You should have sent her to me. . . . And who was asking for horse brasses? No one buys horse brasses any more."

"What are they?"

"Brass medallions for decorating harnesses. The English used to use them as good luck tokens. . . . . Who's the customer who got kissed? That's a devious way to sell a tin knife box."

"She's the wife of our feature editor," Qwilleran said. "By the way, I've brought a present for Arch Riker—just a joke. Would you gift-wrap it for me?" He handed Mary the rusty tobacco tin.

"I hope," she said, reading the price tag inside the cover, "that the Weird Sisters didn't charge you ten dollars for this."

"Ten dollars?" Qwilleran felt an uncomfortable sensation on his upper lip. "They were asking ten, but they gave it to me for five."

"That's not bad. Most shops get seven-fifty."

Gulping his chagrin, Qwilleran escorted her down the stairs, and as they passed Ben's open door he asked, "Does the Bit o' Junk do a good business?"

"Not particularly," she replied. "Ben is too lazy to go out looking for things, so his turnover is slow."

"He took me to The Lion's Tail last night, and he was throwing money around as if he had his own printing press."

Mary shrugged. "He must have had a windfall. Once a year a dealer can count on a windfall—like selling a roll-top desk for seven hundred and fifty dollars. That's one of the great truths of the antique business."

"By the way," Qwilleran said, "we went scrounging at the Garrick last night, but all that was left was a crest on one of the boxes, and I almost broke my neck trying to get it."

"Ben should have warned you. That box has been unsafe for years."

"How do you know?"

"The city engineers condemned it in the 1940s and ordered it padlocked. It's called the Ghost Box."

"Do you think Ben knew about it?"

"Everybody knows about it," Mary said. "That's why the crest was never taken. Even Russ Patch refused to risk it, and he's a daredevil."

After Qwilleran had watched her return to her own house, he climbed the stairs pensively. At the top of the flight the cats were waiting for him in identical poses, sitting tall with brown tails arranged in matching curves. One inch of tail tip lifted inquiringly.

"You scoundrels!" Qwilleran said. "I suppose you've been having a whale of a time, coming and going through the walls like a couple of apparitions."

Koko stropped his jaw on the newel post, his tiny ivory tusks clicking against the ancient mahogany.

"Want to go and have your teeth cleaned?" the man asked him. "After Christmas I'll take you to a cat dentist."

Koko rubbed the back of his head on the newel post—an ingratiating gesture.

"Don't pretend innocence. You don't fool me for a minute." Qwilleran roughed up the sleek fur along the cat's fluid backbone. "What else have you been doing behind my back? What are you planning to do next?"

That was Wednesday night. Thursday morning Qwilleran got his answer.

Just before daylight he turned in his bed and found his nose buried in fur. Yum Yum was sharing his pillow. Her fur smelled clean. Qwilleran's mind went back forty-odd years to a sunny backyard with laundry flapping on the clothesline. The clean wash smelled like sunshine and fresh air, and that was the fragrance of this small animal's coat.

From the kitchen came a familiar sound: "Yawwck!" It was Koko's good-morning yowl combined with a wake-up yawn, and it was followed by two thumps as the cat jumped down from refrigerator to counter to floor. When he walked into the living room, he stopped in the middle of the carpet and pushed his forelegs forward, his hind quarters skyward, in an elongated stretch. After that he stretched a hind leg—just the left one—very carefully. Then he approached the swan bed and ordered breakfast in clarion tones.

The man made no move to get out of bed but reached out a teasing hand. Koko sidestepped it and rubbed his brown mask against the corner of the bed. He crossed the room and rubbed the leg of the book cupboard. He walked to the Morris chair and stropped his jaw on its square corners.

"Just what do you think you're accomplishing?" Qwilleran asked.

Koko ambled to the pot-bellied stove and looked it over, then selected the latch of the ashpit door and ground his jaw against it. He scraped the left side of his jaw; he scraped the right side. And the shallow door clicked and swung ajar. The door opened only a hair's-breadth, but Koko pried it farther with an inquisitive paw.

In a split second Qwilleran was out of bed and bending over the ashpit. It was full of papers—typewritten sheets—a stack of them two inches thick, neatly bound in gray folders. They had been typed on a machine with a loose E—a faulty letter that jumped above the line.

CHAPTER 21

IN THE GRAY-WHITE morning light of the day before the day before Christmas, Qwilleran started to read Andy's novel. The questionable heroine of the story was a scatterbrained prattler who was planning to spike her alcoholic husband's highball with carbon tetrachloride in order to be free to marry another man of great sexual prowess.

He had read six chapters when a uniformed chauffeur and two truckers arrived to remove the roll-top desk, and after that it was time to shave and dress and go downtown. He put the manuscript back in the ashpit reluctantly.

At the *Fluxion* office Qwilleran's session with the managing editor lasted longer than either of them had anticipated. In fact, it stretched into a lengthy lunch date with some important executives in a private dining room at the Press Club, and when the newsman returned to Junktown in the late afternoon, he was jubilant.

His knee, much improved, permitted him to bolt up the front steps of the Cobb mansion two at a time, but when he let himself into the entrance hall, he slowed down. The Cobb Junkery was open, and Iris was there, moving in a daze, passing a dustrag over the arms of a Boston rocker.

"I didn't expect you so soon," he said.

"I thought I ought to open the shop," she replied in a dreary voice. "There might be some follow-up business after the Block Party, and goodness knows I need the money. Dennis—my son—came back with me."

"We sold some merchandise for you yesterday," Qwilleran said. "I hated to let my desk go, but a woman was willing to pay seven hundred and fifty dollars for it."

Iris exhibited more gratitude than surprise.

"And incidentally, were you saving any old radios for Hollis Prantz?" he asked.

"Old radios? No, we wouldn't have anything like that."

That evening Qwilleran finished reading Andy's novel. It was just as he expected. The characters included a philandering husband, a voluptuous divorcée, a poor little rich girl operating a swanky antique shop incognito, and—in the later chapters—a retired schoolteacher who was naive to the point of stupidity. For good measure Andy had also introduced a gambling racketeer, a nymphet, a dope pusher, a sodomite, a crooked politician, and a retired cop who appeared to be the mouthpiece for the author's highminded platitudes.

Why, Qwilleran asked himself, had Andy hidden his manuscript in the ashpit of a pot-bellied stove?

At one point his reading was interrupted by a knock on his door, and a clean-cut young man wearing a white shirt and bowtie introduced himself as Iris's son.

"My mother says you need a desk," he said. "If you'll give me an assist, we can bring the one from her apartment."

"The apothecary desk? I don't want to deprive her—"

"She says she doesn't need it."

"How's your mother feeling?"

"Rough! She took a pill and went to bed early."

They carried the desk across the hall, and a chair to go with it—a Winsor with thick slab seat and delicate spindle back—and Qwilleran asked Dennis to help him hoist the Mackintosh coat of arms to the mantel, replacing the portrait of the sour-faced kill-joy.

Then Qwilleran plunged once more into Andy's novel. He had read worse books, but not many. Andy had no ear for dialogue and no compassion for his characters. What fascinated the newsman, however, was the narcotics operation. One of the antique dealers in the story dispensed marijuana as well as mahogany sideboards and Meissen ewers. Whenever a customer walked into his shop and asked for a Quimper teapot, he was actually in the market for "tea."

After four hundred pages of jumping E's, Qwilleran's eyelids were heavy and his eyeballs were aching. He leaned his head back in the Morris chair and closed his eyes. Quimper teapots! He had never heard of a Quimper teapot, but there were many things he had not heard of before coming to Junktown: Sussex pigs . . . piggins, noggins and firkins . . . horse brasses.

Horse brasses! Qwilleran's moustache danced, and he reproved it with his knuckles. No one buys horse brasses any more, Mary had said. And yet—twice during his short stay in Junktown, he had heard a request for this useless brass ornament.

The first inquiry had been at the Bit o' Junk shop, and Ben had been inclined to dismiss the customer curtly. Yesterday the same inquiry was made at The Junkery. The two buildings were adjacent, and similar in design.

Qwilleran combed his moustache to subdue his excitement and devised a plan for the next morning. The twenty-fourth of December was going to be a busy day: the big party in the evening, another appointment with the managing editor in the afternoon, lunch with Arch Riker at the Press Club, and in the morning—a tactical maneuver that might fill in another blank in the Junktown puzzle.

The next day Qwilleran was waked before dawn by flashing lights. Koko was standing on the bed, rubbing his teeth with satisfaction on the wall switch and turning the lamps on and off.

The man got up, opened a can of corned beef for the cats, shaved and dressed. As soon as he thought the Dispatch Desk was open, he telephoned and asked them to send a messenger at eleven thirty—no later and no earlier.

"Send me the skinniest and shabbiest one you've got," he told the dispatch clerk. "Preferably one with a bad cold or an acute sinus infection."

While waiting for the accomplice to arrive, Qwilleran moved his paper and pencils, clips and gluepot into the apothecary desk. In one of the drawers he found Iris Cobb's tape recorder and returned it to her.

"I don't want it," she said with a sickly attempt at a smile. "I don't even want to look at it. Maybe you can use it in your work."

The youth who arrived from the Dispatch Office was unkempt, undernourished and red-eyed. Most of the *Fluxion* messengers fitted such a description, but this one was superlative.

"Yikes!" the boy said when he saw the newsman's apartment. "Do you pay rent for this pad, or does the *Flux* pay you to live here?"

"Don't editorialize," Qwilleran said, reaching for his wallet. "Just do what I say. Here's ten bucks. Go next door—"

"Lookit them crazy cats! Do they bite?"

"Only *Fluxion* messengers. . . . Now listen carefully. Go to the antique shop called Bit o' Junk and ask if the man has any horse brasses."

"Horse *what*?"

"The man who runs the place is crazy, so don't be surprised at anything he does or says. And don't let him know that you know me—or that you work for the *Flux*. Just ask if he has any horse brasses and show him your money. Then bring me whatever he gives you."

"Horse brasses! You gotta be kiddin'."

"Don't go straight there. Hang around on the corner a few minutes before you approach the Bit o' Junk. . . . And try not to look too intelligent!" Qwilleran called after the departing messenger, as an unnecessary afterthought.

Then he paced the floor in suspense. When a cat jumped on the desk and presented an arched back at a convenient level for stroking, the man stroked it absently.

In fifteen minutes the messenger returned. He said, "Ten bucks for this thing? You gotta be nuts!"

"I guess you're right," said Qwilleran meekly, as he examined the brass medallion the boy handed him.

It was a setback, but the fluttering sensation in his moustache told Qwilleran that he was on the right track, and he refused to be discouraged.

At noon he met Arch Riker at the Press Club and presented him with the tobacco tin, gift-wrapped in a page from an 1864 Harper's Weekly.

"It's great!" the feature editor said. "But you shouldn't have spent so much, Qwill. Hell, I didn't buy you anything, but I'll pop for lunch."

In the afternoon Qwilleran spent a satisfactory hour with the managing editor, and then joined the Women's Department for pink lemonade and Christmas cookies, and later turned up at an impromptu celebration in the Photo Lab, where he was the only sober guest, and eventually went home.

He had three hours before his date with Mary. He went to the ashpit and once more read the chapter in Andy's novel that dealt with the dope pusher.

At five o'clock he dashed out and picked up the better of his two suits from Junktown's dry cleaning establishment that specialized in quick service. There was a red tag on his garment.

"You musta left something in the pocket," the clerk said, and she rummaged through a drawer until she found an envelope with his name on it.

When Qwilleran noted the content, he said, "Thanks! Thanks very much! Have a Christmas drink on me," and he left a dollar tip.

It was the tape measure. Mary's silver tape measure and a piece of folded paper.

Fingering his smooth silver case, he returned to his apartment and looked out his back window. The early winter dusk was doing its best to make the junk in the backyard look more bedraggled than ever. Two station wagons were there, backed in from the alley—one gray and one tan.

Access to the backyard was apparently through the Cobb shop, and Qwilleran preferred to avoid Iris, so he went out the front door, around the corner and in through the alley. After a glance at the back windows of nearby houses, he measured the gray wagon. It was exactly as he had guessed; the dimensions tallied with the notations on the scrap of paper.

And as he walked around the decrepit vehicle he noted something else that checked; Ben's wagon had a left front fender missing.

Qwilleran knew exactly what he wanted to do now. After buying a pint of the best brandy at Lombardo's, he ran up the steps of the Bit o' Junk shop. The front door was open, but Ben's store was locked up and dark.

He stopped at The Junkery. "Happen to know where Ben is?" he asked Iris. "I'd like to extend the hospitality of the season."

"He must be at Children's Hospital," Iris said. "He goes there every Christmas to play Santa."

Upstairs the cats were waiting. Both were sitting tall in the middle of the floor, with the attentive attitude that meant, "We have a message to communicate." They were staring. Yum Yum was staring into middle distance with her crossed eyes, but she was staring hard. Koko stared at a certain point in the center of Qwilleran's forehead, and he was staring so intently that his body swayed with an inner tension.

This was not the dinner message, Qwilleran knew. This was something more important. "What is it?" he asked the cats. "What are you trying to tell me?"

Koko turned his head. He looked at a small shiny object on the floor near the bookcase.

"*What's that?*" Qwilleran gasped, although he needed no answer. He knew what it was.

He picked up the scrap of silvery paper and took it to the desk. He turned on the lamp. At first glance the foil looked like a gum wrapper that had been stepped on, but he knew better. It was a neat rectangle, as wide as a pencil, and as thin as a razorblade.

As he started to open the packet, Koko jumped to the desk to watch. With dainty brown feet the cat stepped over pencils, paper clips, ashtray, tobacco pouch, and tape measure, and then he stepped precisely on the green button of Iris's portable tape recorder.

"Hawnnk . . . sss . . . hawnnk . . . sss . . ."

Qwilleran hit the red button of the machine and silenced the unpleasant noise. As he did so, he became aware of heavy footsteps in the hall.

Santa Claus was lumbering up the stairs, pulling on the handrail for assistance.

"Come in and toast the season," Qwilleran invited. "I've got a good bottle of brandy."

"Worthy gentleman, I'll do that!" Ben said.

He shuffled into Qwilleran's quarters in his big black boots cuffed with imitation fur. His eyes were glazed, his breath was strong; he had not come directly from Children's Hospital.

"Ho ho ho!" he said in hearty greeting when he spied the two cats.

Yum Yum flew to the top of the book cupboard, but Koko stood his ground and glared at the visitor.

"Merr-r-r-y Christmas!" boomed the Santa Claus voice.

Koko's backbone bristled. He arched his back and bushed his tail. With ears laid back and fangs bared, he hissed. Then Koko jumped to the desk and continued to watch the proceedings—with disapproval in the angle of his ears and the tilt of his whiskers. From his perch he could survey the Morris chair, where Qwilleran sat drinking coffee, and the rocker, where Santa Claus was sipping brandy. He also had a good view of the tea table, which held a plate of smoked oysters.

At length Qwilleran said, "Let's drink to our old friend Cobb, wherever he is!"

Ben waved his glass. "To the perfidious wretch!"

"You mean you weren't an admirer of our late landlord?"

"Fair is foul, and foul is fair," said the old actor.

"I'd like to know what happened that night at the Ellsworth house. Did Cobb have a heart attack, or did he slip on the stairs? The snow could have caked on his boots, you know. It was snowing that night, wasn't it?"

There was no confirmation from Ben, whose rouged nose was deep in his brandy glass.

"I mean, sometime after midnight," Qwilleran persisted. "Do you remember? Wasn't it snowing? Were you out that night?"

"Oh, it snowed and it blowed . . . it blew and it snew," said Ben with appropriate grimaces and gestures.

"I went to the Ellsworth house the next day, and there was a bare patch under Cobb's car, indicating that it was snowing while he was stripping the house. The funny thing is: another car had been there at the same time. It left its outline on the ice, and from the shape of the impression, I would guess the second car had a fender missing." Qwilleran paused and watched Ben's face.

"Mischief, thou are afoot!" said Ben, looking mysterious.

Qwilleran tried other approaches to no avail. The old actor was a better actor than he. The newsman kept an eye on his watch; he had to shave and dress before calling on Mary.

He made one more attempt. "I wonder if it's true," he said, "that Ellsworth had some dough hidden—"

He was interrupted by a noise from the desk. "Hawnnk . . . ssss . . . hawnnk . . ."

"Koko! Scram!" he yelled, and the cat jumped to the floor and up on the mantel, almost in a single swoop. "If it's true that the old house has some hidden treasure," Qwilleran continued, "perhaps Cobb got his hands on it—"

The tape recorder went on: "Hawnnk . . . sssss . . . ppphlat!"

"And perhaps someone came along and gave him a shove." Qwilleran was lounging casually in his chair but watching Ben sharply, and he thought he detected a wavering eye—a glance that was not in the actor's script. "Someone might have shoved him down the stairs and grabbed the loot . . ."

"Hawnnk . . . ppphlat!" said the recorder. Then "Grrrummph! Whazzat? Whatcha doin'?" There followed the murmur of blank tape, then "Wool over my eyes, you old fool. . . . Know what you're up to. . . . Think you can get away with anything. . . . Over my dead body!"

It was Cobb's recorded voice, and Qwilleran sat up straight.

The tape said, "Those creeps comin' in here. . . . Horse brasses, my eye! . . . Know where you get your deliveries. . . . You! Scroungin' at the Garrick! That's a laugh!"

Ben dropped his glass of brandy and heaved himself out of the rocker.

"No!" yelled Qwilleran, erupting from the Morris chair and leaping toward the desk. "I've got to hear this!"

The tape said, "Me marchin' on the picket line, a lousy three bucks an hour, and you get ten for a deck . . ."

The newsman stared at the machine with incredulity and triumph.

The tape said, "Not any more, you don't. . . . You're gonna cut me in, Ben Baby. . . . "

There was a flash of red in the room. Qwilleran saw it from the corner of his eye. It moved toward the fireplace, and the newsman spun around in time to see Ben reaching for the poker. Then a big black Santa Claus boot kicked out, and the tea table went flying across the room.

Qwilleran reached for the desk chair, without taking his eyes from the red suit. He grabbed the chair roughly by its back, but all he got was a handful of spindles; the back came off in his hand.

For an instant the two men were face to face—Ben bracing himself on the hearth and brandishing the poker, Qwilleran holding a few useless dowels. And then—the iron thing shot forward. It skidded off the mantel, catching Ben in the neck. As the poker flew through the air, Qwilleran ducked, skidded on an oyster, and went down on his right knee with a thud.

The scene of action froze in a tableau: Santa Claus on the floor, flattened by the Mackintosh coat of arms; Qwilleran on his knees; Koko bending over a smoked oyster.

After the police had taken Ben away, and while Iris and Dennis were helping to straighten up the room, the telephone rang, and Qwilleran walked slowly and painfully to the desk.

"What's the matter, Qwill?" asked Mary's anxious voice. "I just heard the siren and saw them taking Ben away in the police car. What's wrong?"

Qwilleran moaned. "Everything! Including my knee."

"You've hurt it again?"

"It's the *other* knee. I'm immobilized. I don't know what to do about the party."

"We can have the party at your place, but what about Ben?"

"I'll explain when you get here."

She came wearing blue chiffon and bearing Christmas gifts. "What on earth has happened to Ben—and your knee?" she demanded.

"We caught a murderer here tonight," Qwilleran said. "With the aid of your tape measure I placed Ben at the scene of Cobb's accident."

"I can't believe it! Did he admit he killed C.C.?"

"Not in so many words. He merely gave his landlord Godspeed with an auspicious push."

"Was it true about the buried treasure at the Ellsworth house?"

"No, it was a case of blackmail. Ben was pushing heroin, Mary. He met his supplier at the abandoned theatre and bagged the stuff in five-grain decks."

"How did you find out?"

"The cats brought me a deck from Ben's apartment, and Andy's novel gave me another tip. The junkies would identify themselves in Ben's shop by asking for horse brasses."

"That was a clever arrangement."

"But the addicts sometimes wandered into the wrong shop, and Cobb apparently caught on. And here's the incredible part of the story: When Cobb was demanding a cut of Ben's profits, the complete conversation was recorded on tape! I think Koko flipped the switch on Iris's tape recorder when Cobb was trying to make his deal with Ben."

"What a fantastic coincidence!"

"Fantastic, yes! But if you knew Koko, you wouldn't be too sure it was coincidental. It must have happened Sunday morning when Iris was at church and I was at the drugstore."

"Koko, you're a hero!" Mary said to the cat, who was now taking his lordly ease on the daybed. "And you're going to have a reward. Pressed duck!" She turned to Qwilleran. "I took the liberty of ordering dinner. It's being sent over from the Toledo Restaurant. I hope you like oysters Rockefeller and pressed duck and Chateaubriand and French Strawberries."

"But no more rich food for the cats," he said. "They've eaten a whole can of smoked oysters, and I'm afraid they'll be sick." He looked at Koko with speculation and added, "There's one thing we'll never know. How did the Mackintosh coat of arms happen to slide off the mantel at the strategic moment? Just as Ben raised the poker to beat my brains out, that chunk of iron delivered a karate chop."

He gazed at Koko with conjecture and admiration, and the cat rolled over and licked the pale fur on his stomach.

The telephone rang. "Probably our police reporter," Qwilleran said. "I asked him to call me when the police had more details."

He went limping to the desk.

"Yes, Lodge. Any developments? . . . That's what I guessed. . . . How did he find out? . . . He had his finger on everything, that boy! . . . Yes, I've met the guy. . . . No, I won't mention it."

When the newsman hung up, he refrained from telling Mary that the Narcotics Squad had been watching Junktown for three months and that Hollis Prantz was an undercover agent. Nor did he tell her immediately about Ben's complete confession.

Dinner arrived from the city's most expensive restaurant—in chafing dishes and under silver covers and on beds of crushed ice—and Mary presented her Christmas gifts: a case of canned lobster for the cats and a pair of Scottish brass candlesticks for Qwilleran.

"I have a surprise for you, too," he told her, "but first you must hear some painful truths. Andy's death was not accidental. He was Ben's first victim."

"But why? Why?"

"Ben was afraid Andy would turn him in. Both Andy and Cobb had learned about Ben's sideline. Our actor friend was in danger of losing the thing he valued most in the world—an audience—even though he had to buy their applause. On the night of October sixteenth, after he saw Cobb leave Andy's shop, he slipped in and staged the so-called accident."

"And did he kill that poor man in the alley?"

"No. Ben declined to take bows for that one. He police were right that time. One out of three."

Mary caught her breath. "But what will happen now? There will be a trial! I'll have to testify!"

"Don't be alarmed," he said. "Everything's arranged so that you can come out of hiding. For the last two days I've been meeting with *Fluxion* executives and the mayor's aides and your father. I've proposed an idea—"

"My father!"

"Not a bad guy—your dad. The city is going to establish a Landmarks Preservation Committee, prompted by the *Fluxion* and underwritten by your father's bank as a public service. He's agreed to act as honorary chairman. But *you* are going to spearhead the program."

"I?"

"Yes, you! It's time you started putting your knowledge and enthusiasm to work. And here's something else: scrounging is going to be legalized. All you need is a permit and—"

"Qwill, did you do all this for Junktown?"

"No. Mostly for you," he said. "And if you make this contribution to the success of Junktown, I don't think you'll be bothered by those crank calls any more. Someone wanted to scare you—to chase you out of the neighborhood. I think I know who, but the less said the better."

Mary's expression of delight and gratitude was all the Christmas that Qwilleran needed—better, much better, than the brass candlesticks—better, almost, than the $1,000 prize he was sure of winning.

His satisfaction was short-lived, however. The girl's eyes clouded, and she swallowed hard. "If only Andy were here," she mourned. "How he would—"

"Koko!" shouted Qwilleran. "Get away from that wall!"

Koko was standing on the daybed and sharpening his claws on Andy's carefully pasted wall covering.

"He's been working on that blasted wall ever since we moved in," the man said. "The corners are beginning to curl up."

Mary looked across the room, blinking her eyes emotionally. Then she stood up quickly and walked to the daybed. Koko scampered away.

"Qwill," she said, "there's something else here." She pulled at one of the curled corners, and a page of *Don Quixote* started to peel off.

Qwilleran hobbled across the room and joined her on the daybed.

"There's something pasted underneath this page," she said, peeling it slowly and carefully.

"Greenbacks!"

"Money!"

Under the page that Mary was pulling off there were three hundred-dollar bills.

Qwilleran peeled a page of Samuel Pepys and found three more. "Iris told me Andy had used peelable paste, and now we know why!"

"Where did Andy get these?" Mary cried. "He didn't make this kind of money! Any profit he made went right back into antiques." She peeled off another page. "This whole wall is papered with currency. How did Andy—"

"Maybe he had a sideline," said Qwilleran. "Do you suppose he did business with Papa Popopopoulos?"

"I can't believe it!" Mary said. "Andy was so . . . He was so . . . Why would he *hide* it like this?"

"The usual reason," Qwilleran said, clearing his throat diplomatically, "has to do with unreported income."

He said it as gently as he could, but Mary collapsed in tears. He put his arms around her and comforted her, and she was willing to be comforted.

Neither of them noticed Koko as he rose weightlessly to the swanlike daybed. Standing on his hind feet he rubbed his jaw against the carved wood. He stretched his neck and rubbed the nearby doorjamb. He rubbed against the light switch, and the apartment was thrown into darkness.

In the moments that followed, the pair on the daybed were blissfully unaware of two pale apparitions hovering over the dinner table in the vicinity of the pressed duck.